Abo

Lara Temple writes str
about complex individuals who give no quarter but do so
with plenty of passion. She lives with her husband, two
children, and one very fluffy dog, and they are all very
understanding about her taking over the kitchen table so
she can look out over the garden as she writes and dreams
up her happy-ever-afters.

Regency Secrets

Regency Secrets:

The Return
of the Rogues

LARA TEMPLE

MILLS & BOON

First Published in Great Britain 2023
By Mills & Boon, an imprint of HarperCollins*Publishers* Ltd,
1 London Bridge Street, London, SE1 9GF

www.harpercollins.co.uk

HarperCollins*Publishers*
Macken House, 39/40 Mayor Street Upper,
Dublin 1, D01 C9W8, Ireland

ISBN: 978-0-263-31938-5

MIX
Paper | Supporting
responsible forestry
FSC™ C007454

THE RETURN OF THE DISAPPEARING DUKE

This book is for all those who love life, but lie awake worrying.

For those used to shouldering burdens who wish for a shoulder to lean on, even if only for a day.

I wrote Rafe and Cleo's story just for you...

Prologue

Greybourne Hall, Hertfordshire
—Christmas 1800

The day he ran away was the day the lake at Greybourne Hall froze.

It wasn't a thick cover of ice, just enough to glaze over the last dark jade glimmer of water like a dead fish's eye staring heavenwards. Snowflakes frosted the reeds and swirled up the banks in fairy-tale gusts into the open door of Greybourne Chapel. Safely inside, they hovered for a moment to glint in the pale morning sun, before falling to the unusual chequered floor in abeyance, just like all the unhappy people crowded inside.

Unlike most chapels, there were no pews or cushions and no one was allowed to sit on the carved stone benches that lined the wall. Everyone from the Duchess and her son to the grooms and scullery maids were on their knees.

Everyone but Rafe's father, the Duke of Greybourne. The Duke stood above them like a rearing bear, his fists clenched and raised, his voice spewing damnation upon them all.

Rafe had years ago ceased listening to the roaring rumble of his father's morning sermons. When he'd been younger he'd distracted himself with daydreams about great feats of bravery. Now he would soon be sixteen and had other things on his mind.

A month ago, the object of his fantasies had been Lizzy, the very pretty daughter of the postmaster in the village near his school. But that was a whole month ago and now his mind dwelt with delight on the new parlourmaid Susan who was kneeling across from him.

She had big blue eyes and freckles over every inch of her that he could see, which was not very much, but his mind imagined much more. She was some years older than he and he'd heard from the servants that she fancied Lowell, the head groom. He knew, too, that this…*tingling* had little to do with courtly love, but she was so…so everything. She was plump and had the most charming giggle that would make his insides clench and his outsides perspire.

She was also, at the moment, the only reason to be grateful for his father's daily Hell and Damnation sermon. So while his father ranted about descent into sin and something about frogs, Rafe's gaze kept slipping back to Susan's bowed head, her rounded shoulders, the generous bosom not even the unflattering apron could hide…

She peeped up suddenly and caught him. Embarrassment struck him even harder than lust. There was nothing he could do to stop the scalding blush that rushed upwards. Her mouth curved and even through the fumes of his combusting body he could see the compassion there and felt its sting.

They both looked away and, if his father had not reached the apex of his sermon, the incident might never have happened. But just then the Duke's voice boomed. 'Fornication shall bring thee down!'

And Susan giggled.

Silence.

As swiftly as the scalding heat had come it fell away, because he knew his father. They all did. Silence during a sermon was an ill omen. Rafe barely had time to gather his wits before his father lunged. He saw the Duke's hands, great twisted claws, reaching, closing around her freckled throat, raising her clean off the stone floor. Rafe had never seen such horror as in her blue eyes. She gaped up at the Duke of Greybourne, her mouth twisted, her cheeks both pale and stained with colour, the freckles like specks of blood.

No one had yet moved when Rafe launched himself at his father. He saw them all, like chess pieces rooted on their ivory and ebony seats. Then he saw nothing.

The next thing he knew, his face was half in the snow, the flakes dancing in and out of his mouth as he breathed in harsh coughing bursts. He was aflame with pain and something was burying him in the frozen ground. He could see white and dark and the length of his arm flung out to his side. The snow about it was pink.

'That's right, Master Rafe, deep breaths.'

It was Lowell, the groom.

'Susan…' Rafe croaked and there was a moment's silence which made Rafe struggle to rise once more. But Lowell held him down.

'Susan is well, Master Rafe. You stopped him afore he did harm and there's many that's grateful. You stop thrashing and I'll let 'ee be. You've nothing broken that I can see, but you took some blows before we got you away and you'll likely be sore. Best come inside now.'

'I wanted to kill him!' The words burst out, chasing away the new flakes that fell.

'Ay, well,' Lowell said as he took his substantial weight off Rafe. 'Brave words, but best learn to fight proper afore you try next. You're a right big lad and like to be bigger yet, but you'd best put some brawn on those inches.'

Rafe shoved to his shaky feet, twisting away from the groom's attempt to help him. The cold pinched at his skin and tears at his eyes and he stalked away before they came.

* * *

He was shivering by the time he reached his room, but he stopped in the doorway. His mother was on her knees again, but this time by his school trunk. A maid placed a stack of shirts into the half-full trunk and at a signal from his mother she scurried out the door.

'What are you doing?'

'That should be evident, Rafael. I have ordered the carriage to be prepared and you will depart within the hour.'

For a moment he stood in shock but then anger came once again to his rescue.

'I didn't do anything wrong! This is Edward all over again—he did nothing wrong and you sent him away. Where will you send me, Mother? To Egypt as well? Or perhaps to the Antipodes?'

'Do not be dramatic, Rafael. Until term begins you will stay at up at the Lakes. You like it there.'

'In the summer,' he exclaimed.

'Do lower your voice. Dr Parracombe is with your father and has given him something to calm his nerves, but…'

'Calm *his* nerves? He…he tried to *kill* Susan! How many more times will dear Dr Parracombe have to *calm his nerves* when he attacks one of us or the servants? He doesn't need a doctor; he needs a cell in Bedlam!'

She surged to her feet—he was already over six feet, but though he towered over her she was absolutely in control. Her face was as cold as the lake, her eyes grey and flat.

'You will never speak those words again, Rafael. Ever. Your father's religious convictions merely lead to occasional…unbefitting effusions. That is all it is. One day you will be Duke of Greybourne and you must learn that life demands sacrifices.'

Sacrifices.

'So you are sacrificing me,' he said, far more calmly than he felt.

'If that is what you choose to believe.'

'I will tell you what I choose, Mother. If you send me away instead of him, I swear to you I'll *choose* not to return to Greybourne so long as he lives.'

They stood in silence for a moment, then she inclined her head.

'Perhaps that is best. Now go wash and change. And say goodbye to your sisters.'

Rafe leaned his bruised cheekbone glumly against the cold glass of the carriage window and watched the snow-flakes melt and slither down. They'd stopped again to change the team of horses. They were probably close to Manchester because the courtyard was full of gigs and carriages and carts, with ostlers and passengers weaving between them, hunkered against the cold. Everything was in shades of brown and grey and again he felt the same rising choke of misery and fury.

Then at the edge of the courtyard he saw a flash of bright red, like fresh blood on the snow. He took his purse and stepped out on to the cobbles. A crowd had gathered to watch, some cheering, some less enthusiastic, but all curious as some two dozen red-coated soldiers marched along the muddy road.

The soldier bringing up the rear was a rather squat man, with the face of a cheeky gargoyle under his dark stovepipe shako. He stood very straight for his short stature. A little boy dashed out from the courtyard and marched alongside him for a moment and the soldier smiled down at him and patted his head without breaking step.

As the young boy ran back through the courtyard Rafe stepped forward, pulling a coin from his pocket.

'Who were those soldiers?' he asked. The boy stared at the coin, but was as quick to answer as he was on his feet.

'Thirty-Sixth Foot returned from Ireland, sir. That was Sergeant Birdie, sir. My brother served with him, sir.' All this was spoken in a hushed whisper, but with such pride

Rafe smiled for the first time since coming down from school.

'Sergeant Birdie,' he repeated, flashing another coin. 'Which way are their barracks?'

'Over Bolton way, sir.'

'Bolton...?'

'That's north, sir.'

'Excellent. I'm heading north myself.'

'Are you, sir?' the boy asked, a little dubious, but his curiosity was nipped in the bud as Rafe slid him a third coin and stepped back into the carriage.

Bolton. Birdie. Brave new beginnings.

He'd need a new name, too...

Something simple that would draw no attention. Common, unobtrusive...

Grey...

Chapter One

Syene, Upper Egypt—1822

'*Ta'al*. Come in.'

The deep voice was entirely English.

So far, so good, thought Cleo as she took a deep breath and opened the warped wooden door.

The stone floor was hard under her feet, but she knew she was standing on a paper-thin bridge over an abyss. Her next step would either move her towards safety or perdition.

She entered the room and stopped, her hand still on the door, because the man who turned to face her was not at all what she'd expected.

Certainly he was large. Very large. She was a reasonably tall woman, but he would tower easily over her brother's six feet.

More to the point, he was very bare. At least his chest was, but there was a great deal of it.

Not that bare-chested men were entirely unusual in Cleo's experience. Over the years since she and her brother had joined her father on his travels, she had been to places where bare-chested men and sometimes women were not unusual. Still, this man was not what she was accustomed to.

Then there were the scars. They mantled his shoulder and streaked along the right side of his neck. Between his size and his scars and the fear that had taken up lodging in her belly this past week, he was an intimidating sight.

Except for the shaving lather.

A lathered jaw should not make any difference to whether he was to be feared or not, but somehow it did.

'What do you want, boy?' The man wiped his razor on the towel and turned back to the gritty mirror propped on a high windowsill.

At least his words confirmed what she'd overheard in the marketplace—he was English, thank God.

'I'm afraid I'm lost, sir.'

'Lost? This is a rather unusual part of the world in which to lose yourself. How did that happen, Mr...?'

'Patrick.' Cleo offered her usual name, watching as the giant worked away at his shaving, the muscles of his back rippling like the Nile over the boulders of the cataracts. Acting the boy had once been quite easy, but she was out of practice. She cleared her throat and continued. 'I've been in Meroe looking for my father and brother, but they disappeared so I decided to return to Cairo and see if they are there.'

The giant was watching her in the mirror, the speckled glass giving his pale green-grey eyes a strange blank tint.

'Yet here you are in my humble rooms instead of on a boat down the Nile. Would you care to rephrase your predicament?'

'I don't quite understand, sir.'

'Don't you? At least half a dozen *dragomen* approached me the moment I entered town, offering various services. If you only need help reaching Cairo, any one of them would be willing to help for a reasonable price.'

The giant wiped his face with the linen towel and turned. For a moment surprise and a surge of pity chased away her fear. The scars were more evident from the front.

They climbed up the side of his throat like ivy, twisting along his jaw and ending in a whitish blade just at the base of his ear.

She should not be surprised. The merchants she'd overheard in the market had called him *nadab*, or scar. But he was otherwise so alarmingly perfect his face could have modelled for a fallen angel, with pitch-black hair and stormy eyes. Apparently, this angel had not managed to evade the fire in his fall. The whitened skin along his jaw twisted as he smiled.

'Squeamish, boy?'

'No. I can't help thinking how it must have hurt. I'm sorry I stared, sir.'

His smile softened. It felt like a door opening a little wider.

'Staring is honest,' he replied. 'It's the looking away I can't abide. So, what is it you want from me other than directions to Cairo?'

Cleo glanced over her shoulder, listening. She'd sneaked past the innkeeper, but the men would likely search all the inns in Syene. And then... She did not know what would happen then and preferred not to know.

'I'm afraid to travel on my own. I heard in the market you might be on your way north. I don't have much, but I can pay my passage.'

The giant gave one last swipe to his jaw with the towel and draped it over his shoulder as he approached. He was definitely enormous and there were more scars decorating him than she'd realised. They were dwarfed by the burns, but they danced across his bare flesh like decorations— whiteish flicks and weals, as if someone had used him for dart practice. She forced her eyes upwards from the expanse of bare skin and the dark hair that trailed down his chest towards his trousers. His eyes weren't any more comforting—they were a strange metallic greenish-grey and she could discern nothing in them but her own reflection.

He was closer than was wise given her masquerade. But she kept her feet planted. She was just a boy, just a boy...

'Does anyone believe this Patrick nonsense?' He tugged at a lock of her hair. She usually kept it short, yet unruly enough to hide her arched brows. They'd always been her undoing. She debated arguing, but there was something in the giant's face, a lack of both curiosity and censure, that stopped the lie from forming.

'It used to work well enough when I was younger.'

'Much younger, I would imagine. This local garb is doing a poor job of hiding your bosom. If you weren't so gaunt-looking, I would suggest trying for a portly look and padding out your stomach, but you'd just look ridiculous. You should put some flesh in those cheeks first.'

Gaunt-looking. It was true the past few months had been difficult, but...gaunt? Not that it mattered. She glanced down at her chest. She'd bound it, but obviously not rigorously enough. It was rather disappointing to realise it was this and not her face that gave her away.

'Thank you for the advice, sir, but since I can't do much about it at the moment, could you help me? I can pay.'

'Can you? How much?'

Hell. She'd hoped he'd take pity on a fellow Englishman and perhaps even more now he knew her to be female. But clearly this was not that kind of Englishman, despite his cultured voice.

'I have this.' She tugged at the chain around her neck, extracting a pendant from under her *gallabiyah*. The metal setting was tarnished and twisted from when a trunk fell on it; but nothing could mask the quality of the emerald.

'Good God, someone must have disliked you thoroughly to gift you that monstrosity.' The giant plucked it from her hand and the chain tugged against her nape. She resisted the urge to pull away as he inspected it, turning it to catch the afternoon light. This close his eyes were even more intimidating. The green was pale, like peridots, held in by a band of dark steel. They were shaded by long straight lashes that rose as he looked from the stone to her. She was not often intimidated by men, but the hairs on her arms rose in alarm and she kept as much distance between them as the chain allowed.

'Where did you get this?' he asked.

'My mother. It was a family heirloom.'

'That's what people call things when they feel guilty about wanting to toss them on the rubbish heap.'

'I was told it is a small but fine emerald. It is yours if you see me safely to Cairo.'

'No, I don't think that's a good idea. I'm most likely to toss it in the Nile at the first opportunity or hand it to the first blind beggar. Put that devil's eye away.' He finally let the pendant fall and she eased away, slipping it back under her *gallabiyah*. It felt strange against her skin now, as if he'd held it over a fire.

'You won't help me?'

'Help you in what way? The river is all of a hundred yards from here. If you've already made it here from Meroe, which I admit is impressive, why do you need my help on what must be the final and easiest stretch of your journey?'

'Because...'

She fell silent at the sounds outside. Horses, several of them. An unpleasantly familiar voice calling in Arabic for the owner of the guesthouse.

'Never mind.' She headed to the window, but the giant was faster than she, his arm creating a bar across the wooden shutters.

'Not a good idea. If those men are clever, they'll have a man in the back. Are they clever?'

'I don't know... Yes, I... Oof!' Her breath left her as he picked her up and deposited her behind a thick cotton curtain stretched along a corner of the room to create a make-shift cupboard. Behind was a warped wooden dresser and

pegs with clothes. He squeezed her between the dresser
and the corner and planted his hands on the wall on either
side of her.

'You will remain absolutely silent, no matter what I say
or do. Understood, Patrick the prevaricator?'

She nodded, between shock and gratitude.

She ought not to feel thankful. No doubt he would hand
her over with as much emotion as he'd shown at discovering her sex, but somehow she was beginning to hope she
might have made her first correct move in days.

She stared at the thick curtain as it fell back into place.
She hadn't even noticed the dun-coloured fabric closing
off that part of the room. Still, she felt certain anyone entering would look directly at the curtain and through it.
What if she had to cough? She looked around for something to stifle herself with. A white cotton shirt hung from
a peg and she took it, burying her fists in its softness and
raising it like a weapon.

In a tiny corner of her mind not given over to fear and
exhaustion, she thought—*expensive*.

In another corner, far less sensible, she thought—*it
smells so good*. Like the woods behind her childhood
home where the stream created a little brush-covered island. She'd left there half a lifetime ago, but could almost
imagine it lay just beyond the flimsy curtain.

Perhaps the heat and fear were finally melting her mind.

The knock on the door was like a hammer's strike.

'Go away. I'm shaving,' the giant called out, but the
knock repeated, sharper. 'Oh, for heaven's sake, what?'
The door squawked as he jerked it open. 'I said I was busy.
Who the devil are you?'

'We apologise most strongly, *basha*,' said the hated
voice, not in Arabic this time, but in English. 'We search
for a young Englishman.'

'Well, go find him, then. Simply because I'm English
doesn't mean this is a congress of that feckless breed.'

'He was seen coming in this direction from the market.'
'And?'

A few breaths passed and when the man spoke he was rather less peremptory.

'We were thinking that perhaps he might seek out a fellow countryman.'

'Why? Homesick, is he?'

'No. Frightened. He has stolen something from my master.'

'Not a very clever fellow, then. How much will you give me if I find him?'

Cleo froze, pressing the shirt over her mouth even as her heart tried to leap out of it.

'How much…?' The man sounded bemused now and she heard one of the men behind him mutter a colourful curse in Arabic about greedy foreigners.

'I presume your master is paying you for your services. I'm a mercenary myself so I am perfectly willing to have a look for the felon. But if I do find him, what will you pay for him and the stolen property? What is it, by the way? Something valuable?'

'Ah…no, no, not valuable to anyone outside my master. A book. A…a family bible. It is of sentimental value.'

'A strange thing to steal.'

'Indeed. But perhaps the young fool was misled as to its worth. My master is very sad. Naturally, we will offer a reward if—'

'How much?'

'Two hundred piastres.'

The door creaked.

'Five hundred piastres!'

The creaking stopped.

'I'll think about it,' said the giant with a grunt. 'I'm just bored enough to try for the fun of it. Where do I bring this bible-filching fellow if I find him?'

'To the house of Bey al-Wassawi. Ask the servants for al-Mizan.'

'Bay Wassa We. Al Meezan. Good. Now go away. I wish to dress. And you, landlord, find my rascally valet. He went out two hours ago to have my knives sharpened. You'll probably find him at whatever brothel this city boasts.'

The door snapped shut. In the silence she heard the men descend the stairs, their argument fading. Then the scuffle and whinnying of horses as they rode away. Still nothing. Then three heavy treads and a large hand pulled aside the curtain.

'I was beginning to wonder if you'd melted through the wall, Pilfering Pat. What the devil are you doing to my shirt?'

She shook her head, the fabric brushing over her lips.

'I was afraid I might make a noise,' she whispered hoarsely.

'So was I.' He smiled. It lit his face, transformed it. The pull of his scarred skin on his jaw gave it a wry twist, but did nothing to dim its magnificence. No wonder those men had turned tail. This brusque, ill-mannered man possessed the strange magic of charisma.

She knew about charisma. It was as untrustworthy as building a fortress on sand dunes.

She shook out the shirt.

'I apologise. I hope it is not too badly wrinkled.'

He tossed it on to his shoulder to join the towel.

'I don't think the tabbies of Almack's will notice. Now, who the devil was that and why are you stealing bibles?'

'I never stole anything in my life!'

'Not a thing?'

His incredulity flicked at her nerves and absurdly a memory returned…a length of blue ribbon dangling over Annie Packham's bedpost at school.

'A ribbon. When I was at school. It was sky blue and I wanted it. My mother always bought plain ribbons because they were easy to wash.' She snapped her teeth shut. She was truly losing her mind. But at least his smile was back—with blinding effect.

'I think I believe you, Pat. Do you happen to know if there *was* a bible or was everything he said a fabrication?'

For a moment she debated sharing what little she knew. But that was weariness and hunger talking. She shook her head.

'I have no idea why he is following me.'

'No idea? None at all?'

Blast, it was hard to hold his gaze. She decided to offer something to satisfy him.

'I…perhaps it has to do with my father. He dealt in antiquities.'

'One of those fellows who dig holes wherever they go?'

'My father preferred to make copies for collectors rather than dig for originals.'

'You sound as if you prefer he remain above such practices.'

'Naturally I would. He kept claiming he would stop once he found something of true value.'

'Ah. One of those. *"Tomorrow, I promise, dear."*'

She clamped her teeth shut against the need to defend her father. This man was only reflecting her and Dash's thoughts and frustrations, but somehow they rankled coming from a stranger. He smiled at her silence.

'So, what happened to your enterprising father and why aren't you with him?'

'He is dead.'

'I see. Lucky you aren't with him, then. Is this recent?'

She blinked a few times. Dash had often told her she lacked sentimentality, but this man exceeded her by several leagues.

'I don't know. The last letter we received from him was several weeks ago.'

'We?'

'Do we have time for this family history, sir? Or are you merely drawing it out while you consider whether I am worth five hundred piastres?'

The lurking smile extinguished like a candle in a rainstorm. He stepped closer.

'You aren't worth a single piastre to me, *Patrick*. And I certainly don't need that gaudy emerald. You forced your way in here asking for help. I am considering offering it. Don't press your luck. Who is *we*?'

'My…my brother, Dash… Dashford.' Damnation, she was stuttering like a child.

'Dashford? I hope that's a title and not his given name.'

'He has no title. Most people call him Dash.'

His mouth quirked upwards again and relief flooded her. He was a volatile man, this giant, but at least he calmed as swiftly as he stormed.

'Dashford.' He drew out the first syllable. It sounded like a mincing dandy. 'Tell me you are named nothing more objectionable than Patricia?'

How she wished that were true.

'Pattie? Petra? Patience?'

She shook her head.

'*Patrice*. You're half-French. That might account for the dashing Dashford flourish.'

'Do we have time for this? Aren't you worried those men will return?'

'We will hear their horses and you will hop right back behind the curtain. Patsy?'

'Cleopatra,' she snapped and he threw back his head in a shout of laughter.

'Dashford and Cleopatra. What were your parents thinking?'

'As little as possible, I think. What does it matter what I am called? Will you help me?'

'I'll not leave you here at this al-Mizan's mercy, that is certain. But it's damned inconvenient.'

'I'm dreadfully sorry,' she said, unable to keep all traces of acid out of her voice. To her dismay, her voice cracked and she cleared her throat. He inspected her again.

'You aren't about to cry, are you?'

'Of course not. I...perhaps...perhaps if I might sit?'

He grunted and guided her to the table like an old lady. She sat, resting her elbows on it and barely resisting the urge to lean her head on it as well.

'When did you last eat?'

'Breakfast. Yesterday.'

'Idiot.'

'I am not an idiot... I was hiding. Then I went to the market to try and buy bread, but I heard al-Mizan again.'

He rubbed his jaw and her own palms tingled. She laid them flat on the table.

'My friend went to buy food, but you need something to settle your nerves.' He went to the cupboard and took out a bottle. She watched his back as his muscles bunched and relaxed. It was like the sand dunes in the Western Desert—a smooth, sculpted landscape broken occasionally by a jagged scar. His skin looked warm—pliable but firm. She leaned her chin on her hand, feeling a little warm herself.

Hunger and weariness explained a great deal.

'Are you truly a mercenary?'

He glanced over his shoulder. 'Do you even know what that is?'

'Of course I do. A soldier of fortune.'

'Well, fortune is debatable, but, yes. You're lucky I am currently not employed and can act as knight errant.'

She looked about the simple room, noting the scuffed boots and the rather ratty backpack by the cupboard. But then there was the expensive cotton shirt. She could not quite make sense of the man. Perhaps he was down on his luck?

'I can pay. The pendant may be hideous, but the emerald itself is quite valuable.'

He turned and smiled and her gaze slunk away; she felt as though she'd been caught peeking through a spy hole in a bath house. The man finally pulled the shirt over his head. Then he sat, resting his arms on the table.

Thank goodness. Trying not to stare at his chest and arms was exhausting. Clothed, he looked a little less intimidating.

'I have more than enough for my simple tastes,' he answered. 'Keep your beastly pendant for a rainy day, or an overly sunny one. I haven't seen a drop of rain since we dropped anchor in Alexandria. I am beginning to miss England, which is quite an achievement.'

'You have been away long?'

'A while. I must return though. My father died as well.'

'I'm sorry.' Her movement was instinctive, her hand settling on his forearm before she could censure herself. It was so unlike her she left it there for a moment before carefully drawing away. He didn't even seem to notice, just shrugged and uncorked the bottle, pouring two glasses.

'Don't be sorry. He was a right bastard as Birdie would say. The world heaved a sigh of relief when he finally cocked up his toes, but it means I probably must return to England and see how my family fares. Here.'

'What is this?'

'Brandy. Just a little until Birdie returns with something to eat.'

'You are being very kind, but I must pay…' She faltered as his gaze flicked back to her.

'Will you stop harking about payment? I'm not the most reliable of fellows, but I can't desert the Queen of Egypt in the middle of the desert. You asked for help, I'm offering. I'll see you to Cairo…'

The knock at the door had her back behind the curtain before she could even think. His chuckle followed her.

'It's only Birdie. Come in, Birdie. I hope you have brought enough food. We have a guest.'

Chapter Two

Rafe tried hard not to smile as the young woman's honey-hazel eyes widened at the sight of Birdie.

She had an almost unfortunately expressive face. It was like watching a battlefield, constantly changing and frequently surprising. But some reactions were thoroughly predictable—like her reaction to his scars and to Birdie's ugly mug.

To her credit, she adapted swiftly to shocks. She'd done an admirable job keeping her eyes away from his scars without appearing to do so and he'd finally taken pity on her and put on the shirt she'd crushed.

Peculiarly, it felt different against his skin and he tugged at his sleeves and rubbed his forearm where she'd touched it briefly in commiseration. Hers hadn't been the first condolence he'd received after his father's death, but it had felt surprisingly sincere.

He had probably shocked her with his unemotional response, but he refused to add sugar to vinegar. The world was well rid of the bastard and he wouldn't pretend otherwise, not even to a stranger. Certainly not to such a strange stranger.

Birdie placed the basket on the table and turned. After his first glance at the woman, he'd predictably ignored her.

'A guest, sir?'

'This is Miss Cleopatra…something. We haven't been
formally introduced. She is being chased by some unsa-
voury individuals and we shall be escorting her to Cairo.'

'We shall, eh? What about your brother, Master Edge?
He's the reason we've come to this godforsaken place and
now you want to run off before we see this through?'

'We are not running off. We've done everything we
can and left a trail of breadcrumbs the size of pyramids
to tempt his sorry carcase through Egypt. If that doesn't
knock him out of his apathy, I abandon hope for the fool.
Once we reach Cairo we will know if our ruse worked. If
not, I shall arrange with some friends to hit him over the
head and throw him on the first boat to England.'

Birdie shrugged.

'You two were served double…no, treble measures of
stubborn at birth, sir. Even if you fetch him here, there's
no saying it will make a difference. You can bring a horse
to water, but…'

'Yes, yes, the drinking part. All I want is to dump him
in the trough for the moment. Eventually, even that idiot
must drink. He's parched and won't admit it.'

Birdie grunted and began unpacking his purchases. The
wide flatbread, speckled brown and black from the oven,
was still warm and the scent filled the room.

The girl swallowed audibly and Rafe tore off a generous piece, handing it to her.

'Don't eat it too quickly or you'll make yourself ill,
Cleo-Pat. Birdie will prepare one of his famous stews and
some of the local mint tea which will help soothe your
nerves and stomach. Then you sleep and tomorrow at dawn
we'll find a way to sneak you past these unpleasant fellows. Right, Birdie?'

Birdie grunted again, casting her a look as he went to
the door.

'I had the landlord put water on to boil. I'll be back with tea and stew.'

The woman tensed as the door closed behind Birdie and Rafe touched her arm briefly, bringing her eyes to his.

'Don't worry, Birdie is as practised at this as I am. Once you eat, you sleep. If we're to leave at dawn, I want you rested. You will need your wits about you.'

'I don't think I *can* sleep.'

'I think you'll find you can, Cleopatra. Here. Have another piece of bread.'

He had a thousand questions, but he just sat and watched as she chewed slowly, like a dutiful child, even as suspicion was practically rising off her like steam from a bath. Still, when Birdie returned with bowls of the pungent stew and sweet tea she did justice to them with the same careful but methodical approach. Her face was no longer expressive, but as sealed as one of the statues they'd passed along their route. Perhaps it was only hunger and weariness that had left her so exposed.

'More, miss?' Birdie stood with the brass teapot poised over the girl's cup. Unlike the previous three times, she shook her head, casting Birdie a fuzzy smile.

'No more, thank you, sir.' Her voice was slurring and she kept straightening her spine, only to have her shoulders sink under their own weight. Rafe would wager she was so far gone she thought no one was aware of the epic battle she was fighting against sleep.

She'd thanked him as well, but without the smile; warily, like a street dog being offered a scrap and suspecting a trap, but too hungry to keep away.

Pity—she had a smile that completely altered her face. It certainly worked on Birdie, because his usually taciturn friend was beginning to return her smiles, exposing his broken front tooth. That was an honour almost never bestowed on friends, let alone strangers. He was also digging through the stew to find the choicest pieces of lamb for her, something he'd never do for Rafe.

Rafe watched this peculiar blossoming of ease between the two even as he gauged how close Miss Queen of the Nile was to utter collapse. She'd unwrapped her dingy cloth turban from about her head, revealing short hair that fell in feathery swathes across her brow and nape. It was a burnished chestnut colour, like sunlight on wood. Her eyes were also shades of wood and light, with a ring of gold around the increasingly dilated irises.

With her cultured voice, her simple cotton *gallabiyah*, and woodland faerie hair, she was unlike anything he'd come across. Perhaps if he caught her on the cusp of sleep, with her belly full and her head heavy, she might be more liberal with her secrets.

Her lids drooped again and snapped open.

'Thank you, sir,' she recited.

'You're welcome, Miss Cleopatra. So tell me about this book they are after.'

'Book… I don't know. I *told* you.'

'Tell me again. Everything you know.'

She smothered a yawn and rubbed her forehead.

'My father disappeared. More than two months ago. He does sometimes. Disappears for long periods. Looking for objects to buy and sell. My brother went to look for him…'

'Why?'

'Why?' She dragged the word out, her eyes meeting his. He couldn't see any gold in them now, they were all brandy and darkness. The poor girl was half asleep, but he needed to learn a little more.

'Why did your brother go after him if you were accustomed to his absences?'

'Oh. Because Farouq, my father's servant, left him and returned to Cairo.'

'You were worried about your father being alone?'

'*I* wasn't. Dash was. He's nicer than I.'

Well, that was honest.

'Dash didn't return. I was worried. I thought…if something happened and I had not tried…'

'Ah. Guilt.'

'Not only guilt. Dash is too good. My father takes advantage.'

She waved a hand, narrowly missing her cup. Again she seemed to fade, leaning her arm on the table. Her other hand was absently fingering the scabbard of the knife attached to the cloth belt wrapped about her *gallabiyah*. He debated disarming her, but thought better of it. She would feel safer with that toothpick at her disposal.

'So you dressed as Patrick and headed south… Surely not alone?'

She shook her head and yawned again, covering her face with two hands.

'No. I hired a dragoman. He ran away in Meroe.'

'That is unchivalrous. Why?'

'He heard al-Mizan was looking for an Englishman. My description. Dash and I look alike.'

'I see. What did you discover of your father and brother?'

'My father fell ill and died, and I missed my brother by two days. I'm so tired. I must…'

She pushed aside her cup, laid her arms on the table, her head on her arms, and with a little sigh she was asleep.

Rafe looked over her recumbent form at Birdie who had been listening as avidly as he.

'What do you make of that, Birdie?'

'Not much, Colonel. Plenty of holes in that tale. But we can't leave her here.'

'No, unfortunately not. Well, we shall have to change our plans. This sleeping stray here has hired me to deliver her safely to Cairo.'

Birdie gave a snorting laugh.

'Hired you. With what?'

'A tale full of holes.'

'You're an easy mark, Colonel. Beware.'

'She's no threat. Look at her.'

They both looked. She snuggled deeper into her arms. Rafe sighed.

'I'd best put her to bed. Could you find another mattress for me? And not a word to the landlord about our guest.'

'Naturally not. You take my room and I'll bunk on the floor here.'

'No, Birdie. Go speak with Gamal, quietly. Tell him to meet us with the camels by the desert road well before daybreak. That al-Mizan fellow will likely still have people watching the port so we must leave town by the back door.'

'Pity. Gamal was looking forward to selling those camels at market and going home and I was looking forward to a gentle sail down the river.' Birdie sighed and gathered the cups as Rafe came round the table, inspecting his sleeping charge.

'So was I, old man. You are a right nuisance, Miss Patrick Cleopatra. Come along now, into bed with you.'

He was prepared for panic or resistance, but there was none. He held her with one arm around her waist and she went as boneless as a rag doll, her head falling against his chest and her legs buckling. With a grunt he tucked another arm under her legs and swung her up.

She was a tall woman and he'd been right that there were some very pleasant curves under her *gallabiyah* and robe. Her hair was silky under his chin, and beneath the smell of dust and hay was an elusive scent, something cool and green, like a field of wildflowers caught in a late frost. It was totally out of place in a land of browns and ochres.

He smiled at his unusual flight of fancy, but as he laid her down carefully on the narrow bed he allowed himself to breathe it in, her hair just tickling the tip of his nose as she turned to the wall and curled into a ball.

'You are a very peculiar beast, Miss Whoever-You-Are,' he murmured above her and went to fetch a blanket for his new employer.

Rafe stood by the bed. It was still dark and only the occasional sound of an animal—the faint bray of a donkey or yowl of a cat—broke the silence. The girl was still curled up against the wall, taking up a fraction of the long bed. She slept like a hedgehog being sniffed at by a dog.

He rolled his shoulders.

It was time to wake her.

He'd been right to assume the men chasing her would have people at the docks. He'd gone there himself after she'd fallen asleep and seen a couple of the men who'd stood behind that al-Mizan fellow delivering orders to the boatmen. There would be no leaving by that route without having to contend with their knives and the might of the local Bey. It was possible, but risky, and he always preferred the path of least resistance.

Which meant another ride through the desert.

Not his favourite.

He'd told Edge years ago he had no interest whatsoever in visiting his beloved Egypt, being burnt to a crisp by the brutal sun and having what was left flayed by sandstorms. His experiences of the land thus far had only partially changed his mind. He wasn't averse to a nice trip downriver on one of those dahabiya boats, but camels…

Damn, he was getting old.

She sighed, shifting, and the dim light of the oil lamp on the table glinted on her short hair. Even in the pallid light, it was obvious that colour would look magnificent if left to grow long. She'd done a poor job in the back, leaving a tangle of warm waves that gave him a rather clear idea of the magnitude of the offense. Pity. He'd have liked to see that warm chestnut silk in its full glory. Since he'd have her back in Cairo within a week, that was unlikely, but a man could dream.

He leaned over the bed and touched her shoulder and almost fell backwards as she catapulted on to her feet, skidding along the wall.

'Shh…' he cautioned, praying she wouldn't scream. 'It's only the scarred mercenary. It's time to leave.'

She was breathing as if she'd run up four flights of stairs, her hands pressed to the wall. Her eyes were just pale slashes and then they closed as she breathed in very slowly.

'I was dreaming of al-Mizan.'

'I'm sure he'd be flattered.'

'That is *not* what I meant.'

'I'm relieved. I don't see much of a future for you two. Unions should be based on more than a shared appreciation of criminality.'

Her gasp was followed by a little snort of laughter.

'I am not a criminal. I told you, I did not steal anything.'

'I don't particularly care if you did. Mercenaries aren't choosy about their employers, Pat. Now dress so we can slink off into the dark while it is still dark.' He held out his hand and she carefully detached herself from the wall. Her hand was warm in his as he helped her down and, despite her violent awakening, it had the softness of sleep in it. It felt…comforting—a peculiar feeling and not an unpleasant one. He wanted to slip her fingers between his so he could capture that softness, but he let go and turned to take the folded cotton scarf she'd used to cover her head from where Birdie had folded it over a chair.

'You are looking a little better for your rest and food. How are you feeling?'

'I feel…' She paused, her eyes widening in surprise, 'I feel better. That stew was life-giving. But I cannot remember anything after that.'

'I'm not surprised. You were exhausted. Fell face forward into your stew.'

'I did not!'

Her hands, pale smudges, rose to touch her face and he couldn't help smiling at her embarrassment. It was so out of place in this strange situation.

She was out of place.

Hell, *he* was out of place.

Even in the dim light he could see her face turning bright red and he took pity on her.

'I caught you before you landed. It would have been a waste of a decent stew.'

'I don't believe you.'

'Well, I am exaggerating a little. You were coherent enough to put the plate aside before you folded your arms on the table and fell asleep. Don't look so pained, Pat. Amazingly you did not make a fool of yourself, though I would be sure to tell you if you did.'

She glared at him.

'That's right,' he approved. 'Annoyance is healthier than embarrassment. Have at me.'

She surprised him again, her hands dropping, her brows drawing together almost in sorrow.

'You must think me so selfish.'

'I must? Why must I?'

'I did not even thank you or your valet.'

He moved towards the table, tucking his favourite knife into its scabbard and strapping it on before pulling on his coat. He had no problem with people showing their gratitude, preferably in monetary terms, but her remorse made him uncomfortable, as if he'd cheated it out of her, which made no sense.

'You thanked me twice last night, Pat. And Birdie three times. Every time he brought you tea. You drank like a camel.'

'Did I? I…it is all a little murky…but that is not the point. I am truly grateful. And I am sorry you must leave here because of me.'

'Yes, well, we were leaving anyway. You have ten minutes to get yourself in order, Cleo-Pat. I'll wait for you by the stairs.'

He picked up his pack from the table and left the room before she said anything else. Her mercurial transformations were unsettling and he didn't like being unsettled. It was bad for longevity.

Chapter Three

Cleo had lived through many strange days. Certainly stranger than skulking through the narrow roads and the palm groves out of Syene in the pre-dawn hours with two silent men.

Her father's activities had sometimes required hasty scuttlings off in the dark, but the emotions that accompanied those exoduses—a gut-tightening amalgam of fear, anger, frustration, exasperation and weariness—weren't present that dawn. Other than her fear for Dash, she felt surprisingly calm.

Still, she kept glancing over her shoulder, expecting to see al-Mizan and his men materialise out of the dark alleys, but no one followed and only a few stray chickens and a couple of somnolent dogs watched their departure, not even bothering to bark.

Once clear of the town they followed a rough pebbled path towards the low hills. She had little to watch now but the broad back of the mercenary ahead of her. He wore a pale coat that blended well with the desert and he walked with long but light strides.

She was following him without knowing a thing about him other than that he was English and a mercenary. Surely that was a flimsy base upon which to place her trust?

He had a nice smile, her mind offered.

Plenty of scoundrels had nice smiles. '*A man could smile, and smile, and be a villain,*' as Hamlet had said. In fact, it was often their stock in trade. Her father, when it suited him, could smile and beguile with the best of them.

And a marvellous physique, the same treacherous voice chimed in, and she gave it a firm shove back where it belonged. She'd fallen once into that trap and had sworn never to do so again. William had looked like one of the Greek statues he so admired and he'd been a thorough scoundrel in the end.

As always, thoughts of William made her hackles and suspicions rise. She should at least demand to know their destination. It was clear they were heading into the desert, but surely these two men did not think they could get far in this brutal land on foot and with nothing but what they were carrying in their backs.

The mercenary raised his head, scanning the low cliffs, the dawn light turning his scars milky grey.

Was he looking for someone? Perhaps he had struck a deal with al-Mizan while she slept and was delivering her to him in the privacy of the desert...

She slowed, reaching under her robe to grasp the knife attached to the cloth belt wound about her *gallabiyah*.

The giant turned and stopped, his eyes catching the first light of the sun rising sluggishly behind her. Her instincts, usually so reliable, were still as groggy as she'd felt yesterday. Perhaps she *was* still light-headed despite the tea and stew.

She didn't even know his name. That was wrong, wasn't it? To trust one's life to a man when you didn't even know his name?

'What now, Pat?' He sounded impatient.

'I don't know your name.'

'For the love of Zeus... You want society introductions? Here?'

He swept an arm to take in the ragged hills around them and she backed away another step.

'Why won't you tell me your name? Two words. Even one will do.'

'I could just as easily lie to you about it, you know.'

'Yes, but then I'll know you're lying. About everything.'

He sighed. 'And you were so sensible yesterday. My name is Rafe. Now get moving before our guide Gamal decides to continue without us and trades our camels for a bride.'

Rafe. It wasn't much, but it wasn't a lie. Strange name for a strange man. And apparently there were camels and a guide awaiting them.

She took a deep breath and moved forward. He nodded.

'Good. Now stop acting like a skittish foal and keep quiet. I don't want anyone passing through these hills to hear a female speaking in English. So assume you've taken a vow of silence until we're safely in the middle of no-where, understood?'

She opened her mouth and closed it as he raised a brow.

She nodded, annoyance doing a fair job of chasing away her fear. There was no need for him to snap at her like that. Any sane person would hesitate under these circumstances. Skittish, indeed!

She continued this bracing inner dialogue until they passed through the ravine on to a broad plain. Several camels were tethered together by a copse of palm trees, one camel hobbled, his front leg bent upwards and tied to prevent him from running off. A young Bedawi was seated on the rim of a square well and he jumped down and flashed them a grin, sweeping the scene with his arm as if he'd produced the whole oasis from thin air.

Still wary, she approached the closest camel, a cow with a swan-like neck and eyelashes as thick and curling as their guide's.

'She likes you,' the Bedawi said in French as he adjusted

the cow's bridle, smiling at Cleo. Cleo returned his smile
and was just reaching out to pat the cow's neck when a
large camel to her right gave a resentful grunt and stretched
out his neck to nip at her robe with large yellow teeth. She
leapt back and the young man shoved the hairy face away,
but gave it a quick rub on the chin and the grunts subsided.

Cleo rubbed at her shoulder though the camel had done
no damage.

'I don't think he likes you flirting with Gamal, Pat,'
Rafe said beside her. 'Pity you two got off to a bad start,
especially since you'll be riding him.'

'I… *Him?* You must be jesting!'

'Best way to make sure you don't turn your back on
the brute is to be on *his* back, right? Pat here will be riding Kabir, Gamal.'

She was quite certain the giant was making game of
her, but the Bedawi took him seriously, raising his hands
in horror.

'No, *nadab*. Kabir no like women. He al-Shroud. Only
men ride him. Boy will ride Gamila.' He patted the cow.

Well, Gamila wasn't as pretty as her name proclaimed,
but her soft muzzle brushed Cleo's shoulder, as if to compensate for Kabir's bad manners. Cleo smiled into her doe-
like eyes and stroked her wiry neck.

'You're nothing like that great brute, are you, darling?'
she cooed. 'You're a beautiful little sweetheart, aren't you?
Yes, you…*ack*!'

She gave a whoop of surprise as Rafe raised her by the
waist and deposited her on the blanketed saddle.

'Do try to remember you've taken a vow of silence until
I say otherwise, Pat. And if you must talk, try not to sound
as though you're making love to the blasted animal—
anyone hearing you will see through that disguise faster
than I did.'

He strode off and Cleo glared after him. It hadn't hurt,

but her skin tingled where he'd touched her none the less, as if she'd left it exposed to the desert sun.

They rode in silence, Gamila falling into an easy rolling gait, her long neck swinging a little from side to side as if to some unheard tune. Occasionally Rafe glanced back at her with a half-amused smile, as if remembering a good joke, or as if convinced his demand she remain silent was proving a true penance.

Which it was, blast him.

Silence was usually no hardship for her. She'd long ago developed the skill of daydreaming her way through interminable and uncomfortable hours of travel. But now the temptation to demand he tell her his plans was churning inside her like the cataracts of the Nile.

After what seemed like hours he checked Kabir's pace and came alongside her.

'You may speak now, Pat. All those thoughts bouncing about inside of you can't be good for your health. Or my longevity. I should have remembered to take away that little toothpick tied to your belt while you slept before you're tempted to wield it against me.'

She pressed her hand to the 'toothpick' and narrowed her eyes against the glare of the sun as she looked at Rafe. He and Birdie had wrapped linen cloths into turbans to protect their heads like the local *fellahin* and he had tucked the cotton end of it so that it covered the scarred side of his face.

'Where are we heading?'

'To a port further north.'

'Is that wise? Once al-Mizan realises I am no longer in Syene, he will likely search the neighbouring port towns.'

'Not when he hears your brother hired two men to take him to the Red Sea port of Berenice yesterday evening.'

'What? Why did you not tell me? I must return…'

She tugged on the reins and at Gamila's protesting grunt Kabir's long neck snaked out, his teeth bared and heading for Cleo's knee. Fortunately, they closed with a snap just short of her as Rafe angled the animal's head away.

'What the devil is wrong with you, you hairy tortoise? He really doesn't like you, does he? And there is no call to hare off in pursuit. Your brother is not on his way to Berenice. That is what is termed a *diversion*.'

Her excitement fizzled.

'Al-Mizan is too intelligent to fall prey to a trick.'

'Which is why I paid two men to leave town in a highly secretive manner after spreading rumours of taking a furtive, honey-eyed *hawagi* to Berenice.'

'What will happen to them if al-Mizan catches them?'

His gaze moved over her face.

'What a sensitive conscience you have, Pat. Once they provide your admirer with the information they were well paid to deliver, he will let them go.'

'You cannot be certain of that.'

'I am certain of nothing, but I choose my pawns well. They are cousins of Bey al-Wassawi and were in pressing need of some funds. It would not serve al-Mizan's purpose to harm the relations of the local Bey with no cause.'

'And what information were they to pass along?'

'That Birdie and I are on the run from Mehmet Ali after I tried to…ah, elope with his niece and that we presumed al-Mizan came to my rooms using the tale of an English thief as a cover to gauge my defences.'

She tried not to smile. 'That is…elaborate.'

'I thought so, too, but Birdie concocted it and he has an affection for tall tales. To give him his due it did possess the right elements—honour and revenge and cowardly foreigners and all that.'

'No element of truth?'

'Did I elope with the Khedive's niece?' His brows rose in mockery.

'No, I meant…are you on the run?'

'Only from myself. But this wasn't what you were anguishing over just now, though, was it?'

'I wasn't anguishing.'

'If you'd squeezed your lips together any tighter, you'd have lost them. Now that we are a safe distance and can talk I think it is best you tell me more about your predicament so we can be prepared for the worst.'

Suspicion came back with a roar, chasing away her amusement—what if all this openness and charm was aimed at coaxing the information out of her without risking violence? What if he and al-Mizan—?

'There. You're anguishing again,' the mercenary interrupted her thoughts. He looked cross and impatient now, not the kind of expression one expected of a crafty killer. Still, she looked around—they were truly in the middle of nowhere. If he chose to kill her, the only beings to witness her demise would be jackals and vultures and the creepy crawly things that feasted on carrion and…

'Where are we heading?' She forced the question out, her voice as rough as the ground under Gamila's sure hooves.

'I told you, Gamal is taking us further up the river.'

'Which port?'

'You needn't concern yourself with that. Gamal knows what he's doing. I hope. Now, why don't you tell me—?'

She spurred Gamila forward until she came up beside Gamal. Rafe sighed and clicked his tongue, spurring Kabir after her.

'May I ask you a question, Gamal?' she asked in Arabic.

'You speak Arabic!' The young man's eyes widened, accentuating the lines of kohl under his eyes that protected them from sun and disease.

'I learned in Acre.'

'Ah! Far away.' He glanced past her and switched to his lilting mix of French and English. 'She speaks good

Arabic, *nadab*. Now someone understand Gamal and I not speak as to little children.'

'Just remember this little child here is the one paying you,' Rafe replied, tapping his chest. Gamal's smile widened.

'I shall keep your secrets, *nadab*.'

'You don't know my secrets, Gamal.'

'Then it will be easy, yes?' He winked at Cleo and she smiled and answered him in Arabic.

'I don't want to cause you trouble, but could you tell me where you are taking us?'

'*Biltakid!* Of course! To Daraw. We shall reach it by nightfall. There is a small port there where a fishing boat could take you to Luxor and from there you could find a proper *dahabiya*. That would be fastest.'

She thanked him and allowed her mount to fall back again. Unfortunately, Rafe did the same.

'Why didn't you tell me you spoke Arabic?' he demanded.

'You didn't ask.'

'True. Would you have told me had I asked?'

She considered that.

'Probably. I don't enjoy lying unless I must.'

'Good. So now tell me what you spoke of and why it worried you.'

'How do you know it worried me?' she temporised.

'Because when you aren't impersonating a sphinx, your face is as expressive as a toddler's.'

'Ah, I see you are still smarting from Gamal's child comment.'

'No, I merely don't like people talking behind my back.'

'We were right beside you.'

'Don't quibble, Pat. Tell me.' He paused, his gaze holding hers. 'I see. You don't trust me...'

She waited for another flash of panic, but it refused to

come. Somehow facing his scarred and frowning visage made him less fearsome.

'All he said was that we are heading for Daraw, a small port not far to the north. There are only fishing boats there, not the larger *feluccas* or *dahabiyas* that could transport us to Cairo.'

Rafe tapped his hand on his thigh and scanned the horizon.

'I wish we had a decent map of this place. Mine shows nothing between Syene and the temples. I'll have a word with Gamal and Birdie and decide what is best.'

'I'm dreadfully sorry to be such a bother, Mr… Rafe.'

'How very English of you, Miss Pat. And it is either Rafe or, if you are clinging to the codes of civilisation, Mr Grey.'

'Mr Grey.' She smiled at the wholly inappropriate name. Mr Grey had to be one of the least grey men of her acquaintance. 'I am pleased to make your acquaintance, Mr Grey.'

He smiled back and gave a little bow.

'The pleasure is all mine, Miss Cleopatra… What *is* your full name?'

'Osbourne. Cleopatra Osbourne.'

'*Osbourne?* Well, well. The pleasure is all mine, Miss Cleopatra Osbourne.'

Chapter Four

'Tired?'

Cleopatra-Patrick Osbourne glanced up from staring at her saddle and shook her head without a word.

She was proving to be one of those rare people who only spoke when they had something to say. There was even something a little intimidating about the way she made no requests for either sustenance or rest as the hours melted away in the blazing heat. She'd eaten when Birdie brought her dried dates and bread, bestowing that same surprisingly warm smile upon his friend, but otherwise she seemed miles away, as unapproachable as the desert.

The broad, padded saddles were far more comfortable than he'd expected and the camels moved with impressive balance and occasionally speed over uneven ground, but the desert was just as uncomfortable as anticipated. It was mostly rock-strewn plains between stark hills, tufted with thorny trees and bushes. It was nothing like the illustrations of rolling sand dunes he'd seen in his brother's books. He'd have to have a word with Edge about authorial integrity.

It was also empty. He'd seen not one living soul the entire day other than a few lizards poking their snouts at the sun. It was daunting as hell and hot as Hades. The only positive was that it would be impossible for anyone to approach them without being seen. He untucked the cloth that covered his face and breathed deeply.

'Gamal said we are stopping for the night at the end of this plain,' he said to the girl and she glanced up from her contemplation of her saddle.

'So soon? We could cover quite a few more miles before dark, surely.'

'*You* could, perhaps, but there is a well there and I think the camels might prefer to stop and drink. They've been doing the hard work all day, after all. You've only been sitting there scowling and stewing.'

Even under the film of dust that covered her face he could see her colour rise, but then the lines at the corners of her eyes crinkled in laughter.

'You are a strange man, Mr Grey. I cannot tell if you are trying to annoy me or make me laugh.'

'I haven't yet decided. Either will serve the purpose better than you sinking into a brown study. Though to be fair, brown is pretty much all there *is* to study out here.'

She laughed and unhooked the cloth covering her mouth, shaking off a small cloud of dust.

'I love it.'

'You and my brother.' He sighed. 'I wish you would explain what it is about the desert that appeals to you, for I am yet to understand this passion for sand.'

'Now you are being facetious. There is so much more than sand here.'

'Rocks. Thorny bushes and stunted trees.'

'Have you seen none of the antiquities?'

'A little. Birdie and I have been on a forced march, or rather forced sail up the Nile.'

'You said as much before. Why *are* you here if you are not interested in these lands? Has it to do with this brother of yours?'

He found himself on the verge of telling her about Edge

when he realised she had done it again—very neatly deflected attention from herself.

'Miss Osbourne—'

'Look!' she interrupted with a little sigh of pleasure. 'An oasis.'

They'd just come around an outcropping and a burst of blessed green met their eyes—palm trees waving above a clump of bushes and a streak of low green grass marking the run off from a well.

'Thank the lord,' he said with equal pleasure. 'Miss Osbourne, would you care for a cup of tea?'

Rafe held the two chipped cups as Birdie poured from the kettle.

'Campfire tea again, Colonel,' Birdie said with satisfaction. 'It has been a while, no?'

'You have a peculiar sense of nostalgia, Birdie. We had perfectly respectable tea only yesterday. Without the mud. I hope the boiling killed whatever that is that's floating in it.'

Birdie poked at it with the tip of the stick he'd used to stir the fire, adding flecks of charred wood to the brew.

'Looks dead to me. You drink that and give her the other.'

'*Thank* you, Birdie.'

'You're welcome, Colonel.' Birdie grinned unrepentantly and Rafe sighed and walked across to where the young woman was seated on a wide boulder. She was staring hard at the ground, oblivious to the spectacle of the setting sun turning the hills around them into a dance of red-orange fire. She might be dressed like a man, but she looked the image of a desert princess being conveyed to some unwanted fate—resolute but inwardly resisting.

'May I join you, Pat?'

She cast him a guilty look, as if she'd been caught thinking very uncharitable thoughts of him and their little camp.

Well, he'd been thinking the same.

She met his gaze but he felt her thoughts were several leagues away. She did not even appear to notice he was holding out a steaming cup of tea so he raised it, making the steam weave tipsily between them.

'Here. For you.'

She blinked and took the steaming tin cup warily. 'What is it?'

'Tea. Sugar. And something murky at the bottom, so drink carefully.'

Her sudden laugh was even more a surprise than her smile—it was rolling, joyous…irresistible. It took years off her face and he found himself smiling as he sat down on the boulder beside her.

For a few moments, they sipped their tea and watched the sun melt into the hills. The wind was rising, sweeping away the baking heat of the day, and the scent of earth and tea soothed the edges of this stark world.

He knew it was time to discover more about his charge, but the moment was so…peaceful, he didn't want to let it go just yet.

In the end she spoke first.

'The last time I had tea in the desert was with my brother.'

'Tell me about him.'

'He is two years younger than I. Very clever. We write articles together for the *Illustrated Gazette* about our travels under the name D.C. Osbourne. Do you know the *Gazette*?'

'I don't, I'm afraid. A local newspaper?'

'Oh, no. They are London-based and very selective.'

'Impressive.'

She glanced at him as if gauging whether he was being serious. Birdie had given her soap and she'd washed her face and hands and her lashes were still spiked together. With her short hair uncovered and the wind teasing it against her cheeks and brow she could easily have been a model for Leila, the heroine of the *Desert Boy* novels his brother penned. He smiled at the silly notion and she frowned.

'It *is* impressive,' she insisted, mistaking his smile. 'We have had almost a dozen articles appear in the *Gazette*. Do you know how many journalists would give their eye-teeth to achieve that?'

'Many, I presume. I have no idea what eye-teeth are, but they sound valuable.'

Her frown gave way to laughter again.

'They are the pointy teeth, like a dog's, though I am quite certain you know that. You are a strange man, Mr Grey.'

'That has been pointed out to me before, for various reasons. What is yours?'

'I cannot make out what you are thinking.'

'That is a good sign. I've spent many years working to achieve that effect and it is comforting to know I've succeeded. Do you always expect to know what people are thinking, Miss Osbourne?'

'No, that would be presumptuous of me, but few people make the effort to truly hide their thoughts and even fewer do so while appearing so amicable and reasonable on the surface.'

He pressed a hand to his chest.

'Are you implying that I am duplicitous, Miss Cleopatra-Patrick-on-the-run-dressed-as-a-boy?'

'No, I am saying you possess a singular talent, Mr Grey. It was a compliment.'

'I shall return the compliment by telling you precisely what I am thinking, which is that though I find your singular talent for not chattering very impressive, at the moment I need you to tell me as much as you can about your situation so I know what lies ahead of us.'

She sighed and touched the tip of her tongue to the dry

skin of her lower lip. His tongue tingled and he pressed his teeth into it. Down, boy. Wholly inopportune.

'I don't particularly enjoy talking about my family's affairs, Mr Grey.'

'Perfectly understandable. I myself would prefer to share my bed with a dozen warthogs rather than do that, but, given the circumstances, you will have to overcome your distaste.'

'I know that. I am not certain where to begin. With my father, I suppose. He is rather hard to explain. He was a…a collector.'

'Of?'

'Curios. He travelled the world collecting whatever he thought people might have an interest in buying. Masks, statues, anything really. Since we came to Egypt he concentrated on statues and ancient jewellery. And mummies.'

'Mummies? As in…mummies? *Dead people* mummies? Your father was a grave robber?'

'Of course not, mummies aren't…they…he…well, I dare say you are right. Amongst other things. For the most part he worked for a French antiquities trader in Cairo named Boucheron, but he recently tried to find independent sources of income.'

'Such as selling decomposing corpses.'

'They are remarkably well preserved; that is the whole point. He recently sold a shipment of some three dozen mummies to a man named Pettifer in London who also has an interest in Egyptian curiosities.'

'He shipped three dozen dead people to London.'

'They weren't all people. There were also some baboons and cats and even a crocodile…' She must have seen something of his thoughts on his face for her honey-brown eyes filled with laughter. 'Never mind. I know it is ghoulish, but there is a market for them thanks to the likes of Belzoni and Drovetti. People pay to watch them unwrapped.'

'Good God.'

'You are very squeamish for a mercenary, Mr Grey.'

'Having my life almost forcibly removed from me on too many occasions, I have a healthy respect for it. I don't like the thought of my body being…tampered with.'

'Well, I don't think you need worry about that as you are unlikely to be mummified.'

'I prefer not to think about it at all, Miss Morbid. Shall we return to your father?'

'I dare say we must. The point is that my father was a scavenger. Rather like the ibises by the Nile—he collected what he could and hurried away when bigger prey arrived. That is why we moved so often.'

'And this is how you were raised?' That explained quite a bit.

'Not wholly. Until I was fourteen I lived with my mother in a small town near Dover. After she died…eventually we went to live with my father. He was in Acre at the time, searching for Templar treasure.'

Eventually. There was a wealth of possibilities tucked into that word. Curiosity plucked at him again, but he concentrated on his objective.

'I presume he found none?'

Her dimples appeared though her mouth merely gave a small quirk, as if struggling against invisible constraints.

'Naturally not. We were quite hopeful for a while, though.'

'So was I at fourteen. What happened next?'

'He ran afoul of Suleiman, the local Mameluke ruler.'

'What did he do? Try to steal his mummy?'

'I see you find this amusing, Mr Grey.'

'No, merely trying to raise a smile out of you. I'm improving, aren't I?'

Her smile won out over the dimples and he found himself smiling back.

'So you left Acre for Egypt?'

'No, first we went to Greece where Father found someone who made wonderful statuettes which he then made to look ancient by staining them with tea and cracking them. Dash and I enjoyed that part of it. Then they shipped them to accomplices of theirs in England until he was requested to leave after…after his partner returned to England and my father could not pay his debts. From there we went to Zanzibar because he had heard from Mr Pettifer that there was demand for more exotic findings. We lived there until—'

'Let me guess. Until he fell afoul of the local ruler and was forced to leave. Again.'

'No, his searches meant we sailed a great deal along the coast and at one point the ship we were on was captured by pirates.'

'Good God! How old were you? Were you…hurt?'

She tipped her head on one side, considering the undercurrent he could not hide from his question.

'Ever since I came to live with my father I have often been Patrick. He said he could hardly take in a girl and was planning to send me to some horrid convent school in the desert. I refused to go and leave Dash alone with him. Patrick was a compromise.'

He digested this piece of information, adjusting his thoughts and curbing his temper, but it wasn't easy. Fathers were a sore point with him, but hers was shaping up to be someone he most definitely would not have gone out of his way to help.

'Do you mean to say you have been masquerading as Patrick Osbourne from the age of fourteen?'

'Well, only part of the time. It was far simpler than it sounds. We were children and there were very few Europeans where we were and many tended to be associated with the various churches and therefore naturally my father avoided them. The most creditable Englishwoman I met during this period was Lady Hester Stanhope and she was dressed far more outrageously than I.'

'You met her?'

'I did, though not in the best of circumstances. My father tried to insinuate himself into her expedition to Ascalon, but once he realised she planned to surrender whatever she found to the authorities he left. She was very kind to Dash and me and thoroughly approved of my man's garb, having adopted it herself long before. She even gave me a pair of her embroidered trousers.'

'So she, at least, knew you were a girl.'

'Oh, yes. It is usually the women who see through my disguise, but they rarely tell the men.'

'The world in a nutshell.' He grinned and she finally turned to him fully.

'*You* saw through it, Mr Grey. What does that make you?' Her smile, complicit and full of mischievous light, felt like an invitation to step over an unseen barrier... Into what, he had no idea, except that it was probably not a line he ought to cross. He pulled back on the reins he hadn't realised were slipping.

'Observant by necessity. My livelihood depends on it, Miss Osbourne. Now that we have established your father's dubious activities, tell me what happened here in Egypt.'

She shrugged and swirled her tea.

'The French led by Drovetti protect the antiquities trade jealously, sometimes violently. That is why Father decided it was safer to work with them. Boucheron hired him to help set up workshops to produce what they term *souvenirs* for sale in Paris and London and Vienna.'

'Sounds sensible. What went wrong?'

'My father never abandoned his dream of making a great discovery and he felt Boucheron's activities demeaned him. He wanted to be a Belzoni.'

'What on earth is a Belzoni?'

'Not what, who. Belzoni made his name transporting the statue of young Memnon to England and explored as far south as Ybsambul. He is all the rage in England now. My father abhorred him.'

'I thought he wanted to be him.'

'Precisely. Envy is a strange beast, isn't it?'

'I wouldn't know,' he said primly and won another smile.

'In any case, my father decided he would go even further south, to the pyramids of Nubia. There are dozens of them there, more even than in Egypt.'

'There is also an ongoing war, as best I can gather. Hardly the best place to take one's family.'

'That was why I…why Dash and I decided not to go with him.'

'I see. And how did he react to that?'

'He was…upset. He is accustomed to us tending to the practicalities of his life. But he had his servant with him. At least he did until Farouq also decided he had had enough and returned to Cairo where he went to work for Boucheron, my father's employer. By this time Dash and I had already decided it was time to leave Egypt. We'd been talking for a long while that we no longer wished to live like… fugitives. We planned to return to England and set up house and write articles and perhaps Dash could find employment at a university or a newspaper. We began making arrangements and sent a letter to our father to inform him.'

'Let me guess, he wrote back denouncing his ungrateful offspring.'

'No. He never wrote back at all. I told Dash that was an answer in itself as we should leave, but Dash is far nicer that I. He decided he could not leave without speaking with my father directly.'

'Leaving you alone in Cairo?'

She scuffed her boot on the pebble-strewn ground. The sun had sunk lower still and the hills and scrubby trees were casting long shadows, like fingers straining to envelop them. He could feel the struggle inside her.

'Tell me, Cleo-Pat.'

'It's all so complicated. I don't know if there is anything to tell. Dash tells me I am absurdly suspicious by nature.'

'I am glad to hear that. Here is your chance to unburden those suspicions to someone who has plenty of experience in that field.'

'Very well. A couple days before Dash left for Nubia, Boucheron came to our lodgings and told us our father stole something from him before his departure. He demanded we find my father and force him to return.'

'I thought you said your father spent several months in Nubia? If he stole something before he left, why didn't this Boucheron demand it's return earlier?'

'Precisely. I presumed Boucheron only realised my father's transgression because Farouq revealed something when he went to work for him.'

'Strange. Did he not tell you what it was?'

'No. When he realised we had no idea what he was speaking of, he merely said our father would know and that when we found him we should tell him that, unless he complied, Boucheron's Janissaries would resolve the issue. I knew what that meant. He'd once sent one of his servants to "resolve an issue" with a Maltese merchant. We never saw the merchant again.'

It wasn't calm, but iron control that held her voice flat. Probably years and years of expecting the worst. Rafe's hands tightened on his thighs but he didn't speak, just waited, and after a moment she continued.

'I decided right then that enough was enough. Boucheron might just as easily decide to kill one of us to make his point and I wanted Dash out of there.'

'Why didn't you offer him the emerald?'

'I did. He tossed it back at me. It seems no one wants it.'

'Interesting.'

'I thought so, too. I told Dash we needed to leave immediately and at first I thought he would agree—we even made travel arrangements—but then he disappeared to Nubia and left me a letter telling me he'd arranged for me to travel with a family returning to London on the same ship who were willing to provide me with lodging until he arrived.'

'Since you're here I presume that plan fell through.'

'I could not leave Egypt not knowing what had happened to Dash. Besides, the Mitchums were extremely proper and quite shocked with me. I think they were pleased I reneged on my brother's plan.'

'I can imagine. So, tell me what you discovered in Nubia and how those fellows, whom I assume are Boucheron's men, came to be chasing you?'

'It is complicated…'

'I have gathered that. Since we have nothing better to do at the moment you have plenty of time. Tell me.'

She sighed. 'Very well. When I reached Meroe I discovered my father had died and that Dash had been and already left to return to Cairo. But when I reached Wadi Halfa an innkeeper warned me a man called al-Mizan was looking for a young foreigner matching my description. Clearly he was searching for Dash. We are very alike.'

'I'm impressed the innkeeper didn't hand you over. You must have some hitherto undiscovered ability to charm.'

The dimples punctuated her cheeks, but her voice remained dispassionate.

'That was when my dragoman left me, so apparently my charm has its limits. I managed to remain hidden until Syene but when I tried to hire a felucca the owner ran off to find al-Mizan so I went back into hiding. I thought the longer I led them astray, the more time Dash would have to reach Cairo and then leave for London.'

'Wait. Why would he leave for London if you hadn't?'

Her shoulders rose and fell on a long sigh.

'Because I left a letter saying I had left for London as

agreed. If something happened to me on the way to Nubia, I did not want Dash searching for me.'

Rafe shook his head, but he understood sibling loyalty. The only reason he was presently sitting on a boulder in the middle of the desert, with aches in places he hadn't even known existed, was because of his brother.

But what the devil was he going to do with her? Simply conveying her to Cairo was no longer a viable solution.

They sat in silence for a while, watching the last glimmerings of the sun as it melted behind the hills. A pleasant breeze began to stir the dusty green bushes and cooled his face.

'So what shall we do next?' she asked, interrupting his musings.

'Go to sleep.'

'You know perfectly well what I meant, Mr Grey. Should we not go and try to slip into Daraw under cover of darkness?'

'No. Arriving in a new city in the dark draws attention.'

'I would have thought the opposite.'

'Foreigners entering a new town will always be remarked and Birdie and I doubly so. We are safest hiding in plain sight. A foreigner and his Bedawi guide will draw attention, but hopefully not suspicion. Tomorrow you and Birdie will remain here while Gamal and I have a look about Daraw and if it is safe we will hire a boat and then sneak you on board. So there. What say you to that brilliant reasoning, Master Pat?'

'I say your superior reasoning is not matched by superior mathematical skills. There will be a foreigner and two local guides. Birdie can remain to watch the camp.'

'I didn't miscount. Two guides would be suspicious. You will remain here with Birdie.'

'Two is no more suspicious than one.'

'You will remain here with Birdie. If anyone is watching the port, they might see through your disguise as easily as I did.'

'So you *do* think there might be trouble.'

'I always think there will be trouble. It protects me from being either surprised or disappointed.'

'True, but it is an awfully wearying way to live.'

She sounded like someone who spoke from long experience.

'Your father has a great deal to answer for,' he said in a burst of annoyance and she smiled with surprising lightness.

'He was not all bad. People rarely are. Surely there is something you remember fondly about your own father?'

'Not a thing. He wasn't a sweet old thing like yours.'

'Well, at least my father had some sense of duty; he could have abandoned us when we were dropped on his doorstep, but he didn't.'

'Good God, Pat, that's no measure of a father's worth.'

'True. Perhaps I feel guilty I never truly liked him. Is that terrible of me?'

'Terribly honest. I never met the fellow and I'm not very fond of him myself.'

She laughed.

'You are very flippant for a mercenary.'

'We are a surprisingly flippant breed.'

'That is not what one would expect.'

'Have you ever met any?'

'Only some of Boucheron's Janissaries. I think their senses of humour were beaten out of them at birth, poor souls. Are there others like you?'

'I'm afraid to ask what "like you" entails to your mind, other than flippancy.'

She considered him, brushing aside a tangle of hair the wind had blown over her brow. Despite her masculine attire and haircut, he was finding it very hard to believe anyone could possibly be fooled by her masquerade.

'I don't know,' she said at last. 'You are not at all what I would have expected.'

'Another ambiguous statement. You are very skilled at those, Cleo-Pat.'

'I shall be even more ambiguous, then. I am glad you are not what I would have expected. Thank you for coming to my aid.'

With the sun hidden it was already pleasantly cool, but he flushed as swiftly and as absurdly as a boy. For a moment his mind went peculiarly bright and blank, like stepping from darkness into a well-lit room. He searched for something to say. Something flippant and safe.

The breeze was rising and it flicked the edge of her cloth scarf against her cheek and she brushed it away, unwinding it from her neck.

She had taken off her robe and her *gallabiyah* hung loosely about her, but now he could see her throat and collarbone, paler than her hands, just the hint of a silver chain disappearing beneath the fabric. The image of it lying against her skin, with that tangle of metal and vivid green stone nestling between her generous breasts... He tried to stop the downward spiral of his thoughts and blood, but with a sense of fatality he felt his body clench with anticipation of following those thoughts with touch...with taste...

He gathered himself, pushing away his libido's wholly inappropriate response. It was not as if she was making any effort at all to be seductive. In fact, she was one of the least artful women he had ever met. For all he knew, all those years playacting a boy meant she was unaware of her attractions and, as far as he was concerned, it was best to keep it that way.

She laid her folded scarf on the boulder and took another sip of her tea, closing her eyes, her tongue brushing across her lower lip as if to gather every drop of the beverage. Again there was absolutely no reason for his body to lurch like a poleaxed camel, but it did.

'Don't do that.' The words were out of him before he could think them into silence and she straightened in surprise.

'Don't do what?'

'W-wet your lips.' Hell—was he stammering? He hurried on. 'It will only dry your lips further. I will fetch more tea. And food. I'm starving.'

He strode off, relieved to put some distance between them. Perhaps the desert thirst had caught him and this strange, sensitised heat was the outcome. Or perhaps this land of ancient gods and strange tales was affecting him more than he wished to admit.

Another complaint to set at his brother's door.

Chapter Five

Birdie and Gamal were preparing flat loafs of charred bread on stones set on the fire and the earthy scent mingled with the smoke. Rafe's stomach growled in anticipation even as his mind moaned.

'I need a decent meal soon, Birdie. I'll waste away on this regime of bread and cheese.'

'You've gone soft these years, Colonel. A little hardship won't hurt you.'

'Devil take you, Birdie. I don't need any *"It will be good for you"* advice. I shall turn thirty-seven soon.'

'Huh. I was forty-six last month, young 'un.'

Rafe tried to school his smile.

'Forty-eight. And we celebrated in full style on board Chris's pleasure ship.'

Birdie's crooked teeth reflected the flickering firelight.

'Did we? I don't recollect much. The mead that rascally Catalan of his brewed would have been useful against the French. Hopefully we can celebrate yours on board there as well after we bring the young miss back home. She'll be safe there?'

Rafe brushed the sand from his hands.

'I don't know. I don't think so. We may have to improvise something.'

'Hmmm...'

'What does that mean?'

'It means, my fine buck, that you have found another way to avoid coming to terms with your future.'

Rafe stilled.

'Birdie, we do not discuss this.'

'*You* don't. Nothing stopping me from doing so. Only a few months ago you said now the old Duke is dead you had no choice but to return. Then you concoct this plan to bring Edge back from Brazil by counterfeiting your death...'

'You know why I did that. The stubborn idiot wouldn't have moved otherwise.'

'Aye, but don't tell me you weren't considering turning that fiction into something permanent and having your brother assume the title.'

'I considered it for all of two minutes. I wouldn't do anything which meant I could no longer see Edge.'

Birdie's face softened.

'I know. Those two years you spent with him and his son were your best. All the more reason why you should have your own children. And that means going back to England, putting your hand on what's rightfully yours and settling down. I'm not saying you shouldn't help Miss Cleopatra reach Cairo, but after that it's time to go home. No more lost souls.'

Rafe shifted uneasily.

'I don't want the damn Duchy; all I have of Greybourne are bad memories. That place will sap my soul. I enjoy what we do, Birdie.'

'You enjoy solving other people's problems and you were a fine officer. I dare say having a few hundred people under you as the Duke of Greybourne won't be much different. You'll make your own memories to chase away the old. I've never seen you dragged down by fate, Rafe. Not when you stomped into barracks twenty-odd years ago and demanded I take you on and not when you near lost your life when you pulled McAllister and Cates from the fire at Los Piños.'

Rafe instinctively rubbed at the marbled skin of his neck. He might have saved two of his men from the fire at the gunpowder depot, but it had been Birdie who'd saved his life and nursed him back to health. Another on a long, long list of debts he owed him.

'Don't talk rot, Birdie. Fate not only dragged me down, but stomped me into a pulp when Jacob died.'

'I know you loved your nephew like your own, Rafe. I was there with you at Chesham those two years, remember?' Birdie answered softly. 'Fate dealt you and Edge a vicious blow, but it didn't fell you. You saved your brother from drowning in grief and you're still trying to save him, but at some point you will have to stop trying to save others and do something about yourself.'

'What the devil is wrong with me? I like my life, Birdie.'

Birdie shrugged, which only made Rafe angrier.

'You're a fine one to talk. You've no more roots than I do.'

'That's true, but I'm coming to regret it, Colonel, and it may be well too late for me. You've made me a rich man, but I told you when we began this voyage it would likely be my last.'

'You've said that a dozen times before.'

'Aye, well, that's my problem. I'm as scared as you.'

'Scared.'

'Shaking in my dusty boots. Elmira told me so and she is right.'

Rafe fell silent. He knew Birdie and the rather taciturn widowed housekeeper they employed at Tarn Cottage had an arrangement, and he was glad for Birdie, but he hadn't realised it went beyond mutual convenience.

'I didn't know it was that serious, Birdie,' he said a little weakly.

'Well, neither did I for as long as I could ignore it. I

never expected a woman to want to look at my ugly mug day in day out, but the truth is I've come to admit I want that. When we return… I think I will stay. I'll be there if you need me, that will always be the case, but…'

Rafe touched Birdie's shoulder briefly.

'I'm happy for you.'

'Well, don't say that yet. She might have come to her senses and changed her mind by the time we return. But if she hasn't… I would rather see your children born before Elmira kills me with her cooking.'

Rafe smiled, but he didn't feel it. The sick feeling was only growing. He'd known this moment was coming since the day he'd received news of his father's death.

Birdie had known him longer and better than anyone and yet he still could not explain to him the deep, sick sensation that rose up in him every time he thought of returning to Greybourne. He'd built a whole new life, a good life, well away from that dank pit. His brief return to it when Edge's son was born had only provided more proof of precisely how dank it was.

He'd returned, expecting to find Edge and his wife Lady Edward happily celebrating the birth of their son. Instead, he'd found Edge alone with Jacob, a happy but sickly babe, while Lady Edward had been whisked away to Bath by her mother to recover her strength. As the doctors shook their heads in despair over Jacob's health and Lady Edward kept extending her stay in Bath, Rafe had abandoned all thought of leaving Edge and Jacob.

His resolve to remain had received an extra boost when a month after his arrival his father descended on Chesham unannounced, spewing his usual vitriolic concoction of doom and damnation. The Duke proclaimed the infant an abomination to God and demanded he be sent away so Edge could beget a healthy heir for Greybourne since Rafe's seed was clearly not going to bear fruit.

That had been a day Rafe would prefer to forget. If it

had not been for Birdie and the swift arrival of his mother, accompanied by the ever-ready Dr Parracombe and his sedatives, he and Edge might well have committed patricide. If ever he'd needed a reminder of the poison that was Greybourne, he'd seen it that day. He wanted nothing to do with it. He would do his duty by the estate and the welfare of his tenants and not a hair's breadth more.

'I think you'd best look elsewhere for someone to dandle on your knee, Birdie. But you are right that I must at least make provisions for the management of the estate. It will be damned strange going back there. It feels as though I'm willingly stepping into a pit full of vipers.'

'There'll be naught but old snake skins by now.'

Rafe wasn't at all certain of that, but he shoved that thought aside.

'That is just as unappetising an image. Speaking of which, isn't that ready? I am so hungry I could eat your cooking.'

Birdie tipped the plate he was in the process of extending and Rafe rescued it before its contents slid into the fire.

'Now, now, Birdie. I thought you had a tougher hide than that.'

'I need one with you about. Go feed the young lady before she blows away. And watch yourself over there.'

Rafe took the plate and shot a look at his friend.

'What is that supposed to mean?'

'She might come to like you all too well if you go on as you are and then you'll be sorry.'

'What the devil do you think I was doing?'

'Making her smile. And laugh. And liking it.'

'I was making her tell me the truth, which is rather necessary under the circumstances. That is all.'

'If you say so. Now go feed her. *That* is necessary.'

Cleo watched the two men talking by the fire. The contrast between them could not have been more marked.

Even with his scars, Mr Grey was a splendid specimen of a man. His size and patrician features only served to accentuate Birdie's squat ugliness. But as she watched the easy, smiling communication between the two it was evident that contrast was lost on them.

'Love looks not with the eyes but with the mind...'

She shoved the foolish quote away and shifted her gaze to the hills once more.

Perhaps she had been too honest with Mr Grey. In his rough and sardonic way, he'd charmed the truth out of her. He'd cleverly made her relax her caution, lean into his warmth that made the world sag a little in his direction. She hadn't even noticed it until he'd moved away. For those brief moments she'd felt utterly natural sitting here with him. Unthinking, un-calculating, just...herself. It was so rare a feeling she only recognised it when it was withdrawn.

She shook her head. The events of the past weeks must be addling her brain.

It was a little mad to allow someone else to assume custody over her fate. She'd never done it before, but in truth it was a wondrous sensation.

A dangerous one, too. All she knew with certainty was that this handsome, scarred giant was a walking deception. He instilled confidence, made her lower her guard, yet she knew he could be ruthless. It was obvious in the way he watched the world, the ease with which he'd faced al-Mizan and dismissed him and then orchestrated their departure with a minimum of fuss. The way he accepted the change in their plans and the annoyances it must bring without any sign of discomfiture. It was as if he expected life to be full of rocky shoals and murky pits. It was unfair that he should convey such an air of calm and humour when he was no doubt eternally alert beneath. His was the behaviour of a man who did not rest, who did not trust.

And if a man did not trust, he could not be trusted.

'*"There's no trust, no faith, no honesty in men; all perjured, all forsworn, all naught, all dissemblers,"*' she muttered at the desert floor.

'Well, that's a miserable philosophy. Here. You'll feel better once your belly is full.'

She looked up, startled. She hadn't even heard him return. She would make a horrid mercenary.

He waved the plate at her and the flat bread slid tipsily across. She caught the plate, the warm, doughy aroma overlaid by the tangy smell of goat's cheese. Her mouth watered and her stomach rumbled like approaching thunder. She leaned forward, embarrassment flooding her once more.

'Who was the dismal fellow or lady who had such a poor opinion of men?' he asked as he sat down, placing his own plate on the boulder and tearing a strip of bread.

'Shakespeare. Juliet's nurse speaks those words to Juliet after Romeo kills her cousin. I didn't mean to…' She foundered, worried he would think she had been referring to him. Which she had.

'Shakespeare. Of course. It's always Shakespeare that's trotted out to bolster one's beliefs. Still, it's always good advice to keep your expectations low. Like expecting this bread to be inedible and then discovering it is delectable. I must be growing desperate indeed to think that.'

She relaxed once more. Flippant had its advantages.

'*"Nothing is good or bad but thinking makes it so,"*' she offered and took a bite of the hot, pungent combination of bread and cheese.

'Shakespeare again? I don't think I agree with him here. There is plenty that is categorically bad and no thinking otherwise could make it good.'

'I believe he meant we can shape our perception of the world. If we always expect evil, then we will perhaps miss the good.'

'A fair point,' he conceded with clear reluctance.

'Dash tells me I have a sad habit of quoting Shakespeare,

but one of the few possessions we managed to always take with us were his plays and I have reread them dozens of times. I shall try to restrain myself.'

'No, don't. It appears you've had to restrain yourself far too much in your short life, Cleo-Pat. Enjoy your unfettered freedom while you can, because once you're safely in London, you will face restraints aplenty. Now eat up. You'll need your strength for what's ahead.'

Unfettered freedom.

Cleo turned over on the thin pallet Gamal had placed for her by the fire and pulled her robe more tightly around her, tucking her fist under her chin. A few feet away the dying fire glittered at her. A short distance behind her was the substantial bulk of Mr Rafe Grey stretched out on another pallet.

She knew she must sleep, but she'd never felt so wide awake in her life. As if she'd swallowed a sackful of shooting stars and they were slamming about inside her like fireworks.

It made no sense. She was exhausted, weary to the marrow of her bones, her legs and back aching from the interminable ride.

And afraid she might never sleep again.

This is absurd, she told herself. Last night she had fallen asleep with her head on a table. The previous night she'd curled behind a stack of reed baskets in an empty market stall, convinced she'd wake up to the tip of a knife. Tonight she was blessed with a mattress of sorts, a blanket and a mercenary who was literally watching her back.

And she couldn't sleep.

She *needed* to sleep, but his words kept bouncing about in her head, butting against her worries like a goat at a gate.

Unfettered freedom...

If all went well she would be returning to England after more than a decade away.

To what?

To a great gaping blackness, greater than the enormous night sky above them.

She breathed in and out slowly, trying to focus on the world around her and not the panic inside her. Over by the well a camel groaned and then came the faraway ululation of a jackal. The mercenary behind her stirred and settled. She could not tell if he was awake and was struck by an urge to turn over and check. She shifted on to her other side as quietly as she could.

Oh. *Not* sleeping.

His eyes looked black, the last flickers of the fire sparking them with stars. He lay on his side facing her, his head resting on his bent arm and folded coat. The moonlight stripped half his face of colour and cast the rest in shadow.

'It's only a jackal,' he whispered.

'I know,' she whispered back. 'They won't come near. It isn't that. I can't seem to sleep.'

'That's not good. Surely your beloved bard had something to say about the importance of sleep. He seems to have something to say about everything short of how best to boil an egg.'

She smiled, absurdly relieved by his nonsense.

'He says sleep is the *"balm of hurt minds"* and something about stealing us away from ourselves, and knitting unravelled sleeves of care, and then of course there is Hamlet's famous—'

'I regret asking,' he interrupted. 'In any case, take his advice, close your eyes and begin knitting.'

'I am trying. I cannot stop my thoughts.'

That was more honest than she wished, but he merely raised himself on his elbow.

'Annoying little bastards, aren't they? Send them over here and I'll give them a talking to.'

A laugh huffed out of her and she untucked her hand and cast an imaginary object at him.

'Put them in a sack and drown them, please.'

'You're a merciless little thing. No need for such measures, I'll just dust their jackets for you and send them back on their best behaviour.'

'That sounds more nursemaid than mercenary.'

He did not answer immediately and she worried she'd offended him. Then a different smile tugged at his mouth. Not jesting. Warm and intimate and yet distant.

'I will have you know I am a fine nursemaid, Cleo-Pat.'

'You have children?' Her thoughts leapt to children far away, wondering where their father was...

'I had a nephew, but he died. Jacob. He was all of two years old.'

'Oh, no. Oh, *no*! I am so, so sorry.'

'So am I. He charmed everyone who knew him. Well, almost everyone.'

'Your brother's son?' she asked. 'The brother you came to Egypt for?'

'The same.'

'What happened to him?'

'My brother or Jacob?'

'Jacob.'

He sighed.

'He was ill for a long time and then he died. I didn't mean to add my ghosts to yours. There is something about sleeping under the heavens that loosens the tongue. Go to sleep, Queenie.'

He turned on to his back, his profile etched against the darkness behind him. She felt he was tempted to turn his back to her completely, but was resisting the urge. For a mercenary he was very considerate of other people's feelings.

Fair play would be to turn over herself and give him the privacy of his thoughts, but there was something comforting about the sharp-cut lines of his profile. She could feel the strange sink and jerk of sleep and in that floating moment before her eyes sealed themselves against her will she wished one could embrace someone in pain without a thought to propriety or consequences.

It might have been the jackals that woke her, or the grunt of the camels. Whatever it was, sleep dropped her from its embrace and she landed flat on her back, her eyes wide and staring at the moon. She turned immediately, half expecting to see a wild beast crouched, ready to leap, but instead there was nothing.

Not even a sleeping giant.

Mr Grey's pallet was empty, the blanket neatly folded, and at the edge of her vision, between the boulders, a dark shape was moving. Away.

No…two dark shapes. She rose to her knees, squinting into the ink of night. They moved lightly and quickly eastwards. She could still hear the faint rumble of snoring near the trees—probably Birdie asleep by the camels.

She knew she had not been asleep for long—the stars and moon had barely moved. She rose, pulling her robe about her and attaching her dagger. Her mind tumbled through possibilities but one held firm above all—the path between the boulders led down towards Daraw.

Rafe watched the band of stars shimmer above him, cold and bright like shards of crushed ice scattered on the darkness. Without even looking he could feel sleep weigh Cleopatra Osbourne down, long lashes lowering over her intense golden-brown eyes.

He closed his eyes as well, willing everything away, willing himself not to turn and look at her. Then he turned on his side and watched her after all, wondering what on earth he was going to do with her. Eventually she gave a little puff of a sigh and her body relaxed as she sank into a deeper sleep.

He rose carefully and went towards where Birdie was leaning against a boulder.

'She's asleep,' Rafe whispered, motioning to Gamal to join him. 'We'll back as soon as we take a look at this port and the lay of the town. I don't want any surprises tomorrow.'

Birdie yawned widely and nodded.

'She won't like you doing this behind her back.'

'I can handle her dislike. It's her mistrust I have a problem with. If I tell her, she'll insist on coming and that might prove dangerous. I want her here where it's safe.'

'What do I tell her if she wakes?'

'Hopefully she won't, but if she does, tell her the truth.'

Birdie cast a glance towards the fire.

'Just come back quick like, will you?'

'As quick as we can.'

On this side of the Nile the village was a small one. He and Gamal made their way to the north of the village to where they could see the feluccas and fishing boats tied to the two simple wooden wharves that spanned the reedy shallows. The small open space by the wharves was surprisingly full for such an hour and small port.

'Is the port always so crowded at this hour, Gamal?'

'No, *nadab*. This is the hour for home and *shisha* and *kahwa*, the coffee place. I do not like this.'

'Neither do I. Blast...' Rafe shifted further back into the shadow. 'See that man, the tall one just at the edge of the port talking to the fat one?'

Gamal leaned a little past him.

'You are right, *nadab*. It is al-Mizan speaking with the Sheikh.'

'Devil take him.'

'Al-Shaitan is more likely to take us, *nadab*.'

'Good point. Come. There's nothing for us here. We

shall have to keep to the desert until the next—' He stopped as Gamal's hand clamped on his arm.

'Anzur!'

Rafe had no idea what that meant, but he followed Gamal's gaze towards the other end of the wharf where the reeds took over. Beyond, the half-moon was a shattered reflection on the inky water and the pale blur between the reeds might have been a large bird looking for frogs, but somehow he knew it was not. He motioned Gamal back the way they came.

Coming round the north of the village, they found her easily enough. She'd chosen a good vantage point to watch the port, but was so intent on the figure of al-Mizan as he stood talking to the rotund Sheikh she did not even notice Rafe approach until he was three feet from her.

He found himself praying she would not cry out. He never liked to employ force, but in this case… Just as he was wondering if indeed he could do it, she turned on her haunches, her hand dropping to the ground as if ready to propel herself forward. He touched his finger to his lips, his eyes locking with hers in the darkness.

They remained like that for a moment and for a second her gaze flickered over to where al-Mizan was standing. There were two other men with him now and they were conferring and looking about them. When her eyes returned to Rafe's he shook his head and pointed into the darkness behind them. Finally, she moved to follow him.

They were halfway back to the camp before he felt capable of speaking calmly.

'What did you think you were doing?'

'I woke and you were gone,' she replied. 'I thought—'

'You thought we'd gone to sell you out.'

He'd been betrayed often enough through the years and he rarely took it personally. He *shouldn't* take it seriously, but somehow this show of mistrust after everything she'd told him…everything he'd told her…

He tried to tell himself it was understandable—she was frightened, worried, and all too used to thinking the worst of people. He should not be angry with her.

Well, he wasn't angry with her, he was *furious*. He'd forgotten what that felt like—like molten steel filling him. He felt as though he had to do something or explode, but there was nothing he *could* do. He did not understand this volcanic pressure inside him, but he knew it would, it *must* pass.

'I had to be certain,' she whispered as they entered the encampment. Her voice was low but insistent, on the verge of a plea. Gamal cast them a worried look and slipped off towards his pallet by the camels where Birdie's snores still rumbled gently. Rafe drew a deep breath, but the expected calm didn't follow.

'Go to sleep, Miss Osbourne.'

'You are being unreasonable…'

'*I* am being unreasonable?' He dragged his voice down and she sighed.

'Yes, you are. You are in a temper because I disobeyed you, but you should have told me of your plans.'

'I would have you know I am a model of good temper when dealing with *reasonable* people, Miss Osbourne,' he snapped.

'I think it very reasonable to insist on taking part in deciding my fate.'

'That is not what happened and you know it! You knew full well you were meant to stay at the encampment!'

'And I decided not to. That is my prerogative. I am after all paying for your services, Mr Grey. I am not obligated to follow your advice.'

'You aren't paying me a scuffed piastre, Queenie, and if you don't want to find yourself alone in the middle of the desert, you *are* obligated to follow my advice.'

* * *

Cleo rarely felt truly angry. Long ago she'd often felt this kind of impotent fury at her father as he'd dragged them from one disastrous venture to the next. But her anger had faded into frustration and finally sloughed off her altogether. She'd forgotten how hot and cold and confusing it felt.

It also felt alive. Vivid. Bubbling inside her more powerfully than fear.

Amazingly, it felt *good*.

'Do you often issue threats you won't act upon, Mr Grey?'

'How do you know I won't act upon them, Queenie? You don't know the first thing about what I am capable of.'

She snorted.

'I know you are capable of dismissing perfectly good advice. I told you Daraw was too close to Syene to be safe, but you had to go sneaking about at night just to prove me right. What if al-Mizan's men or someone in the village had seen you?' She was well aware she was fanning the fire and perversely she was enjoying it.

'The only person they almost saw was you, Queenie, and the only time I and Gamal were at risk was trying to stop you from putting your neck into al-Mizan's noose!'

Her anger faded a little at the thought that she had endangered them as well. She tried for dignity instead of righteousness.

'If you had discussed your plan with me, I would have happily complied—'

'Ha!' he interrupted. 'You wouldn't recognise compliance if it kicked you in the backside. You may be used to ruling the roost, but if you plan on spending the next few days haranguing me and ignoring my directives, I'll happily leave you here.' He snatched his pallet from the ground and stalked off towards the camels.

Cleo lay awake for a long while, her cheeks stinging

with a swirling contradiction of heat and anger and hurt.
She watched the last glimmer of embers die, very aware
of the emptiness behind her.

Chapter Six

'Tired?' Birdie asked as helped her dismount at the end of the following day's ride. It was the first word any of them had spoken to her since they'd set out that morning. Concern was writ large on his puckish face so she managed an almost-smile and shook her head.

She wanted to tell Birdie the truth—she wasn't tired, she was exhausted. With the look on Rafe's face haunting her, it had taken hours to fall asleep. Even admitting his anger was justified, she didn't know why it affected her so. He wasn't her friend, so she could hardly lose his friendship. Yet it felt precisely as if she had.

The closest thing she'd felt to this was when they'd been forced to leave Acre after living with the Tawil family in their sprawling house just north of the port. But that had been a real loss—a loss of love and friendship built over years. Her father had hardly given them a chance to say goodbye to the people who'd become their family. It was absurd to feel the same deep wrenching sensation merely because a man she hardly knew was angry with her.

She glanced at Rafe's broad back as he helped Gamal remove the saddles while Birdie set out his pots by the fire. It was the same scene as the previous night and yet she felt they were already excluding her.

If he hadn't been a mercenary, and a flippant one at that, she might almost believe he'd been hurt by her mistrust.

'Here, miss.' Birdie approached her and held out a steaming cup. She took it and bent her head over the steam to hide the pricking of grateful tears.

'Thank you, Mr Birdie.'

'Just Birdie, miss. That's not good for the heart, you know.'

She started and some of the tea splattered over her hand. He handed her a surprisingly clean handkerchief and she dabbed at the stinging liquid.

'What's not good for the heart?'

'Worrying when you can't do a thing about it. It was my fault for falling asleep, but next time just give me a good kick and wake me before you go off on your own so I can calm your worries.' He hesitated. 'We've been in far worse situations than these, believe me. And if something happens to him I'll see you through.'

She breathed through the burn of tears. These men hardly knew her and yet somehow they were more committed to her safety than her own father ever had been.

'Thank you, Birdie.'

He flushed and frowned. 'No need. Best thing to do is keep yourself busy. Finish your tea and go draw more water for those thirsty beasts while Gamal and I prepare supper.'

The brusque order calmed her far more effectively than empty reassurances. She finished her tea and went to unhook the water gourd by the well. She'd watched men and women work the wells, but doing it herself was harder than she anticipated, the rope burning her palms as she dragged up the heavy leather buckets.

How the women who filled large clay jugs with water carried this weight on their heads over miles back to their villages or tents, she had no idea. She tried not to spill the precious water as she poured it into the trough and was concentrating so hard on her task that the blow caught her completely by surprise. She landed neatly on her behind in the mud and found herself staring up into the bulbous eyes of Kabir as he ambled past her to the trough. Her nemesis looked well pleased with his victory as he slurped noisily at the water.

'I'm doing this for you, you ungrateful wretch. You might at least show some respect,' Cleo muttered as she struggled to her feet. The other camels approached, Gamila huffing gently and batting her long, curled eyelashes at Cleo as if in apology for Kabir's behaviour. Cleo stroked Gamila's neck as they both stood and watched the slobbering Kabir with what Cleo was certain was shared disgust.

'Typical male. No consideration or manners,' said Rafe behind her and Cleo turned in surprise, her hands covering the muddy patch on her behind.

His comment sounded like an olive branch, but his expression was as blank as it had been all day. They stood for a moment in silence before he jerked his head towards the campfire.

'Supper is ready.'

Unlike the previous evening, supper was a subdued affair. The tension between her and Rafe was palpable and both Gamal and Birdie exchanged glances and ate in silence. When Birdie poured out the last of the tea, she gathered her courage and turned to Rafe.

'May I know where we are heading next, Mr Grey?'

Rafe put down his cup.

'I was wondering how long before you started making demands.'

'It is not a demand, merely a question.'

Birdie directed a frown at Rafe. 'We've decided the ports are too risky, miss. Gamal suggested we go by way of the camel route and take a boat from Asyut, which is too large for them to control.'

'Asyut! That means several more days in the desert.'

'That's right, miss. So we'd all best catch some rest now.'

She took her pallet and followed Rafe to arrange it by the fire, searching for some way to ease the tension that strummed between them.

'I am sorry you have had to extend your journey because of me.'

He shrugged. 'Never mind. Hopefully we have confused them sufficiently to give your brother time to reach Cairo and leave Egypt. That is your object, no?'

'Yes. Yes, of course. I only hope Dash acts immediately once he sees my letter.'

'So do I. Was he named for his speed or for his dashing manners?'

There was a hint of lightness in his voice and her relief bloomed.

'Neither. An ancestor of ours from Ashford in Kent went to France and took to calling himself d'Ashford. My mother decided to perpetuate that foolish vanity in Dash's name. She was very…poetically minded.'

'So she's to blame for you quoting Shakespeare?'

'She'd be proud to accept that blame.' She smiled and turned away to unfold her blanket, surprised by the burning in her throat. It seemed so long, long ago—those evenings reading with her mother in their small back parlour where it was warmest because it shared a wall with the kitchen. She'd thought that was her life—simple and safe and happy, just the three of them with occasional visits from her father. Now it felt far less real than sitting in the desert with a mercenary.

But it was still there, that memory—of warmth, her mother's deep voice as she read, holding the book a little away from her because she always misplaced her spectacles…

'You miss her.'

His voice was brusque but not unkind and she both shrugged and nodded, waiting for him to move away. To her surprise, he spread his pallet between hers and the desert once more and came to sit on a boulder by the fire. He picked up a twig and traced neat little rows on the ground. The sand rushed into them like raindrops into a crack in the pavement.

'I'm sorry, Cleo-Pat.'

'It hardly matters. It was so long ago.'

'Some things never stop mattering. Was she responsible for you name as well?'

'Of course. She said it was part tribute to Shakespeare's play and part tribute to my father. In Greek it means "glory of the father". All the Ptolemaic queens were named Cleopatra and all the kings Ptolemy, which means "warlike".'

'Well, that says it all. Name the kings after violence and the queens after kings.'

She laughed. She'd always hated that aspect of her name, but somehow his words blew away that slight with a puff of laughter. He smiled and the knot of tension in her stomach unravelled further.

'I'll call you Cleo, then. Or Glory.'

'Not Glory, please. Besides, you already appear to have far too many names for me.'

'Cleo, then. Or I rather like Cleo-Pat. Osbourne doesn't suit you, though. Do you know what it means?'

'I...no, I never thought it meant anything at all.'

'It's old Norse. It means the bear god...*os bjorn*.'

'Does it? I rather like that. Do you actually speak Norse?' She couldn't keep the scepticism from her voice and he gave that grunt she was coming to recognise was a mix between amusement and annoyance.

'I know some odd bits. I lived with my brother for a couple of years, after his son Jacob was born, while I recovered from my burns. The boy never fully escaped the rheumatic fever and needed to be watched closely. He loved being read to and I soon made my way through most of

Edge's mythology collection, including a tome on the significance of names in old Norse. Jacob was particularly fond of that. Perhaps it was my ludicrous accent.'

Strange how well she could imagine Rafe holding a somnolent babe in his arms, reading aloud in his deep purr of a voice. She didn't want that image in her mind; she had enough to unsettle her at the moment.

'Does Rafe also mean something in old Norse?'

'Yes. Wise wolf.'

'How apt. So I am a bear god, you a wise wolf, Birdie can be a kind, resourceful bird and Gamal the handsome camel named Camel.'

His smile flashed in the dark.

'We sound like one of Aesop's fables. Except in my case, Rafe is nothing more impressive than Rafael shortened.'

'Rafael,' she repeated, and the sound rolled outwards, warm and liquid in the darkness. 'God heals. An archangel's name.'

'I know. I was definitely misnamed.'

'I don't think so. Raphael saved people.'

'Even less appropriate. I'm a mercenary, remember?'

'Of course I do. You saved me.'

He snorted.

'You hired me to do just that. I might as easily have handed you over to that al-Mizan fellow if he'd been more generous. I don't think Raphael haggled with God over his fee.'

'You didn't haggle over the fee either.'

'I don't think he could have matched your offer. That grotesque green gewgaw is worth a couple of months' lodgings at least.'

Her hand groped for the chain that held her little treasure and closed on it.

'You could take it now and still hand me over to al-Mizan.'

'Even mercenaries have their principles, Queenie.'

'I think you make a better bear than I do, Mr Rafael Grey. You are long on brawn and bluster. I know you weren't even considering handing me over to that man.'

'You know nothing of the sort, as you proved by following us into Daraw. You should try living up to your namesake, Cleopatra—trust no one.'

She considered his words, and his warning, and tried to understand why, other than her still being alive, she *did* trust him now. Perhaps it was the foolishness that often comes with fear and despair—clinging to a rock protruding from the ocean though one knew it was as dangerous in its barrenness as the great wide sea.

Yet she did trust him and it worried her. Trust meant lowering one's guard and that meant...trouble.

For a moment the darkness settled on them again as the fire dimmed. Then a spark shot upwards, followed by a lick of flames as the fire found more to feed its hunger. It lit his profile against the fading light on the horizon. He had a profile worthy of a coin—strong and sharp, as if the winds of life had hewn him down to his elements. The only imperfections were his scars. She wondered what had happened to him.

Trust no one. It was excellent advice, but...

'I rarely do trust anyone,' she said tentatively. 'I do not mean I trust you wholly, but I think, if I am right about you, you will try to fulfil your bond and that is far more than most men...most people do.'

He actually squirmed, raising his eyes skywards as if beseeching the heavens for deliverance. She smiled and continued. 'Also I don't know that Cleopatra didn't trust anyone. She appeared to trust both Julius Caesar and Marc Anthony enough to have children with them.'

'That was good political sense, not trust. Or trust in her ability to direct her fate by whatever means at her disposal. A very sensible woman, that illustrious lady.'

'I agree. But being sensible doesn't preclude trust. You

strike me as a sensible man, but you trust Birdie. And your brother.'

'What do you know of my brother?'

'Nothing but what you said yourself. But I know love when I hear it. Your brother is a lucky man to have you.'

'You are damned annoying, Pat.'

'That is the second time you have damned me, Mr Grey.'

'I have a suspicion it won't be the last, Miss Osbourne.'

Chapter Seven

Desert travel was strange.

Almost a week had passed since they'd left Syene and, though they were always in motion, it seemed to Rafe as if they never truly made any headway. The pinkish cliffs gave way to dunes and plains and then again to cliffs. The shadows of the camels marked the passing of the day—long and fuzzy into the west, shrinking and darkening as the day passed, scrunched beneath them, like an oily puddle, and then stretching out into the east once more until everything began to glow orange and dim to purple as the sun expired.

Gamal set a brisk pace and it was too hot and dusty to talk during the day, but at night by the campfire, the four of them settled into the easy camaraderie of soldiers on the march. Ever since he'd enlisted in the army at sixteen he'd come to love these times—sitting around a fire, talking and listening.

It had been a way of life for him and Birdie and it was also in Gamal's blood, but Rafe was surprised how naturally Cleo fitted into their little troupe. Perhaps this was what came of a life adapting to circumstance. She rarely complained and whatever snaps of temper and impatience she allowed herself were directed solely at him. Strangely, he welcomed these chinks in her defences.

He watched her helping Birdie. The two of them were talking and laughing, the evening breeze sifting through her short hair and every so often she shoved it away from her eyes with the back of her hand.

His mind was still struggling to resolve her contrasts. Her clothes and some of her gestures were boyish, yet she looked as feminine as Venus rising from the sea. Her voice, too, was all woman—deep and warm and with a dash of spice, like winter cider. Especially when she laughed. Her laugh was as generous as her curves and he really had to stop trying to coax it out of her.

He sighed again at the pity of it all. His body had crossed the Rubicon with her and was having a grand time thumbing its nose at him from the other side. He knew he would do nothing about this attraction, but it was a damnable nuisance.

She came and sat cross-legged on the pallet beside him without a word and they both watched the sky succumb to the night.

He'd heard the desert was a strange and deceptive place, but he'd assumed that referred to its physical nature, not a spiritual effect. And yet it didn't feel at all logical that anything bad could happen to them in this elemental place. He felt…peaceful.

He should and would do well to keep in mind that the desert…in particular this desert and in this strange woman's company…was not at all peaceful.

It was a jackal who broke the silence. The howl went on so long he felt it begin to reverberate inside him. Finally, it broke into a series of sharp yaps and stopped.

'It sounds lonely,' she said.

'I know, but it likely isn't. Gamal said they almost always live and hunt in packs.'

She nodded. 'I saw a mother jackal playing with her

pups once. They were the sweetest things—with enormous ears that looked as though they would tip them over. It was beautiful—I know some people believe animals do not possess emotions, but you could see how much pleasure they took in one another.'

Her voice was deeper than usual and its rawness plucked at him.

'Is that what you want? A pack of your own?'

'Is that so wrong?'

'Not wrong… It depends.'

'On what?'

'Whether you know its limits. Families aren't a magic antidote to loneliness. We of all people should know that.'

'I do know that. I'm not…' She gave a little laugh. 'I am an awful liar. I cannot even lie to myself. I envy *jackals*, for heaven's sake.'

He could feel it. Of course she was lonely. So was any reasonably sensible human being. Sometimes every cell in his body ached with bone-deep loneliness. It was part of being alive. Belonging to a pack could temper, but not eliminate, it.

'I hope Dash is safe. I hope…' Her voice quavered and she stopped, her hands fisted on her thighs. Without thought he put his arm around her, cursing himself.

Her breathing was still shallow, stuttering. He wished she would cry. It was better than this…drowning. She was drowning in the desert and it was his fault.

'Cleo… Please…don't listen to me. I'm no authority on anything. You'll have your family.'

She shivered, pressing her forehead against his neck. He could feel the contours of his scars against her skin and started pulling away, but her hand curled into his shirt, her fingertips dragging the fabric against his ribs.

'We come from a long line of soothsayers,' he whispered against her hair. 'I can see you'll have a dozen children—six girls, six boys… No, better have more girls, they are less trouble.'

She gave a little huff of a laugh, her breath cooling the perspiration on his throat, and he stopped himself from tightening his arms.

'*I* am trouble…' she whispered hoarsely, but he could hear the glimmer of a smile there and a wave of gratitude rushed through him.

'That's true. Serious trouble. Perhaps we'll change that to more boys than girls since you are likely to have a bevy of little warrior queens. You'll never have a moment's rest.'

Her hair was soft and he rubbed his cheek against it, just turning his head a little so that it skimmed the corner of his mouth. He breathed her in again, trying to reach that enticing core. It was unfair that she smelled so good despite everything and he probably smelt like one of the camels by now.

'I don't want a dozen children,' she murmured. 'I want two or three. The more you have, the more you worry.' Her voice was creaky, but he could tell she was back. Which meant he should let her go.

He didn't want to. She was warm and soft against him and it took every ounce of his will to sit still. To remind himself he was comforting her. That he had nothing to offer and no right to take. They sat in silence until the words were dragged out of him.

'I'll find your brother for you.'

She sighed and pulled away a little.

'It isn't your place to find him, Rafe. You are doing more than enough helping me. I'm sorry I…fell to pieces. Thank you for being so patient.'

She took his hand and rubbed it gently between hers. He'd been simmering already and her touch was fire set to dry hay. It spread so fast and so hot he couldn't do anything but sit there as the heat flayed layers off him.

He must have made some sound because she untangled

herself, murmuring a stifled apology and went towards the well. He walked in the other direction, chased by images that had nothing to do with reality—of spreading her out in the middle of the desert, discovering every curve and line and taste of her. Of pulling her on top him so he could watch her body against the starred sky as they moved.

It would pass. These little fevers always did—they dragged him back to his youth, twisting his view of the world and convincing him he wanted something he didn't really. But they never lasted. Eventually they ran out of tinder and went ashen and dull. It was only that her foolish, pointless yearning had infected him for a moment. Like jabbing an old wound.

It would pass, all he had to do was wait it out and one day he would wonder why on earth it had caught him so hard.

'We are almost at the end of Darb al-Arba'in. Asyut is past those hills,' said Gamal, pointing eastwards over his camel's neck. He'd kept them at a fast pace that day to reach the oasis and though Cleo was grateful to see the shadowed grove of palms that promised rest, his words caused a sharp twinge in her chest. Beyond those hills was the Nile and the end of their journey.

Gamal had told her he would be leaving them in Asyut. He would sell all of the camels but Kabir and Gamila and then return to his family, wealthy enough to marry.

Rafe and Birdie would likely proceed to Cairo in search of traces of his brother, and she… Once she reached Cairo she would know more. There was no point in worrying unnecessarily. Worrying had made her blabber about jackals and loneliness last night and forced Mr Grey to comfort her like a child.

She'd held on to that sensation last night as she tried to sleep. The warmth of his body around hers, his scent— earthy and cool. His hand between hers, large and rough with a warmth that sparked fires through her like a field of thorns in summer. It was foolish to indulge these sensations, but she did anyway. All too soon she would be on her own again and life would snatch her back in its talons.

'What is Darb al-Arba'in?' Birdie asked and she welcomed the distraction.

'It is the forty-day camel caravan road from Nubia to Asyut. Asyut is quite large so we can probably find a boat there without drawing too much attention. I doubt al-Mizan will be there. If he persisted in looking for Dash at all, he would most likely have gone to Luxor.'

She glanced at Rafe, but if he was relieved they were near their journey's end, she could see no sign of it. Or of anything, for that matter. When he wished, he could keep his face as blank as a rock.

'Look at that, Colonel!' Birdie exclaimed as they passed through the last line of palm trees. Out of the ochre plain before them rose the palmiform pillars of an ancient temple. Either design or time had left only several separate structures standing and a row of half-buried sphinxes. She loved these small temples in Egypt—they were as delicate and sturdy as life, with their exuberance carved and painted on their walls and pillars.

She wished Dash were there with them. He would have loved to see this.

As they watched, a goat and kid ambled up the alley of sphinxes, the kid skipping and bucking over the sand as they headed into the shade of the palms. Kabir huffed in disgust at such frivolity and Gamila nudged him in the neck.

'I think that is a hint, Kabir.' Cleo laughed.

Gamal smiled. 'Kabir is stubborn.'

'I place my faith in Gamila,' Cleo replied, patting the cow. 'Please tell me we may set camp near here and explore the temple a little?'

'You'd think we were on a Grand Tour,' Rafe said drily,

but then added, 'Setting camp here sounds like a good idea. We could even sleep inside. What do you say, Gamal?'

'Very good. But I will sleep with the camels and keep them safe from thieves, *nadab*.'

'So will I,' Birdie said. 'You won't find me stepping inside a tomb until it's my turn to fill it. But you enjoy yourself, miss. No telling what tomorrow brings.'

'I know precisely what tomorrow brings, Birdie,' Rafe said as they moved towards the temple. 'More dust and wind, more dry cheese and burnt bread and dates, and more aching muscles and sulky camels. I'd trade my kingdom for a bath, a feather bed, and a slab of sirloin.'

'I thought I already won your kingdom for a glass of whisky several times over, Colonel.'

'Well, I wish you would do a better job hanging on to it, old friend. I don't want it.'

'So you say, but duty has a way of sinking its teeth into our tail, Colonel. Now you and Miss Cleo go have a look at your new lodgings. And try not to fall into a pit or come across a snake in there and make this all a wasted trip.'

'You two sound like a married couple,' Cleo said as she slipped off Gamila.

'Birdie sounds more like a mother hen. He's picked up some bad habits since I met him twenty-odd years ago,' Rafe said as he followed her past the staring sphinxes and between the pillars that rose like stone flowers out of the sand.

'You've known him twenty years?'

'Since I enlisted in the army.' He must have seen the surprise on her face for he gave a wry smile. 'I'm thirty-seven. Almost.'

'Your parents did not mind you enlisting so young?'

'I ran away.'

'Why?'

He shrugged, waving her inside, and after a moment's hesitation she entered the temple. Inside, the heat dropped sharply and the rising afternoon breeze made the dust dance and flicker like gold flecks in the shafts of sunlight poking through the cracked roof.

Rafe followed her over the sand drifts into the depth of the temple, pausing beneath the carving of a pharaoh with one hand upheld and the other outstretched and balancing a bowl. They went deeper, past carvings of humans with animal heads, birds with long curved beaks, a large baboon seated on a pedestal, and endless rows of hieroglyphs.

'Think,' she whispered as she unwound her turban, her voice shivering the still air. 'This has been here for thousands of years. Created at a time when Egypt was as great as any empire. I wish I had my notebook and a pencil here. This would make a wondrous tale for the *Gazette*. If only I knew who they were…'

'They are ashes and dust just like everyone else.' His voice was so flat she knew he was still elsewhere. She turned to watch him as he stared blankly at the wall.

'Why did you run away, Rafe?'

His eyes flickered to her and away.

'I had a fight with my father.'

'What did you argue about?'

'I said fight. Not argument. No one argued with the… with my father.'

'Well, then, what did you fight about?'

'Him trying to kill a maid because she giggled.'

The air squeaked out of her lungs. He turned at her silence, his smile wry.

'I come from bad stock. Are you certain you want to be alone in here with me?'

'Don't be foolish. Whatever your father was, you are as sane as I.'

He walked along the wall, his gaze moving over the carvings, but she could feel things shifting about inside him. She wanted to stop him, turn him to her and have him tell her…everything. He seemed so open sometimes but with every snippet he revealed she felt the mystery grow. And her curiosity. He must have come from a well-to-do family—it was in the way he spoke and a certain ease, that expectation that people would follow. But there was much more and that was mostly hidden in darkness. Now she felt he was finally twitching back a corner of the curtain and it shocked her how much she wanted to pull it away completely. He remained silent so long she was certain he had no intention of continuing his revelations, but he surprised her again.

'I used to have dreams that they would come and switch me, as well.'

'Switch you? Who?'

'Whoever kept switching him into a violent fanatic. It almost made me believe in demons and possession, which would have made my father very happy. He was a fire and brimstone zealot.'

'Perhaps…perhaps it was an illness?'

'Perhaps. Since we never spoke of it, I never asked. Whatever it was, that was why I ran away.'

'But…your mother? She must have been frantic.'

'Frantic is not a word one would associate with my mother. Her object was always to keep the surface of her world calm. She was a master…sorry, mistress of control. If it calms your conscience, I did write to her after I enlisted.'

'And she didn't object?'

'She objected to my choosing to enlist rather than purchasing a commission. She told me she preferred I join the Dragoon Guards so I didn't have to mix in low company.' His voice rose in a mincing falsetto and she smiled.

'I have a notion your mother does not sound like that.'

His mouth relaxed into a smile. 'No. She's a true martinet.'

'So? Did you join the Dragoons?'

'Hardly. I joined the Rifle Corps when it was formed

and that summer I was already losing my first battle in Spain. The next year I won my first battle in Copenhagen.'

'What did your mother say about that?'

'I have no idea. I did not speak to her until Edge's son was born. I was thirty by then and since I was already several years into this mercenary business, the issue didn't arise.'

Each of these lightly delivered revelations were blows that made her heart give a heavy, painful thump before hurrying along again. He didn't sound angry, but she was; she was furious for him. It was burning and crackling inside her. She wanted to reach through time and space and shake sense and love into his parents. How could they not have cared?

'Well, I am very happy Birdie found you. He strikes me as a far better person than your parents.'

'Undoubtedly. Though to be fair, I found him. One of my many talents—I know a good egg from a bad one.' He grinned at her over his shoulder and she felt a flush of pure pleasure.

'I've never been called a good egg before. As far as compliments go… I like it.'

His smile softened and for a moment they stood there in silence. She'd never felt so cut adrift from life and yet so very right where she should be. Home. The thought shook her but before she could even pull away from it, Rafe turned back to carving of a woman standing beside a crowned man holding a staff.

'Could this be your namesake?' he asked, his voice curious, calm and distant. She recognised the question for what it was. The end of his revelations.

'No. From what I understand this style is much earlier than Greek times. By that disc I think this is Amun, god of the sun. You said your brother is a scholar, he would no doubt enjoy this.'

'No doubt.'

'When I was a child I always wanted to see the places my father mentioned when he came to visit us in England,' she said. 'But I never imagined I would. When we were at the orphanage...'

He turned abruptly.

'You were in an orphanage?'

'After my mother died; but only for a year. Then a ship's captain arrived with a letter from my father saying he would take Dash.'

'Only Dash?'

She shrugged.

'Well, to be fair, I can understand his dilemma. Being saddled with a girl, especially in this part of the world, is not easy. But I couldn't allow them to take Dash without me so I cut my hair and took his second-best set of clothes and we both presented ourselves at the ship and said the message must have meant sons, plural, not son, singular. I am quite convinced the Captain saw through our ruse, but he was a kind man and probably took pity on me. The orphanage was not very salubrious.'

In the gloom of the temple she found it hard to read his expression but her pulse picked up, like a camel sensing predators beyond the cliffs.

'I did not tell you about my childhood to make you pity me, Mr Grey.'

'I don't pity you. Between an orphanage and your current life, I think you chose well. But forgive me if I think your father was a complete louse.' He spoke with barely suppressed violence. 'I cannot understand people who abandon their children. If you don't want them, don't have them.'

'Perhaps that is something one does not know until one has them?'

'That is no excuse.'

'I don't understand why you seem angrier with my father than with yours.'

'I used to be viciously angry with him,' he said finally, to the pharaoh.

'Not any more?'

He shrugged.

'When I heard he had died, I thought it would come back, but I can't find it. I think…if he *was* mad it is unfair to be angry with something beyond his control. Don't ask me about my mother, though. And I mean that seriously, Prying Pat.'

His smile was back so she didn't mind the rebuke. They stood for a moment in the darkening silence. It occurred to her she'd never felt more comfortable with anyone. She didn't want to return to Cairo, or England. She wanted to stay right here, with Rafe. She saw her hand rise just as he turned towards the entrance.

'I'll fetch our belongings and we'd best eat and have an early night. We should reach the river tomorrow.'

Chapter Eight

An hour later Cleo was heading back towards the temple through the palms, her arms full of brush for the fire, when she saw Rafe by the well.

He stood with his back to her, his shirt off, his back glistening with water as he shaved. The lowering sun was adding red and gold to everything and it transformed his back into a landscape far more arresting than any she'd seen on their trip. Like the desert, its power was rough and raw. Beautiful.

She stood rooted, like Lot's salt pillar of a wife. She couldn't look away. Her heart began thumping viciously, her skin burning, and a moan bubbled up inside her. It had been building this whole week, images and thoughts and sensations knitting together into one stifling fabric of need.

She would never have imagined a week ago that one of her chief worries was an increasing tendency to daydream about a brusque and flippant mercenary. She couldn't even blame him. All he was doing was shaving peacefully. She, in turn, was on fire. She wanted to skim her tingling palms down that sculpted expanse, feel every curve and contour, slip them round to his flat abdomen until her fingertips brushed the dark hair arrowing down...

She knew she should move on, but she remained where

she was, wishing he would turn to her, not with his teasing laughter or compassion, but mirroring the heat she felt flooding her, making it hard to breathe.

He poured water from the gourd over his head and face, rivulets forming shiny stripes down his back. She swallowed as he dried his face with a strip of linen, his touch slowing and softening as it moved over his scarred shoulder.

Her heart squished itself into a little ball, shoving back the lascivious storm. What she wanted more than anything was to wrap her arms around him and touch her lips to that shattered, tortured skin. Soothe it…him…

Oh, this is not smart at all, Cleopatra. Lust is one thing, caring is another matter altogether.

Their journey was about to come to an end. In a couple of days she would never see him again.

Repeat after me: you will never see him again.

He turned, his hand still on his scars, his eyes locking with hers. She didn't know what she looked like, but she was afraid he could see *everything*. His hand descended slowly from his scars and she watched it with something like horror, as if waiting for him to extend an accusing finger. She'd been hot before, but her face blazed like the noonday sun. She swallowed and stepped back, stumbling a little.

'If my scars bother you so, you must stop sneaking up on me when I am shaving, Cleopatra.'

His voice was utterly flat and her mind utterly aghast, so it took a moment for her to register his words. She dragged her gaze up from his chest to his eyes.

'That's not… I wasn't… They *don't*…'

He walked towards her, still with that same flat look. She tried to gather her thoughts, explain…

Explain what? That's she'd stood lusting after him behind his back? That even now she wanted to reach out and take…

Perhaps if he had stood still she might have been able to think of something sensible and mature to say, but he kept coming towards her and her mind joined her body in the wishful clamour—perhaps he would not stop…he would put those big hands on her, touch her, bend down to press his half parted lips on hers…

He was within an arm's reach from her, he extended his arms… God, she would combust faster than dry papyrus if only…

With a faint, unamused twist of his mouth he took the bundle of twigs from her arms and walked past her.

She stood for a moment, heat and horror warring inside her for dominion.

It was only a few short moments but it felt as though she'd been down to the rings of purgatory and back.

Nothing like that had ever happened to her. Not even with William when she'd been young and foolish and—despite her father—still believed in love and dreams come true. She'd thoroughly enjoyed their embraces, even if they'd led to humiliation and disillusionment. But she'd never felt…fire.

She'd never felt afraid.

Already the flood waters were lowering, leaving behind the usual debris—a wincing embarrassment and frustration. It took another moment for the real sting to wake her as his words finally sank in—he hadn't thought she had stood there like a lust-struck ninny, but stricken by disgust and dismay because of his scars.

Shock held her silent for a moment. He treated his scars lightly, but there had been disappointment in his voice, his eyes. No—not disappointment, *hurt*. She'd hurt him.

She turned and hurried towards the temple, her mind tumbling over itself.

Rafe was kneeling in the central chamber of the temple, his head bent as he worked to kindle the fire. He'd put a shirt on and it clung damply to his back. He must have heard her enter, but did not look up.

'I'll be out of your way once the fire is ready.'

She hurried into speech.

'Rafe. You were wrong. Your scars don't bother me in the least. I've seen them before, remember?'

He pressed some dry weeds gently on to the flicking flames, careful not to smother them.

'You were half-dead that day and you had a hard enough time looking at me even then. You don't have to hide it, Queenie. I'm used to it.'

'But…'

'You looked as though you'd seen a ghost. So unless one of your mummy friends was making faces behind me…'

'Just *listen*.'

He stilled, but didn't turn. With his shoulders bowed over the fire, the rising flames casting gold lights on his dark hair and making the wall carvings shiver and dance, he looked like a supplicant come to beg mercy of the gods.

'That's is not why I looked…however I looked. I wasn't even thinking of your scars…no, that is not quite true. I *was* thinking of them, but they don't frighten me. The truth is…' She came forward and took a deep breath before resting her palm lightly on his scarred neck. His skin was both cool and hot, or perhaps that was her. 'I don't know you very well, but I hate the thought of you being hurt.'

Rafe froze.

I hate the thought of you being hurt…

It meant nothing, nothing at all. He'd seen people react a thousand and one ways to fear and loneliness. It took everyone differently. It clearly took Cleo into unnecessary realms of compassion.

So said his mind. His body, however, already on its knees, dropped at her feet like a panting puppy. There was nothing he could do to stop it marshalling the troops against him. It gathered the feel of her hand on his skin, the warmth of her legs close behind his back. It added images from the long, hot, dusty days—the way she wiped the perspiration from her cheeks or tilted her head back to catch the first breeze of the afternoon, exposing that little dip at the base of her throat where her scent would rise with each beat of her pulse.

He kept still, waiting for his mind to reassert dominion over his body. It was usually faster in coming to his defence, but the heat kept rising like the Egyptian sun—becoming incomprehensibly hotter, spreading from her hand like a curse, seeping through his skin into his veins and skidding along merrily to attack him from within. It bothered him far more than the erection that pulsed into life within seconds of her touching him. This heat felt far more dangerous than a lustful surge—it felt as though it was plotting against him.

What the devil was wrong with her to touch him like that? It would serve her right if he'd do what every base cell in his body ached to do.

He drew away, very carefully, as one might from a poisonous snake.

'I don't need pity, Miss Osbourne.'

'That is good. I haven't any for you.'

He uncoiled himself and stood. She stepped back and again he saw that same widening of her eyes and pupils. Damn it, he knew fear when he saw it.

'You tell a fine story, Cleo-Pat, but you have to work on not flinching or blushing with embarrassment.'

She gave a small, strangled laugh, surprising him.

'I wasn't flinching and it's not embarrassment. I'm beginning to think Birdie has grossly exaggerated your knowledge of women, Mr Grey.'

He clasped her arm before his mind even fully registered her meaning. She didn't pull away, just stood there. He had been right—she looked flushed and flustered. But he had been absolutely, peculiarly wrong—it wasn't fear, or disgust, or even compassion. The latter had been in her touch and voice, but not in her eyes, at least not now.

She could as easily have looked away, lowered her lashes, anything, but she let him take it in—the almost sleepy look in her eyes, the sultry heat colouring her cheeks, the tension in her parted lips. It wasn't an invitation; it was an admission. She wanted him to see the truth because she would not allow him to believe the alternative—that his damage either frightened or repelled her.

He had no idea what to do with this gift.

Oh, hell.

He laid his palm gently against her cheek. It shook slightly, reverberating against her skin, his index finger resting on the impossibly soft lobe of her ear.

'I apologise, Cleo.'

'Don't. There is no need, Rafe.' Her fingers rose to brush across his jaw, her gesture mirroring his. 'How did it happen?'

It sucked him in, that gentle question. It rang with concern and an echo of pain, as if she'd been there with him those long, agonising months when he'd been tempted to take whatever path available to relieve the pain.

'Stupidity. Mine. I walked into a burning building and would have stayed there if not for Birdie.'

She shook her head, her fingers feathering over his damaged skin, her mouth a sad, tense bow as her eyes followed her fingers, making his skin burn all over again.

'There is more to it than that. Don't make light of it.'

'I'm not… I must. I don't like remembering it.'

'Yes, I can see. I'm sorry.'

'It was a gunpowder depot. We were sent to salvage what we could when their cannon fire hit the building. I was already outside, but five of my men were still inside.' The words were dragging themselves out of him, just as he'd tried to drag out McAllister and the others. 'Birdie and I went in to find them. We pulled two out and I went back...'

He could remember the smell—acrid, evil—and the sound—snapping and sizzling. He'd just anchored his hand in McAllister's coat when the explosion hit him. He had no other memory until days later. And then the first memory was pain. For a long time.

He breathed in and out.

'It was a long time ago.'

'Some memories defy time. They're carved on our minds like those walls. If we lived a thousand years, they would still be there.'

He nodded slowly. Right now it felt as if this moment was being carved in stone, too. He didn't want it there any more than those long painful weeks in Los Piños, but it was unstoppable.

'I didn't mean to pry, Mr Grey,' she said as the silence stretched and he shook his head. He didn't want her to call him Mr Grey right now. Not that he wanted her, or anyone, to call him Greybourne, but for the first time the lie felt wrong. What would happen if he just...told her? If he laid it all bare. He'd already revealed so much more than he'd ever intended. What would happen if he added his true name? Not Mr Grey... Rafael Edgerton, Duke of Greybourne...

The image reared up again—that dark-eyed, twisted beast of a man with fingers tighter than steel bands and a mouth spewing hate. His heart stuttered. That wasn't him any more than he was Mr Grey.

'Rafe,' he said, brushing his thumb across her lips as if to imprint it on her. His voice was raw. He knew touching her was wrong, dangerous. Birdie had warned him precisely of this. He could not take advantage of the situation. Not with her. Even more so now she'd given him this strange gift.

His heart, already booming like that infernal cannon, quickened its barrage. She was important. Somehow in this short, intense week, she'd become important enough to demand another level of care, from himself as well. Whatever lay in her future, it wasn't him. He figured in no one's future, hardly even his own.

But his thumb was still gently brushing her lips, gathering her breath, his fingers resting on the soft sweep of her cheek, on the pulse at her neck. Sharp, urgent...

'Rafe...' It was a slow exhalation that made his body tighten, his mind fizzle and fade as her lips seemed to continue moving against his thumb, murmuring something. Very gently she laid her hand on the centre of his chest. The impact wasn't gentle at all. A swirling miasma of heat and iciness swept outwards from his centre, lighting his body from within.

There was a snap as a twig cracked in the fire and a surge of flame lit the walls around them with sunset colours. She smiled, a slow smile that rumbled through him like a herd of wild beasts on the hunt.

'You look like a pharaoh with the carvings behind you,' she mused, her gaze moving over his face and making his skin tingle as if her fingers were doing the exploring. 'Beautiful.'

He half laughed at the absurdity of that word, but it was another layer stripped away from him. He shook his head, trying to gather his strength against the assault of his own senses, but she merely brushed her palm up his chest, his shirt no protection at all. 'Don't laugh. You *are*,' she insisted. 'You have eyes that take in the whole world and I like the way those lines near your eyes always deepen when you try not to laugh at me.'

She touched his jaw, her fingers trailing again over his scars. 'You think these disgust me, but they don't. I wanted to touch you. I wanted to do this...'

She rose against him, her breath caressing his jaw, her hair tickling his cheek and temple as she brushed the lightest of kisses over his damaged skin.

'God. Cleo…' His throat moved with her name, his hands closed on her waist. He needed to put her away from him, but she was so warm, she smelled so…*so* good… He breathed her in, that faraway coolness of the fields after the first winter rain that brings life to everything. It was doing the same to him.

He must be going a little mad.

A lot mad.

She sighed deeply against him, her lips parting to allow her tongue to taste the tense sinew of his throat. Painful pleasure unfurled inside him like smoke from the camp-fire, flickering embers into firestorms.

He couldn't stop himself from arching his neck to give her better access. She moaned encouragingly, her hands skimming up his back and he realised she'd slipped them under his shirt. They felt so damn good against his skin. So damned right.

So absolutely wrong.

Her nails trailed down his back and with a shattered groan he caught her arms and drew her away before she utterly destroyed him.

'Cleo, *please*. This is a mistake.'

A mistake.

There was such anguished insistence in his voice it muted the drums of warmth beating inside her. Cleo leaned back to inspect his face. He *was* beautiful. But he was look-ing worried and angry again. She desperately wanted him to feel what she did—as warm and doughy as fresh bread and as light as sunbeams. She knew this was not proper, but it felt *right*. How could he not feel that, too?

'It doesn't feel like a mistake,' she murmured, resting her palms against his chest. His muscles shivered beneath them and it spread to her. She *liked* that sensation. It filled the great big echoing cavern inside her with incandescent light.

She had no idea what the morrow would bring but for the first time in…she did not know how long…she felt truly herself. Cleo.

'But it is, Cleo. I can't take advantage of you.'

'May I take advantage of *you*, then, Mr Rafe Grey?'

'No!'

'In two months I shall be twenty-seven years of age. Twenty-seven!'

'What on earth has that to say to anything?'

'Twenty-seven and I have never felt this before…this fire. That *cannot* be right. Even when William and I—'

She squeaked as his hands tightened briefly on her arms.

'*Who* is William?'

Clearly mentioning another man while propositioning one was not a good idea. She had a lot to learn about seduction.

'It doesn't matter. He was an antiquarian friend of my father's and just as dishonourable. But that was a long time ago and I never felt like this when he touched me. I *like* feeling like this. It feels as though you are lighting fires inside me, as though—'

'Cleo, please, *please* stop.'

'I don't want to stop. Tell me why it is so wrong to wish to kiss you? I am not asking for anything else…'

'Cleo…'

There was such an entreaty in that one word her fires doused a little further. He looked tense and miserable and with a shaft of pain she realised he really did not wish to do this.

'Is the idea so distasteful?'

'No, Cleo—'

'You think me mannish in these clothes…and ugly.'

'Are you mad? I think… I *know* you are torturing me. Believe me, I would like nothing better than to do precisely what you are asking. And more. But you placed yourself in my care. Try to understand what that would make me if I gave in to base instincts. It would be a betrayal.'

'I wouldn't hold you responsible.'

'But *I* would.'

For a moment they both remained there, facing each other in the firelit temple.

She should not argue with him. Lust had not completely killed her common sense, yet she couldn't stop herself.

'And if I weren't in your care?'

'I don't…dally with innocents.' He would have sounded priggish if his voice hadn't all but cracked midway through the sentence.

'What a silly word. What if I weren't *innocent*?'

'You're impossible.'

'Oh, just tell me the truth.'

'If you were experienced and not in my care, I would fall over myself to coax you into the nearest bed, Cleopatra. But you aren't and you are. And that is that.'

'No, I'm not and it isn't. I'm not an *innocent*. William saw to that.' Again, possibly not the best thing to reveal to a man one is trying to seduce. 'So you see, you would not be doing anything wrong.'

'What did the bastard do to you?'

She shrugged, the memories dousing her passion. Ten years later, it still stung. She'd been almost eighteen and he close to forty, her father's age. But to her he'd been… freedom. He'd listened to her and made her laugh and made her feel…beautiful. Day by day, he'd peeled away her embarrassment and prudish concerns with teasing and little fleeting touches that seduced her. Little gifts and complicit smiles and then…promises. Of a shared life, a house and a family in England. A home, children. Security.

Except he already had a home and children. And a wife.

At least he'd had the decency to tell her the truth before he'd scuttled off. There'd been some mercy in that. Amputation was healthier in the end than the slow gangrenous rot of wondering what she had done wrong. She'd told her father, still naive and hopeful enough to think he'd take her side, maybe even comfort her. Well, another lesson learned. He'd been more furious at her having chased off his partner and ruining their trade in faux Greek statuettes than at William's betrayal.

That was the last time she turned to her father for comfort or aid. From that moment on it had been her and Dash and she'd been better for it.

'Cleo. Answer me. Did he hurt you?' Rafe said insistently, dragging her out of the past.

'You needn't sound as though you want to hunt him down and shoot him. It happened ten years ago and he did nothing worse than take what I offered willingly and then tell me he could not marry me because he already had a wife in England.'

'Nothing worse? Where the devil was your father in all this?'

She gave a little laugh. 'He was blaming me for chasing away his business associate. But it was *my* mistake for trusting either of them and it has nothing to do with now.'

He drew a deep breath, as if pulling back on invisible reins.

'Cleo, these feelings are natural. Especially when you are in danger and afraid. But they wear off and when they do they leave a bitter taste because you think you are choosing, but it is not a true choice. You deserve someone who can promise you happiness.'

Somehow this hurt more than everything he'd said before.

'I don't want anyone to promise me anything and certainly not something as ephemeral as happiness. My whole life has been built around a string of empty promises, being shunted about from one dream to another, none of which were mine, and watching all of them turn to cinders.'

He did not answer and they stood in silence for a long

while. He still held her lightly, his fingers gentle against the sensitive inside of her arm. She could hear his breathing—slow and deep and forceful, like the surf beating on the stone walls of Acre. She'd always felt those waves were the sound of the whole world breathing.

'Right now the sum of my dreams is to find my brother, reach England safely, and make a life there. All I want from you is…this.' She rested her hand once again, very gently on his chest. 'Rafe…'

He let go her arms abruptly and stepped back.

'I'm going for a walk. I'll sleep at the entrance tonight.'

Rafe spread his bedding outside the entrance to the chamber and pulled his blanket over him. He settled heavily on his aching shoulder and lay still for a long while, watching the moon blur as a ragged cloud crept up on it in the dark. He heard nothing from inside the temple but the snap and crackle of the small fire. The temptation to go inside was excruciating, but he remained where he was, a solid, aching barrier between her and the world.

He waited, as tense as a drawn bow, for her to come to confront him. Even for her to wish him goodnight. But no sound came. It was hellishly unfair that she could fall asleep so easily after kicking him off a cliff into purgatory.

It didn't help that a pack of jackals was carousing somewhere in the darkness. The jackals' long yowls reminded him of drunken soldiers after a battle—caught between the relief and sadness of surviving, and the need for human touch.

He wished the pack would find some other corner of the desert to annoy.

He turned on his back, staring at the immensity of the sky, and drew his leg up to ease the thudding pressure in his groin. A whole year without a woman was bound to wreak havoc, but that was no reason to indulge his body's juvenile fascination with Cleopatra. Or her fascination with him.

I like feeling like this.

So do I, damn it.

He turned on to his side again and opened his eyes, trying to chase away the ruinous images playing across his closed lids. But his mind was busy stacking the cards against him, pulling them out one by one like a vindictive Tarot card reader—what if she was no longer under his care? After all, she said she was not a virgin…

His mind stumbled over that for a moment. William. Of course she would fall in love with someone named after her precious bard.

You're an idiot, Rafe. Lust is bad enough right now. Don't add jealousy and anger to the mix.

But he couldn't help it. Every time he thought he'd plumbed the depth of her father's callousness, she let drop another pearl. What kind of bastard blamed his daughter for being seduced and lied to by his own friend? Osbourne was very lucky he was dead because if he'd been alive…

Except he wasn't; he was dead and Cleo was alone and for the moment she was his responsibility. Which meant there could be no *'all I want from you is this'*.

He groaned and rubbed his face, blocking out the filigree of stars. He could have come just listening to her. That voice and her big gold-brown eyes all sleepy and warm and… He was so tempted to go back into that temple and curl himself around her and feel her mouth on him again, that soft sweep against his neck…

There was something wrong with this world that women had to deny animal desire unless sanctioned by ceremony. He'd turned his back on that nonsense; why should he impose it on someone as unconventional as Cleo? She wanted it honestly and that was all she wanted from him…

The pin finally fell into the groove and with it the snap of affront.

Of course, that is all anyone wanted from him—some

service to be performed: save me, solve this problem, scratch this itch...

God knew he wanted to scratch this particular itch, just not at any cost.

She was no different in the end. She'd dragged admissions out of him he'd only ever told a handful of people, charmed them out of him with the lightest of touches and that aphrodisiac tincture of compassion. Then she'd come in for the kill with those impossibly sensual eyes pouring honeyed heat over him.

'May I take advantage of you, then, Mr Rafe Grey?'

He should have said yes and the hell with worrying about being manipulated and used. He didn't care. He just wanted...

He half rose, only to lie back down.

In the end, the only thing that should matter was that she was in his care until she was safe. He had so few codes left in his life, so few truths. If he took advantage of her... and it would be taking advantage of her as much as she wanted to take advantage of him...

A shiver of heat raced through him, like a rat roused from its hiding place.

Blast and double blast the woman.

He kept his eyes resolutely closed. A stone-hard cock had yet kept him from sleep when he knew he had to be rested and he was damned if he was going to let it do so now. He had trained for years to deal with situations where he needed sleep and his body rebelled.

He began counting backward from one hundred, each number taking him down a step towards a blank door. At fifty he vaguely noticed he wasn't holding his pistol as he always did during the count. Strangely it was suspended beside him without any contact. A railing had appeared there instead, smooth under his hand. He kept counting even as he wondered where it had come from.

He started floating at thirty, much later than usual, and

even then almost lost his count when a dark-eyed little boy sitting on the steps holding a toy horse smiled up at him.

He felt his hand settle on the familiarly warm downy hair and then the numbers finally fell away.

Chapter Nine

Cairo—three days later

'Home sweet home.'

Rafe dropped his pack on to a scuffed wooden table at the centre of the room and rolled his shoulders. Cleo laid hers down more gently and looked around.

The house was well situated, close to the wharves of Boulaq, but within easy distance of the centre of Cairo. It probably belonged to a well-to-do merchant for it was large and clean and the wooden latticed shutters were in good repair. She peeked through the shutters—the sun was low and beyond the rooftops the Nile was a swathe of silver and copper scarred by the white sails of feluccas and the flat ferries cutting towards Giza. Below she could hear the shopkeepers and the distinctive gaggle of men from the coffee house, and above the scent of the river and the spice store below she caught the warm scent of coffee and the muskier tang of the *shisha* pipes.

She closed her eyes and let the sounds and smells waft around her.

Home sweet home.

For a little longer only.

She had not thought she would miss this city, but now

she knew her days here were numbered she felt the squeeze of sorrow that this, too, must be left behind. She was becoming truly maudlin. She hadn't cried when William abandoned her, yet she'd cried on Gamila's hairy neck, saying goodbye to her and to Gamal.

Gamal, wealthier by five camels and several gold coins, had reassured her it was in the stars that she would return one day to the desert with her man and children and then they would ride Gamila's calf. It was a lovely image, however unlikely, and she'd accepted it for the gift it was.

'Hungry?'

She nodded at Rafe's question. He was still by the table and was watching her. The back of her nape tingled with awareness and the resurgence of embarrassment. Neither of them had referred to the events in the temple at Kharga and Rafe had made every effort to behave as if the interlude had never happened.

Perhaps to someone like Rafe, who'd seen so much in the world, her behaviour was easy to dismiss. Still, he'd been uncomfortable with her ever since. When they'd reached Asyut and she'd curled up to sleep at the bow of the felucca they'd hired, he'd gone to sit at the stern.

'Tired?'

She nodded again.

'You look like you're propped up with scaffolding, Cleo-Pat. Take off that turban and sit down.'

'I should go to Ezbekiya and see...'

He came towards her and she tensed as she had every time they'd come within touching distance since her failed seduction. He looked even more like a corsair in this civilised setting. Nothing had outwardly changed—his plain cotton shirt was open at the neck, his dark hair disordered and his jaw covered with stubble except where the scars left it pale and bare. In the desert his raffish air looked far more natural than the rigid dress code of many visiting Englishmen. But here in the small room with its prosaic table and chairs and a faded painting of some Mameluke patron, he looked like what he was—a mercenary. Capable, dangerous, calculating.

He untucked the edge of her scarf from under her ear and unwound it, his dark brows drawn together with concentration. When he brushed his knuckles from her temple to her cheek that side of her face lit like an oil lamp and she held herself stone still, hope springing to life. But he merely moved away, tossing her scarf on to the pile on the table.

'You've brought half the desert in here with you, Queenie. You aren't going anywhere but into a bath. Everything else will wait until the morrow.'

'I must see if Dash is there—'

'Do you know what they call animals that rush into traps?' he interrupted and she frowned, well aware this was a trap in itself.

'No...'

'Supper.'

'Oh, *very* amusing.'

'Sarcasm doesn't work if you're laughing, Cleo-Pat.'

She didn't bother to deny the accusation. It was very hard to remain serious when he was in this mood. No doubt this lightness was relief at finally reaching the safety and relative comfort of Cairo and knowing he would soon be shot of her and her problems. Tomorrow he would be on his way to find his brother and she—

All her amusement and the glimmerings of pleasure were doused as swiftly as if she'd been tossed headfirst into the Nile.

He frowned. 'I don't care what mouldering mummy of a thought your tortuous mind has conjured, Queenie; you aren't going anywhere today. Come, I'll show you to your room.'

He went towards the door, but she wavered and he glanced back.

'It's not a trap, Cleo.'

'I know that. It's only… I've forgotten what it is like to be indoors.'

'After a week, miss?' Birdie asked as he entered the room with a wooden tray bearing a steaming long-spouted teapot and plate of honeyed cakes. She smiled at him with relief.

'It feels much, much longer than a week, Birdie.'

'Is that a jibe about how heavily our company weighed on you, Queenie?' Rafe asked.

'Stop that bickering, you two, and come drink.' Birdie filled the *finjans* and the scent of coffee and cardamom filled the room. 'Naguib brought this fresh from the coffee house. His son's heating water for Miss to wash and I've sent him to fetch us a good piece of lamb for supper. You'll go to the baths by the square, sir?'

Rafe drained the small cup and rubbed his hand over his jaw, but his gaze was on Cleo. 'You go, Birdie. I'll make do here with hot water and a blade.'

'No, you won't, sir. I'll keep a weather eye here, never fear.'

Cleo saw the yearning mix with hesitation in Rafe's eyes and sighed.

'I am not foolhardy, Mr Grey. I won't disappear while you are at the *hammam*.'

'Your word.'

'My word.'

He nodded but there was still a peculiar hesitancy about him. Finally, Birdie gave him an unceremonious shove towards the door.

'Off with you. Faster you go, faster you're back and it's my turn.'

When the door closed behind him Birdie smiled at her.

'Come along, miss. I'll show you to your room.'

'That sounds very grand, Birdie.'

'Well, it's not that, but right now I'd venture we'd be happy in a hayloft, miss.'

* * *

It wasn't the laughter or the scraping of some string instrument from the coffee house down the street that was keeping Rafe awake. It was a blank wall.

Behind the straw-coloured wall was Cleo's room and her equally narrow wooden bed. In essence, he lay closer to her now than he had in the desert where nothing but a couple of yards of cooling air separated them.

Except now he couldn't see her and it was wreaking havoc on his ability to surrender to sleep. She'd become a talisman, like those prayer beads the men in the coffee house clicked between their fingers. He'd grown accustomed to seeing her just before he fell asleep—marking it in his mind: One Cleopatra Osbourne, present and asleep.

Other than that hellish night in Kharga, for a week now this had been his nightly rote. He hadn't noticed it had become a habit. He certainly hadn't realised it had become a necessity.

Strange to think he'd watched her sleep more than he'd watched any other woman. He'd spent a fair share of time in bed with women over the years, but he could not for the life of him remember ever watching them sleep. If he'd thought about it at all, he would have considered it an imposition—he didn't like the thought of anyone watching him while he was unconscious, so he had done unto others as he wished to be done unto him.

He had no idea why she was different. Perhaps it was the desert—that thick but crystalline darkness, or the absence of walls to protect them from whatever dangers lurked in the darkness so he had to check she was safe.

There was also that niggling confusion—he could not quite get to the bottom of the puzzle that was Cleopatra Osbourne. She was at once so direct and so very convoluted. He found himself searching her face for some clue that would settle the question one way or another. Perhaps in sleep she would reveal that essence. But her face, free of wariness and tension, her lashes twitching like feathers as she dreamt, only confused him further.

Not that it should matter. He'd never before thought it necessary to understand his charges in order to protect them. Why he should feel that impulse now, he didn't know. It was there, though. A discomfort, like sitting on a poorly stitched saddle.

The confusion was rubbing him raw.

Having a real bed, a room and a solid wall between them should have been a relief. The last thing he would have expected was to be lying awake staring at that wall, as alert as if a pack of rabid jackals was scratching at the door.

He'd felt the same at Chesham when Jacob was ill. He and Edge had taken turns keeping vigil and he'd been terrified he'd fall asleep on his watch and wake to find his nephew dead. In the end Jacob had died snug in Edge's arms in the middle of a sunny day. It made no odds if they were awake or not, but something deep and atavistic told him it mattered. The same overpowering urge to assure himself she was well was pressing on his chest like an incubus. He needed to *see* that she was sleeping.

Absurd. Besides being improper and unnecessary and offensive.

He groaned and rubbed his stiff shoulder.

He would compromise by ensuring all the doors and windows were secured. In a few days she would be on her way to England on his friend Chris's ship and there would be no checking on her, sleeping or waking.

His stomach clenched and he stood. A thousand things could happen to a woman travelling to England. Cleopatra might be more resourceful than most people of his acquaintance, but he knew the world—it stacked the deck against women and even the most agile fox could find itself cornered if the hounds were set upon it.

Even if the *Hesperus* was still docked in Alexandria... Even if he trusted Chris with his life... Even then the thought of watching her set sail to an unknown future felt like a betrayal. Worse, it felt…frightening. Wrong.

He felt a little ill with it. Like the days before one fully succumbed to an ague. His insides felt rough, raw, miserable.

It was damn lucky he no longer depended on his skill as a mercenary to pay the bills because he'd clearly gone soft.

He padded into the corridor and his stomach clenched again.

The door to her room was ajar and the narrow bed empty. Fear was chased by anger—she could not possibly have been so foolish to have gone off alone? He strode into the room and the anger dimmed at the sight of her boots, now clean and shiny, set by the small table-cum-dresser. But that merely made way for fear to return. He did not believe they had been followed, yet…

He hurried down the corridor to the salon and stopped in the doorway.

She half turned, her eyes dark and gleaming like an animal's. She was wrapped in a cotton blanket and it trailed on the ground like a cape. She looked more than ever like a faerie being with her short hair and large eyes. A breeze was slipping through the shutters, but his body was heating up far too fast for the cool air to soothe him.

With a mixture of anger and resignation he felt it take hold. He might as well have been that blasted princess chained to the rock in the sea—there was no escaping this wave. It swept out from his centre like kindling tossed into a keg of gunpowder.

He'd wanted to feel young again, but not like this. Not overwhelmed by a need he didn't even understand. He *liked* lust—liked it fierce and hot and immediate. But not when it was laced with fear and this strange loss of balance.

It had happened before, in moments of weakness. This welling of need for some place to set down roots and grow. Someone…

But it dragged up every doubt and demon inside him, his mind mapping the future down a hundred paths to perdition. It ended in his father's madness, his nephew's death, with the murky image of the woman who might marry him realising her mistake. It ended with pain and emptiness and a loneliness worse for being shared.

He *liked* his life. There was no reason to change it only to make it worse. He had no faith in his ability to be anything but a temporary haven. That was the essence of his being. Temporary.

Cleo deserved everything her father and that bastard of a lover had denied her. She deserved her pack of jackals, a safe, good man who would help her set down the roots she'd been denied by the men who should have stood by her.

He knew as much about roots as he did about camels. Less.

He should stay away.

However much his body was waxing lyrical about her at the moment, she was only a page in a very brief chapter of his life. She had no place in his tale any more than he had in hers.

'Why aren't you in your room?' He tried to keep his voice low and authoritative.

'I can't sleep,' she whispered. 'The room feels…stifling after the desert. It's foolish, but I needed to breathe. Did I wake you?

'I wasn't asleep.'

'Oh.' She turned and touched the shutters briefly. Through the perforations of the *mashrabiya* he could see the inky shimmer of the Nile. 'I came to look at the river. It always calms me.'

'You sound as if you will miss it.'

'I think I will. Or perhaps that is only because my future is so uncertain. Better the devil one knows…'

'What will you do when you reach England?' He hadn't meant to make it sound like a demand, but she reacted as to the flick of a whip, her back straightening and her lips flattening.

'First I must be certain Dash has left Egypt. I am very grateful for your help, Mr Grey, and I will find a way to repay you, but you are under no further obligation to me.'

'If I were your friend al-Mizan, do you know what I would do once I realised you'd slipped through my net?' he said, ignoring her stilted formality. 'I would wait for you to do precisely what you appear determined to do—return to your home ground. You might as well declare your arrival in Cairo from the nearest minaret.'

'I'm not quite the fool you think me, Mr Grey. I do not plan to parade around Cairo for all to see. Besides, I doubt my father took anything so valuable from Bey al-Wassawi he'd send al-Mizan all the way to Cairo.'

'You know as well as I al-Mizan is not in the employ of Bey al-Wassawi. He came from Cairo and carried a letter of recommendation from the French consul general.'

'Why are you only telling me this now?' Her voice rose in anger.

'I might just as easily ask why you didn't tell me you knew al-Mizan was in Boucheron's employ?'

She turned her head back towards the shutters.

'I've never met any of Boucheron's mercenaries.'

'Yet you knew he employed a man by the name of al-Mizan.'

'It might have been a common name for all I knew.'

'Not at all, according to Gamal. You didn't mention it for a reason.'

Her chin lowered like a bull considering whether or not to charge.

'Oh? And what reason do you ascribe to me?'

'Two reasons. At first you didn't trust me. It was one thing for a foreign mercenary to shield you from a local bruiser, quite another to expect him to take your side against another foreigner and a wealthy and influential one at that. A sensible mercenary might have decided you and your beastly bauble were not worth the risk.'

'And the other reason?'

'The opposite consideration. You were worried you might not be so easily rid of us if we thought the source of your threat was here in Cairo.'

'You appear to think you know the workings of my mind, Mr Grey.'

'Some of them, certainly. You are too honest a person to lie convincingly, Cleo-Pat.'

'I did not lie.'

'Omitting to tell the truth is still being dishonest.'

'The same applies to you. You don't appear to be at all bothered by the fact you lied by omission.'

'Not terribly. You did not need to know it. Now you do.'

'Magnanimous of you.'

'Merely practical. It makes it clear why I cannot allow you to charge into town tomorrow.'

'He will be on the lookout for Dash, not for Miss Osbourne. Miss Osbourne left for London with the Mitchums weeks ago.'

'Yet what happens if you are recognised? Boucheron will surely be interested why Miss Osbourne, who as you say left for London, has returned to Cairo in record time. No reason for him to consider that at all suspicious.'

She crossed her arms. With her short hair and the plain cotton nightshirt Birdie had procured her she did not look like any young woman of his acquaintance. Her hair feathered over her dark brows and his hand twitched with the need to sift through it, brush it back, shape his hands over her head, her nape… He wanted so very badly to walk over and…

And nothing. It was not going to happen.

'I shall naturally not advertise my return, Mr Grey,' she replied. 'All I wish to do is go to our rooms and see if Dash is there. Perhaps I shall discover this is all a foolish misunderstanding and that all is well…' She wavered, but clung doggedly to her shrinking island. 'There is no reason to always suspect the worst.'

'There is one reason to always suspect the worse and that is one's wish to survive.'

'*"A coward dies a thousand times before his death, but the valiant taste of death but once."* That is from *Julius Caesar* in case you were interested, Mr Grey.'

'Not Old Willie again. And if you must quote him, try not to choose a quote where the character is dead by the next act.'

Her reluctant laughter rippled out.

'I concede, but my point is still valid as well. Living in fear is a dreadful way to pass through this world.'

'I disagree; it is far preferable to be a coward than valiant. As a coward I've died many times and will likely do so again before I do so irretrievably. But, unlike Caesar, for now I'm still here to argue with you.'

'Don't be coy, Mr Grey. You are certainly no coward.'

'You think not? By your definition I most certainly am. My cowardly little mind maps the world with a hundred ways my candle can be snuffed. It could be anything— from having my throat slit by one of your enemies to being poisoned by Birdie's culinary efforts. Every night I go to sleep is another temporary victory over that catalogue. I am only alive today because I am a coward.'

His anger grew with his words. She wasn't attacking him, but it felt like an accusing finger. Rafe Grey's life was based on the actions of a coward, or running away from burdens—his father's anger, his mother's indifference, even his true name. He'd escaped them all, tail between his legs. He didn't need some misguided miss spouting romantic nonsense about being valiant to him. It was a little late for that.

'Then I'm very glad you're a coward.' She spoke softly and there was still a remnant of a smile curving her lips.

It was either the smile or something in her words, but he felt a little stunned, as if he'd walked into a tree he'd not realised stood right in front of him. Of all the risks he prepared for daily, he was not prepared for her shifting moods.

'If being brave is forcing your way again and again through your fears, and I agree it is, then you are a very brave man, Rafe.'

Damnation.

'Are you buttering me up for a purpose, Cleo-Pat? I still have no intention of allowing you to run about Cairo unchecked.'

'I am not buttering you up, but cannot in good conscience continue to impose upon you. You have your own matters to see to.'

'Do you wish me to help you or not?'

'Of course I do, but...'

'Good. Then stop arguing about everything. Tomorrow we will decide how to proceed. Right now, take advantage of having a decent bed.'

He sounded sensible and authoritative. But inside a voice was pleading—*Please go to sleep before I do something my conscience will hit me over the head with.*

'Very well. Thank you, Rafe,' Cleo murmured and he shrugged, clearly uncomfortable with gratitude or praise. He looked like an overgrown, embarrassed schoolboy. She almost enjoyed saying nice things about him just to watch the confident man turn into a squirming mass of discomfort.

She enjoyed far too much about him.

What would he say if she told him it wasn't only her worries about tomorrow that had kept her awake, but the realisation that it was over? This brief, frightening, and yet beautiful adventure.

She smiled at him. She would miss him awfully when they parted ways, but she wouldn't allow that to take away from the gift he'd unknowingly helped her uncover. Somehow during their passage through the desert she'd come to feel she belonged. She'd been right there at the centre of her own world, instead of alone or an observer. It wasn't that Rafe Grey had moved into the centre of her world. *She* had. Whatever happened from that moment onwards, she would hold on to that.

Still, she wished so much she could take something more before they parted ways tomorrow... The thought was suddenly so unbearable she reached out and took his hand. Strange how well she knew it already—its size, the roughness of his callouses and the softness of the heart of his palm. She'd held it sitting by the fire in the middle of the universe and nothingness.

In the dark, with the city hushed around them, his hand was like that campfire—it became the centre of a vast universe, the point from which everything was mapped. She wanted to feel it against her cheek and neck with a need stronger than a desert thirst. Her own skin was half on fire, half icy.

'Cleo...' His voice scraped at her nerves, his hand tightening on hers for a moment, but then he stepped back and turned resolutely towards the door.

'Goodnight.'

Chapter Ten

Rafe was at the table when she entered the sitting room the next morning, the remains of breakfast to one side and a cup of coffee at his elbow as he scribbled on a sheet of paper. He glanced up as she entered, but then returned his frown to his letter.

'I need the direction of your house,' he said to his letter. 'I will go there this morning.'

Cleo took a piece of bread and poured cardamom-scented coffee into a small cup.

'I'm coming with you.'

'No, you are not.'

'I most certainly am. Aside from everything else, you will never find it without me.'

There was a distinct sound of grinding teeth, but he remained bent over his writing. She watched his hand moving in a steady dance over the paper, dipping into the inkwell, flexing. Her own hands were tingling.

He laid down the pen, but did not look at her.

'I concede you know a great deal more about Egypt than I do or will ever wish to know, Pat, but I know more about thieves and murderers than I hope you ever will.'

'Excellent. Then between the two of us we should be prepared for everything.'

'You have hired me...'

'To bring me to Cairo. Which you have. You are no longer in my employ and I am no longer your charge.'

'You are merely strengthening my case that you are not in command. I work alone.'

'That is not very kind to Birdie.'

'Birdie and I are considered a unit for the purposes of my occupation. You, however...'

'Know my way around this city and my own home, which is more than you do. Even if I were to give you the direction, several other families have rooms in that building. You will likely become lost and go into the wrong rooms if you go alone.'

'Must you always insist on having your way?'

'Only when I know I am right.'

He sighed.

'I don't know why I even bother arguing with you.'

'We are not arguing. We are conferring on how best to proceed.'

'No. I was telling you... Damnation, never mind. You may come. But otherwise you will do precisely as you are told. If I tell you to run, you pick up your skirts and run. Understood?'

Cleo paused at the corner of the road, between an open-fronted shop stacked high with rugs and another glittering with pots and pans.

The street looked the same and utterly different.

It was not as busy as Boulaq, but this part of Ezbekiya was still crowded with shops and narrow streets populated by foreign merchants and mid-level officials of the Khedive's court. Her father had always hoped their fortunes might so improve as to allow him to move to the more prosperous parts of Cairo, but Cleo had enjoyed the anonymity of this crowded corner of the city. No one appeared to know or care whether she appeared in her boy's garb or in one of her few dresses.

Now the noise and the crowds felt as oppressive and foreign as the first time they'd come here four years ago.

'Is one of those buildings where you live?' Rafe put a hand on her arm, not to guide her across the road, but to restrain her. He needn't have. She'd become as wary as he these past weeks.

'Yes, we have rooms in the building just by that little passage halfway down.'

'You have that look on your face again. What is amiss?'

'I don't know. Perhaps I am being over-cautious, but something feels…wrong,' she murmured.

'Cautious is good. Especially when a group of unpleasant men are on your tail. You should trust those sensations—your mind sees more than you do. Is there something out of place on the street?'

'No, it is merely…yes, yes, you are right—something *is* out of place. I left the *mashrabiya* shutters closed and Dash would never leave them open in the middle of the day. See upstairs?'

He raised his eyes to scan the house, his hand moving a little on her arm. It was a reassuring rub. For such a big man he had a gentle touch.

'Perhaps your landlord came to look around?'

'He has never done so before and would have no reason to. Our rent is paid through to the end of the quarter.'

'I see. Is there somewhere you can wait for me? Or perhaps I'd better take you back to Boulaq now I know my way here.'

'We agreed I was to come with you!'

'And you have. There is no need for you to go any further, Queenie. We passed a spice shop just around the corner. Wait for me there.'

'No!' It was her turn to grab his arm. It was a substantially thicker and more solid affair than hers and she added her other hand to secure her grip. He looked down at her hands, his brows rising. Embarrassment hit her like the blast of an open oven and she dropped his arm, tucking her hands into her *gallabiyah*.

'Listen to me. The buildings along the north side of the street were once part of a Mameluke palace and they've been separated into lodgings in the least sensible manner. Corridors and doors head in every direction so you might never find the right door and even then you won't know if anything has changed since my departure. Besides, I am far safer with you than on my own out here and—'

He sighed. 'Very well, you will probably only follow me anyway and make matters worse.'

'There is no need to be insulting.'

'And there is no need to take offence when you've already won the draw. Now, lead on, MacDuff.'

'It is *"Lay on"*. Why must everyone misquote that?'

'Because it is an improvement on the original.'

'An improvement on *Shakespeare*!'

'You look ready to run me through. You shouldn't idolise anyone, Pat. Not even a man who's safe by dint of being dead. He can still disappoint, you know.'

'I don't idolise him. There isn't even a *him* to idolise— it's his writing that means something to me; not the man himself. He could be a three-legged, one-horned goat for all I care.'

'Yet you still allow him to sway your judgement.'

'I do not.'

'You are standing here on a street corner, arguing with me while al-Mizan's minions might be roaming your house. I'd call that being swayed.'

'It's not… I'm merely…not ready.'

'I know, but it's always better to know the truth.'

'No, it isn't. Oh, devil take it. Let us go see.'

* * *

'Your housekeeping skills leave a lot to be desired, Queenie.'

Rafe watched her as she scooped up a pile of clothes and a bonnet from the floor. 'What are you doing?' he asked as she began laying out the clothes on the narrow bed.

'Checking.'

'What?'

'Clothes.'

'And why are you checking clothes?' he asked carefully.

She placed her hands on her hips and looked around the room.

'Dash has been here.'

'I don't know much about your brother, Cleo, but I don't think he made this mess.'

'Of course he didn't, but someone has taken at least one set of clothes—warm clothes—as well as his best shaving kit and his old writing case. The note I left him is missing as well. I doubt the thieves would have been interested in that.'

'I see. But we don't know if he came before or after the people who decided to redistribute all your possessions on the floor.'

'After. This picture frame is broken, but the likeness it held of my mother is gone. It was hanging on that wall and had it been intact when he came he would have taken it with him, frame and all.'

'Good point.' He rubbed his chest as realisation set in that had Cleo not gone in search of her brother, she would have been here when they came to search the rooms. If he'd had any lingering doubts about the need to remove her from Egypt without delay, the casual violence inherent in the ransacked room removed it utterly. By hook or by crook he would see her safe to England and be done with this.

He watched her as she continued inspecting the room. Her face was imperturbable again, except for that stubborn jutting of her lower lip. He could see no fear there, but she was no fool. She *must* realise the danger to herself. He followed her into the next room.

'This means that your brother has likely been through here in the last few days, seen this chaos and realised it was time to leave Egypt in your wake post haste. That is good news.'

'Yes.'

'You don't look relieved.'

'I should be, I know. But I don't understand what they are looking for. My father may have been many dubious things, but I've never known him to steal something outright. I cannot make sense of any of this.'

She was gathering and stacking the discarded slips of paper, the same ferocious frown cutting lines in her brow. He wanted to tell her to forget about making sense of her sire's leavings and concentrate on the future. Except that he was as aware as she must be that her future was even cloudier than her present.

She placed the stack of papers on the desk and straightened a small framed print of a very English landscape on the wall. He could see where she had done her best to give this depressing set of rooms some character—there were colourful cushions and carpets and a few framed drawings of temples and landscapes.

He followed her into the next room and stopped in the doorway, absurdly embarrassed as he realised it was her bedroom. It, too, was a jumble of discarded clothes, cushions and books and she bent and untangled a simple muslin dress from the pile in the middle of the floor. There was hardly anything untoward about the sight of a plain cotton frock, but he took a step backwards and went back to the main salon.

It was only a dress. He'd seen hundreds of them—on and off women. He wasn't merely getting old; he was becoming addled. Next he'd be blushing at the sight of a bonnet and getting hard at the mention of a reticule.

Pathetic.

After all, the simple Egyptian belted robe she wore showed as much of her anatomy as a gown. Well, not as much of her magnificent bosom. He wouldn't mind at all seeing that on display in one of the low-cut London fashions. With her height and physique and those elfin features she would probably attract a great deal of attention. She would look best in vivid colours, desert colours, that reflected the honey of her eyes and skin and the chestnut warmth of her hair. Earth and fire.

Ah, *hell*.

'We should be going.' His voice was more growl than suggestion and he cleared his throat, calling himself to order.

'In a moment...' Her reply was muffled and her shadow moved about the room, the dark length of an arm slipping across the floor and touching the bed as if beckoning him.

Seeking a distraction, he picked up a book from the desk and flicked open the cover. With a jolt of annoyance, he realised that the fates were having a grand time toying with him—it was a well-worn copy of Edge's first *Desert Boy* book, the one he himself had all but forced his brother to write. He flicked the page, his heart contracting at the familiar drawing of a cat riding a camel and the printed dedication.

To J.- My heart, my home, for ever.
And to R.- My brother and my rock.

Combating lust with sentiment was not a tactic he had tried in the past. He couldn't even vouch for its effectiveness because at that second a far more immediate peril intervened.

He could never later make sense of this lapse in his caution.

A bout of juvenile lusting, even combined with surprise at seeing Edge's book, was no excuse for becoming so pre-occupied he completely missed the man's approach. He couldn't even console himself that his near-murderer had been unusually stealthy because Cleo did hear him. One minute he'd been glaring at the book and the next there'd been a cry and a blur of movement as Cleo barrelled past him and into the man rushing towards him with a dagger, her hands fastening about the attacker's wrist, driving it upwards.

The man cursed, swinging his arm back at her and there was a dull thud as his elbow struck her head and she hit the wall, sliding to the floor. The assailant hardly changed his trajectory as he continued towards Rafe, his whole body behind the thrust of the knife. But the momentary check Cleo had provided was more than enough.

Rafe raised the book he held and gave a brutal whack to the man's knife hand and then swung the volume back to connect again with the side of his attacker's all too fa-miliar face. The knife flew in one direction and the man in the other, his head hitting the doorjamb behind him with a thud. Rafe advanced immediately, but before he could even grab him al-Mizan's eyes rolled backwards and he slipped to the ground.

'You killed him,' Cleo whispered, rubbing her shoulder as she struggled to her feet. She did not appear to be very shocked by the prospect.

Rafe's blood was still boiling, but too many thoughts were going through his mind so he focused on what mat-tered right there and then.

'He's not dead and he'll probably come out of this faint any moment, so help me. Bring me a cravat or scarf to tie his hands and then go into the hallway and I don't want to hear a peep from you. Not one word.'

She hurried out and returned with a stack of linen strips and he hauled al-Mizan on to a wooden chair and set about tying his hands and legs to it. The man was already beginning to stir and Rafe shooed her towards the hallway.

'Stay out of his sight and for God's sake don't say a word. Promise me!'

She bunched her fists, but nodded, and he picked up the man's knife and waited.

It did not take long. Al-Mizan groaned, cursed and looked as though he was well on his way to casting up his accounts, but he controlled himself, finally focusing on Rafe.

'Hello, al-Mizan.' Rafe smiled. There was a livid bruise along his cheekbone where he'd knocked against the door-jamb and another along his jaw where the book had caught him. Rafe tapped the tip of the dagger to the already swelling flesh and al-Mizan winced, shying away.

'Looks as though you are going to have quite a black eye. I suggest applying wet compresses and avoid trying to skewer people for a few days.'

'You lied to me in Syene,' al-Mizan snarled.

'Did I? I only remember turning down your less than generous offer.'

'You knew of this Osbourne. You are in league with him.'

'Not at all. It is simply that his offer was better than yours. I am merely trying to help return him to England in one piece. I assure you he neither has nor wishes to have whatever it is you are looking for.'

'I saw you this moment holding a book!'

Rafe picked up the discarded *Desert Boy* book and opened it.

'This? I applaud your master's taste in reading, but he could have saved himself great expense and trouble and bought a copy at a bookshop.'

Al-Mizan glared at him, but there was a growing puzzlement in his eyes.

'Perhaps I was mistaken about this instance, but the son of Osbourne took his father's possessions from the lodgings in Meroe. The book as well. My master did not think the boy was in his father's confidence, but then why take the book and why disappear?'

'Perhaps because a murderous fellow was on his trail?'

'He was not to know I meant to harm him.'

'You're not that stupid, al-Mizan. What else was he to think when mercenaries begin to make enquiries about him in the middle of Nubia? Of course he ran. He told me the day he came to find me he did not know why you were chasing him.'

'If he does not have the book, then who does?'

'I neither know nor care. My role is to ensure Mr Osbourne is put safely on a ship to England. I am happy to enquire if he took any books from his father's possessions and, if he has, I will ensure we deliver them all to your master, Monsieur Boucheron.'

It was a gamble. Rafe saw Cleo's shadow shifting in the hallway as she listened and he hoped she kept quiet.

Al-Mizan's eyes narrowed and he gave a tug at his bonds.

'I never spoke my master's name. You reveal yourself, *basha nadab.*'

'Not at all. It does not take a great mind to realise Osbourne's father took something from his employer. Neither I nor Osbourne the Younger have any interest in entering that feud.'

'I see no reason why I should trust you. When last I did my men wasted a day chasing two of Bey al-Wassawi's cousins.'

'Only a day? They were even more ineffective than I thought. As for trusting me, you should because you strike me as a sensible man and, more to the point, because at the moment you are tied to a chair and I could easily make away with you right now.'

'It would be foolishness to harm me, *nadab*. If you know aught of my master, you should know he possesses a great deal of influence here. He could have you thrown into one of our prisons. You would not like it, I assure you.'

'Don't waste your time threatening me, al-Mizan. You would have an easier time of it if you killed me outright rather than trying to put me in a local gaol. But having failed in that endeavour I suggest you pass along a message to your master. My only interest is in returning Mr Osbourne to England. I have no interest in stolen goods and neither does he. All I want is the man, on a ship.'

'Why? Of what value is he to you?'

'I could ask the same of you.'

'I told you...'

'You told me a tall tale about some family bible. Now we have each other's measure, al-Mizan, you know I don't believe that. Tell me what it is you are really after and I might be able to help you. I don't believe you have gone to all this trouble for a mere book. As best I understand antiquities in this country, there are no valuable books. All writing was on papyrus scrolls. Therefore, I presume it is the contents, not the book itself, that is of value. I also find it curious that your master apparently didn't send you in pursuit until Mr Osbourne's servant defected to his service. Therefore, either he didn't notice this extremely valuable book's disappearance, or, more likely, he did not know of its existence until told of it by the servant.'

Al-Mizan's mouth pressed down hard. Rafe pressed forward his advantage.

'A more romantic fellow than I might have begun to dream of a book filled with clues to a treasure Mr Osbourne was pursuing in Nubia, but since your master did not give you any instructions to make enquiries regarding

Mr Osbourne's activities there, I can discard that fantasy. He wants this book and only that.'

'How do you know he gave me no such instructions?'

'I can count, Mr al-Mizan. I enquired when you passed through Syene on your way south and by my calculation you must have turned around the moment you discovered Osbourne the Younger had been and gone and ridden hard to close the gap. Answer me one question, Mr al-Mizan. Do you know why your master wants this book? Just yes or no will do. No details necessary.'

Al Mizan sighed, his shoulders lowering a little.

'In my position, it is best not to know all the details. It is enough that he wants it and that he pays me well for my services. But I tell you, for him it is of the highest importance.'

Rafe nodded. He knew truth when he heard it. It was a sensible man who did not seek knowledge that could redound against him.

'Then perhaps I should have a word with him myself.'

'I would usually counsel wise men against foolishness, *nadab*, but in this case I need not bother. Monsieur Boucheron is not in Cairo.'

'Where has he gone?'

'He does not inform me. He ordered me to remain alert for Osbourne's son's possible return and then he left.'

'I see. In any case, if we should discover aught of it before we depart Egypt, I will see it is delivered to him. We want nothing of it, merely to return to England now that Old Osbourne is dead. Understood?'

Al-Mizan nodded. It didn't count for much, but it was the best Rafe could secure at this juncture.

'Good. Now I think it is best we part ways.'

'You will not leave me tied to this chair!' al-Mizan protested and Rafe picked up a discarded cravat and twisted it into a gag, tying it around al-Mizan's mouth.

'A few knots won't hold back someone of your skills,

I'm sure,' he murmured reassuringly as he went towards the door. 'Clearly you have paid someone in this building to send word to you if anyone enters these rooms. Make enough of a racket and I feel certain they will come running.'

Cleo was waiting in the narrow hallway, her honey eyes wide, her mouth a thin, determined line, and a broom held firmly in her hands. He waved her towards the door just as a loud crash sounded. Clearly al-Mizan meant to dismantle the chair himself. Good fellow.

Chapter Eleven

Within moments they were wending through the narrow alleyways, skirting stalls and laden donkeys, water boys and women balancing baskets and jugs on their heads. Eventually, Cleo stopped looking over her shoulder every few yards, but she did not speak until they were within sight of the river.

'Why did you tell him I was Dash?'

'Because while they think you are your brother they will be looking for him in the wrong place, giving him more time to leave Egypt unobstructed.'

'Of course. I see. Thank you.'

Her voice was brisk and Rafe realised again how grateful he was for her calm, though she had looked anything but calm as she had launched herself at his would-be killer.

The memory still formed icicles in his chest. The blur of movement, the realisation of danger, the shock. He'd made mistakes in the past and they'd cost him and others, but this...

He didn't want to think about it.

'Don't ever do that again, Cleopatra.'

The words were out of him before he could stop them.

'Do what? Ask questions?'

'Throw yourself at someone wielding a knife.'

They'd reached the house in Boulaq and with a last glance down the street he ushered her inside. She went, but her frown showed precisely what she thought of his comment. He couldn't blame her—he wasn't happy with himself either at the moment, but he couldn't help it.

'I would think you would be grateful, Mr Grey. You might now be sporting another impressive scar in your collection if not for me.'

'I *am* grateful, but I am also serious. Never do that again.'

'You prefer I leave you to be skewered?'

'I prefer you not try to skewer yourself on a trained killer's knife.'

'So do I. Very well, if you prefer to play the hero, next time I shall leave you to it.'

He stomped up the steps beside her, not sure he was pleased with her compliance.

'Do you think he believed you?' she asked.

He considered lying to her and discarded the notion; his prevarication skills weren't at their best around her.

'Men like al-Mizan don't believe anyone. I rather like the fellow.'

'How broadminded of you. After all, he only wished to kill us both.'

'I don't think he was intent on blood—his brief was to find this book and bring you back to Boucheron so he could ascertain what you, I mean your brother, knew. His attempt at violence right there was sparked by personal pique and was a sore mistake. He is well aware of that. Hopefully once you, or rather your brother, leaves Egypt they will forget all about you. Now I need to find Birdie. I want him to run a couple of errands for me.'

She continued up the stairs.

'What errands?'

'I need some new…cravats.'

'Please don't bother to lie, or, if you must, at least make an effort at being convincing.'

'Yes, ma'am.'

'You don't intend to tell me?'

'No, ma'am.'

'You don't trust me.'

'Like al-Mizan, I don't trust anyone. For their own good. The more you trust someone, the greater the burden you place upon them. If I don't trust you, you needn't worry that you might let me down.'

'Another truly abysmal philosophy, Mr Grey.'

'Says the young woman who trusts not a single person on this fair earth.'

Her foot slipped on the step and he caught her elbow, steadying her.

He waited for her to proceed, but she remained where she was, staring at the floor.

'That is not true,' she muttered finally.

'Not true? You told me yourself you never truly trusted your father and we've established you don't trust your brother, not when it truly counts. Either tell me who you trust or stop denigrating my hard-earned right to mistrust everybody.'

'I trust you.'

She had to stop *doing* this.

He hadn't earned it; he didn't want it. Trust like hers demanded trust in return and if he let himself trust her... He had no idea what that even meant except that it had the power to terrify him, as if he held Pandora's box in his hands with warnings from the gods etched deep on to its surface. There would be no closing this box once opened.

She turned to him, chin raised. 'And Birdie, though I know you will say I should not trust either of you.'

'I have already told you precisely that. I don't enjoy repeating myself.'

'I trust you to do the best you can. Not for me, but because you think it is right.'

He put his hands on her shoulders and turned her, marching her towards her room.

'Stop this blathering mawkishness and go wash. I'll see about food. I'm hungry.'

Thankfully she didn't argue and he hurried away before he followed her. Lurching between lust and embarrassment was putting a strain on his ageing heart. The sooner he put her aboard a ship to England, the better.

Cleo sat on her narrow bed, listening to Rafe's receding footsteps. She rubbed her hands on the rough cotton of her robe. They were still shaking. *She* was still shaking. The sick jingling that had plagued her from Nubia to Syene and then quieted during the long days in the desert was back.

She unwrapped her turban and shoved her hands into her short hair.

Her bonnet...

She'd rescued it from the wreckage of their lodgings. And her dress and books and... They were all still there. Dropped on the floor when she'd seen the shadow move behind Rafe, the arm rising and the afternoon sun glinting off a dagger.

He was right. There hadn't been a coherent thought in her mind at that moment. Only images—the shadow, the dagger, Rafe holding a book, his back to his attacker. Then her own hands stretched before her as she found herself in mid-air.

It took being thrown against the wall to wake her mind to fear and denial, but by then it was all over.

Rafe's face had been utterly blank as he administered those two blows which stunned the man. Then he'd looked over at her, a quick look that was like a nail being hammered straight into her heart—sharp, painful, terrifyingly final.

At that moment he'd mattered more than life.

She'd done as he told her. Half her mind had listened to his interrogation of al-Mizan, but the other was still ringing with terror at what might have happened to him.

At some point it *would* happen. It happened to the best of them, he'd said. A moment's inattention. A mistake...

Today it had almost happened because of her.

She could not even think it. She was scared for Dash, for herself, but this felt different—almost superstitious. She *needed* him to exist and she did not even understand why.

'Supper!'

Rafe's call penetrated the door and her fog of confusion and her stomach grumbled hopefully.

In the small room that served as salon and dining room Rafe was putting plates on the table.

He glanced over at her, his pale green eyes sharp and alert.

'Sit.'

'I shall go bring...'

'Everything is ready. Sit.'

She was too tired to protest. She sat as he served her from another of Birdie's mouth-watering stews.

'Where is Birdie?'

'Out.'

'You are not going to tell me where?'

'It has to do with my brother.'

'You have news of him?'

He didn't look up from his plate, but smiled at the excitement in her voice.

'Only that he did indeed arrive in Egypt and continued south. Either on our trail or to my uncle's house in Qetara.'

'Are you not worried for him?'

'For Edge? No, not now he's here. He might be as pig-headed as a mule, but he was an excellent officer during the war. Until he was shot, that is.'

Her knife clacked against the plate and he glanced up.

She kept her own gaze lowered. She hated how shaky she still felt.

They ate in silence until he spoke again.

'Thank you.' His voice was low, resonant, like the rush of the Nile against the felucca's hull.

'For what?'

He leaned back, the cane chair protesting.

'I should have thanked you properly. For coming to my aid.'

'I'm certain you would have managed.'

He shook his head.

'Anyone can die, Cleo. I've seen skilled men make the most foolish mistakes. You should take credit where it is due.'

'I don't want to.'

'I know. And that is a bad sign. You can't go around believing I'm infallible. Until we get you safely on your way to England you need to remain alert.'

'I *was* alert. That is why you are sitting across from me and not dead or being stitched by a Cairene surgeon, which is not a fate I would wish on my worst enemy.'

He grinned and tapped the table with his palm.

'That's better. Moping does not suit you.'

'I was not moping!'

'Blue as a witch's…never mind. I keep forgetting you are a lady.'

'And I keep forgetting you're a grown man.'

'Excellent. Now throw something at me.'

'*Ladies* do not throw things,' she snapped.

'They damned well do. They can't easily throw a punch at me like a man might when riled. Though, like you right now, they might wish to. And my ragged face discourages slapping, so I've had the odd plate or tankard tossed at me. Go ahead if it will make you feel better.'

'Breaking something merely because one is angered or frustrated is childish and serves no purpose.'

'Says someone who's never done it. And you're frightened, not frustrated.'

'How precisely would breaking something alleviate fear?'

'I didn't say it would.'

'Then why are you telling me to break something?' Her voice was rising, shedding all pretence at calm.

'To distract you. It's working, too.'

'You. Are. *Infuriating!*' She ground her teeth, thumping her fists on the table. Part of her knew his object was not merely to distract her, but to break the strange tension that was binding them and that made her even angrier. She didn't want him to be flippant now, not when she was still shaking inwardly. She wanted something completely different and he knew that and that was precisely why he was trying to make her angry. Well, he'd succeeded.

If her plate had not still been half full of Birdie's stew, she might have succumbed and done just what he suggested. Smashed, shattered, razed, crushed it into tiny bits and stomped on them until they were dust. Until fear and need and confusion were consumed in the fireball of her fury. Until she was free of everything, including the most impossible man she'd ever met.

Rafe leaned back and watched the fire snap and crackle in her. It was there in the rush of colour up her face, in the narrowed gold fire eyes that were stripping layers from his skin, in the white-knuckled fists.

It was magnificent.

It was also singeing him inside and out. He mastered his breathing, but he couldn't stop his heart from going into a faster gallop than it had when that knife had slashed towards him.

That had been a very different kind of heartbeat. Fear was well and good, but terror was something he could not afford and that was precisely what had slashed through him as he'd watched her launch herself at the man.

That had been new. Icy. A shriek of denial.

Now she was sending his pulse out of control once more, except this time he wasn't cold—he was boiling inside. She looked like a queen about to cast him into the pits of hell and the madness was that he was as hot and hard as if she'd spent the past week seducing him.

Which, to be fair, she had.

If only he could do something about it.

He shifted on the uncomfortable chair, wishing his morals were significantly more flexible. He could only imagine all that fury and heat and frustration and determination in bed...

If only...

'Do I amuse you, Mr Grey?'

'Do you...?' He floundered.

'If you are going to sit there grinning at me, I will go elsewhere.'

She shoved to her feet, her chair squawking and teetering. He managed to reach the door before her.

'Cleo, wait, I am trying...'

'You *are* trying. I've never met a more *trying* man. If you try me any further, I might...' She appeared to physically struggle with her unfinished sentence and then tossed up her hands in despair. 'Kindly move aside, Mr Grey.'

Her glare alone would have been enough to incinerate a stack of papyrus scrolls. He leaned his full weight back against the door, not because he was afraid she would slip past him, but because he very much wanted her to come close enough to try.

'You are right. I meant well, but...'

'People always mean well, *but*—'

'If you would only listen to me.'

'I have done little else but listen to you this past week. I know full well what you wish to do. You wish nothing more than to deposit me on the first ship to England and have done with me...'

'I do not—'

'Yes, you do and I do not blame you in the least—I am just as tired of my problems as you are. However, that does not mean I will allow you to dictate my actions. Now, kindly step aside.' She reached past him for the doorknob and the opening door knocked him from behind.

It wasn't a serious blow, but the devil in him gave a yelp and he stumbled forward. Her hands shot out, steadying him.

'I'm so sorry, Rafe! I did not mean to hurt you!'

'When I advised you to throw something, I did not think you would start with doors. As usual you are highly precocious, Cleo.'

Her concern crumbled as swiftly as her anger and she burst into laughter and gave him a little shove. He didn't step back and she stayed there for a moment, her hands on his chest. Then she rose on tiptoe and touched her lips to his cheek.

Absurdly, that shock was on par with his earlier terror. His skin turned into a carapace of ice and his insides to a chaos of thumping heat. He didn't even realise he'd closed his arms around her waist, pinioning her to him, until she leaned back against their confining band.

She'd been flushed with anger before and the laughter was still there in her eyes, but also the softening, speculative heat she'd shown before.

She pressed upwards again, bestowing the same light kiss, but this time she stayed there, her lips parted against his skin, moving gently. He let his eyes close, his hand moving against her back, mirroring the motion of her lips.

God, it felt so good. Even her touch against his scars felt...

It was a sign of how addled he'd become that he only now realised it was his scarred cheek. He let her go faster than she'd charged at al-Mizan, but she'd already anchored her hands in his shirt and her mouth came to rest against the corner of his. She seemed to be gathering herself, either waiting for a signal or preparing to withdraw.

All he had to do was nothing. Ignore the warmth of her breath against his skin, the pressure of her body leaning against his, the heat trapped between them like a captured sun. The thudding, demanding, hungry, ravenous heat he was tired of shoving down.

He felt the tensing of her muscles as she prepared to push away and with a smothered moan he wrapped his arms back around her.

Not yet.

Just a little more.

Just an inch. Not even an inch. That was all it would take to bring her lips to his. He wanted so, so badly to kiss her. Properly, thoroughly. All of her, every warm living inch of her.

Step aside?

Like hell.

He turned his head, his lips touching hers. Hers parted just a little, fitting against his. She breathed in, sucking the soul from his body and setting the rest on fire. He heard the sound deep inside him and the answering buck of her body against him and he felt his reins slip from his hands.

Just a taste.

He let his lips move against hers, just gathering the feel of that warm, pillowy bow. He kissed it very gently, catching the corner of her mouth with the tip of his tongue, just where it hovered between smile and laughter. She gave a little moan and then her tongue touched his, a galvanic shock driving their bodies together, hard. His hand was suddenly in her hair and he felt it shake a little as her short feathery hair slipped like shattered silk between his fingers. God, he wanted to do that again and again.

He wanted…everything.

She had her hands in his hair now, too. Was on her tiptoes as she met his kiss, her breasts flattened against his chest. From a slight, brief embrace they were fast approaching combustion and he waited for the sword's thrust of conscience, he even went in search of it, hoping it might come to his rescue, but there was nothing inside him now but fire and the deafening thump of drums...

Not drums, someone was clumping up the stairs...

She must have realised it before him because she disentangled herself with the rapidity of a cat escaping a dipping.

'Birdie is back.'

'I don't care.' He moved towards her.

'We are in the dining room. He is sure to come here...'

Before he could even admit she was right the door opened. She was halfway across the room by then and Rafe scraped his hands through his hair, but clearly their attempts were unconvincing because Birdie stopped whatever he was about to say, looking from one to the other. Then at the plates on the table.

'Hungry, were you?'

Starving.

He didn't say it. He couldn't think of anything sensible to say and in the end it was Cleo who spoke, moving past them to the door.

'We were, thank you, Birdie. It was delicious. The stew, that is,' she added just before closing the door behind her.

Birdie placed the sack he was carrying on the table. When he spoke he pitched his voice low, but it did nothing to hide his anger.

'Sooner she's on her way to England the better, sir. Not like you to play fast and loose.'

'I am not doing anything of the kind.'

'Made her an offer, then?'

'What? No, of course I haven't.'

'Not well-born enough for the likes of you?'

'Birth has nothing to do with it. At least not hers. I don't even exist. Rafe Grey is nothing more than the figment of a boy's imagination.'

'Aye, but the Duke of Greybourne is real enough and that's what you are now, like it or not.'

'You know damn well I don't and that is precisely the point. With any luck Edge will have another son. I'm not going back to that place...that life. *This* life is all I know and all I'm good for, and it sure as hell is no place for a wife even if I wanted one, which I don't, so keep your opinions to yourself.'

'I will if you only keep your hands to yourself.'

'She kissed me first.'

'Jumped on you, did she?'

'No,' Rafe admitted. 'Hit me on the head with a door first.'

'Good for her. I might try that myself. Except you might kiss me, too.'

Rafe grinned in relief that Birdie's ire was fading.

'We had an incident with al-Mizan. At her lodgings. I was trying to distract her and I admit it got out of hand.' Far, far out of hand. 'I won't do it again.'

There wasn't as much conviction in his voice as he hoped, but Birdie's attention had been diverted by his previous comment, his ragtag brows climbing into his hair.

'You found the scoundrel?'

'He found us and almost introduced me to his dagger. That little hellion stopped him. The sooner we take her to Alexandria the better. With luck Chris and the *Hesperus* will still be in port.'

'She might take issue going aboard a privateer's ship.'

'Chris isn't a privateer. There's no war on that I know of at the moment.'

'Smuggler, then.'

'No one has ever accused him of smuggling.'

'Not yet.'

'If I see he has dubious goods aboard, we can find her

other means of travel, but you know she'll be safer on the *Hesperus* than travelling alone on a merchant ship.'

'That's the truth.' Birdie sighed. 'So, that's the plan? We hand her to Chris and wash our hands of the whole affair?'

Rafe poured the wine, but did not pick up his cup.

'No,' he said at last. 'Now I know Edge is safely in Egypt, it's time we returned to England ourselves. As you said—I can't run for ever. I need to take stock of Greybourne so I can get on with my life. That way we can see Cleo safely to England as well. With any luck her brother will already be there and that will be the end of that.'

He waited for Birdie to raise objections, but all he said was, 'Have you told her?'

'No. I don't think I should.'

Birdie picked up his glass.

'It sits ill with me to lie to her, Colonel.'

'With me, too, but we're between a rock and a hard place. Unless we prove that nuisance brother of hers is safely on his way to England, her conscience won't let her sail. But she's not safe here, Birdie. It's not al-Mizan that worries me any more, it's how he spoke about this Boucheron fellow. I don't want her in his domain any longer than absolutely necessary.'

'Very well. I'll pack our belongings. You go with Naguib to speak to the Captain of the *dahabiya*. Best not leave you here alone, just in case she throws herself at you again,' he added with a snap and headed into the kitchen.

Chapter Twelve

Alexandria

Cleo had not been to Alexandria since her arrival in Egypt. It had changed since then, but it was still rather a ruin of a town. Like many port cities she'd seen, there was a sense of miasmatic menace. Rootless people came and went and one knew little of them—perfect for the venal, the criminal, and the lost.

A small closed carriage drew them through the town and past the shattered structure of an old Roman tower. Behind it the sail-studded turquoise sea stretched away, and in front stood an obelisk, stark and tall and covered base to pyramid-pointed tip with hieroglyphs.

'*There* is my namesake,' she murmured and Rafe turned to her from his inspection of the view. With a word he motioned to the driver to stop.

'That must be some sixty feet tall,' Birdie mused and she nodded.

'It is called Cleopatra's Needle. I've seen illustrations in *Description de l'Egypte*, but I've never seen it myself. I wanted to come here when we arrived in Egypt, but my father said we hadn't time. It's…amazing.'

Rafe swung open the low door and held out his hand.

'Come along, Queenie. There is no one here but the camels and donkeys to see us and we can spare a few moments to pay homage to your birthright.'

Cleo had reason later to be doubly grateful for their short excursion to see the obelisk and climb the tower to look over the expanse of the Mediterranean. From the moment they reached their rooms in a lovely Mameluke palace overlooking the bay, her curfew began. She'd given Rafe her word she would remain indoors for the rest of the day as he and Birdie made enquiries, but the inaction sat ill with her.

By afternoon she was seriously contemplating going in search of her errant knights, but just then she heard voices from the courtyard. She hurried into the sitting room, but it was only Birdie, instructing a servant to place a large wicker basket on the table. He glanced up with a smile, but immediately shook his head.

'No news yet, miss.'

'Oh.'

'But we've set matters in motion. Tomorrow we'll go see Captain Carrington. This is not a large city and the Colonel's friend is still docked here, which is good news as he knows many people. If your brother is here, or if he has recently sailed, we are likely to know very soon.'

'Dash might not have travelled under his own name.'

'I hope he hasn't, but there are still ways to trace him. There cannot have been many ships sailing for England this past week so the options are limited.'

'Unless he sailed to another port...' Her heart constricted. That would make the possibilities multiply. And the risks.

'It is possible. Tomorrow we should know more. I've bought you some new clothes.'

She looked absently at the shirt he was unfolding, but her attention was elsewhere. 'Did Rafe not return with you?'

Birdie glanced up.

'Don't worry, miss. He stopped at the *hammam* and paid the fellow to have the place to himself. I'm off to prepare supper. Go rest. It will be a long day tomorrow.'

'I've been resting all day,' Cleo said in frustration.

'I know it isn't easy, miss, but you agreed it would not do for Miss Osbourne to be seen in public when we want it known she already left for England.' Birdie sighed and extracted something from his pile and placed it on the table. 'Here. This is from the Colonel. To keep you occupied.'

It was a rather beaten volume in ochre-coloured leather with most of the gilt worn off, but still enough to read the print on the spine.

Shakespeare. Vol. IX. Taming of the Shrew.

She snorted.

'Very amusing—and it is my least favourite comedy of the lot, Mr Grey,' she muttered and went to her room. She stared at the wall for a few long moments, cradling her farewell present to her chest.

Tomorrow was likely her last day with them. Whatever they discovered or not about Dash she knew she had to release Rafe to seek his own brother, by force if need be. So, if this was her last day of unfettered freedom, she should not be spending it moping in her room. She wanted an altogether different farewell present.

She wrapped her turban round her head and slipped quietly downstairs.

She'd seen the unobtrusive entranceway to the bath house on their arrival. It stood just a few steps from their lodgings and she gave herself no time to think before she plunged inside. Her heart, already rushing downhill at a swift pace, slammed into her ribs when a man in a long white robe stepped out of the overseer's room.

'The *hammam* is closed. Come tomorrow,' he said, shoo-ing her with his hands.

'I am the *hawagi*'s servant,' Cleo said in Arabic. 'I have an important message.'

The guard shrugged and went back to his little room.

Cleo proceeded, her heart thumping in her ears as she pushed aside the heavy curtain covering the entrance to the *maghta* and a burst of steam enveloped her.

'*Ijo de cabron*... Cleo!'

She stood frozen for a moment. He'd thrown a long cot-ton towel over his shoulder, like a Roman toga, but it did little to cover his steam-slicked body. She knew men were required to cover their hips with a *futa* in *hammams*, but Rafe was clearly taking advantage of his privacy.

'What are you doing here?' he demanded. 'Has some-thing happened? Where is Birdie?'

She shook her head, gathering back her scattered thoughts.

'Nothing happened. Birdie thinks I'm resting.'

'Then what in the name of all the rings of hell are you doing here?'

'I wanted to see a male *hammam*.' She looked around, trying to sound casual and wondering why this had seemed a good idea. 'It's not very different from the women's. I thought it would be larger.'

He didn't answer and she went to look at the nearest por-tal. A small pool with stone steps stood as flat as a sheet of ice and several buckets of water stood beside a spout. Above her a murky light entered through the ornate glass pieces that studded a low dome.

It was almost dark outside and she was alone with a mostly naked man in an Egyptian bath house.

'You shouldn't be here, Cleo.' His voice was muffled by the steam.

Her heartbeats reverberated through her like the clang-ing of a deep bell but she unwound her turban and breathed in the hot, scented air. Once again her life was about to change, through forces beyond her control. But how she acted, what she did, was hers. Soon this man would be gone from her life. It felt absurd and wrong, but she knew it to be true. Therefore, she had to choose how to act now.

'I think I will miss being a man when I return to England,' she said.

He didn't answer, so she took off her robe, folded it and placed it on a wooden shelf by the room with the dipping pool. She gathered the skirts of her *gallabiyah* and there was a curse behind her as he grasped her arm.

'Enough, Cleo. Go back to the rooms.'

This close she could see every sinew and muscle. His skin shone, water tricking slowly over the landscape of his body. He *was* beautiful. Not just the force of his body, but remnants of his mistakes. He might be built like a Roman statue, but it was the damage that made him real. She knew she would probably never again see anything so beautiful.

'Cleo, *stop.*'

'I'm only looking,' she murmured and he groaned and dropped her arm, turning away.

'You're mad, you know.'

'I don't think it is mad to enjoy looking at you, is it? I'm certain enough women have done so before me. Why am I different?'

He gave a slight laugh and went to sit on a bench, his back to her.

'I told you I won't take advantage of you.'

'We are in Alexandria. Tomorrow we either find Dash here and you consign me to his care, or I will secure passage to England. Either way you are relieved of your protector's duties.'

She took off her *gallabiyah* and closed her eyes, breathing in the spice-scented air. Sage and mint. She would miss those scents. She would miss Egypt.

She would miss this man most of all.

Her breath shortened and she swallowed. There was nothing for it. She knew the world kept moving beneath them.

'I'm going to wash myself. You may leave if you wish. Or stay.' She went into the next room and poured the warm water over her. She'd washed in the small tub the servant had brought to her room, but this was different. With the steam all around her and the warm water streaming over her she closed her eyes to explore the image of Rafe's body, slick with steam, the pressure of his hands on her body, shaping her...

Rafe stood helplessly in the doorway. His code required he do as she suggested and leave, but he couldn't.

She stood with her back to him, her body shimmering like pale marble in the dimming light from the dome. She might as well have been a statue come to life, the line of her back and the rounded rise of her behind as she rubbed the soapy palm fronds over her arms.

He'd been right—she had a lovely body, generous and beautifully curved. Perhaps she was right, he was making too much of this. She was no virgin, no English miss. She was Cleo, a wholly strange and independent entity. If she wanted this, why not allow this temporary breach?

He picked up another ball of stripped palm fronds, lathered it with soap and moved towards her. He knew she felt his approach because her chin rose a little, but she did not turn.

'I'll wash your back,' he said.

She gave a little nod and straightened. He touched the slope of her shoulder and closed his eyes for a moment. He was as hard as the rock floor. All he had to do was one step closer and... He breathed in and out, clasped her shoulder gently with one hand and brushed the fronds down the curve of her back.

He went slowly, watching the lather slide down as he

worked, over her buttocks and down her legs. He let his fingers and knuckles graze her warm, slippery skin. It was addictive, this touch. He wanted to spread her out on the cold floor and do the same to every inch of her—look, touch, taste...

He swallowed and kept to his agenda, ignoring the howling need that pulsed in every cell and gathered into a ravenous demand in his loins. He didn't want this to end, not even in satisfaction. He knew what would follow then— regret and reckoning. No, he wanted to stay like this, his hands on her skin, standing so close to her he could see the wet spikes of her short hair clinging to her nape, a pulse just at the side of her neck, the curved line of her cheek between that determined jaw and the uncompromising cheekbones.

He didn't want to ruin this moment, not even with pleasure.

She turned her head, her eyes gleaming. She looked the way she had in the temple—shadowed, whisky-coloured eyes that were absolutely honest in their need.

She leaned her hand against his chest and he realised he'd let his own towel drop. He didn't have time to think before she moved, her arms around his back, pressing her full length against him. His body blazed like a molten sun against her cool skin, his erection pressing hard against her, their skin slick.

'Our lives could end in a flash and I don't want to regret not taking this. When we leave this room, we leave this behind if you wish.'

He shook his head at the absurdity of that, but it was such a seductive fiction. And at least one thing she'd said was true. Their lives could end in a flash. This was honest, this burning wish—it was just now. It, too, would pass, but right now...

He let his hands finally settle honestly on her skin, without the lie of washing her. He let them slip from her shoulders down to her thighs, fitting her to him as he went so he could feel the full pressure of her breasts, the tension of her abdomen on his erection, her legs shifting gently on his, so much softer and smoother. He slipped his knee between her legs and she hummed, letting her leg rub the length of his.

'Yes,' she murmured, rising to touch her mouth to his neck. He arched it to give her better access, urging her on with words while his hands talked to her as well. For a long while he explored her, watching every expression that flitted across her face as his hands travelled over her, tracing her lines gently as he felt her body relax into his touch. Her mouth moved along his neck, his chest, not quite kisses, just breathy answers that heated and cooled his damp skin.

He kissed her, teasingly light at first, drawing her to him until she rose into the embrace, her body moving with his as if to music, and she was humming gently, almost purring. His whole body reverberated with that sound, like the lasting shimmer of a bell.

Her eyes were half closed, gleaming amber and gold as she explored him as well, her hands shaping themselves over him, stopping to rest gently against his damaged skin in a way that made him clench hard around something he didn't want to open.

He slid a hand down the curve of her back, cupping her behind as he leaned back, tracing his fingers gently over the curve of her breasts. They were beautiful, round and warm in his hand, her nipples rose-coloured like her lips, but darkening as they hardened at his touch. He brushed his lips over them and she gave a little mewl, deep in her throat, her fingers threading through his hair and tightening painfully.

'Yes, I want that...' she whispered in her gravel and honey voice and he shuddered, resisting the beating rush of need that was demanding he act *now*. End it now.

He didn't want it to end. He wanted this to go on for ever. He kissed the tightening crown of her breast, flicking it with his tongue and revelling in the answering clenching of her body against his, in her soft encouraging murmurings. Her hands mirrored his, caressing his back, slipping lower to sweep tentatively over his behind in a way that nearly felled him, gaining in confidence and only faltering when he shifted to touch the soft skin on the inside of her thigh.

She tensed, reminding him that his desert queen might be devastatingly passionate and not an innocent in society's terms, but one lover years ago did not mean she was comfortable with the intimacies he took for granted. He slowed, taking his time until that hum returned. Then he brushed his hand very gently down her abdomen and over her wet curls.

'May I touch you here?'

She breathed in sharply, pressing her face into the curve of his shoulder, her arms tightening about his nape.

'Yes.' Her voice wobbled but her legs parted further as he trailed his fingers up and down her thighs. 'I like that, just like that...'

He pressed his eyes shut, hard. Every word she spoke was like a hand stroking him. Her skin was already slick with steam and it was so beautifully simple to slip his fingers over the silky skin of her parting.

He anchored his hand in her short hair, kissing her deeply, hungrily, as he touched her. She kissed him back with the same hunger, her breath catching in little helpless gasps, her hips moving now against his hand, searching, reaching... She'd dropped all her defences and he saw everything, every confusion and pleasure and that soft secretive smile that knocked his heart on its side. He pressed her against the tiled wall and her head fell back, baring her breasts to his mouth as she clung to him until she cried out her release in a series of long shudders.

They stayed like that for a long moment, surrounded in milky swathes of steam, his arm hard around her back, his mouth pressed to the thudding pulse in her temple, his palm warm against her. Then she gave a long sigh, her muscles relaxing.

'I'm so glad I came here.'

He gave a choked laugh against her hair, but he was in too much pleasurable agony to make the obvious glib remark. He drew away a little, but her arms tightened on him, her hips moving, rubbing herself against his erection.

'Cleo, perhaps we shouldn't…'

'Yes, we should. I want you to be glad I came here, too,' she murmured against his skin, her hands moving down his back with purpose. His heart, already beating far too fast, stumbled.

'It felt so, so good,' she continued. 'I don't remember it at all like that. William didn't…'

Rafe nipped gently on the lobe of her ear and she shuddered and mercifully fell silent.

'A piece of advice, Cleo. When making love to one man, never discuss another.'

He felt her smile against his skin. He took her hand, his fingers sliding between hers, and guided it to his erection. She gave a little sigh and wrapped her hand around it and he couldn't hold back a groan of sheer pleasure.

'It's so soft,' she murmured, sweeping her palm over its length.

'Soft?' he demanded in a choked voice.

'The skin.' She half laughed, her gaze on her hand as she explored. 'Underneath it's hard as stone, but here…soft…' Her voice was almost as much a torture as her hand. 'Like this? Do you like it?'

'I love it,' he answered, not caring about anything but that she not stop. He wanted to stay right there, in this pitch of agonised pleasure, with her body and mouth torturing him and her hand wringing his soul into ecstatic oblivion.

He guided her until she caught the rhythm, kissing her, stroking her head and back as she kissed his neck, his chest.

When her mouth stroked past his nipple he felt an explosion of joy and she paused.

'You like this as much as I did,' she murmured against him and he nodded helplessly, his mind pleading—*don't stop.*

She held him as he came and they stood afterwards in a hard embrace, the steam still rising in fluffy billows, but weakening. He could feel the cooler air snake about his legs. Everywhere she was not pressed against him felt bare, exposed. He detached himself carefully and went to fetch a bucket of the cooling water. He rinsed her off gently and dried her with a cotton towel and she stood there and let him.

They dressed in silence and left, passing the guard who was nodding at his post. Rafe placed another coin on his tray and followed Cleo out into the darkening evening.

At the bottom of the stairs to their rooms Cleo turned and smiled.

'Thank you, Rafe. I won't forget that.'

A burst of pain radiated through him and he didn't even know why.

'I don't think I will either.'

She hurried up the stairs and slipped into her room. He could hear Birdie moving around the kitchen-cum-dining room and he went to his own room and lay down to stare at the ceiling, torn between ebbing bliss and rising guilt. His conscience had already been flaying him about what was in store for her the next day; he hadn't thought he could feel any more culpable.

Apparently he could.

Chapter Thirteen

They walked along the stone jetty towards the rowboat rising and falling on the waves. Beyond it was the deep blue of the Mediterranean, blooming with sails. She slowed, her cracked heart lightening at the sight despite her sorrow. She remembered the salted breeze and the sound of the waves so well from those years in Acre—it was like listening to a heartbeat under a blanket.

Rafe had told her his friend might be able to shed light on Dash's whereabouts, but she knew the chances were slim. In a matter of days, she would probably have to leave for London and this wondrous sea would lie between her and her past, between her and her new friends.

She didn't want to leave. She was not ready.

Rafe stopped by the rowboat, holding out his hand peremptorily.

'Come.'

His voice was clipped, his eyes cold and distant, and her old instincts came to the fore. 'Why could this Captain not meet us on shore?'

'Because he's the Captain and he has other matters to attend to, Prudent Pat.'

'Stop calling me that,' she snapped. 'You called me Cleo easily enough in the *hammam*.' For a second before he withdrew his gaze she knew he was back there as well, steam wrapping around them, his body hard and hot against hers, his mouth…

She'd wanted a memory and now she had it…branded on to every inch of her.

A trickle of sweat ran down her neck and between her breasts and she was grateful for the sea breeze that cooled her as she stepped into the rowboat. It rocked and tipped as Rafe entered and she grabbed at the side.

'Careful. You'll tip it.'

'Now that is unkind. I've all but starved myself of decent food seeing you through the devil's desert and now you're complaining I'm fat?'

'I did not say that. You are merely big…' Her cheeks flamed in sudden embarrassment.

'You do look like you could use a cooling dip, Pat.' His hand rose and settled back on his thigh, but her cheek tingled as if he'd brushed his fingers across it.

'In these clothes I'd likely sink to the bottom like a rock.'

'I'd save you. Again.'

'I seem to remember saving you the last time we had a brush with danger,' she replied. Possibly it was the wrong thing to say for he fell silent, his almost-smile flattening out. She felt he was gathering himself for something and for a moment wondered what history he and this mysterious Captain had together.

They did not speak again as they cut through the waves to draw alongside a large two-masted brigantine. The sailor called up their arrival in French and there was a clacking and a series of thuds as the Jacob's ladder was unrolled for them. Rafe stood, his feet apart for balance, and helped her to her feet. But again his gaze seemed to slip away from her.

Once on board he moved swiftly and she had no more than a brief impression of a wide and impressively uncluttered deck before they entered the quarterdeck and proceeded down a corridor. He opened a cabin door and as she stepped inside she couldn't hold back a gasp of surprised pleasure.

She'd been on many ships in her short life, but she'd never seen such quarters. The bed was long enough to accommodate someone Rafe's size, there was a gilded sofa with embroidered silk cushions, a large rolltop writing desk, and two substantial-looking chairs framing the door like sentinels. The floors were covered in multicoloured rugs and the walls in cupboards and shelves stacked with books, crockery and rolled charts.

'What a beautiful room. It looks as though a sultan should be reclining on that bed eating sweetmeats,' she whispered. 'I've never seen anything like it.'

'That's because there is nothing like it. Chris is unique.'

'That sounds ominous. Are you certain he might know something of Dash's whereabouts?'

'He knows a great many things, the scoundrel,' Rafe replied and went to open one of the cupboards, taking out a bottle and two glasses. He unstoppered the bottle and sniffed at it, then poured himself a measure and took a deep swallow from his cup. His eyes closed and he expelled his breath on a groan that made her legs tense. 'Including where to find the finest spirits in the Mediterranean, damn his black soul. Try this.'

She took the glass cautiously and sipped. Her mind filled with sunset colours—deep burnt orange to purple-black cherries.

'It's wonderful,' she said hoarsely as it stopped exploding in her mouth and the fiery skies she'd swallowed settled into a soothing afternoon haze. 'What is it?'

'I don't know, but I agree, it's wonderful.' His voice was muted and she risked a glance at him, but he turned away again, moving towards a painting on the wall.

'Perhaps we shouldn't have drunk from it?' she said, looking into the innocuous-looking liquid. The ship was swaying gently, adding to the soft sensation left by the spirits. She'd heard of drugging potions used in harems. 'Are you certain it is wine?'

'Of course it is wine. Chris knows the best vineyards in Europe. He sells most of it to the highest bidder, but if anything makes it to his private chambers, it is tried and tested and true. Drink up.'

'If I drink up, I will likely fall down and I must still go search for Dash once we speak to your Captain.'

He took a deep breath and set his cup down. She tensed, setting her cup down as well.

'Rafe. I *know* there is something you are not telling me. Please...have you word of Dash?'

He squared his shoulders.

'Nothing yet. After I speak to Chris, I will continue with our enquiries. You will remain here.'

'I most certainly will not. I agreed to wait while you made enquiries yesterday and I came with you to see this Captain of yours, but our agreement ends there.'

'Boucheron is in Alexandria. I won't risk him seeing you.'

'Boucheron... You knew this yesterday.'

'Yes. You will be safe here on the *Hesperus*.'

'On a ship full of felons?'

'They aren't felons; they are...enterprising sailors. The point is they are loyal to their Captain and their Captain is loyal to me.'

'You cannot place me here like a trunk and expect me to sit twiddling my thumbs. I am not your property, Mr Grey.'

'You hired my services, Miss Osbourne. Now you are stuck with them. I've kept you safe so far and I have a distaste for watching my good work go to waste. So begin twiddling your thumbs. I will return soon. And don't drink all the wine, I'll want a glass when I return.'

'What? No!' She leapt for the door, but it closed with a

thick thump before her hand even touched the knob. Then there was a click as the key turned.

He'd locked her in.

It was so obvious and yet her mind struggled to accept it. In all their long journey together he'd never yet done something like this.

She rattled the knob and gave the door a kick, cursing Rafe in every language she could summon.

How *dare* he. Like hell she would stay there. She turned and spotted another door and strode towards it, but it merely led to the Captain's quarter gallery. It comprised a dressing room, then a room fitted with a large copper bath and finally a small latrine. They were all as pristine as the Captain's quarters, as if they had only now been delivered from the shipyard. But since they offered no other exit other than the small windows that opened directly over the rolling waves, she was too furious to be impressed.

The waves were lazy and rhythmic, but large. She could hear their distant boom against the rocks. It would be possible to squeeze through the open quarter-gallery windows and try to swim ashore, but the ship was anchored well out of the bay—a long and dangerous swim with the current against her...or she might be taken up by one of the fishing boats and God only knew what they would do with her...

And when Rafe discovered her gone? He cared about the charges he took on. It wasn't merely pride—protecting his charges was a measure of his worth, of who he was. He would search for her just as she had searched for Dash, possibly putting himself even further in harm's way. Now she knew Boucheron was in Alexandria her foreboding escalated. Now she had not only Dash, but Rafe to fear for.

She returned to the cabin and sat down with a thump on the sybaritic bed and picked up a crimson cushion, hugging it to her. It was not natural—sitting here while they were out there.

If something happened to Rafe because of her...

At times like this she envied devout people. They would have their gods to pray to, to place their faith in, to blame if aught went wrong. All she could do was hug the tasselled cushion and wait.

She'd never expected to fall asleep. One moment she was seated, hugging her cushion, and the next she was lurching out of darkness into darkness.

For a moment she thought she'd been tied into a sack, but it was only a blanket. She twisted off the bed, misjudged its height and fell with a grunt on to her knees.

Hands brushed against her, closing on her arms and pulling her to her feet. She should have been scared, but she knew immediately who it was.

'Are you all right?' he whispered, his hands skimming down her arms. Rising to touch her face.

'I fell asleep,' she stated unnecessarily. 'What happened? What...?' She stopped speaking, realising something was very, very wrong.

'We're moving! Rafe, the ship is sailing. Oh, hurry, we must stop it!'

She surged past him, groping for the door; instead she found herself blocked by a large body once more.

'Rafe! Tell the Captain...'

'We sailed two hours ago.'

'What?' Her voice faded. She could hardly see his face, but she could feel him and not merely through her hands, which were fisted in his shirt. He was stone again. Grey.

'It's Dash.' She forced the words out. 'You've discovered he's dead.'

His hands grabbed her arms, tightly this time.

'No. No, I haven't. I don't know if he's dead or alive. We could not discover if anyone of his description sailed for England in the past couple of weeks. I bribed the harbourmaster to keep an eye out for him and to tell him his sister has sailed to England and that if he has an ounce of sense he'll do the same if he has not already.'

She let go of his shirt. Her hands were burning, her face, her chest. There was a boiling blaze at the centre of her forehead. It wasn't the heat of lust that had carried her into a dreamful sleep. It was rage.

Fury.

'You *bastard.*' It was like the hiss of a kettle. She could barely part her teeth to let the venom through.

He laughed.

'Chance would be a fine thing.'

'You had no *right*. Oh, God, if I were bigger I would… I would… How *dare* you! You tricked me! You might very well have left my brother to die!' She groped around in the dark, searching for something, anything, to wield. She bumped into a chair, wrapped her hands around its back and raised it, but it was absurdly heavy. She threw it anyway and it dropped, narrowly missing her foot.

She bumped into the shelves and glass clinked on glass. The bottles! She stroked upwards, over the wooden shelf guard to the smooth glass. She grabbed a bottle by the neck and hoisted it.

She knew it was pointless and pathetic, but she couldn't stop. She was choking with something, suffocating with it, and he just stood there like a lump in the dark while they moved further and further from the *only* person who mattered, leaving him to whatever fate awaited him. Alone.

Because she'd trusted this man. Hadn't she learned anything from her feckless father? From William? She'd walked into this trap without a second thought, like the blindest of the blind, smitten, fools. She'd learned *nothing.*

She'd wanted so desperately to trust him not only with her fate, but with Dash's, too. She *had* trusted him. Despite everything, she'd felt lighter, happier these past days than any time she could remember. She should have known it was too good to be true.

She hated him, but she hated herself far more.

Her eyes were better accustomed to the dark now. He was still an outline against the door; watching her. He'd done nothing to stop her frantic search for weapons. His face was blank, but his shoulders were slumped. She knew he wouldn't move if she threw the bottle, which was stupid. She didn't want him to accept her anger. She wanted him to toss it right back at her and tell her the truth. That he was only doing what mercenaries do—she was to blame for trusting him. That she'd known all along what he was, but she'd closed her eyes and dreamed. And while she'd been dreaming they'd cast off their moorings and sailed and left Dash to his fate.

No hurled bottle or chair would turn this ship back. She had nothing to threaten him with or bribe him with. It was done.

She replaced the bottle and pressed her hand to the lump of blazing coal embedded in her forehead.

'No.'

'Cleo...' His voice was husky and he pushed away from the door, but she raised her other hand, palm out.

'Go away. You win. Now go away.'

He shook his head and righted the chair.

'I'm staying.'

'I don't want you here.'

'I'm staying and you're listening.'

'No.'

'Yes. It was the right course of action. The only course of action. For you *and* for your brother if only either of you are intelligent enough to understand that.'

'Don't you dare belittle him.'

'Or what? I'm sick and tired of you endangering yourself as if he's a five-year-old lost in the forest. He's a grown man and if he has an ounce of the integrity you claim every time you sing his praises he'll be thanking me for getting you out of Egypt.'

'*If* he isn't killed by al-Mizan. If he hasn't already been killed by him.'

'He hasn't.'

'You can't know that—'

'I can. Boucheron is no fool. I told him—'

'You *told* him…you spoke with him?'

'Shh. You've already woken half the ship. Do you want to wake the other half? Yes, he owns a palace in Alexandria and was in town awaiting a ship to France, or so he said. Al-Mizan must have sent him word of our encounter because he wasn't in the least surprised when I arrived. Boucheron might be a dangerous man, but he's no fool. I made clear that whatever idiocies your father engaged in, your brother had no part in it. As long as your brother leaves Egypt swiftly, Boucheron will let him be.'

She swallowed her bile and lowered her voice.

'That sounds like quite an amicable discussion you had.'

The chair squeaked as he leaned forward and the gleam of the night sky turned his eyes luminescent, like foam on the sea.

'I negotiated with an enemy, that is what I do. Hopefully Boucheron will now be wary of interfering with your brother knowing he is not unprotected. What the devil do you think would have happened if you stayed in Egypt? Even if your brother discovered you were still there, he could not contact you for fear or putting both of you at risk.'

'Why did you not tell me any of this?'

'Because I knew you wouldn't wait here simply because I asked. So I told Chris to sail as soon as I came back aboard. There is a trunk with some of your clothes over there by the wall, by the way. We rescued them from your lodgings.'

She gave the trunk no more than a cursory glance. She had more important issues at hand.

'Did you drug me?' she demanded, thinking of that wine

and her dreams. Perhaps that explained why she'd so low-ered her guard to fall asleep while effectively a prisoner.

'What? No, of course not! You can lay quite a bit on my doorstep, but don't blame me for falling asleep.'

'It was convenient, though.'

'It damned well was. Believe me, I wasn't looking for-ward to…this.'

This.

She reached for her anger and found there was noth-ing there. Not anger, not fear, not anguish, not…caring. Nothing.

He was probably right about everything. Even that she was a risk to Dash as long as she remained in Egypt.

It didn't matter anyway. They had sailed. *That ship had sailed.* What a silly little phrase. Nothing you can do, that ship has sailed. And here they were. On their way to Eng-land. And nothingness.

'I hate that you went about this without me. Without telling me anything.'

'I know,' he answered.

'You told me I could trust you.' She couldn't stop the words or her voice from shaking.

'Trust me to do my best to keep you safe. Not actually trust *me*. Those are two different things.'

'Apparently.'

He didn't answer. He was just another bulk in the gloom. Like the cupboard and table. She wanted her anger back. Something to make her tilt her head back and howl at the skies; she wanted to find Dash—safe, alive. She wanted to turn the clock back six months and make everything go away, including Mr Rafe Grey. Now she was on her way to England, to a world she no longer knew and a future she couldn't imagine.

She lay down on the bed, turned her back on him and stared at the whorls on the wooden wall.

A night breeze was slipping in through the galley windows along with the sound of the waves lapping against the hull. A fast, sleek ship suspended between two worlds and she belonged in neither. Perhaps it would never reach anywhere and they would sail and sail, the two of them with a band of pirates.

It was a mark of her confusion that she could consider that fate the best of all possible outcomes.

Rafe stayed where he was, watching the slow rise and fall of her shoulder and arm. She was curled up tightly and he wished he could wrap himself around her, absorb her confusion and fear until it drained away.

A fantasy even more likely to remain a fantasy now he'd made her hate him.

The swift collapse of her justifiable anger didn't reassure him in the least. He'd have preferred the storm to stay high.

He considered leaving the cabin so she could have the privacy of her misery. But he didn't fully trust her either, so he shifted a chair so that it blocked the door and sat down. He didn't know what Cleo might do, but he couldn't leave her here alone with her pain and frustration. She was still his responsibility, whether either of them liked it or not.

Chapter Fourteen

He had no memory of falling asleep, but the next he knew the bed was empty and the daylight was bright in the open windows.

The open windows…

He surged out of the chair with a strangled sound. She wouldn't. She…

The door to the quarter gallery swung open and Cleo entered. Rafe sank back into the chair, rubbing his face and waiting for his pulse to slow. His tumbling, panicked mind struggled to right itself.

He was too old for this. Not that anything in his past was truly equivalent to *this*. *This* was proving far too much of a strain on his tattered soul. He watched warily as she moved towards him. He searched her face for the volcanic anger that had welled out of her last night, but her face showed nothing but weariness.

'Please let me pass. I would like to ask where I may prepare some tea. I am thirsty and there is nothing here but wine.'

He half stumbled to his feet, shoving the chair to one side.

'I will fetch it.'

'There is no need, thank you, Mr Grey.'

'Cleo…'

'Miss Osbourne, please, sir. We are no longer in the desert,' she said haughtily as she swept past him into the narrow corridor.

The sailors Cleo came across as she passed through corridors and crowded holds didn't seem shocked to see her, but they did tend to melt away, as if unsure whether she posed a threat. When she reached what must be the sleeping quarters—a space hung with hammocks, some still populated by snoring sailors—her steps faltered and a luckily slim man of indeterminate years approached her, his deep black eyes reflecting the light of the lamps.

'Mees? I help?'

Yes, please. Help. Take me back to Alexandria and help me save my brother.

'I'd like some tea. *Thé. Shai.* Please,' she answered, the last word a little wobbly.

He smiled and beckoned her to follow and to her surprise he led her on deck. The wind held the sails taut and the air was filled with the sound of water slapping against the hull and the creaking of ropes and masts. The view all around was the same she had seen from the window of the Captain's cabin. A blue, liquid, anchorless desert.

The brigantine was far swifter than the heavy merchant ships she'd travelled on and she could feel the gentle burst and skip of the ship as it cut through the low waves. She felt a strange detachment—she was suspended between England and the East, the two halves of her past. She wished she could stay here—all she needed was tea and a book and she could sail like this for ever.

'You rang for tea?'

Rafe stood before her holding an elaborate silver tray, his feet braced apart for balance and his expression that of a punctilious butler. She wanted to hate him, knock the tray out of his hands and let loose the howl inside her. She let the image come and go and even that tired her.

All she wanted now was tea.

'Thank you.'

He hesitated, watching her as if waiting for something else. Then he placed the tray on the table before her. The ship shifted and the tall, elaborate coral-coloured teapot with delicate paintings on either side teetered.

'Goodness, careful!' She steadied the pot, inspecting the gently drawn landscape rising from a river to jagged mountains along its side. 'This looks like it is Qianlong. Or more likely a marvellous fake. If so, my father would likely have brokered a deal with the forger on the spot.'

She poured the tea into both cups and the scent, as fine as the crockery, mingled with the salt air. Rafe sat on one of the wooden chairs. It was a little small for him and he shifted uncomfortably.

'Knowing Chris it's not a fake. He's too finicky.'

'Not finicky; *discerning*,' said a deep voice and she turned. The man did not in the least resemble the image conjured by a wine-loving Captain with a taste for luxury. He was quite tall, though not as tall as Rafe, but it wasn't his stature that was the source of his impact. His hair was a deep shade of mahogany brown, gilded at the edges into fire by long exposure to the sun, his eyes as blue as the sea, shading to dusk around the pupil, and he was one of the handsomest men she had ever seen.

Rafe grunted and stood, confirming his superior height, if not manners.

'*Finicky.* Chris, this is Miss Osbourne. Cleo, this is Captain Christopher, or Chris. They don't use surnames on this vessel of knaves. And whatever you do, don't call him Kit.'

Their host shot Rafe a look that could have felled a forest, but by the time he turned back to Cleo he was smiling and she smiled back without thinking.

'You are quite right, Miss Osbourne. It is Qianlong. You have a good eye.'

So do you. Two of them, even, she almost said before she recollected herself.

'I apologise for commandeering your cabin and now your chair, Captain Christopher.'

'They are both honoured. I am sure if they could speak they would be thanking you for the improvement in their terms of employment. Besides, I owe this ugly fellow a favour and this allows me to discharge it while enjoying the company of someone who appreciates beauty. Any chance you can go read a book somewhere and leave us to discuss the long and convoluted history of Chinese crockery, Grey?'

'No. And fetch your own cup. That's mine.'

The Captain's mouth curved up at the corners, but he put down the cup and beckoned to the sailor who had helped her earlier. When that was done the Captain leaned back in his chair and began the tale of how he had acquired the Qianlong teapot. It involved actual pirates—rather than *faux* pirates, as Rafe disdainfully called Chris—a beautiful Chinese princess, a malevolent wizard, a dragon's egg and the daring rescue of the princess's beloved Shih Tzu puppy.

Meanwhile a sailor brought more cups, tea and delicious little almond-and-hazelnut-filled cakes sprinkled with cinnamon which Cleo devoured without even realising.

'If you like I will show you a collection of Sèvres *théières* I'm transporting for a friend, Miss Osbourne. Did you find the book, Benja?' he asked as the sailor who had brought the tea returned.

Benja handed a book to Cleo with a little bow. It was all very ceremonial and she had to resist the urge to bow in response.

'I am quite certain you will enjoy this,' said the Captain as he rose. 'If you will excuse me?' His smile shifted from her to Rafe and deepened into a near grin as he headed towards the bridge.

'One day he'll hang,' Rafe said just loud enough to be heard.

'Shhh… I thought you were friends.'

'Of course we're friends. Doesn't mean he doesn't annoy the cr— the hell out of me. He probably invented that story.'

Cleo sighed, licking a sliver of hazelnut from her fingers before wiping them on her handkerchief and picking up the book.

'I don't care. It was a wonderful tale. Oh, look, it is *Captives of the Hidden City*, the fourth of the *Desert Boy* books! How marvellous.'

She was struck with sudden guilt. Just an hour ago she was railing against fate and here she was enjoying tea, laughing with her nemesis and blissful at the prospect of sinking into this wondrous book.

'Ah, don't go that way again, Pat.' Her face must have shown her thoughts, because Rafe leaned forward, his hand rising, but falling back on to his thigh. 'You're alive. If your brother hasn't already left Egypt, with any luck he'll do so soon and will find you in London.'

Don't go that way.

He was right, it wasn't like her to become maudlin. She leaned her head against the back of the armchair and met Rafe's storm eyes straight on. He smiled a little.

'That's right, Cleopatra. No asps for you.'

'Of course not. But there is no comparison. Cleopatra likely believed wholeheartedly in the afterworld where she would reign as queen and goddess. Death was merely a rite of passage.'

'Still a mad thing to do. I'd rather stay and fight.'

'Evidently.' She smiled. 'You and your Captain Krees are of that breed. Taking on life headlong and making the most of it. I'm envious.'

'You're not that different, sweetheart. I don't know a handful of women, or men, who would have made it this far from Meroe. Whatever misguided vision you have of yourself, take it from someone who has seen a little of the world—you have a deep, strong core. You'll survive and thrive.'

She couldn't stop her mouth from wavering out of shape or her eyes burning. She didn't want him to say things like that.

'I've said the wrong thing again.' He sighed. 'Have some more tea.'

She shook her head.

'Tell me about our Captain, instead. How do you know him and why does he owe you a favour? And why does he hate being called Kit?'

'More bedtime tales?'

She shivered a little, remembering lying on the desert floor, watching the stars shimmer as he spoke. Amazingly she wished they were back there. Foolish.

'No tales, just the truth.'

'They aren't my tales to tell. But he's a good man and a better friend, that's all that matters. Is this general curiosity or are you smitten already?'

She smiled. She would not have thought someone with Rafe's looks and physique might be envious of the handsome Captain, but there was definitely a sour tinge to his voice.

'Not yet. I shall inform you when it happens.'

'Very amusing. I've seen women fall prey to his charms more times than I can count. I don't want to bear that burden of guilt as well.'

'I shall try and spare you, then.'

'You can laugh all you want, but it was evident you were enthralled with his pretty face, admit it.'

'I was enthralled by the teapot as well. And the sunset

over the cliffs in the desert and a host of other beautiful things. But that doesn't mean I want to stare at that sunset for ever. There is a vast difference between appreciating and wanting. Once he began telling that story I forgot how he looked and, in truth, I liked him better then.'

He picked up the book, leafing through it.

'Just be careful. His charm runs deeper than his handsome face. I didn't consider...just be careful.'

She wanted to tell him his concern was absurd. Even a little insulting. Only the day before they'd shared an intimacy that to her at least had been utterly transporting, and today he was suggesting she might become infatuated with another man.

Perhaps this was how his world operated. Perhaps he was used to falling in and out of lust with women and thought little of it. She wished she could do the same. She would be quite grateful if Captain Chris could inspire a tenth of what she felt towards Rafe. She didn't want to be stranded with these feelings, whatever they were—lust, need...love...

'I'm in no danger from Captain Chris.'

He shrugged again. Sometimes he looked and acted like an overgrown boy, uncomfortable in his rough frame. She wanted to take the book from his hands, take them in hers and tell him that she wanted *him*, not handsome Chris. His vanity might enjoy the tribute, but the rest of him would shy away, raise that barrier even higher.

Just be careful. His warning had come too late and she wondered if such warnings were ever effective.

'You're angry at me again, Cleo-Pat.'

She met his gaze and told him the truth.

'I'm...worn and worried and, yes, I'm still angry at you, Mr Grey. You may have thought you were acting in my interest, but your chief concern was *your* peace of mind and *your* conscience. Now go away. You are blocking the sun and I wish to read.'

* * *

It cost Rafe, but he did as he was bid and went away. He'd known she would take it ill, but somehow he'd hoped she'd understand.

He found a frowning Chris in the map room with Benja.

'Trouble, Chris?'

'No. A few Barbary pirate ships have been harassing merchant seamen south of Malta. Just marking their possible route so we can avoid it. What's on your mind? Disembowelling me?'

'The thought did occur to me, yes. Don't toy with her. She has been through enough. The last thing she needs is you charming her into a broken heart.'

Chris straightened, directing a very peculiar look at Rafe.

'I don't think I can, but in any case I shall try to rein in my desire to charm my way into the heart of every female within twenty leagues of me.'

'I didn't mean it like that and you know it.'

'You're in a foul mood. I've never seen you so worried about your customers. You've fulfilled your brief. She's alive and on her way to London. What more can you do?'

'Nothing,' Rafe grunted.

'Is she even paying you?'

'There's this great big horror of an emerald. Like the ones we used to see in the mountains in South America.'

'A fine payment. You're not taking it, I presume.'

'She'll need it once she reaches London. I doubt she'll make much from her writing, even assuming they'll accept articles from a woman.'

'Hmmm.' Chris stared off at the wall, his fingers tapping on the map. 'I like her.'

Rafe straightened in alarm.

'There's no currency in that, Chris.'

'What? Oh, not in that way. I meant I like her and she'd

best find a position that can support her. I think I shall have a word with my Aunt Mary when we arrive.'

'Anyone ever tell you what a useful fellow you are?'

'Never the ones that matter, Grey. And what will you do while I am relieving you of your burdens?'

Rafe almost objected to his calling Cleo a burden, but stopped himself. He'd probably revealed too much already. How had he become so enmeshed in all this? He wished he could just…disappear. Run away again and escape this tangled confusion. Perhaps that would be best. He'd done it before and been perfectly fine. Happy. Content. He could do it again.

'Whether Edge returns to England or not once he digs himself out of Egypt, I'm afraid I can't put off going to Greybourne any longer. If my mother refuses to continue to manage the estate, I'll need to make arrangements to administer the place from…wherever.'

'Why not from Greybourne?'

'No, thank you.'

'Your father's dead. It's yours now.'

'I'm aware of that.'

'And you're getting too old to play this soldier of fortune game.'

'Say's the gentleman smuggler.'

'I don't smuggle. I trade.'

'You just admitted you're still smuggling.'

'What, Boucheron's antiquities? That doesn't count as smuggling. The crates were marked for customs as marble and building materials. That was close enough. Besides, that was a year ago.'

'So you've turned respectable? What are you carrying now?'

'Cotton, spices, quite a bit of excellent wine, a damsel in distress and the very ugly Disappearing Duke.'

Rafe raised his hands, hushing his friend, and Chris sighed.

'Very well. I won't reveal your silly secret. You're just Rafe Grey, mercenary. Still ugly, though.'

Rafe rubbed his scarred cheek.

'Thank you, I find being ugly quite useful. Adds mystique and ups the price.'

'Except you just said you aren't taking a fee this time.'

Rafe kept his hand on his scars, grounding himself in them.

'No, every so often one has to do an act of charity to balance out the rest. This is mine.'

'I thought tricking Edge into travelling to Egypt was yours.'

'That is different. Edge matters.'

'And she doesn't?'

'She...' Rafe waited out another of those annoying flashes of tingling heat as it headed inexorably for his groin. Blast, he hated being sixteen again. The sooner they were off this ship the better. 'She is different, yes. But she doesn't matter, not in that way. Perhaps this whole Greybourne thing is throwing me off balance.'

'Ah, is that your excuse for kissing her?'

'I never said a word about...anything of that sort.'

'True. I was merely guessing. Now I know.'

'You blasted devil. Besides, it isn't true—*she* kissed *me*.' And quite a bit more.

'Of course you resisted wholeheartedly.'

'It might surprise you that I did...initially. She's lost her father, mislaid her brother and has no future to go to. What kind of cad would I be if I took advantage of her natural need for comfort? All she wants is a little solace in the midst of chaos,' he continued doggedly. 'Right now I'm all she has, but she'll land on her feet.'

Chris made a mark on the map. 'Useful trait to have. Are you worried she might develop expectations if she knows of your title and fortune?'

He considered it. 'No. Not in the least.'

'You sound almost disappointed, Grey—' He broke off as Benja returned and Rafe jumped at the opportunity to escape, leaving the two men bent over their charts, plotting the course to England and to a life he did not want.

Chapter Fifteen

'Hallo, Birdie,' Cleo said as Benja left her by Birdie's bunk in the sailors' hold. Birdie grunted and hauled himself into a sitting position. 'No, don't rise. Captain Christopher said you are feeling poorly so I brought you some tea.' She looked around the surprisingly clean hold.

'Don't worry, now. It's always the same when I first come on board.' He rubbed his beard, inspecting her over his cup. 'You're looking a little peaked yourself. The Colonel said you're angry.'

She shrugged. 'Not at you, Birdie.'

'It was the right thing to do, Miss Cleo.'

'He should have asked me.'

'Should he? And saying he told you we thought your brother might still be in Egypt, you would have come quietly?'

'Of course not. He is my little brother.'

'Well, there you have it, miss. Captain Chris couldn't wait any longer in Egypt.'

'I would have found another ship.'

'Not one where we could know you were safe. It is only fools who turn their noses up at an offer of help. I don't oft think you're a fool, but…'

She sighed. 'You are probably right, Birdie. I am mostly

disappointed in myself. I should not feel so relieved to have had choice taken away from me. But why did you and Mr Grey also leave? I thought he meant to find his brother?'

Birdie sipped his tea, considering the ceiling.

'The Colonel has business to see to back home. He'd done what he set out to—tempted his brother to Egypt; Edge will have to find his own way from there.'

'I hope both our brothers do. I should not have been so angry with him.'

'He expected nothing less. But don't make him suffer long.'

'Don't exaggerate, Birdie. He's hardly suffering.'

'I've known him a few days more than you, miss.'

'Devil take you, Birdie. Now I feel guilty myself.'

He gave a jaw-cracking yawn.

'Good. So go tell the lug you don't wish to feed him to the crabs.'

Rafe lowered the book at the knock on the door. Bunking in the map room meant he had to accept interruptions with good grace, but he was in a particularly foul mood at the moment and would have appreciated some privacy. He put down his book.

'Come in.'

'Mr Grey? May I have a word?'

He stood, his simmering anger at Cleo transforming within seconds into a different heat altogether. These shifts of mood were happening far too swiftly for his liking.

'Is there anything you need, Miss Osbourne?'

'I did not mean to interrupt.'

'You aren't. What do you want?'

His question was both ungracious and childish, but he felt a snap of satisfaction at her blush. Still, she stepped into the room and closed the door. He was suddenly absurdly conscious of the bed behind him. His hands curved of themselves, as if they were already closing on the cool sweep of her skin, and his mind conjured the image—Cleo in his bed, her short hair tossed into charming chaos by his hands just as it was now by the wind...

For the hundredth time his body scrabbled at his control, cursing him for taking what she'd offered and branding all those sensations into him. Odysseus's sirens he could deal with, but Cleopatra Osbourne was another matter entirely.

She shifted her weight. He was probably making her nervous. Good, she was making him writhe.

Finally, she drew a long breath and plunged in.

'I wished to apologise, Mr Grey.'

'Ah, yes. I heard you went to speak with Birdie. Did he instruct you to apologise?'

'Yes. He told me I have been monstrously unfair to you and that you are huddled in a corner, weeping and smiting your brow at the injustice of it all. I presume that is what the book is for. You couldn't possibly be reading it.'

Damn her.

He planted his tingling hands on his hips and managed not to smile.

'Naturally I wasn't reading the thing. I keep one by me in case I need to chase off a rat.'

Her dimples appeared before her smile did.

'Thank you for the warning. I had a close escape, then.'

'Very. The only thing that held me back was that it was one of your friend Shakespeare's and you'd probably have snatched it and scampered off.'

Her eyes went wide and bright. 'Oh, how marvellous! Which one?'

'I'm not telling you. You will ruin the ending.' He caught her sleeve as she moved towards the bed.

'No. Do stay away from my bed unless invited, Queenie.'

She stopped immediately. She'd flushed before, but now she turned as crimson as Chris's cushions. He had not meant to ruin their tentative return of rapport, but there were limits and sometimes her naivety sent her hurtling over them. He'd never thought that gaining her trust would become such a burden.

'I am sorry. I think... I know I have been living in my own little world for too long. I was angry because you imposed your will on mine, though I knew you did so because you felt I was at risk of real harm. Yet I did the same to you and can't claim that defence. That day in the *hammam*...' His heartbeat shot ahead, but she wasn't looking at him, her hands twisting into each other as she struggled with the words. 'I keep pushing you into a corner, don't I? I wanted something and I...oh, I am no good at explaining myself. I don't think I have had enough practice.'

He breathed very carefully, as if a flickering butterfly had settled on his hand.

'I think you are doing a fair job of explaining yourself, Cleo, but you have nothing to apologise for.'

'Yes, I do, Rafe. I never thought myself particularly impulsive, yet I have been doing all manner of impulsive things since I met you and every time it is you who must pay the price.'

He half held out his hand.

'I think it is more a case of honesty than impulsiveness, Cleo. And I prefer you be honest, even if it tests my fortitude at times. Friends...' he tried the word tentatively '...should be able to allow themselves more latitude with each other. I shall take it as a compliment that you allow yourself that latitude with me. I show Birdie sides of me I would never show the world and I trust him not to run in horror if I misstep.'

'Then thank you for not running in horror.' She pressed her hands together and to his surprise he saw they were shaking. He resisted the urge to touch her cheek, to make her look up so he could see the shifting storm of thoughts he knew were pounding inside her.

'You mustn't lay my weakness at your door, Cleo. I

could have been stronger and sent you on your way. I didn't.'

'But you would never have done anything had I not forced you into that situation.'

'Probably not. I don't have many codes, but the ones I possess are important to me. But I don't... I can't regret that it happened. It was...beautiful.' He wanted to say so much more, but his own thoughts were chaotic and jumbled, as if his mind had begun to speak a foreign language. 'I'm sorry, I've never had a conversation like this before.' He laughed a little and she smiled and heaved a hefty sigh of relief.

'Neither have I. I rather like it, though. Thank you.'

'I declare a moratorium on apologies and thanks for a while, Cleo-Pat.'

'Very well. I still feel quite guilty, though,' she said as she went to the door.

'Still? I told you...'

'No, about something else entirely.'

He knew he shouldn't ask. He knew it. And yet he did. 'About what, then?'

'Your bed. It is so much smaller than mine.'

The door closed behind her.

Even passengers on a smuggler's ship are ruled by routine.

After a week at sea Cleo woke, dined, and went to sleep to the tune of the ship's bells like everyone else on board. She particularly waited for the bell calling them to dinner. It wasn't the surprisingly excellent food she looked forward to, it was that Rafe was most relaxed with her when in the Captain's company.

Her apology had defused much of the tension between them, but Rafe seemed to have traced a circle around himself, like a druid's mark of protection. She could not tell if he was shielding her or himself; if it was her, it was failing miserably.

At least during dinner and sometimes seated with them on deck she felt utterly, vividly happy. Rafe and the Captain had clearly known each other long and enjoyed the peculiar and rare camaraderie of men who were completely comfortable with one another and therefore enjoy outdoing each other in pointing out each other's foibles.

The Captain was also more than willing to indulge her love of Shakespeare, especially when he realised how much it goaded Rafe. One dinner he brought his collection of the plays, all dog-eared from frequent reading.

'I'll leave these here for you to take what you want. Perhaps you'll even convince this philistine to give them a try. He used *Hamlet* in school to even the table legs.'

'It kept wobbling when we were playing whist. Very distracting,' Rafe defended himself.

Cleo's attention sharpened. Rafe continued to parry all her questions about either his past or his future. She gathered any glimpse of his life like nuggets of gold from a river.

'What was school like?' Cleo took the opportunity to ask.

'Rafe was very instrumental in making sure I survived my first two years in school.'

'I was also two years older and a head taller. It was no great effort to keep those damned bullies at bay.'

Captain Chris's smile twisted a little.

'It cost you a beating by the headmaster.'

'Only once. It was well worth it to see Barnsley and Greaves waist deep in the mud.'

'What happened?' Cleo demanded.

'Curious, Cleo-Pat?' Rafe grinned and Chris leaned his elbows on the table and told a tale which had Cleo laughing so hard she spilled her wine.

Rafe took her glass from her.

'Here, you may laugh at me all you wish, but I won't condone the waste of Chris's precious nectar.'

Cleo dabbed at a spot of wine on her dress with a napkin.

'I cannot afford to spill it either. This dress might be years out of fashion, but it is my most respectable one and I shall be needing it when I present myself to Mr Fulton, the editor of the *Gazette*.'

'What a pity I didn't know previously,' Chris said. 'We sold a dozen bolts of Chinese silk to a merchant in Alexandria. There was the most amazing embroidered orange silk that would have suited you perfectly, Cleopatra.'

'Stop flirting, you bacon-fed knave,' Rafe growled.

'Rafe! That is from *Henry the Fourth*! Oh, very good!' Cleo commended, taking back her glass.

'It's all your fault. Between the two of you quoting that mawkish pap at each other morning to night I'm surprised I'm not dreaming in Shakespearean blather. I'm only glad Chris doesn't share your fascination with mummies.'

Captain Chris raised his brows.

'Mummies?'

'You know, dead bodies wrapped in sheets.'

'I know what mummies are, Greybeard. Are you interested in mummies, Miss Osbourne? How wonderfully ghoulish.'

'My father was interested in them and only because they fetched a good price. Just before he disappeared he sent a shipment of three dozen mummies to a Mr Pettifer in London, who apparently unwraps them in front of an audience.'

'Ah. Pettifer.'

'You know him?'

'Yes. He's well named, that petty scoundrel. Opened what he calls a "Hall of Wonders" on Piccadilly. I don't advise you follow up on the acquaintance.'

'But I must. He is always late in payment and it is usually not until he wishes for Father to procure him something else that he pays his bill. I plan to demand he honour his debt when I reach London. Besides, if Dash did indeed succeed in leaving Egypt already, then Mr Pettifer might know where he is. Dash mentioned Pettifer's connections in the antiquarian world might prove useful.'

'If it is antiquarian connections he needs, I'll introduce him to John Soane. He is a close acquaintance of my aunt's and I often procure objects of interest for him. In fact, my aunt is an excellent person for you to meet. In fact, I think…'

He leaned back and stared at the ceiling, but whatever thoughts were being conjured in his mind were interrupted by Benja's appearance.

'Wind is changing, *Capitán*.'

'Hold that thought, Cleopatra. I shall return anon…'

He left the cabin, taking the carefree atmosphere with him.

Of late, each time she found herself alone with Rafe she had to rearrange herself, like the moment after stumbling on a perfectly straight road. He also appeared to find these moments a strain because he would usually hurry to make a remark, but this time it was she who rushed to fill the void.

'It is very kind of Captain Chris to offer his assistance, but I have imposed on him enough. He needn't go out of his way on my account.'

'Since he is certain to visit his aunt when we reach London, he will hardly be going out of his way.'

'You know what I mean. I cannot continue to hang on your coattails. When we reach London I must make my own way.'

'Oh, God, not that again. You have the rest of your life to make your own way, Cleo. But right now you haven't the tools to do so.'

'We must agree to differ on that head, Mr Grey.'

'If there is any phrase I dislike more than that, I cannot recall it at the moment. No, we will *not* agree to differ. This is a very simple issue, Cleo. Do you honestly believe I will deposit you on the dockside and go about my business? What the devil do you think I am?'

'The stubbornest man of my acquaintance, sir. You make me sound as if I will wander about the docks like a stray lamb just waiting for the first scoundrel to fleece me. I am neither an imbecile nor reckless.'

'I think you qualify for both those epithets if you refuse a perfectly reasonable offer of assistance.'

'I have already accepted a great deal of assistance from you. I cannot be forever hanging about your neck, like those fictional swooning damsels you so deride.'

He flushed.

'I never lumped you in that category. For pity's sake, you are the least susceptible female I have yet come across.'

'Somehow that does not sound very complimentary.'

'I was making a point.'

'That I am case-hardened and bull-headed. I should fare just fine on the London docks, then.'

'Don't twist my words, Pat. What great scheme of the heavens might be upset if you surrender your vaunted independence for a brief moment and accept our help? Is there some Greek curse that will be unleashed? Is the fate of civilisations at stake? Or is it simply your wish to give me more sleepless nights than you have already?'

She pushed back her chair and went to the windows and stared into the darkness. The waves were slow inky swells that rose and fell like the breath of a sleeping, slimy beast. In the distance she thought she could just see the glimmer of a light—perhaps another ship or even the shores of Portugal.

Soon, all too soon, she would be returning to a country where she knew no one. Why *not* accept Rafe and Captain Chris's help?

Not because of a Greek curse, but something far more mundane. She *knew* Rafe. He would not be able to walk away without making absolutely certain she was safe. It was simply the way he was. Her insistence on independence was rubbing on his conscience and his peace of mind… She almost smiled as the wheel finally settled into the groove.

How *petty* of her. She *did* want him to worry, she did not wish to be put away, score settled, like his past assignments. She wanted him awake at night, worrying about her fate. She wanted him thinking of her.

Petty and unfair.

She rubbed her eyes and returned to her chair.

'I'm too tired to argue with you, Rafe. Can we not resolve this later?'

'No. I refuse to have this argument with you in the middle of a dockyard, which is precisely what will happen if we don't resolve this now. The sooner you come to terms with it the better. We will be in London in a matter of days, Cleo.'

'I *know* that. Stop growling at me!'

'What are you two arguing about now?' Captain Chris asked as he re-entered, bearing a tray of cakes. 'On second thought, don't tell me. I might have to take sides and hurt the big lug's feelings. These will make you both feel better. Benja prepared it especially for you, sweet Viola. He is clearly smitten, which shows excellent taste on his part.'

'Is senility setting in, Chris? Her name is Cleo, not Viola.'

Chris settled into his chair and took one of the cakes himself.

'If you'd minded your lessons with the same assiduity as you spent trying to escape school, Rafe, you might realise it is perfectly apt.'

'Oh, God, not Shakespeare again.'

'Yes, philistine.'

'Which one was Viola? The one who lived in the forest dressed like a shepherd and made men run rings around each other?'

'That was Rosalind and I do *not* do that,' Cleo objected. 'Though I am flattered by the comparison—Rosalind is a fine heroine. Captain Chris was referring to Viola from *Twelfth Night*. She also dressed like a boy and is mistaken for her brother, but the resemblance in our tales ends there.'

Cleo considered the cakes and took a generous slice. She'd eaten better since boarding the *Hesperus* than she had in years. Any more of this and she'd be bursting out of her few dresses.

'Oh, there's more to her story, I think. A very resilient young woman, Viola. She thinks she has lost everything, but rather than abandon hope and bemoan her fate she takes on the guise of Cesario, becomes page to the Duke of Orsino, falls in love with him and, though he is a blind fool for most of the play, she ends up marrying him.'

Rafe grunted and crossed his arms as well.

'Sounds like the plot of a third-rate Haymarket play. No wonder I cannot remember it.'

'I agree it is not one of my favourites,' Cleo admitted, giving in to temptation and taking a second slice. 'I found Viola's devotion to Orsino rather tiring and his adoration of Olivia even more annoying.'

'The two of you haven't a sentimental bone between you.' Chris laughed. 'I find other parallels, though. There is the fact that Viola disguises herself as Cesario which, of course, is quite apt, given Caesar was Cleopatra's lover. And then Orsino means bear in Italian. You have a fascination for names, don't you, Rafe? I thought you might find that curious.'

'Do you mean because of the "bourn" in Osbourne, Captain Chris?' Cleo asked, perplexed by the exchange between the two men. This clearly touched on something that lay between them.

'There is that, too.' Chris nodded. 'I applaud all things symmetrical.'

'You are lucky you're pretty, Popinjay, because you are about as amusing as an arse boil,' Rafe snapped.

'We can't all be endowed with your ample measure of charm, Grey Bear... I mean Grey *Beard*.'

'Don't you have a ship to sail?'

Captain Chris laughed and stood.

'I do. And a storm to beat if we're lucky.'

Cleo glanced worriedly towards the windows. She'd seen no signs of storm clouds in the dark sky.

'Another storm?'

'A big one this time. Past the straits the sea is a different beast altogether. It will either speed us towards the Channel or make fish feed of us all. I'd better go ensure the former. I'd hate to follow literary parallels and have my Viola cast ashore in an untimely manner. Unless, of course, you find your Orsino in said manner.' He winked at her and left.

'Addle-pate,' Rafe muttered.

'What on earth was that about?'

'I neither know nor care. As for you—until you know your way about London you will accept whatever position Chris can conjure out of his family's ample hat.'

'Have a piece of cake, Greybeard. It might sweeten you up.'

'I'm serious, Cleo.' His tone softened. 'I need to know you will be safe. I would say you owe me that. Think of it as a way to erase your debt.'

'By owing you more?'

'By granting me peace of mind. I'm not asking that you commit yourself to a nunnery. Merely meet with Chris's aunt so she can see if there is some position she can secure for you. If her suggestions do not appeal to you, you are free to reject them. Would that be so terrible? You are not signing over your soul, you know.'

She looked down at Benja's cake. She'd already given Rafe a large portion of her soul. What difference would it make whether she agreed? Whether Dash survived or not—her life as she had known it was over.

'I'm sorry, Pat.'

She pressed the heels of her hands to her eyes. She hated how he could sometimes see right through her. He rarely called her Pat any longer, except to tease her, but he wasn't teasing her now. Soon he would no longer call her that, or call her anything at all.

'Pat is gone, Mr Grey. Henceforth I am Miss Osbourne. Whoever she is.'

'You'll find your way again. You have that…gift,' he said, but his voice was strained as if he was trying to convince himself.

'I might, but I don't particularly wish to.'

'I can sympathise with that. Life is not very considerate of our wishes, is it?'

'No. What do you wish for, Rafe?'

He turned his glass in his hand, watching the light from the lamps dig deep into the purple. His expression didn't change, but she could feel him slip away again. When he looked up and smiled she knew he'd marked the boundary between them once again.

'Oh, I'm easy. Good food, good wine, good company. At the moment I am lucky to have all three. What else would I need?'

Me, said the treacherous little voice inside her. She took a third slice of the cake and stood.

'Where are you going?' he asked, rising as well.

'To find *Twelfth Night* among the Captain's books. Perhaps I shall learn something useful.'

Chapter Sixteen

She would have done better to have read *The Tempest*.

At first she'd thought it was the Captain's wonderful wine that was making the room roll so alarmingly. But she doubted it would account for the ship behaving more like a barrel rolling downhill than a sea-going vessel.

She managed to change into her nightshift and lie down, only to find herself dumped summarily on the floor as the ship tipped on its side.

There were times when hammocks were definitely preferable to bunks, she thought as she grabbed the shelves, spreading her legs wide to battle the roll and pitch. She could feel and hear the waves lashing at the hull, the desperate creak and wail of wood being strained to its last fibre.

Then the worst happened. She could feel the ship rising, straining and shuddering as it was lifted up. She knew it could not last, any moment the laws of nature would have their way with them. When the inevitable drop came, it took the ship, but not her stomach. The latter lurched up into her chest only to be thrown down again as the ship tipped over on its side.

Any moment now and the Captain's prediction about them becoming a treat for the fish might very well come to pass. She clung to the polished wood, her heart slamming far faster and more brutally than the shrieks of wind and raging waves.

But her mind was amazingly quiet and clear. All she could think was—she did not want to die and she did not want Rafe to die.

She wanted him here, with her.

The door slammed open and something between a squawk and a shriek burst from her, but it wasn't the ship being torn apart. Rafe stood braced in the doorway as the ship rolled back. His hair and face were slick with rain and the coat he was shrugging off fell with a wet thump to the floor.

I've conjured him, she thought. Her relief was so great it took quite a bit of restraint and common sense not to abandon her grip and throw herself at him precisely like a Haymarket heroine.

The ship gave another mighty effort to shake her off. She lost her hold on the shelf, but managed to grab one of the solid chairs that was grinding sluggishly back and forth across the floor, dragging her as she clung to it.

Rafe came towards her, using the shelves as anchors.

'Stop dancing like a drunken goat and sit down.'

'I am trying! It's impossible to stay still.'

She was beginning to feel queasy. She couldn't remember suffering from seasickness before, but there was a first time for everything. Her first relief at his entry was dissipating fast. It was bad enough she must look like a fright in the oversized nightshirt; casting up her accounts in front of him would add injury to injury.

'I am perfectly fine. Go away,' she said, trying not to sound desperate.

'No. Not while you're rolling around like a billiard ball.'

'I'll sit down.' She aimed for the seat and promptly fell to the floor as the boat went the other way. The blow to her bottom was so sharp she lost her breath and sat gasping.

He helped her to her feet, planting his feet wide against the roll.

'Come, sit.'

'I think I am safer on the floor.'

He laughed, tucking her against him.

'You'll roll around the floor like a loose cannon, Queenie. Come.'

To her surprise he sat at the end of the bed and propped his boots against the cupboard. Before she could understand what he was doing he used the roll of the ship to pull her off her feet and on to his lap. His arm curved about her waist, his hand on her hip, flexing as he held her through the particularly enthusiastic roll.

'See? Nice and snug. We roll with the ship, rather than try to battle it. You can't win that one, sweetheart.' His voice was a rumbling purr against her side and his breath warm on her temple.

His warmth radiated through the thin, damp cotton of their shirts and her hands began tingling at the memory of sliding her hands over his chest in the bathhouse. How his muscles had hardened under her touch, bunching and flexing in that strange dance of invitation and rejection. Her hand was so close to his waist, a simple tug could separate shirt from trouser and...

The ship gave another leap and dip and she grabbed at his shirt.

'Ouch. Watch your nails, hellion.'

'You've been stabbed more times than a roast ham. I hardly think my nails will have an impact on you.'

'God, you'd be surprised.' There was a laugh in his voice, but also a rawness, and she leaned back a little to look at him.

He was half smiling, but there was tension there and demons in his eyes.

She released his shirt, gently rubbing the spot she'd abused, still watching him.

His pupils widened, turning storm into thundery dusk, and under her thigh she felt him harden. It was definite, immediate, and so was her response.

All fear of the storm, the queasiness and embarrassment just…evaporated. Her body shimmered with heat, expanded and woke into awareness of every point of contact, of the tingling warmth between her legs, of the need to *do* something…

Oh, lord, she was in trouble.

'Maybe this was not the best idea.' His voice was even rougher than usual, but he didn't remove her from his lap. 'I think you'd be safer on the floor.'

'But not as comfortable.' She was *purring*. She'd never purred in her life.

'Comfortable isn't the word that comes to mind,' he muttered, but his arms tightened around her. 'Just try not to move.'

The ship pitched again, as if rolling in laughter at their pretence at civility. His legs braced harder against the side of the cupboard.

She rubbed her feet together and tucked them against his thigh.

'Stop it. Or I'll drop you.'

'My feet are cold,' she protested. He dragged the blanket towards them and drew it round her shoulders. She snuggled into it.

'I'm so glad Captain Chris appreciates fine things like cashmere. Isn't it soft?'

His answer was more grunt than corroboration, but his arms closed around her again under the fuzzy cocoon, one hand warm and heavy on her hip, the other tucking the blanket under her feet and staying there.

She sighed. If this storm was the end for all of them, at least she would go down more comfortable than she had been in…in for ever. She snuggled deeper, flexing her feet. His hand tightened, his fingers firm against her instep. She smiled.

'Thank you, Rafe.'

'Please don't. Just…stop moving.'

'It's the ship, not I.'

'Liar. I know I deserve to be tortured for all my sins, but this is beyond my dues. Please try to sleep.'

'I don't think I can.'

'Try. *Please.*'

She did try. She tried not to think of how addictive and unique his scent was or wonder what it was about it that made her wish to fill her lungs with it and keep it with her always.

She tried, not very hard, not to take advantage of the rolling ship to expand her map of his body against hers. To be quite fair, he was not helping. His arms and hands tightened with each roll and pitch, his legs tensing and relaxing. He was no more still than she and she could not tell how much was necessitated by the workings of gravity and how much driven by the same demons that were hard at work undermining her control.

She kept waiting for the next wave—his hands would close tightly on her hip and foot, sending sweet waves of bliss through her like music from a chime. She risked flexing her foot against his hand as they rolled and his fingers pressed hard against her sole, sending a shiver all the way up to her scalp. It felt… Oh, yes…marvellous!

'And stop humming, blast it.'

'Sorry. I feel a little fuzzy. Can one become tipsy from being cuddled?'

'I don't know, but one can and is becoming addled by it.'

'Sorry,' she said again and kissed the side of his neck. He seemed to collapse like a house of cards, with a protesting groan that echoed the creaking of the boat. She was no longer cocooned but crushed—stretched out on the bed with a very heavy and warm giant on top of her, her arms still tight about his neck.

'I know this is my fault, but there are limits, Cleopatra, and we've just passed mine. I'm going on deck where it's safer. Now go to sleep.'

'I don't want to sleep. My future…my whole life is a great unknown, but this feels so right. How could it be so wrong?'

His breathing was deep and unsteady, his chest brushing against hers with each breath.

'It certainly is in the world you are heading to.'

'But we are not there yet. We are not anywhere yet. We might not reach anywhere if this storm worsens. Would it be so terrible if we take this pleasure?'

He raised himself a little. In the dark his eyes were even more menacing—twin shards of a northern sea. If she hadn't felt his heart thudding against her, she might have worried she was alone in this drugging need.

'You are under my protection…'

She unhooked her arms.

'Oh, God, not that again. I am no longer under your protection, but under Captain Christopher's. I am, however, under *you* and I like it here. If there is one thing I have learned in my addled life it is to take what pleasures come my way as long as they harm no one.'

He didn't answer immediately, but the muscles of his jaw were working away, making the scarred skin ripple.

'This isn't good. I'm far gone enough for you to be making sense, Queenie.'

'I *am* making sense. You said yourself lust is the manifestation of a natural need. Or were *you* prevaricating?'

'No, but it is different for you. You're…'

Her eyes narrowed.

'I am what? If you dare say *a woman*—'

'Well, you are.'

'You have taken others of my genus to bed, haven't you?'

'Yes, but they were...more experienced. Stop glaring at me like that. It matters. At least, it matters to me. Right now you are lonely and scared. Hell, I'm the same. I would like nothing better than to drown my mind for a while in this madness, believe me. Nine out of ten parts of me are hitting me over the head for not saying yes at the top of my lungs.'

'Those are the nine parts of you that I like, Mr Grey.'

He smiled, his hand coming up to clasp hers where it was still pressed to his chest.

'The tenth part is deeply wounded, but it likes you best of all and doesn't want to sacrifice our friendship for the price of pleasing my damned libido.'

'Tell Mr Tenth to keep its nose out of the other parts' affairs. And I mean that literally. What happened in Alexandria was not an aberration; I want this honestly.'

He sank his head on to her shoulder. She could feel the battle inside him, the rigid weight pressing down on her. She wanted to tell him the battle was for naught. She would never hold this against him, but despite his strange life, he had rigid standards and she was not certain she wanted to force him to break with them.

She sighed and turned to brush his soft dark hair with her lips.

'Just a kiss, then? And then I promise I shall stop torturing you.'

'Just a kiss?' He raised his head and she wasn't certain if there was relief in his voice or disappointment.

'Yes. That is all. For tonight at least,' she amended conscientiously.

'Then you sleep?'

'As best I can. Yes.'

He adjusted himself on his elbow, gazing down at her. After moment he gave a small, determined sigh and brushed his fingers from her cheekbone to her jaw, his thumb settling on her lower lip, brushing gently.

'Just a kiss,' he repeated and she nodded.

'Just a kiss. After what we did in the *hammam*, how much harm could a simple kiss do?'

'At this rate a simple kiss might burn me to cinders, Cleo.' His fingers were tracing the lines of her face, gliding over her cheek, the curve of her ear and the sensitive skin below it before returning to her mouth. 'This is probably not a—'

She slipped one hand into his hair and drew his head down into the kiss.

Just a kiss.

Just the whole world cracking open and revealing itself like a ripe fruit, just her body saying—yes, finally...more.

For a few moments he let her explore his lips with hers, doing nothing more than holding himself above her, his hand as gentle as a down feather against her cheek.

This was *hard* for him, this control, she realised with glee. She wanted it to be hard. She wanted him to *need* this. To be buffeted by it just like the waves outside, just like the forces inside her that kept pushing her towards him.

She wanted him to want *this* as much as she did. No, she wanted him to want her. Not her kiss or her body, but *her*. This was different from Alexandria. She didn't know how; she just knew it was.

He raised himself suddenly, his hand pressing into the cushions, his face taut.

'Hell, I want more than a kiss, Cleo. I want to watch you come like you did in the *hammam*. Just listening to you makes me hard...your voice, your laugh...it lights me up inside...' His voice was rough and shaky, his hand sliding down between her breasts, pushing aside her pendant, down over her abdomen and up again, splaying across her ribs.

Her pulse chased his warmth, but it was his words that were working on her now, his voice a drug pouring through her, pumping heat and need through her veins.

'You amaze me, Cleo,' he murmured against her skin, his mouth following his hand, his breath shaping the words over her breast, along the surprisingly sensitive curve of her waist. 'You hold so much inside. But you're so generous, so true.'

He kissed the softest point just beside her hip bone and her legs drew up in a convulsion of need. He was driving her to the brink.

'Touch me,' she urged, rubbing his shoulders, reaching as far down his back as she could without stopping his destructive, beautiful progress. He pushed back for a second, pulling his shirt over his head and tossing it aside and then did the same to hers, much more gently.

'I will,' he promised. 'Trust me.'

'I do,' she whispered and he went still for a moment and then very gently eased her thigh to one side, his breath warm on her skin as his mouth lightly brushed kisses from her hip downwards. It felt foreign and a little frightening for him to be so close to her there.

'I want to hear your voice when I touch you,' he murmured against the inside of her thigh, his tongue tracing slow circles that made her skin skitter and pulse. 'Tell me what you like.'

She shook her head. That was beyond her.

'Whatever you're doing, I like it. Just do it more.'

His laugh was its own torture, a puff of warmth that rushed up between her legs and she clenched her jaw. When he slid one hand under her behind, raising and adjusting her, she let him. When he pressed a trail of gentle kisses to the sensitive skin of her inner thigh she held herself still until he reached the soft centre of the thudding heat between her legs. Then she couldn't hold back a spurt of breathy laughter—embarrassment and pleasure and gratitude all clashing.

She draped one arm over her eyes, as if hiding from the world could protect her. Her other hand hovered near his head, brushing at his soft dark hair until he threaded his fingers through hers and brought her hand to her breast, his thumb catching at her nipple and making fireworks explode.

The sensation was sweet and sharp and as it met the rising pulses of pleasure at her core she knew it had to stop, but it didn't. She tried not to cry out as the pleasure whipped itself into a storm, but the sounds burst from her—soft, then urgent, and finally imploding in a long breathy moan as honeyed heat crashed through her, sweet, molten. She was drowning in it…

She went rigid and he stilled, just holding her as wave after wave swept over her, softer each time until she lay there, exhausted but still humming.

'Listening to you is better than any aphrodisiac, Cleo.' His voice was raw and she could feel the tension in him. She turned lazily to press against him, her hand slipping down to see…oh, yes, he was hard and hot, the skin velvet-soft.

His breath hitched and he tucked his head into the slope of her neck.

'Wait a little…don't hurry.'

'I'm not,' she said idly, her hand gently stroking—her palm, the back of her hand, testing each sensation, mirroring the swaying of the ship. She whispered, 'Look, the storm has calmed.'

'Has it? Doesn't feel that way.' His voice was muffled against her neck. He held himself very still and she turned to kiss his temple, his flushed cheekbone. He was big and warm against her and it felt so absolutely right to have their naked bodies intertwined like this. She nudged him on to his back and raised herself above him, her legs slipping against his, her breasts half pressed against his chest. She traced a long line down his chest, over his stomach and up his erection, resting her palm on its heat and slowly closing it into a gentle squeeze. His eyes fluttered closed and a rumbling groan caught deep in his chest.

She smiled and trailed her hand the other way, right up to the dip at the base of his throat and back again. As her fingers and nails travelled up and down his muscles contracted and goosebumps rose on his skin. She could feel the vicious control he was exerting, but he couldn't control the shudders that struck, especially when she reached a certain point just by his navel or when her hand brushed his nipple. And when her fingers closed on his erection, each time a little tighter, a little longer, his breathing began coming apart at the seams. It made her feel hot all over again, powerful...*happy*.

He might keep himself from her, but she felt so close to him she could not believe there wasn't at least part of him that cared, that wanted to take what she was so willing to give.

'I like to make you feel like this,' she murmured, brushing her mouth across his, in long slow sweeps just like her hand. He said something in reply, but it might have been old Norse for all she knew because he dug his hand into her short hair and kissed her—a long, drugging kiss that began spinning its own magic through her body. His other hand anchored on hers, guiding her until his head arched back on a hoarse groan, his body tightening in release.

The storm had released the ship and it settled into a gentle swaying, like a great hammock. Rafe held her close as their bodies cooled and pulses slowed.

As the wondrous warmth began to fade, one thought rose like a jagged rock out of the mist—he had to tell her the truth of his identity. He could no longer hide behind the cowardly fiction that there was no need to do that since they would soon be in London and each heading on their merry way.

She kept condemning his conscience and right now he

wished he could send it to the devil himself. But whether his bond with her went any further or not, he had to tell her who he was.

For the first time in his life he was about to voluntarily reveal his identity to someone other than Birdie. It terrified him and he did not know why. Perhaps he was more superstitious than he thought, as if revealing his title, his origin, would somehow unleash a curse he'd escaped when he repudiated his name. It was absurd, childish, but it made his stomach roil.

He had to tell her.

He stroked a hand down her arm and she gave a little hum, stretching against him. A greedy shudder ran through him in response and set his heart pounding, not with desire this time, but with fear. The web his body and mind were weaving around her was tearing down all his defences, all his control.

She pulled away, rising on her elbow. Her smile faded as she met his eyes.

'What is it?'

'Nothing… I used to have some semblance of control. Apparently not any more.' The words were wrenched out of him and she placed a hand on the centre of his chest. Now he could feel his heart slamming against his ribs—like a fool pointlessly throwing himself against a wall.

'Rafe. You keep telling me not to go that way. Now I am telling you—don't let your conscience ruin this moment.'

'I can't help it; this is who I am, Cleo.'

No, it isn't, said the mocking little voice of his detested conscience. *Who you are is Rafael Edgerton, Earl of Braden, Duke of Greybourne. Tell her the truth.*

He slipped her off him and stood, searching for his clothes. It was still pitch dark outside, but he could hear the men hurrying about the ship, no doubt righting the chaos of the gale. They'd weathered the storm outside, but he had no idea how he would fare in the storm ahead.

Tell her.

The coward in him dressed in silence. Once she was safely on her way to her new life he would tell her and risk whatever curse life chose to toss at him next.

'I must go help Chris. A storm like that was bound to cause damage.'

'Of course,' she replied and he cast her a quick glance. She sat curled into the corner he'd occupied only a few hours ago, the blankets cocooning her.

'Your hair is getting longer,' he said inconsequentially and her hand snaked out of the warmth of the blankets and touched it.

'It must look a mess.'

'It looks beautiful.'

She shook her head a little and he fought the urge to walk back to that bed, to her, and send the world to the devil.

'I must help Chris,' he said again and left the cabin.

Chapter Seventeen

The Thames, England

'Good morning and welcome to England. Land of horrible weather, worse food, and plenty of phlegm.' The Captain's morose greeting was a perfect echo of Cleo's sentiments. They stood for a moment watching the flat, reedy shores slide by as Benja steered the *Hesperus* up the estuary.

'It looks soothing, though,' she replied, trying for cheerfulness. 'All that green.'

'True. There is a great deal of green.' He looked up at the sky and wiped the mist of rain from his hair. 'And grey.'

'Speaking of which—where is Mr Grey?'

He turned to look at her. Evidently her attempt at nonchalance left much to be desired.

'He spent hours with us cleaning up after the storm and he looked exhausted, so I sent him to rest a little before we dock and must face the real world.'

'I wish we could keep on sailing for another month at least. I'm not ready,' she blurted out and Chris sighed.

'Neither am I. In fact, quite a few people on this ship are dreading going ashore for one reason or another, including your knight errant, Viola. Perhaps our concerted repulsion will send us back out the estuary. I can't very well wish my sister remain unmarried merely for my own convenience, but I do wish her letter had missed me in Alexandria.'

'I think it is very noble of you to honour her so.'

'Pure fear. She will complain to my grandmother and that formidable woman terrorises the lot of us.'

Cleo smiled, as he'd intended, but she could hear a dozen conflicting currents in his tone. He seemed so open and yet, like Rafe, he kept himself mostly hidden below his handsome surface.

'I hope it is not as bad as you think.'

'I hope the same for you, Viola. But meanwhile I want to make a suggestion. Until I speak with my aunt I would like to suggest you remain on the *Hesperus*.'

She pushed away from the bulwark.

'Captain…'

'Don't reject my offer out of hand, Cleopatra. Accepting help does not diminish you, quite the opposite.'

'You sound like Rafe.' She sighed. 'But I *need* to go back to managing on my own. I'm beginning to worry I will have forgotten how.'

'I gather your resilience has been challenged before and will likely be so again. It would be rash, even arrogant, to reject our offers, and you don't strike me as being either. Be sensible.'

'I once thought I was a very sensible person. Or perhaps that was merely in comparison with the world we inhabited with my father. I have recently come to realise I am not at all sensible.'

'I wouldn't go quite that far. I've known you to show glimmerings of good judgement.' Rafe spoke behind her and she stiffened, her body giving her ample proof of her utter lack of sense.

'Cleopatra is eminently sensible,' Chris intervened. 'She's agreed to stay on the *Hesperus* while we conclude our first round of enquiries regarding her brother, a position and that weasel Pettifer. Much easier to co-ordinate our plan of attack from here than from some busy lodging house with suspicious matrons on the watch. Correct, Cleopatra?'

The wind whistled past them and far into the distance she could see a farmer's cart moving along a straight, empty road. It looked as foreign and outlandish as Acre had appeared to her a dozen years ago.

She did indeed need to manage on her own, and soon enough she would, but for the moment these two men were offering to smooth her path. Cleopatra the Queen would have expected nothing less. In fact, she would have demanded it.

'I agree. Thank you, Captain. However, my agreement is conditional.'

She directed the last part to Rafe and a smile picked up the corner of his mouth.

'Conditional on what, Queenie?'

'On your promise that you won't do anything behind my back.'

'I rarely make the same mistake twice, Cleo. I promise.'

She sat down with a thump at the Captain's table and re-folded the letter. She had expected nothing else, but the moment Rafe returned bearing Mr Fulton's response from the *Gazette*, her heart had gone into a hopeful gallop. It was doing that far too often these past months and usually for the wrong reasons.

'I presume that means your editor has not heard from your brother?' Rafe asked as he watched her.

'No, he hasn't. He presents his compliments to C. Osbourne and informs *him* he is interested in continuing his association with us at the same rates as before when D. Osbourne arrives in England.'

'Well, that is good news at least.'

'The only good news we have.'

'A first swallow of spring,' he replied, hiking his voice up and waving his hand with a flourish, and she smiled.

'You are in a fine mood. Have you visited your mother?'

'I would hardly be in a good mood if I had. That joy yet awaits me. But I have two more swallows in my pocket.'

'News of Dash?'

'No, Queenie. Not yet. The first is courtesy of Chris—he spoke with his aunt and by a stroke of good luck a widowed cousin of hers is in need of a companion while she is waiting for her sister to return from India to come live with her. I told you that family is a source of endless surprises, good and bad.'

'Oh.'

'Don't sound so glum. She is staying with her relative, a Mr John Soane. According to Chris, the house is a veritable museum of antiquities. You should feel right at home.'

'I was thinking of swearing off antiquarians for a dozen years or so.'

'You may do so soon enough with my best wishes, but not quite yet. Which brings me to my other swallow, or rather pigeon to be plucked—Mr Pettifer. I will be meeting with him this afternoon.'

She surged to her feet, a martial look in her eye.

'You mean *we* will be with meeting him this afternoon.'

'I think it is best you remain here.'

'It is *not* best. This is not merely a matter of collecting on his debt to us. Pettifer and my father often corresponded and he might know something of what happened between my father and Boucheron. We might be in England, but until I am certain Dash is here and safe, I must have a clearer idea what my father was involved in so I understand the risks.'

'I can do all that. I'm quite a hand at subterfuge.'

'I know you are, Mr Grey, however—' She broke off, examining his careful lack of expression. 'Are you making game of me?'

'Ever so slightly.'

'So you *did* intend for me to come with you?'

'Not precisely. *We* will meet with him, but *you* won't.'

'That makes no sense.'

'You will meet him as Patrick, not Miss Osbourne. Miss Osbourne will only make her appearance in a safe and proper setting as Mrs Phillips's companion. And *I* will ask the questions. Now go change back into a boy. If you *please*, Miss Osbourne.'

He shot her a half-mocking smile as he left the cabin and she changed as swiftly as possible and was still arranging her cravat when she hurried down the gangway to the awaiting carriage.

Rafe watched her struggles with the starched linen as the carriage drew off, his scrutiny making her fingers clumsier than usual.

'I feel as though someone is strangling me,' she muttered. 'I hate cravats. Why can I not wear a neckcloth like you?'

Rafe clicked his tongue impatiently. He, too, had changed clothes and was dressed in a rough serge coat and simple waistcoat and scuffed boots, yet he still looked far more impressive than she ever would in her respectable gentleman's clothing. It wasn't merely his size and the scars, but a quiet yet undeniable potency that was even more apparent here in the dank heaviness of London than in Egypt.

'Chin up. I shall try and salvage that disaster.'

She did as she was told, trying to keep her eyes on the squabs behind him and not on his face as he leaned towards her. His lids were lowered and his silvery eyes intent as he unravelled her knot and set about retying it. The pressure of his fingers at her throat was gentle, fleeting, but it was hard to breathe. She had an overpowering urge to touch him, even just rest her fingers against his thigh that was so close to hers. She counted out her breath and gave in to the need to look at him. It was absurd to be so happy that he was so close when all he was doing was fixing her cravat, but she was gathering these memories like fireflies in a jar.

She could count his lashes from here, see the fine meshing of grey and green in his eyes, the pressure of bone beneath his cheek and the moonscape of his scarred skin. She wanted so desperately to touch it again. In her mind she leaned forward just a little more, pressing against his fingers, brushing her mouth against his cheek, slipping along his freshly shaven jaw, absorbing the tension of his mouth, soothing it with hers until it softened…

'There.' He sounded as strangled as she felt and when he looked up she stayed there like a beached boat—bare and helpless.

'Cleo… No!'

'I wasn't doing anything.'

'You were thinking it hard enough. Damn it, we are in England now.'

'Is it outside the law to think about kissing in England?'

He leaned back, shoving his hands deep into his pockets.

'You know what I mean.'

'Yes.'

She fell silent and turned to look out the opposite window. It wasn't raining, but it certainly did not look like springtime. She'd expected the city outside the boundaries of the docks to look more like her memories of her village or the murkier memories she had of Dover, but here there was no hint of the green shores they'd passed—just brown and grey buildings with dark, blank windows. The people were also dressed in sombre colours and walked swiftly, heads down.

Very soon she would be swept up into this world and Rafe would continue in his. He had fulfilled his task—she was in London and safe, at least for the moment. Today or tomorrow might well be her last day in his company.

It was over. The most harrowing, intense, terrifying, exhilarating, confusing month of her life was over.

She would have to make the best of this as she had always done before, but for the first time in her life she wondered if she could. With this strange friendship she'd let slip the protective shield she had not even realised she wore until it fell away. Without it she felt both weaker and stronger. She'd allowed herself to feel and show need for the second time in her life and, unlike William, she knew that Rafe was worth it. Whether or not he could love her in return, she loved him.

She'd known she was heading down this path, but somehow she'd hoped she might avoid the destination. It felt like another part of her come home. Another wing unfurling as she crawled out of her chrysalis. There was so much of her that was coming to life these past weeks she wasn't certain she recognised herself any longer, but she was certain it was right. All this—this unravelling and knitting back together was right. Even if loving Rafe led to pain, it was still right.

She hugged herself against a sudden convulsive shiver. Without a word Rafe unfastened his coat and draped it over her legs. She tried to hand it back to him.

'I don't...'

'You are freezing. I don't want you falling ill.'

His arms were a folded bar across his chest. The shirt was of rough cotton and the sleeves a little short, just showing the fine dark hair on his forearms. They were rising in goosebumps and she realised he, too, must be cold. She shifted close to him on the seat and spread his coat over both their legs.

'We'll share.'

His arms were shifting, rising and falling where they rested against his chest. Her leg wasn't quite touching his, but she could feel its warmth, as if he was reaching out to her despite himself. She eased a little closer still, stopping when the fabric of his trousers touched hers.

'Cleo.' There was entreaty in his voice.

She moved away a little and wet her lips, the words forcing their way through the sudden ache in her throat. 'I liked being close to you, that is all. I'm not asking for a cottage and a garden. Just…some warmth.'

'Ijo de cabron.' He slipped his arm around her waist, pulling her on to his lap just like he had during the storm, tugging the coat around them both. 'There. Now we're close. But it's only for warmth in this mud puddle they call English weather.'

'Fine.'

She leaned her forehead against his cheek, her stomach contracting at the transition between the stubbled jaw and the smooth but twisted skin. He didn't like when she touched his scars, but she did, it was almost a compulsion. It took her closer to that fear of what might have been—he could have died, just as she could have died in Syene. As her mother and father had died. As Dash might even now be dead. Life was fleeting and gave no quarter. There was no fate, no faith, no guiding force watching over her, either evil or good. There was only life—this moment before it passed into another and was gone. She would weather this, too, but for now she wanted to be close.

As the tension eased from her she sighed, letting her eyes drift shut a moment. His arms jerked about her, as if he'd been prodded, and he seemed to relax them by force. But his voice was as tense as his muscles when he spoke.

'This is madness…'

She nodded and they stayed like that, shifting with the coach, his fingers resting on the back of her hand, brushing gently at the soft skin just at the junction of her fingers. He had such a gentle touch, as if she were a little chick dropped from a nest. But it didn't mask the strength beneath. That was as evident as the arousal that pulsed into life beneath her thighs as the carriage rumbled on. A moan bubbled through her at that telling pressure. He wanted her, too. For whatever reason and for however long, he felt at least a little of this burning. She could feel the urgent pressure of the blood pulsing at his neck—warm and alive—and she turned to touch her mouth to it. He tasted of the desert, of open space and vast nights and…hers.

When she was like this it felt so absolutely true. That he was *hers*.

This man, this touch.

She arched her hand, slipping his fingers between hers and clasping them. She should have resisted the urge because he groaned, moving her off his lap and leaning his head back against the squabs as he addressed the roof.

'Blast it, I'm doing it again. This is too serious to be taken lightly, Cleo. When we've dealt with Pettifer and are back on the *Hesperus*, you and I are going to talk. There is…something I must tell you.'

Something I must tell you. That sounded as ominous as al-Mizan's voice coming to claim her in her nightmares. Or William's voice the last time she'd seen him—in the dark evening outside their lodgings in Greece, two furtive figures, one with a very furtive secret. They'd often met like that, but this time his message had said he had something to tell her. She'd been in seventh heaven, certain he meant to propose and they would marry and return to England together. She'd never considered 'something' meant a wife and three children back in England. She'd learned a lot that week.

'What *thing*?' she asked, her voice dull and flat.

'Not now. We've arrived.'

The carriage turned off a main thoroughfare and slowed to a halt. Rafe reached across for the door and paused.

'Remember you are not to speak, Cleo. I will do the talking.'

His voice was abrupt and it snapped her temper back to her defence.

'What am I to do if I have questions? Write you a note? Whisper in your ear?'

His shoulder rose as if she'd done just that and tickled him in the process.

'*Carajo.* Very well, but keep your voice low and let's hope he just thinks you're young and effete.'

'I will speak like this.' She dropped her voice into a husky rasp. 'Will this do, sir?'

He exhaled a harsh breath.

'It will if you're trying to find a position on the stage at Drury Lane, or worse. If you must speak, try mumbling. I will translate. I'm not being stubborn for the sake of it, Cleo. People like Pettifer are dangerous; they are always on the verge of capsizing and seize at everything they can to stay afloat. Let's make certain it is not you.'

Mr Pettifer was a small man with eyes like a curious calf and a halo of soft brown curls and a bright red waistcoat embroidered all over with birds and flowers. He looked... sweet. Cleo mistrusted him immediately.

Rafe rejected his offer of ale and asked the innkeeper for whisky. Cleo wanted to demand some for herself as well, but refrained. She watched as Rafe picked up his glass and inspected Pettifer with such leisure that the man slowly began turning red. He gave a little laugh and tilted his head to one side, rather like the robins on his waistcoat.

'Well, sir? Your...friend was most insistent I meet you and here I am.'

'So you are. We have a mutual acquaintance, Mr Pettifer.'

'We do? I mean...how wonderful. May I ask whom?'

'A Mr Arthur Osbourne, lately of Egypt.'

'Osbourne. Charming fellow, charming. Good eye. Very good eye indeed.'

'So I hear. You share a penchant for mummies, yes?'

'We share a fascination with all things extraordinary.'

'Have you heard from him of late?'

'Oh, not for a year, I think.'

Rafe set down his glass and leaned forward.

'Lying will only make this conversation longer and more painful than necessary. You corresponded with him and you recently took shipment of several cases of mummified remains. Nod if you agree with those facts.'

Pettifer's head wobbled before it settled into a reluctant nod.

'Good. You owe payment on that shipment, Mr Pettifer. I am here to collect it on his behalf.'

'I assure you, I dispatched payment...'

Cleo leaned forward, but Rafe raised his hand.

'I said do not lie. I haven't the patience.'

Pettifer's smile held, but his eyes darted from side to side as if surveying an internal inventory of lies. Finally, he sighed.

'I am certain some accommodation could be made.'

'*Will* be made. A man of mine will come to collect first thing tomorrow. Be certain to have payment ready or those mummies just might take on a life of their own and do a little damage to your exhibits during the dark hours.'

'Surely there is no need for violence.'

'That is completely up to you, Pettifer.' He paused. 'Now that we've settled that, tell me what Osbourne did to set Boucheron on his tail.'

Pettifer's cherubic face flushed from his shirt points to his carefully brushed curls. He flapped his hands.

'Pray lower your voice. Osbourne may have been so foolish as to challenge that man, but I am not.'

'Challenge him? How? Don't slide away now, Pettifer. Just answer the question.'

'I do not know for certain. Osbourne always had more ambition than sense. It was clear from his correspondence he did not enjoy taking part in supplying antiquities of… dubious origin to creditable establishments and collectors. It went against his fantasy of becoming respectable. In his last letter he asked me for the direction of someone trustworthy at the British Museum and whether I had heard who had acquired a large granite statue of Horus sent recently from Luxor.'

Cleo clenched her hands but Rafe gently pressed his boot on hers.

'And what did you reply?' he asked.

'I asked what he meant by trustworthy. He did not write back.'

'In other words you evaded his questions.'

'Well, I felt it best not to become involved. Boucheron has connections in my little world, even in England. I tend my little garden and keep out of others'.'

'Of course. So do you know who acquired this statue?'

'Not in England, though I did hear a statue of Horus along with a most excellent sarcophagus were acquired by the Louvre for well over one thousand pounds.'

Cleo swallowed. No wonder her father had begun to turn against Boucheron—she was quite certain he had never seen a fraction of those sums.

Rafe's gaze captured hers before turning back to Pettifer.

'Have you by any chance heard from Osbourne's son?'

Pettifer frowned.

'No. I have never had the felicity to meet him. Why?'

Cleo wished she could have heard a shadow of a lie in his answer, but she felt he spoke an uncomplicated truth. If Dash had arrived in England before her, he had not contacted Pettifer.

'Never mind why,' Rafe answered. 'Should you hear from him or of him you will place an advertisement in *The Times* saying Mr P. has an item for Mr G. and then watch the advertisements the following day for instructions. Do you understand?'

'I really don't see why—'

'Think mummies in the night, Pettifer...'

Pettifer sighed and nodded. '*The Times*. Mr P. has an item for Mr G.'

'Good.' Rafe stood and Cleo followed suit. 'Anything else, Patrick?'

Cleo shook her head. She felt deflated and weary as she followed Rafe outside into the drizzle. It wasn't merely what they'd learned from Pettifer.

We need to talk.

'Thank you for helping me, Rafe.'

'You are welcome. You had no idea those so-called souvenirs were being sold as actual antiquities, did you?'

'No. Boucheron must be mad, selling them to museums. The risk is enormous.'

'That depends. If a single piece was suspected, Boucheron could claim he himself had acquired it in ignorance. But if your father had intimated this was no innocent mistake, but a large-scale endeavour, his reputation would be ruined and no one would buy from him. I would wager the infamous book al-Mizan was sent to retrieve was a record your father was keeping of these items. Chris told me he heard Boucheron transported a large shipment of antiquities on a ship to Marseilles only a few weeks before we sailed. God knows how many of those were forgeries.'

'What shall we do?'

'I will have a word with Chris. He knows these people. I don't want you involved in this in any way... For your brother's sake.'

She had been about to speak, but his last words stopped her, as he must have known they would. It galled her to be shut out like this, but he was right. Clearly Boucheron had ties in London as well. Until she was certain Dash was safe, she must keep out of it.

He appeared to be waiting for her to say something, but the only words that came were, 'I wish I was a man. Being a woman is like running uphill with pebbles in one's shoes.'

His smile was weak and there was no sign of humour in his eyes—they were far more grey than green and the scars were grey-tinged as well.

'I wish you'd been a man, too. This would have been much easier. But you will be safe with this widow and surrounded by a host of mouldy antiquarians. For all you know you might discover you enjoy being in a household like Soane's. Whatever slurs you cast on them, I can see how much you love that world. I'll wager you'll all too soon be fending off sonnets and marriage proposals by the dozen.'

There was conviction in his words, as if he'd already settled her future in his mind and was casting her away on the current like a paper boat.

'Don't be foolish,' she snapped, struggling to contain the gnawing pain in her chest. But then the anger, too, faded away, a paper fire only, leaving her cold and ashen and resigned.

She'd known what he was—he was far more a nomad than ever Gamal was, because Mr Rafael Grey had no set route to travel. His very being was defined by chance—chance encounters with those who might need his services for a while before cutting themselves loose again once their objective was fulfilled. He was instrumental, incidental. He had no substance of his own to anyone except Birdie, his brother and, for a brief tragic while, his little nephew.

And for an even briefer while, to her.

Which was her mistake, not his.

Chapter Eighteen

Rafe followed Cleo out of the carriage and up the gangway, gathering his resolve with each step.

He could no longer avoid the inevitable. They'd crossed the issues of Cleo's finances, lodgings and occupation from the list. That meant she was safe. More importantly, she was no longer in his care.

It was time to tell her the truth.

She stopped in the middle of the deck, raising her face to the first drops of rain.

'I'd forgotten about English rain,' she said. 'It's so different from rain in Egypt or the storms at sea, but it feels like…home.'

Home.

He raised his own face to the sullen flicking of cold pins and needles and rubbed his chest. His pulse felt thick, as if struggling through a peat bog.

'Come inside.'

She followed without a word. Once inside the cabin, she went to stand by the table, leaning one hand on its surface.

He felt as anxious as she looked. The time of truth had come and he had no idea why this was so very hard. Why he had not just said it weeks ago. It was not such a great matter after all, was it?

My name is not Rafe Grey, though that *is* who I am… whom I have been for most of my life.

My name is Rafael Edward James Braden Edgerton and I happen to be the Duke of Greybourne and it is now time for me to face my past and my future and I would like to ask you to be part of it.

Perfectly sensible speech.

I am the Duke of Greybourne.

Just say it.

'Rafe? Are you well? You look…pale.'

'I…uh. My name is not Rafe.'

Her brows drew together.

'I know that. It is Rafael.'

'No, what I meant to say was…' Oh, hell, why was this so hard? It felt as though he was about to voluntarily walk off a cliff.

No, it felt as though he was about to kill Rafe Grey. Reach in and murder him with his own hands just as his father had once tried to murder that poor maid.

And he had no idea what would take his place.

He finally opened that door an inch wider. Time to let her in.

'My father was a violent man.' The words left him in a rush. 'My first real memory of my father was when he broke my brother's arm. I have no idea why. Not that there had to be a reason—it could be anything. That final time, before I left, we were in chapel and he tried to strangle Susan, our maid, simply because she laughed. I remember every second of that day except for the few short moments when I lunged at him to pull him off and was thrashed by him. Those moments are…gone, as if I'd slept through them. They've never come back. The next day I ran away to enlist and that's where I met Birdie. For years I tested myself to see if that strain of violence was in me. I was certain it would find its way to the surface sooner or later. So I became a soldier and a mercenary and—'

'It isn't in you, Rafe,' she interrupted with finality.

'You don't know that.'

'Yes, I do. I think you do as well; at least I hope you do. There is a different between using force when you must and being ruled by it or being blind to its effect on others.'

He gave a small laugh.

'Is there?'

'I believe there is. I don't think you allow yourself to be ruled by anything but conscience and caution, and you are certainly anything but blind to others. You must know you are not like your father.'

He breathed in and out. 'I prefer to believe I am not. I have never felt the pull of it, but the fact is that violence has shaped my life in too many ways to count. But that is not what I wanted to tell you...it is merely so you can understand why I did what I did...'

He rubbed his forehead, wishing the words would somehow appear out of the muddle. Now that the moment was here he wanted to stop it, delay it just a little further. Tell Chris to raise anchor and take them back into the emptiness of the ocean so she would have time to absorb the truth. Not when the very next moment she must go play companion to a widow and her lapdog and he must go confront his living ghosts.

He'd made ill use of his time with her, hemmed in by conscience and pointless convention, just as she'd said. He might not wholly be his father's son, but perhaps he was more his mother's son than he'd hoped.

He breathed deeply, searching for that elusive streak of valiance that would propel him forward. Cleo came and took his hands; they felt clammy in her warm clasp.

'Rafe? Something is wrong. I can see it is. What is it? Just *tell* me.'

He'd known this was coming the moment he'd received the letter informing him of his father's death. Rafe Grey, all of twenty years old, was about to be extinguished. Rafael Edgerton, Duke of Greybourne, had to step back on to the stage and he had not the faintest idea who he was.

Just tell her and make it real. Rafe Grey is no more… He'd never truly existed.

Just *tell* her.

'Cleo. I'm not…'

There was a clumping as someone ran along the corridor and Cleo dropped his hands. Rafe hoped whoever it was stopped before they reached Chris's cabin, but then the door swung open and Birdie strode in, a letter in his hand and his usually equable countenance twisted with anxious tension. Cleo moved towards him, her eyes wide with concern.

'Birdie, what is it?'

'It's a letter from Paul, Elmira's brother.'

Rafe caught Birdie by the shoulders and felt them shaking. If he'd ever wondered how much Birdie cared for Elmira, he knew now.

'What happened?'

'She's not dead. But he writes she's ill. This letter was sent three weeks ago, Rafe. Three *weeks* ago. I must leave *now.*'

'Of course. We'll ride out as soon as we find horses.'

'You needn't—'

'I'm not letting you go alone. It's a long way to the Lakes and you'll need someone to see you don't ride yourself into exhaustion and a ditch. You'll be in no state to help Elmira if you do.'

'You have your own affairs—'

'They've waited until now; they will wait a little longer. Go pack and I'll hire the horses.'

Birdie nodded, his mouth a tense downward bow. He cast a quick look at Cleo.

'I'm sorry, Miss Cleo.'

To Rafe's surprise, and Birdie's as well, Cleo hugged him fiercely.

'Don't be foolish. Godspeed, Birdie.'

He mumbled something incoherent and hurried out.

'Is there anything I can do?' Cleo asked. Rafe considered and discarded blurting out his admission. Cleo was safe for the moment and what he had to say was something he could barely manage when he was coherent, let alone with Birdie's fear hanging over him.

'Yes. Go with Chris to this Mrs Phillips and wait for your brother. When I return London we will finish this conversation, but now I must go with Birdie.'

'Of course you must. Please be careful, both of you.'

He nodded and made it to the door before turning back, almost by compulsion. He had no idea what to say that could be said in the minutes ticking by at Birdie's expense, so instead he crossed the room back to her. He raised her and placed her neatly on the table before clasping her face gently between his hands. They were still cold and now also shaking a little as he brushed the feathery hair back from her cheeks and brow. He wanted to take her with them, have her ride by his side and Birdie's. He had no clear idea what he was doing, but he didn't want to leave her here. He didn't want to leave her.

She smiled and brushed her hands over his, slipping her fingers between his.

He kissed her hard and she opened to him with her warm generosity, her hands threading through his hair and over his nape before drawing back.

'You must hurry.'

'I know. Stay out of trouble, Pat.'

Chapter Nineteen

Lincoln's Inn Fields, London—two weeks later...

The tall arched windows of Soane House were bright with candlelight though it was only just turning dark. It seemed to stand forward from the row of rain-drenched, dark-windowed and dark-bricked houses, a happy invitation to enter and be amazed.

Rafe shoved his hands deeper into his pockets, gathering his resolve. Somewhere behind that cheerful façade was one Miss Cleopatra Osbourne, companion and thorn in his side. He'd rehearsed his admission *ad nauseum* during the interminable ride north and back, but now the moment of truth was upon him he felt the words fizzle and fade once more. It wasn't the words that would matter in the end; it was Cleo.

In a matter of minutes Cleo would decide which path his life took. There had been times when others held his life in their hands, but strangely he'd never felt as powerless before fate as he did now.

He'd missed her every moment of these long, long two weeks. All his faculties for gauging danger, for scanning the future for pitfalls, had been engaged with her. His mind had populated the dank grey skies and muddy roads and indifferent posting houses with an accounting of the past weeks from the first moment she'd appeared in his room in Syene. He'd leafed through every image, fixing it in his memory as if it was already fading in the damp of his new life.

It scared him because that was what he'd done after Jacob's death as he'd tended to Edge's misery, holding his own inside. He'd held each memory of his nephew like a drop of dew, willing it not to break and spill. And now he was doing the same with her as if she'd already turned her back on him and begun walking her own path, without him.

Sometimes he was convinced she must care for him as he did for her. That it could not merely be friendship and gratitude and the physical fascination of an undeniably passionate woman. But he couldn't get past the fact that, despite all that had happened between them, he recognised in her that strength that would allow her to move on despite tragedies and loss. She might already be consigning him to the trash heap of her past, determined to make the best of what she now had.

He'd thought...he'd truly believed he was the same, but she'd snatched that fiction from him. He knew he could manage if he had to, but for the first time in his life, he didn't want to. He needed her—her love, her hands holding his, her eyes telling him she wanted to be with him. He wanted to make her smile and keep her safe. With him.

He should be happy for her if she was settling into her new life. It was unfair to want her to be as confused and agonised by this separation as he was, yet he wanted precisely that.

He wanted, quite desperately, for her to need him.

He squared his shoulders and brushed the drizzle from his face, preparing himself. He'd just stepped on to the path when the door opened and a figure stepped out, leading a small mop of a dog. Rafe shifted back into the shadows and watched as they crossed the road towards the square, his heart picking up speed as if in the presence of danger.

The storm had left leaves all over the path and the dog snuffled happily at the damp debris, its long hair gathering samples as it went. With her face hidden by a bonnet, a pelisse most likely borrowed as it was both too large and too short, and her purposeful stride reduced to the dog's shuffle, he might easily have walked by her on the street without even noticing.

But then she looked up at the sky as if out of a deep hole and it was like waking up in the vastness of the desert, the soft halo of a sunrise behind the hills. Again he felt the same blessing of being alive that had begun to unfurl in him since he'd met Cleo. Those weeks in the desert and on the *Hesperus* he'd felt...content.

He rubbed his chest, trying to still the nervous thumping. Then he took a deep breath and came up the path behind her.

'Hello, Cleo-Pat.'

Both she and the dog jumped. The dog gave a throaty cough, but after its first outrage came to snuffle at his boots. Rafe crouched down to pet the tubby ball of hair, buying time.

'How does he see where he's going?' he asked, pulling the soggy skeleton of a leaf from its fur. 'What's your name, little fellow?'

'Perseus, but we call him Percy.' Her voice was muffled and it was a moment before she spoke again. 'Thank you for sending me word so promptly that Mrs Herndale was recovered. I was worried for Birdie.'

He risked looking up and wished her face was in its expressive mode. It was unfair that just when he needed her to show something, she could flatten everything out. Her skin was still darker than the approved English complexion and strands of her short hair were escaping the confines of her bonnet, feathering on her forehead and cheeks.

He scratched the dog's head, took another deep breath and stood. Now she had to look up to meet his gaze, but it gave him no real advantage. Her uptilted face and the sweep of her throat were so familiar he felt his throat tighten with something between pain and relief. It was still Cleo.

'You look tired, Rafe.'

Definitely still Cleo.

'I have just arrived from the north.'

'Have your affairs not gone well? Is aught wrong with your family?'

'I don't know. I haven't seen them yet.'

Her brows took wing.

'Why not? I thought that would be your first order of business.'

My first order of business was to see you.

He didn't say it because she was right. Once he told her the truth, going to Greybourne should be his first order of business. He had to face his demons and discover precisely what he was about to offer before he did. She deserved a home, stability…the promise of her own pack of jackals. If he could not find it inside him to offer her that, he should not offer her anything at all. She must be able to trust him and that meant he would have to trust her.

He waited for the slap of fear and it didn't come. Of all the shifting, roiling chaos inside him, that was solid—he might not know who the Duke of Greybourne was, but he knew who Cleopatra Osbourne was and he trusted her.

'You needn't answer me if you don't wish,' she said, cutting into his thoughts and hurrying on before he could recover his wits. 'Chris wrote to me yesterday. He has been very good at following your orders to keep an eye on me. He has even offered to review the article I am writing for the *Gazette*.'

'Has he? Kind of him.'

Her brows rose slightly at his tone.

'It is kind. He is a good man.'

His unwelcome burst of jealousy faded.

'He is. The very best. I'll be happy to review it, as well, if you like. What is it about?'

Her dimples finally appeared.

'It is an account of my journey to Nubia and back. Expurgated, of course.'

'No mention of scarred mercenaries, I hope? I prefer to operate in the shadows.'

'You are very inconspicuous, indeed, Mr Grey. And, no, you are not featured in my article. I knew you wouldn't appreciate the notoriety. I am writing about al-Mizan, however. I wish I knew more of him; I find myself regretting I did not speak with him after all.'

'I find myself grateful you didn't.'

'I thought you liked him.'

'I do. I appreciate sensible people.'

She smiled, but her tone was wistful. 'I don't think I am very sensible, not truly. If I were, I wouldn't be talking to a man in a darkened square within sight of my employer's window.'

'I'll amend that. You are part-sensible, part-impulsive, and an assemblage of several dozen other conflicting parts.'

'Goodness. I sound like a mad aunt's quilt.'

'Hardly. More like one of those Dutch paintings with everything happening all at once, but at the centre there's a joyous, steadfast core.'

It was hardly a gallant compliment, but she flushed and looked a little stunned. He had no idea where that strange thought had come from and it wasn't until he'd spoken the words that he realised how true they were. All those conflicting parts might turn him into a confused, lustful boy, but it was that deep, calm core of hers that made his breathing ease and settle when he was with her. It was a strange feeling and he hadn't noticed it until he'd felt its absence these past two weeks.

God, he'd missed her.

Leaves skittered along the path around them, whispering against the damp earth. Above them the trees were rustling with growing impatience.

Make a move, man! Just tell her.

He shoved his hands into his pockets, encountering the little parcel there. He fished it out and shoved it at her.

'I brought you something. I saw it in the market in Ambleside and remembered the story you told me. It's nothing. A jest.'

She took it with a quick glance at him and unfolded it to reveal a rolled length of blue ribbon.

'Rafe! It is just like the one I stole from Annie Packham.' Her voice was muted, but he could feel that welling of emotion in her she fought so hard to keep at bay. He felt absurdly accomplished that he'd found something that could do that to her. He wanted to wrap his hands around hers and cocoon that silly strip of ribbon between them.

He took a step forward.

'Miss! Miss!'

They both turned to see a small figure bundled in a shawl and mobcap hurrying up the path.

'That's Betsy, Mrs Phillips's maid,' Cleo said with resignation just as the young woman came to a stop several paces away, eyeing Rafe warily.

'Is this fellow bothering you, miss?'

Cleo's dimples quivered.

'No, Betsy. He is a friend of the family and, despite appearances, he is quite harmless.'

Betsy's face hid none of her scepticism.

'Mrs Phillips saw you from the window and sent me to fetch you and Percy back so you can be ready in time for the guests, miss.'

'Thank you, Betsy.'

If Cleo's quiet words were a hint, Betsy ignored it. She

stood, arms folded, all five feet of her radiating disapproval.

'It's coming on to rain, miss,' she added pointedly. It was true—the heavy clouds were succumbing once again to their weight, dropping big melancholy drops through the leaves.

Cleo sighed and looked back at Rafe.

'I must go. I'm glad Birdie and Mrs Herndale are well.'

She hesitated and he pushed back his frustration, but there was nothing he could do.

You're not in Egypt any longer, fool. This is London.

'I will come by tomorrow to make a more formal entrance, Miss Osbourne. Will you be here?'

She smiled, brushed away a drop of rain that splattered on her cheek and gathered the snuffling dog in her arms.

'Where else might I be?'

Chapter Twenty

'Well, about time you returned to London,' Chris said as he handed Rafe a towel. 'And in the nick of time, too. Cesario has come on stage.'

Rafe dried his rain-soaked face and hair, but his mind was still in the windblown square, kicking him for having once again let the moment slide away. If ever he'd needed proof of his cowardice, his fear of putting his fate to the touch was conclusive evidence. It should have been the first thing out of his mouth: 'My name isn't Rafe Grey. It is Rafael Edgerton, Duke of Greybourne, and by the way—will you marry me?'

Well, perhaps not quite like that…

'Are you even listening to me?' Chris demanded. 'I said Cesario is here.'

'Who is where?'

'I'll translate. Dashford Osbourne is in London.'

That finally penetrated Rafe's self-flagellating fog.

'Are you certain?'

'Benja has been keeping an eye open on new arrivals and when he heard the *Nightingale* was arriving from Egypt he went to watch the disembarkation and spotted him right away. He said the resemblance to Cleo was unmistakable. He followed him to the Four Bells where the boy took a room. Gave his name to the innkeeper as Thomas Mowbray.'

'Don't tell me. That's the name of some Shakespearean fool.'

'Of sorts. In the play he's a nobleman loyal to King Richard the Second who banishes him for a crime he himself committed.'

'Hmph. Clearly he has issues with the deceased Mr Osbourne.'

'Fathers do appear to be a bone of contention of late.'

Rafe cast him a malevolent look.

'Don't tempt me to strike back, Chris.' He tossed the towel over the back of a char. 'Let's go there.'

'Unfortunately, he's no longer there.'

'You lost him?'

'I didn't know you were in London so I went there, but the room was empty. Apparently the boy used it as a decoy. Benja and the others are out searching the other inns.'

'Come along, then. I want the young pup secured as soon as possible.'

'Where will you take him? Here or your place in Lambeth?'

He hesitated.

'I'd best take him directly to Cleo. Then…we shall see. I need to see Edge, too…' He hesitated. 'I've had my contacts keep track while I've been up north. Apparently he is back and he is married.'

'What? Good Lord, when did he manage that?'

'In Cairo, apparently. To Lady Samantha Carruthers.'

'Lady… Isn't that Lucas Sinclair's sister?'

'The same.'

'Is that good? Bad? Horrific?'

'It is excellent. I hope. The timeline worries me. Three years he stays in Brazil scribbling away, then in a few weeks he apparently traverses Egypt, marries Lady Samantha and returns to England. He's being impetuous and that's out of character. I don't want to see him hurt.'

'Then put him out of his misery and tell him you're alive and well.'

'Once we find Cleo's brother I'll go see him and hope he doesn't plant me a facer. I'd hate to have to pay my visit of ceremony on Cleo tomorrow with a black eye.'

'Your visit of…well, about time. All the more reason we should find Dash before he absconds again.'

'Damn and blast the fool.' Rafe stood in the middle of the Eagle and Crown's courtyard, glaring at the shuttered windows. The room let to Mr Mowbray was as empty as the one in the Four Bells. 'Where the devil has he gone now?'

Chris yawned and wound his scarf tighter against cold air.

'I thought you said he was a scholar? He's being damned cautious.'

'He is a scholar, but he's also Cleo's brother. Clearly mistrust runs in the family.'

'Well, we'll pick up the trail tomorrow. At least we know he's alive and on dry land. Go tell Viola. That should please her.'

He wandered off and Rafe headed in the other direction, staring at nothing as he wove through the alleys towards the main thoroughfare.

Of course he had to tell Cleo right away. Perhaps her delight would melt those careful barricades she'd mounted. Perhaps enough to… To what? She was not the type of woman who would accept a proposal because he'd produced her brother. Or a title and fortune. She would either accept him on his own merits and her own feelings or not at all…

It was the faintest of sounds, but what caught his attention was that he'd heard it before, just after leaving the Eagle and Crown.

One of the most distinctive sounds was that of a man walking with unnatural caution. The denizens of the docks bent on mischief knew better than to make such a mistake.

He paused in the centre of a crossing. There was not enough light for anyone to cast shadows and he did not bother trying to trick the fellow into revealing himself.

'Dash Osbourne, you're lucky Cleo is fond of you because I'm tempted to break your leg so you'll stay put and not cause us any more headaches.'

He waited.

A figure moved out of the alley and the faint light from the tavern down the road raised a reddish glint off the man's dark hair. Rafe felt an absurd, almost painful relief. Finally.

'You're the one who left the message for me in Alexandria?' the man asked.

He even sounded like Cleo. Rafe was so tempted to grab the boy and truss him up safely before something happened.

'Yes. What the devil are you about, setting up lodgings at half the taverns in London?'

'I thought I noticed someone following me when I disembarked. I thought perhaps there'd been someone on the ship with me after all and I needed to be certain I was wrong before I went to look for Cleo. Then I heard you speaking with that man about me.' He took another step closer, but there was still a good six yards between them. 'Do you know where Cleo is?'

'She's companion to a Mrs Phillips at the house of Mr John Soane in Lincoln Inn Fields.'

'Companion? *Cleo?*'

'I know, it doesn't sit well, but for the moment it serves its purpose. I will take you there now. I think under the circumstances we will be forgiven for the late hour.' He moved forward, but the younger man stepped back, holding up his hand to stop him.

'I shall go on my own.'

'Cleo will have my hide if I don't see you there safely.'

'I'm going on my own. I've heard of Mr Soane and can find my way.'

'This is ridiculous. I'll follow you, you know.'

'If you insist. Waste of a cab fare.'

Rafe debated actually trussing the fellow up, but though delivering him to Cleo held an appeal, delivering him bruised and hog-tied didn't. Instead, he followed at a reasonable distance and when Dash Osbourne waved down a hackney on a busy thoroughfare, he did the same.

When his hackney stopped before the distinctive house of Mr Soane, Dash Osbourne was already on the steps. He looked back as Rafe descended from his cab and gave him a slight salute of the hand. Then the door opened and light and the sound of company poured into the cool street.

Rafe cursed beneath his breath as he paid the cabbie— he'd forgotten Soane was entertaining that evening. He stood on the other side of the road until it began to drizzle once more. England thus far wasn't proving very welcoming and he wished once again he could somehow transport himself and Cleo back to the desert. Back to travelling with Birdie and Gamal, helping her evade Kabir's jealous nips and talking into the night. Knowing what he knew now, he would make better use of his time with her.

He wished he could see the look on her face when Dash appeared, but he had no intention of walking into a social event. He could hardly present himself as Mr Grey to people who might already be Cleo's friends and certainly not as the Duke of Greybourne. That was not how he wished for Cleo to discover the truth about him.

He turned westwards, walking swiftly. The frustration that had been plaguing him now for weeks was reaching fever pitch. He should be happy, delighted even. He'd brought her safely to London, found her a position, found her young fool of a brother. But he wasn't. He didn't know what he was any longer. He was becoming soppier than Hamlet—swinging between antic moods and melodrama. He was becoming ridiculous.

And careless.

On the docks he'd been cautious and alert, but as he headed through the drizzle on to Duke Street, his mind remained by that well-lit house on the square. When he felt the oh-so-gentle tug he acted out of instinct to disarm the pest. He couldn't even blame the cutpurse for what happened.

As he knocked away the hand trying to separate his purse from his person, the pickpocket gave a surprised squawk, lurched backwards and slipped on the slimy cobbles. Rafe had just managed to grab the man's coat and haul him upright when he felt the sting to his thigh.

He was acquainted with that sensation through long experience with the wrong end of a knife. He shoved the man against the wall and pinned his knife hand. It wasn't a large knife, but sharp enough to slit a man's purse from its strings without being noticed. The man stared wide-eyed at Rafe and then down at the darkening stain on Rafe's trouser, visible even in the dark.

'Gad's truth, I didna mean to—'

'I know, you fool. Blast it. I don't have time for this. Go away.'

'Ye'd best bind it…'

'I don't need barber's advice from a cutpurse. What the devil were you thinking, going after someone my size?'

'The big ones are oft the slowest…begging your pardon, sir. I didna ken you was a blooming soldier. I don't go after swads less they're boozy. I'm no Tyburn blossom.'

Rafe let him go, untied his neckcloth and wound it around his thigh.

'I was in the rifles, not a redcoat, but you've made certain I've a set of red breeches now. What are you still doing here? Waiting to see if I drop dead from this scratch so you can turn scavenger?'

''Tis more than a scratch, that is. Ye might be needing a crocus.'

Rafe gritted his teeth as he tightened the knot.

'I don't need a blasted surgeon. You've done a fine job of cupping me already. You sound like a soldier yourself.'

'Aye, sir. Invalided at Ciudad Rodrigo, sir.'

Rafe sighed and opened his purse. The world could always be depended upon to remind one to count one's blessings.

'Here, take the night off from knuckling.'

'I can't take that, sir!'

'Why not?'

'*Why not?* I've pinked 'ee. T'wouldn't be right.'

'Don't quibble. I deserve to pay for lowering my guard. Try not to guzzle it in one night.'

The man drew himself up. 'I don't indulge in spirits, sir.'

'You're a better man than I, then.' Rafe tested his weight on his wounded leg. Pain slashed up and down like a dozen razors had been sown into his flesh.

There would be no visit to Sinclair House tonight. He would be lucky to reach his rooms.

'You can earn it by finding me the closest hackney, Soldier.'

'Fair enough. Pitch yourself at the corner there and I'll nab one for 'ee.'

Rafe had no idea how old his attacker was, but he was undeniably swift on his feet. By the time Rafe dragged himself to the end of the road, there was a hackney waiting, the driver squinting at him suspiciously.

'I don't want trouble with the Watch, see?' he growled, waving his whip, but the pickpocket merely snorted in disdain as he helped Rafe into the grimy vehicle.

'Pipe down, Jarvis. He's a flash swell and well equipped.' And then to Rafe, 'Best see a barber, anyhow, sir.'

Rafe shook his head and shoved the coin into the man's hand and after a moment's hesitation the pickpocket melted back into the dark. Rafe gave the hackney driver the direction of the rooms he kept for his use in London, leaned back carefully and prepared himself for a long, painful ride.

Chapter Twenty-One

There were benefits to living, however temporarily, in what more closely resembled a museum than a home, Cleo thought. It wasn't merely Mr Soane's wondrous collection of antiquities that filled every corner of his house, but the fascinating people it drew like moths about a scholarly flame. They were very different from the dubious characters in her father's circles. Right now, for example, her employer Mrs Phillips was happily engaged in a heated discussion about the origins of the myth of Medea with two scholars and a few moments ago Cleo had a fascinating discussion regarding the latest news on the decipherment of the hieroglyphics.

Dash would undoubtedly enjoy himself in such a setting. Usually so would she, except she was…distracted. Her thoughts returned stubbornly again and again to the dark square and to Rafe. She could almost feel the blue ribbon burning a hole in her reticule.

A strange, gleeful, hopeful ball of warmth kept appearing somewhere deep in her chest, like a bubble struggling to rise.

He'd brought her a ribbon and would visit her tomorrow. A formal visit.

His tale of his father's violence made sense of so many

things about him and had even given her hope… She knew he liked her, was attracted to her. She'd seen it even in those brief moments in the square. She didn't know if there was more than that, if he felt any of the harsh, deep-cut need that struck her every time she thought of him or saw him or woke to a day empty of his presence.

She knew so little of his history and he knew all of hers, yet she felt she knew him better than she'd ever known a person, perhaps even better than she knew herself, for she was discovering she was not at all as she had thought all her life. Not cold, not wholly self-sufficient, not accepting of her fate.

She was alive and bursting with a need to be with him. Not just for what he might give her, but because more than ever she felt she had so much to give him. She was right for him.

He'd brought her a ribbon and was coming tomorrow. All she had to do was make it through this evening and the night and…

The crowd before her parted, creating a temporary path between her and a tall, dark-haired man who stood speaking with Mr Soane. Her heart catapulted up into her throat and for one joyous moment she thought Rafe had decided to act sooner than anticipated on his promise to visit.

But then her heart fell to the floor, flapping like a landed fish. The resemblance was uncanny—the slightly aquiline slant of the nose and the determined chin, the sun-warmed skin and that slow curve of a smile… But this was not Rafe. It was the jaw, bare of scars, that which made her chest contract and her eyes burn as they had each time loneliness caught her these past weeks.

Mr Soane's footman was just passing and Cleo rose quietly and stopped him before he entered the servants' passageway. 'Who is that tall man speaking with Mr Soane, Henry?'

The footman glanced over her shoulder.

'That is Lord Edward Edgerton, miss. He is here with Lady Edward.' His nod indicated a tall woman with laughing blue eyes and dark hair.

Cleo knew from his tone Henry had more to tell her so she motioned him towards the back stairs leading to the kitchens. It was no doubt not at all the thing to gossip with the servants, but she *had* to know.

'What do you know of them, Henry?'

'Well, miss, they are new back from Egypt and newly wed, too. She's a Sinclair,' he said and she nodded though it meant nothing to her. 'Everyone's talking about how it's he and Lady Edward that wrote those *Desert Boy* novels.' Henry allowed himself a gratified smile at her expression of shock. 'It's true, miss! They appeared tonight quite by surprise, too. Not that they would be turned away, not in a million years. Not the authors of *Desert Boy* books and brother to the Disappearing Duke, to boot. I don't doubt Mr Soane is right pleased they've come.'

'The Disappearing Duke?' she whispered.

'Yes, miss. Everyone knows the story. Lord Edward's elder brother, heir to the Duke of Greybourne, he ran away to the army when he was a boy. He's the new Duke a year now, but there's been not a peep from him. There are even rumours he's dead, which means Lord Edward will be the next Duke. Now if you'll excuse me, miss. I must bring these downstairs.'

She nodded and stood aside, staring at nothing.

Was this what Rafe had wanted to tell her? Her mind had taken her fears quite a few places these past weeks—a wife, children, an engagement, an illness, a crime... She'd imagined them all.

Or at least she thought she had. She hadn't imagined a duchy. It should be a relief compared with all the scenarios her mind had conjured, but it wasn't. And just now in the square...

That was what he'd meant to tell her. Not her foolish dreams, just his conscience giving him no rest once more.

No wonder he'd tried so hard to keep her in her place all this time. He was no fool, he must have seen she'd begun to weave him into her dreams...her cottage and her pack of jackals... He done his best to gently dismantle the bridges she kept insisting on building between them.

He might not be a scoundrel like William, but she'd been as blind with him as she had been ten years before. And of the scenarios she imagined, this revelation set an ocean between them as solidly as if he *were* already married.

Perhaps this was what it would feel like to suddenly discover the secret of the hieroglyphs—signs that had been before her all along were blindingly suddenly clear. Discussions between Rafe and Birdie, Captain Chris's taunts... Bears and Dukes and Viola and Greybeard...

Greybourne. Grey. Bourne.

She welcomed the anger, opened the door for it and dragged it in by the collar.

He and Captain Chris had talked over her head as though she was a child. All along he'd treated her a little like a child, hadn't he? Stay here, Cleo. Eat. Sleep. Be good, Cleo.

Throwing plates was too good for him! She should drop a pyramid on him. Feed him to Kabir and toss the remains to the Nile crocodiles.

She shrank back into the shadows as a group came through the passage. It was Mr Soane and the woman Henry had pointed out as Lady Edward. They headed to the display room which was filled floor to ceiling with prints and paintings.

It was impulse that sent Cleo after them and made her wait until Lady Edwards remained alone in the room. When Cleo entered, the other woman was looking through framed drawings that filled a specially made cupboard that opened like pages of a book, each one hung with framed prints.

'You are Lady Edward Edgerton, are you not?'

Lady Edward turned at Cleo's overly brusque question, surprise and wariness evident on her attractive face.

'Yes. I'm afraid you have the advantage of me, Miss...?'

'Miss Osbourne.' Something flickered in the other woman's eyes and curiosity turned to intentness. Without a doubt her name meant something to Lady Edward. So Rafe had discussed her with his brother, perhaps even consulted on how best to deal with her. 'Are you here because of me?'

'I beg your pardon?' The woman's eyes widened.

'I knew the moment I saw Lord Edward that he must be closely related to the man I knew as Mr Grey. He did mention a brother and, if that is the nature of their relationship, I can understand why he did not see fit to share his true name with me. But that is hardly the point. If you are here by coincidence, I apologise, but if you are here on my account, pray tell him I do not need to be watched like a newborn lamb. He has done enough already.'

Lady Edward hesitated before answering.

'The Greybournes are a stubborn lot. They mean well, though.'

'So I have noticed on both counts. Truly I am grateful for his help thus far, but there is nothing more to be done. And if he is indeed that... Disappearing Duke everyone is gossiping about, clearly he has his own affairs to see to.'

'I find that Edge... Lord Edward has a fixation with seeing things through. Perhaps his brother suffers from the same weakness?'

Cleo snorted.

'That is putting it mildly. I am grateful for his help—I know I might not have succeeded in returning to England without him, but I could have secured a companion's position without his interference. Mrs Phillips might have agreed to employ me as a favour, but she might yet decide to find someone who is not accosted at night by a giant with no manners and a dubious sense of humour.'

'Are you quite certain there is nothing more to be done?' Lady Edward enquired cautiously and Cleo turned to fiddle with the latch on the cupboard, breathing carefully.

Nothing more to be done. Those simple words ripped another hole in her tissue of hope. This revelation meant she had well and truly lost Rafe. Perhaps soon she might have to accept she'd lost Dash as well. Perhaps it was best to accept it all at once. There was no Rafe, no Dash. Time to grow up once again and move on. She dropped the latch and raised her chin.

'Since my brother may have suffered the same fate as my father and I do not believe in the occult, then, yes, there is nothing to be done. Gone is gone.'

She couldn't hold the woman's compassionate gaze. Any moment now she would break and she did not want Lady Edward to report back to Rafe that Miss Cleopatra Osbourne was a hopeless watering pot.

'I had best return to Mrs Phillips before her argument with Mr Thorpe regarding the true nature of Medusa comes to blows.' She tried to smile and went to the door, but compulsion made her turn and the words tumble out of her. 'I do hope Rafe keeps out of trouble. He was very kind and helped me, though I was nothing but trouble for him. I hope to repay the favour some day, though I cannot see how.' On a final impulse she added: 'I dare say you will think it forward of me to say so, but I do hope you and Lord Edward are working on another book. I cannot tell you the pleasure they gave me and my brother while... Never mind. Thank you for listening to me, Lady Edward.'

She didn't return to Mrs Phillips. She couldn't face anyone else just now.

She'd barely sunk on to a chair in Mrs Phillips's small parlour when there was a tap on the door and Betsy poked her head in.

'There you are, miss. I didn't see you downstairs.'

Cleo rose to her feet guiltily. 'Is Mrs Phillips looking for me, Betsy?'

'No, miss. A man. Not the big fellow from the square, another one. Very polite. Says he's your brother…'

The darkness welled up like sinking into a pool of ink and the air rumbled with the galloping of at least a hundred horses, but when the light returned the maid was still in the doorway, waiting.

'Dash.'

'Shall I show him up, miss?' the maid asked hesitantly.

'Show him…? Oh, yes, please, Betsy. Yes.'

When Dash entered she was standing, her hand braced on the table, still prepared for disillusionment. But it was him—her little brother, smiling. She stood, spread her arms and he walked into her hug. They stood like that a long while until he squirmed out of her arms just as he had as a little boy. But he was grinning.

'I'm honoured I merit a few tears, Sis. I can't remember ever seeing you cry.'

'I'm becoming soft in my old age. I'm so happy you are here and safe, Dash. I was so afraid.'

'So was I,' he replied, inspecting her head to toes. 'When I saw the damage to our rooms I was frantic until I found your letter saying you'd left for England. I wasn't certain you would have. I took what I could and left for Alexandria that same day.'

'But then why did you not leave for England immediately?'

'Because our friend Boucheron was in Alexandria and he controls everything there. I decided to lie low and wait for him to leave, but the blasted fellow looked set to stay there for a while so I finally risked coming into port, only to find myself waylaid by a sailor who knew my name. I almost had an apoplexy, but he just gave me this and disappeared. I realise now that your large friend with the scars must have set him on to me.'

Her breath hitched at the mention of Rafe, but she merely took the worn and limp piece of paper Dash handed her and unfolded it. Rafe's voice filled her mind immediately.

'I'm seeing your Patrick safely to London. Your friend B. is serious about retrieving whatever your father took from him, so if you have it I suggest you find a *safe* means of returning said property—I find it's always best to hide a needle in a haystack and make a great deal of noise about the hay. Whatever you do, don't turn your back on him—make sure there are other people about if you speak with him. And if a fellow named al-Mizan finds you, tell him *nadab* will make it well worth his while to send you safely on your way. I have a feeling he will show me that courtesy, one mercenary to another. Don't dither.'

Cleo rubbed the paper a little as if she could feel him.

'Who is he?' Dash asked, watching her closely, and she sighed. There was no point in telling Dash the truth about Rafe, at least not yet.

'His name is… Rafe. It's a long story. First tell me the rest of it. What did Father take from Boucheron?'

'I don't wish to show disrespect for the dead, but our fool of a father kept a notebook listing all of Boucheron's transactions. He listed which antiquities were sold where and there were markings which I think showed which were real and which forgeries. Farouq must have seen the notebook.'

'Oh, no. No wonder Boucheron wanted Father back under his thumb.'

'Yes, he must be well pleased he's dead.'

'Did you find the notebook among his belongings?'

'I did, though I had no idea of its significance until I read your friend's note. I only took it because it was Father's and I wish I hadn't been so sentimental. If I'd left it there for Boucheron's people to find, none of this would have happened. I returned it to Boucheron, though.'

'Dash! That wasn't wise. Now he might think you know about the forgeries!'

'I wasn't that obvious, Sis. I took your big friend's advice and gathered a stack of Father's most recent notes about the pyramids of Meroe, bought some books about Upper Egypt and was lucky enough to find a volume called *Hidden Treasures of Nubia* in an Alexandrian bookstore. I put it all in a parcel and waylaid Boucheron at the Ptolemy Club in Alexandria so there would be other people around. I think I played the wide-eyed innocent to perfection. Told him I presumed Father stole his plans to find a treasure cache in the Nubian pyramids and conveyed what I hope was the right amount of scoffing disdain at the idea. Then I proclaimed I was only too delighted to finally be able to leave Egypt for England. He said how delighted he was to recover the books, but it was the notebook that he slipped into his coat pocket as I was leaving. You know what he's like—a damned clever fellow. He was even so kind as to offer to put me in contact with some friends of his in London if I needed occupation. He assured me he had excellent connections here.'

'How sweetly ominous.'

'Exactly. I thanked him, but said I was looking forward to taking up an offer of a fellowship in Edinburgh. I felt that was far enough away to calm his concerns.'

'I'm so proud of you, Little Brother. But mostly I'm just happy you are finally here. I've missed you.'

He grinned and gave a jaw-cracking yawn.

'Same here. Now about that giant of yours—'

'He's a mercenary and he's not mine. Now you are safe he will no doubt consider his obligation fulfilled. He must return to his family.'

'Pity. I wasn't very gracious just now.'

'Just now? You saw him?'

'By the docks. He had people on the lookout for me. I thought they might be Boucheron's people who somehow followed me aboard the *Nightingale* and to England and was a little rattled.'

'Oh. What did he say?'

'That you'd have his hide if he didn't deliver me safely.'

She smiled, pressed her hands over her face and burst into tears.

Chapter Twenty-Two

Rafe leaned on the hackney door, giving his leg a moment to adjust as he looked up at the imposing façade of Sinclair House. Even after a day lying abed he was not yet well enough to be up and about, but his conscience was causing him more grief than his leg. He'd put off this moment far too long; it was time to see Edge and face his future. At least his injury might soften his brother's well-deserved ire.

The door to Sinclair House was opened by a butler almost before he'd released the knocker.

'Mr Grey to see Lord Edward,' Rafe announced and the butler opened his mouth but then paused, his eyes widening. 'Lord Edward is in residence, isn't he?' Rafe asked cautiously.

'He is, Your Grace.'

Ah. He'd forgotten how alike he was to Edge. Though given his current state, he would have thought it would take a man longer to make the connection.

Thankfully the butler said no more, merely stood back. 'This way, Your Grace.'

Rafe limped in his wake, concentrating on his steps. Each one was an adventure in discomfort. He was used to pain, had lived with it for quite a long time after the fire.

But strangely he felt this cut even more. He was not as re-silient as he had once been. He just wanted it to be over. He wanted...

He wanted Cleo to be there and hold his hand and scold him for his stupidity in wandering around London at night without paying attention to his surroundings and to tell him that only an idiot tended to a knife wound himself. He wanted to see her frown and her smile and he just... wanted her.

Oh, hell, he was a mess.

'In here, Your Grace. I shall fetch your brother.'

He hesitated as Rafe lowered himself on to a sofa, bit-ing back a groan of pain, and then hurried out.

Edge burst into the drawing room and Rafe smiled, far more relieved than he would have believed possible to see his brother. He looked fit and well. Far better than he'd looked the last time he'd seen him in Brazil. Apparently he didn't return the sentiment for his gaze swept over Rafe and his frown deepened.

'Good God, Rafe. You look like hell. Are you ill?'

'Blunt as usual, Edge. No, I had a little altercation with a cutpurse. I wasn't paying attention. My stupidity entirely.'

Edge seemed to waver as if contemplating pulling his brother into a hug, but then he strode over to the bell cord and gave it a tug. 'You need a doctor.'

Rafe sighed and nodded.

'I hoped to manage without a blasted surgeon, but that was probably optimistic. I think I might need a few stitches'

Tubbs appeared promptly at Edge's summons.

'We will need a doctor, Tubbs,' Edge said and the but-ler nodded.

'I know just the one. What shall I tell Lady Edward? She is worried.'

'Ask her to wait.'

'Not your run-of-the-mill servant,' Rafe commented

when the door closed behind Tubbs. 'I've heard the Sinclairs have their little battalion of efficient minions.'

'Yes. And, knowing him, that doctor will be here in moments so I suggest you take that time to explain why you have put me through hell these past months. I thought you were *dead*, Rafe.'

Rafe winced at the mix of fury and pain in his brother's voice.

'Don't look like that, Edge.' He tried to rise. He was not comfortable facing Edge's justified anger stretched on a sofa like an ailing aunt. But his leg, having carried him thus far, gave a shriek of outrage and buckled. He sank back down, breathing heavily. 'Damn this leg. I know you're furious and you've every right to be, but I knew it would take something drastic to drag you back into the land of the living. Every time I told you to return to Egypt you told me to jump off a cliff. So I did, figuratively. A contact of mine forged that letter from the embassy claiming I was presumed dead. I knew you probably wouldn't believe it, but you couldn't ignore it. I planned to leave clues along the way and wait for you in Luxor and have you finally show me this precious Egypt of yours.'

'So what happened to that charming little plan?'

Rafe shifted his leg with both hands and wiped his forehead.

'I came across someone who'd become separated from her family in a very inhospitable corner of the world.'

'Miss Osbourne,' Edge confirmed.

Rafe looked up with a grimace.

'I was wondering about that advertisement in *The Times*. It wasn't quite accurate so I knew it wasn't that unctuous little worm Pettifer. Still, it was clever of him to change the text to warn me. At least this saves me the need to visit him to find out why. How did you figure it out, by the way?'

'We had some help. But what has that to do with being stabbed?'

'That was purely my foolishness. I thought I had a lead on finding her brother.'

'Brothers appear to be disappearing at an alarming rate recently.'

'As amusing as ever, I see. I never really disappeared. I always knew where I was.'

'As *annoying* as ever, I see. You do realise you are now the Duke of Greybourne and have been back in England for several weeks and have not yet even contacted the lawyers, let alone the brother who you led to believe was now about to assume your title?'

'I planned to do so once I resolved this little issue. And I made sure that fellow you paid to look out for me in Cairo followed me to Alexandria so you would know I was alive and well and on my way to England.'

'I would have appreciated a note to that effect. The fact that you disappeared again once you reached London wasn't precisely encouraging.'

'Yes, well, I was distracted. I needed to arrange some matters.'

'Yes, meeting with fraudsters and convincing them to pay debts they'd never considered paying and then securing a companion's position for Miss Osbourne. I can see why your only brother's peace of mind would rank below those.'

Edge set to pacing the room, following the geometric design of the rug, regimented even in his anger.

'I'm sorry, Edge. If it's any consolation, you dealt me quite a shock when I heard you had somehow managed to marry your Sam while chasing me down. Good for you. I don't know quite how, but I feel I ought to receive some credit.' Edge continued his pacing and Rafe hesitated. 'That is good, isn't it, Edge? I mean, you've wanted her for ever, as far as I could tell. We've never talked about it, but devil take it, man, I would have had to be blind and dumb not to realise how important she was to you. The only times I've ever seen you light up were around Jacob or when you received the drawings she made for your books. And when I came to haul you out of Chesham after the funeral you were quite voluble about—'

'I was drunk,' Edge snapped, not stopping.

'*In vino veritas*, as they say. When I heard she was widowed as well I thought…if Edge had an ounce of sense he'd go see the lay of the land. But, no, he stays stuck in Brazil like a barnacle. So I decided to scrape you off and see what happened. You can only write love letters so long, Brother mine.'

Edge snorted in disdain. 'I've never written a love letter in my life.'

'No? I've read four of them so far and so have thousands of other adoring readers. Damn long ones, too, but at least there's some adventure and excitement and history along the way while we all wait for Gabriel and Leila to come to their senses and admit they are batty about each other. That's why this last book has everyone swooning, from what I hear. I've been damn busy these past few weeks, but even I've heard the raving. I managed to leaf through my housekeeper's copy and those last lines, on the cliff? *"It was only ever you."* Damn romantic. No wonder Sam agreed to marry you. She finally discovered the romantic pudding under that dour exterior.'

Edge shook his head and sank into a chair, suddenly looking as shaky as Rafe felt.

'My God, I'm pathetic.'

'Damn it, Edge, that's not what I meant. Any woman would kill to have someone write masterpieces about her and for her. Don't tell me Sam doesn't appreciate them— her illustrations are a work of love in themselves.'

'Not to me. She had no idea I was the author. That is just the way she is.'

'But…you told her, didn't you?'

'She found out a week ago. In a book store.'

'Oh. Well. That must have been…uncomfortable.'

Edge shoved his hands through his hair.

'Yes.'

'Do you mean to say you proposed to her, but didn't think of telling her the truth?'

'I didn't propose. She did.'

Rafe couldn't hold back a sigh and Edge gave a bitter laugh.

'I told you I am pathetic.'

'No. Stubborn. Wary. And luckier than you deserve. What is wrong, then? You should be in seventh heaven.'

Edge laughed again.

'I was on fourth and climbing, but I've fallen a few rungs. I knew from the beginning Sam wanted to marry me because she wanted a family and a home and I was willing to make that devil's bargain. This shouldn't make a difference, but it does.'

'What shouldn't?'

Edge scrubbed his hands through his hair once more.

'It's a damn long story.'

'I've nothing better to do until the sawbones arrives… Ah, hell.' He broke off at the sound of voices approaching. 'He could not possibly have found—'

'Mr Haversham, Your Grace. A skilled and discreet man of medicine,' Tubbs announced and stood back to allow a short man with unruly white hair to enter.

'Your Grace, Lord Edward,' the man said hurriedly, as if in a rush to dispense with niceties and get to the business of carving up his patients. 'What have we here? Bullets or swords?'

'A knife. To the thigh,' Rafe admitted.

'Excellent. Bullets are a nuisance. Give me a good clean cut any day. We'll need a bed, hot water, linen and a good fire. And some brandy if there's stitching to be done so we can celebrate a job well done when I'm through. Not for you, Your Grace. You look feverish enough as it is. Gruel for you, I'm afraid.'

For the first time since he arrived Edge grinned outright and Rafe was too pleased at the sight to resent it.

'Her Grace, the Duchess of Greybourne, is in the drawing room, Your Grace. I thought you might wish to know.' Tubbs stood in the doorway to Rafe's bedroom at Sinclair House, a distinct twinkle in his eyes. Rafe lowered his brother's book.

'Ah, hell.'

'Precisely, Your Grace. Your brother and Lady Sam are with her already. Here is your cane.'

Rafe debated claiming he was too ill, but that would not only be cowardly, it would leave Edge to face the dragon's wrath alone. Besides, he'd slept most of yesterday after the doctor was done with him and needed to get back on his feet. He had a visit to pay that was already overdue.

At the thought of Cleo, a surge of yearning coursed through him and he took the cane and let Tubbs help him to his feet. They had not gone three steps in the hallway when Edge came striding towards them, his mouth so tightly held it looked as though his jaw might shatter.

'Rafe...'

'Tubbs already told me she's here. Bad luck.'

'I know. Come. Before she says something to Sam I might regret.'

'You left Sam alone with her?'

'Hurry.'

The drawing room door was ajar and Sam's voice carried towards them, tight with fury and pain.

'I am sorry, Your Grace, but you must excuse me for a moment. I... No, I am not sorry. I am so very, *very* grateful to you. You will never know how much.'

'Grateful, Lady Edward?'

Rafe flinched a little at the sound of his mother's voice, as cool and distant as ever. Edge surged forward but as

Sam's voice rushed on, Rafe caught his brother's arm, stopping him.

'Yes, grateful, Your Grace,' Sam answered. 'I did not understand how you could have given away your child, a boy of six, but it was the very best thing you could have done. His uncle and aunt loved him with all their enormous hearts, unconditionally. They helped make him the marvellous, unique man he is. It broke their hearts when your...when *their* grandson died. It broke their hearts when Edge went even further away and they had to let him go and hope he would return. I saw their faces when he arrived in Egypt. *That* is love. And that is why Edge will always turn to them when he needs to see what he is really like. Not to you.'

'Yes. I know. And now to you. So, if you refuse to call my son by his given name Edward, what *do* you call him when you wish to annoy him?' the Duchess asked, her tone tinged with absolutely unfamiliar amusement. Rafe felt the jolt of surprise run both through him and Edge at the same time, finally propelling them into the room. Sam turned to them, her cheeks blazing, but her eyes confused and searching. Rafe took pity on her and spoke.

'Yes, Sam. What do you call this lug when you wish to annoy him? I could use some leverage. Hello, Mother. I admit you have succeeded in surprising me.'

'I dare say I have. You are not looking well, Rafael. The years have not dealt kindly with you. Do sit down before you fall down.' She patted the sofa by her, but Rafe eased himself into an armchair. Edge took Sam's hand and sat with her on the sofa opposite, turning to their mother.

'What game were you playing just now, Mother?'

'Game?' Sam asked.

'I do not indulge in games, Edw... Edge. I was curious about your wife, that is all. She is nothing like Dora.'

'No. Thank God.'

'Yes. Dora was a charming girl, full of light and laughter as long as the sun shone, but not built for hardship. A delightful lapdog to your current lioness.'

'You were *testing* me?' Sam's voice squeaked in outrage, but the Duchess turned to Rafe and Edge.

'I am aware my choices when you were young mean I will always have but limited access to you and I have accepted that. I still believe it was the best decision under the circumstances after the effects of your father's accident became apparent. Now that Rafael has little choice but to assume the responsibilities of his title...' she glanced at Rafe as he shifted in the armchair '... I will remove to the Lancashire property. I have only remained until now to ensure Greybourne does not fall into disrepair and I hope I have not done too ill a job. I know neither of you will voluntarily seek my company in future, so naturally I wished to take what is likely to be a singular opportunity to see if this woman will make you a good wife. I see that she shall and I was wrong to worry.'

Something flickered in Rafe's mind at her words, but it was Sam who asked the obvious question.

'What accident? And what has it to do with sending Edge away?'

'I am surprised you have no memory of this, Rafael,' the Duchess replied, her grey eyes fixing on him now. 'You were, after all, seven years old at the time. The Duke was thrown from his horse and suffered a severe injury to the head. For a long time, we thought he would not survive. He did, but it soon became evident he was no longer the same man. He became most pious and intolerant and...occasionally violent. After the incident when he broke your arm, Edw... Edge, Dr Parracombe and I decided it was judicious we limit his access to the children. There was no question of having him confined. The scandal would have stained the Greybourne name beyond repair.'

Edge clasped his left arm.

'He broke it? My father broke it? How?'

'That day...you were reading to me and Greybourne walked in and tried to take the book from you. You were always stubborn, my boy, and unfortunately you held on. Before I could even think he threw you against the wall. By the time Dr Parracombe treated you and sedated him I had made a pact with myself. I would protect my children by whatever means possible and that meant removing you from danger.' She smoothed her dress again, but as no one broke the silence she continued. 'I could hardly expect the Duke to condone sending his heir to Egypt, Rafe, but I ensured you spent most of the year at school or up by the Lakes, and the girls lived with the governess in their own wing. Naturally we could allow no taint of madness to cling to the Greybourne name and as far as I know there have never been rumours. Rigid religious beliefs served as a fine excuse for his...spells. Now he is dead we need no longer be concerned with discovery. Dr Parracombe is completely trustworthy.'

'Trustworthy... Mother, why did you never say a word of this? We have not been children for a long while. We *deserved* to know.'

'I thought it the best course of action.' She turned to Rafe. 'Greybourne is your cross to bear now, Rafe. I do hope you find someone to share it with who will make it a happier place.'

Rafe shook his head, feeling utterly shattered. He wanted to be angry at her for having kept the truth from them, for having them live in doubt and fear and loneliness. He could see now she'd meant to protect them, but this...

And just as quickly came a slashing sense of loss. A completely different life had been snatched from them, from all of them, through no one's fault but fate and a bad fall. Had his father understood anything of the tragedy? He hoped he hadn't. He didn't wish that on anyone.

What a waste. His whole life could have been different. Edge would not have been sent to Egypt and he would not have run away.

And neither of them would have met the women they loved.

He met his mother's gaze as it moved over his face. Her fingers reached out, hovered within reach of his scarred jaw.

'I hope...no more of this for a while, Rafe?'

He shook his head again. No. No more of this. Time to go home.

'Good,' the Duchess said briskly as she rose and fastened her dove-grey pelisse. 'I have promised to visit with some friends while I am in town and then I must prepare for my departure to Lancashire now I have seen all is well. Do ring for my carriage to be brought round.'

Chapter Twenty-Three

'A Mr Grey to see you, miss.' Betsy's voice held more than a smidgen of disapproval.

Cleo's pen stuttered mid-word, the ink creating erratic constellations over her description of Cairo.

Mr Grey.

She'd expected him to arrive yesterday, as he'd promised, and she'd resolved to show her gratitude and not a hint of all the other emotions crashing about inside her like billiard balls in an earthquake. But as evening fell she'd come to accept he was not coming. She'd even kept Percy out longer on his evening walk, scanning the darkening square, but it remained stubbornly empty. She could only surmise that he'd heard from Lady Edward that Cleo was now aware of his true identity, and was too much of a coward to face her until she absorbed the news and calmed down.

Well, she had not calmed down in the least.

Mr Grey.

No matter how many times she repeated to herself he was not like William, not like her father…that he owed her nothing and had promised nothing, yet had done more for her in the short time she'd known him than anyone since her childhood world fell apart…that she could and did trust him…that he owed her nothing in the end…even that he had every right to keep his identity to himself—she *knew* all this, but it still hurt to her core.

No wonder he'd tried to keep her at bay. He'd probably realised that despite all her protestations that she did not want anything beyond the moment, she was weaving him into her foolish dreams of cottages and her little pack of jackals.

The Duke of Greybourne, even returned from the wild, could have no part in that fantasy. Whether he wished it or not he was about to be swept back into a world in which she had no part.

What is in a name?

A chasm. A line as deep and treacherous as an ocean.

She knew why he was here. She knew his subterfuge weighed on him, she'd seen it every time he'd been on the verge of telling her the truth. Now it was time for him to complete his confession.

Third time unlucky.

The only thing that should matter was that he had helped Dash. Everything else *must* be put aside. She tried to clear her mind from everything but her gratitude, but there was quite a great deal to clear.

'Shall I send him away, miss?' Betsy said hopefully as the silence stretched.

'No. Show him in, Betsy.'

The first thing she noticed when he entered was the pallor that gave his sun-warmed skin a grey tinge. She'd not noticed it in the square, but then it had been dark. Surely it was not the result of merely two weeks in the rainy north? Her anger began to fizzle and she tried to pull it back about her like a slipping shawl. For all she knew he was feeling the weather after a round of dissipation. Perhaps that was what had prevented him from calling on her yesterday. She was not at all certain it was better than cowardice.

Her anger received another blow when he took a step

into the room and she noticed he was leaving heavily on a cane.

'Rafe! What happened? Was it Boucheron? This is all my fault!'

His mouth quirked for a moment. 'Hardly. You attribute far too much omnipotence to that French fraudster. I had a disagreement with a cutpurse, that is all. My mistake.'

'When?'

'When?'

'When did this happen? Yesterday?'

His eyes fell from hers.

'The day before.'

'After you saw Dash. It *is* my fault.'

'No, it is mine; I wasn't paying attention. I meant to write you a note, but I was a little…indisposed yesterday after the doctor stitched me. I slept most of the day. It isn't serious, just uncomfortable.'

'Then why are you on your feet?' she demanded. 'You should not be standing, I am sure.'

'Well, you haven't yet invited me to sit,' he said reasonably and despite everything she found her mouth curving.

'Besides,' he added as he limped towards the sofa and eyed it, 'sitting down has become something between ordeal and penance.'

She had no integrity at all. Her defences cracked and she hurried forward, taking his arm and weight as he lowered himself into the chair with a grunt, his leg extended. His arm was hard and warm under her fingers and as she reluctantly let it go he brushed the back of her hand briefly with his fingers, sending fire up her arm.

'Thank you, Cleo.'

She returned to her seat and folded her hands in her lap.

'You're welcome, Your Grace.'

He stiffened, a slight flush spreading over his cheekbones. Guilt personified.

'Edge mentioned you spoke with Sam that evening. I wasn't certain if you'd realised... I'd intended to tell you...'

'It is said hell is paved with good intentions, Your Grace.'

'Shakespeare?'

'Samuel Johnson. And don't think you can distract me.'

'I don't intend to. I know I was wrong not to tell you. Not initially, but certainly on board the *Hesperus* I should have told you the truth.'

'Why?' she challenged. 'You owe me nothing. I hired you to help me, which you did. There was never a requirement of honesty, as you made clear several times.'

Her words wiped all expression from his face. He looked his full ducal self now—hard and cold. She was being childish, but she couldn't help it.

'Nevertheless,' he continued, his voice as flat as his countenance, 'my name...my origins have always been an issue. When I ran away I decided to turn my back on them so when I enlisted I gave my name as Rafe Grey. At the time it felt fitting, a reminder of what I was turning my back on and a reminder that I had to be watchful and unobtrusive.'

His mouth twisted at the absurdity of that, but Cleo held herself still, her hands firmly in her lap, and he continued, 'I knew as long as I was Rafe Grey I could have no...permanence in my life, and I accepted that because I knew that as my father's son it was probably best I not inflict any more Greybournes on this world. I know you told me I am not like him, but I lived most of my whole life under the cloud of fear that I might be, or that, God forbid, that strain would manifest in my children if not in me. I did not want to willingly embrace a legacy of uncertainty and pain.'

'I told you before, Rafe. You are not like your father. I *know* that. Whatever happens, please don't let this rule you.

I've never met anyone more deserving of being happy and living your life to the fullest. You *aren't* like your father.'

She reached out and clasped his hand, trying to anchor him with her certainty. But she could not do that for him any more than she could be anything but what she was, Cleopatra Osbourne, daughter of a rootless fraudster.

He drew his hand from hers very gently, fisting it on his thigh before he spoke again.

'The mad thing is that I've just learned it wasn't like my father either.'

'I don't understand.'

'I'm not the only one making confessions. I've just come from a meeting with my mother...'

As Cleo listened to his account of his mother's visit, more and more layers peeled away from her flimsy defences. She didn't want to abandon the defence of her anger, but it was slipping away from her, leaving only a sense of oppression and loss.

'What a sad story,' she said when he fell silent. 'Your poor mother. I cannot imagine what she must have felt. To have your world ripped apart...the poor woman.'

'I suggest you don't say that to her face. She's likely to freeze you with a glance. She's as tough as an old boot.'

She smiled at the return of some colour to his voice, but shook her head.

'No, she isn't. Perhaps outside, but not inside. I'm so sorry you had to experience any of this, Rafe.'

He shifted uncomfortably.

'It's old history.'

'No, it isn't and you know it. I wonder if your father even understood the change that came over him. In a way I hope he didn't. To be cut off like that from yourself... to be aware in any way of what you've become. I cannot imagine a worse fate.'

His mouth finally softened, though not quite into a smile.

'You'll be making me feel guilty I wasn't more compassionate towards him.'

'I dare say you might have been if your mother had trusted you enough to tell you the truth. But she must have felt as though she was clinging to a branch in a flood. How sad.'

They fell silent and once again the truth rolled back to fill the void.

His Grace the Duke of Greybourne. Her little dream of a family with this man would remain just that. She didn't even have grounds for anger. He'd warned her, tried to avoid her, worried about hurting her. He was no William, as much as she might want to cast him in that role so she could cauterise pain with anger. He was Rafe. The man she loved with all her heart and soul and body.

'I hope knowing this will make going back to your home easier, Rafe—' She broke off and managed a smile. 'I can't quite call you Your Grace, you know. It just doesn't feel right.'

He waved that away, his gaze fixed on her face. 'I didn't come merely to tell you my name, Cleo, long overdue though that was. I came to offer it to you. Will you do me the honour of marrying me?'

The words came out in a rush, as if he was forcing them out before a door closed. Cleo sat very still. The mantelpiece clock tut-tutted away.

'Well?' he demanded. His hand was still fisted on his thigh and the other held his cane in a death grip. She tried several times to form the words, pulling in air only to have it slip out again, as shapeless as her thoughts.

Her fingers began to ache and she looked down at them. As he'd talked she'd wound the blue ribbon he'd gifted her tightly about them without even realising. She unwound the ribbon and the blood rushed back, beating hard.

'Did I ever tell you what happened after I stole that ribbon, Rafe?'

He shifted impatiently but his voice was flat when he answered.

'No. You didn't.'

She wet her lips and smoothed the ribbon on her lap. 'I kept it hidden in my drawer and agonised over it for days and days. I made myself ill worrying about it. It wasn't that I believed in damnation or sins, it was merely that I *knew* it was wrong to have taken something that did not belong to me. In the end I went to Annie and told her.'

'What did she do?' The words sounded as though they, too, were wrung out of him.

'She was angry. And hurt. She said, rightly, that I had no right to take what wasn't mine simply because I wanted it.'

'If you don't want the damned thing, then toss it on the dung heap. It is only a ribbon.'

'That isn't what I meant and you know it. I think you are the bravest and most wonderful man of my acquaintance, Rafe Grey. Which is why you must understand why I cannot accept your proposal—it would feel like stealing for me. I don't take marriage lightly.'

'You think I do? Then how the devil did I manage to avoid it for thirty-seven years?'

'With your soft heart? I have no idea.'

He smiled reluctantly, but it didn't show in his eyes.

'I am serious, Cleo.'

'I know. So am I.' She leaned forward and touched his arm and his hand closed over hers, warm and large and so inviting.

'You deserve so much, Rafe. I'm honoured that you are willing to overlook the difference in our births, but even if your conscience is telling you it is the right thing to do, it isn't. You are my finest friend and you deserve to love and be loved and so do I. If I agreed to enter into such an uneven match—'

'I don't give a sainted damn about my title,' Rafe bit out and she shook her head.

'I wasn't referring to differences in birth, but in sentiment, Rafe. It is a burden when one side loves and the other doesn't. I saw that all too well with my mother. If I said yes, I would be robbing you of that possibility and I cannot do that. Don't you understand?'

His hands rose, as if warding her off. For a moment he remained with his head bent, silent and frozen.

'I understand...' he said at last, but his voice scraped to a halt and he cleared his throat. 'God knows I wish... more than anything...that I could make that true for you. You deserve that more than anyone. Obviously I haven't that power.'

She watched his lowered head, her chest a knot of pain and her eyes filling. She tugged her chair next to his and took his hand. She hadn't realised her tears had slipped free until he raised their clasped hands to her face and his knuckles grazed her wet cheek.

'Don't cry, sweetheart. Damn your soft heart. I won't break. I promise. I refuse to have you pity me. I'd rather love you and have you kick me to the curb than be a cause of hurt to you. At least I've had the good sense to give my heart to someone worthwhile, even if she cannot love me back. I won't... I can't give up your friendship and, if all we can be is friends, I shall have to make do with that. Perhaps one day you'll...feel more. I won't badger you, though. And if one day you...find a man who will give you what you wish, I will do my damnedest not to make a fool of myself or strangle the life out of him. I want your happiness, Cleo-Pat. I wish it could have been with me, I will always wish it, but I wish for your happiness above that.'

Cleo's mind fiddled with his words like a child racing to complete a puzzle against the clock of doom. Surely it was impossible the picture that was forming was correct. She had misheard...he had misspoken...she had finally allowed sentiment to overpower sense...she...

Rafe loved her.

Not conscience, charity, not even lust...

Rafe *loved* her.

Rafe loved *her.*

She pressed their joined hands to her lips and his hand tightened convulsively on hers.

'No, Cleo... I don't want pity.'

'Pity! You ought to pity *me* for a blind fool, Rafe. And you are one, too, to so completely misunderstand me. I *love* you. I have for weeks. My poor heart has been cracked so many times it's a wonder it is still beating, but it is.' She pressed his hand to her chest. 'Can't you feel it? It's spilling over with love. I *love* you, Rafe Grey.'

Rafe felt as though he'd walked straight off a cliff, but forgotten to fall. He just hung there, in a strangely silent world, even his own breathing far away, as if he was seeing this all from a distance. But beneath his palm her heart was beating a matching rhythm to his.

He could not remember ever seeing real joy, he certainly had never felt it. Now he saw it in her face—in her smile, her eyes, in the pressure of her hand that held his to her heart. And he felt it—in the centre of his chest, expanding and making it hard to breathe.

'You mean it,' he said a little absurdly, his voice rough. Her hand pressed harder against his.

'Of course I mean it. I've meant it for ages. Why on earth do you think I have been gathering every moment with you, every touch, and begging for more?'

He touched his fingers to the corner of her beautiful mouth, to that tugging smile that ruled his soul and senses.

Cleo.

'You've never begged. You demanded,' he replied and was rewarded by her warm laugh.

'Because you are absurdly stubborn. If only you'd told me you loved me sooner...'

'A brave man might have. I told you I was a coward, Cleo.'

'I won't have you calling yourself that, it isn't true. You are cautious and caring and so giving to others that you forget to take. And I *love* you.' Her voice shook, deepened. 'I love you, Rafe. You told me I was one of those who... who manage and it's true, but I don't *want* to manage. I want to feel the way I do when I am with you. Alive, and happy, and myself, even when it hurts. I'm even happy being miserable with you.'

He knew well what she meant. He didn't understand the alchemy of it, but there it was—love had replaced a part of his soul with something that twined the two of them together. She was part of him now and he needed her. This.

'I only wish you didn't have this stupid title, Rafe. Otherwise I would throw caution to the wind and ask you to marry me. But even if we cannot wed, I want you to know I am yours in every way that matters.'

'Do it, Cleo. Throw caution to the blasted wind.'

She stilled, her eyes fixing on his.

'I don't expect it, Rafe.'

'You should. You should demand it. I've let the Greybourne name and legacy shape too many things in my life, Cleo. I won't let it ruin the best thing that ever happened to me.'

Her hand hovered over his chest, just brushing his shirt, and she took a deep breath.

'Rafe Grey. Will you marry me?'

'I will,' he said, capturing his hand against his chest. 'Today if I could. But two hasty marriages in our family might be a little much. My mother can finally begin atoning for her mistakes by helping us do this properly.'

'I doubt she'll be happy about this.'

'She will be ecstatic about anything that ensures I settle down, sweetheart. Not that she'll show it.'

'I shall just have to show it instead of her,' Cleo said as

she pulled the long chain with the emerald pendant over her head and placed it round his neck. 'There. I haven't a ring to give you, so this must do.'

The emerald lay heavily against his chest. He could feel his heartbeat against it, as if trying to reach through a cage and grab.

She leaned back to inspect it.

'I should say it matches your eyes, but they are much prettier.'

He half laughed and managed to force the words through his clogged throat. 'I cannot take it. It's yours.'

'You aren't. You are safekeeping it for our daughter. You promised I would have daughters, didn't you?'

'Yes. And sons. A wild pack of jackals.'

She touched his cheek lightly, her smiling eyes seeing right through to the pain that was still lodged in his stomach.

'And sons. You promised and you are a soothsayer, after all.' She snuggled against him, careful of his leg as she tucked her head into the curve of his shoulder as she had on the *Hesperus*. 'Do you know; I think I am going to be a very demanding wife.'

'I hope so.'

'And spendthrift, too. You *are* wealthy, correct?'

He leaned back a little, warmed by the laughter in her gold-flecked eyes.

'I am. What are you plotting? Building a pyramid on the front lawn at Greybourne?'

'No, a *hammam*. All marble and with a dipping pool, but with something to lie on right in the very middle so I can lay you down and wash you all over…' Her voice trailed off into a husky rumble, her hand slipping under his coat and down his chest.

He felt as though he'd been shoved into a steam room right now—the heat was spiralling through him like steam, half melting him, half turning him as hard as the emerald pressed between his chest and her glorious breasts. Mrs Phillips's parlour was *not* the place…

'And then…?' he prompted.

'And then I will take you on an adventure you will never forget, Mr Grey.'

Epilogue

Greybourne Hall—1824

'Well?' Cleo demanded as she removed Rafe's blindfold. He stood for a moment squinting at the sight. The spring sun outside was powerful, cutting through the milky glass windows and transforming the marble and granite surfaces to cream and gold. The light caressed the cushions that lined two *chaises longue* and then sped on, dancing off the flat surface of the raised stone bath.

His mouth quirked—he reckoned the bath could comfortably accommodate four people, or one large scarred mercenary and his pregnant wife. Only last night he'd had a delightful time bathing Cleo in the brass tub in their dressing room, taking his time soaping her beautiful breasts and the taut skin of her stomach.

The thought of being able to join Cleo in the warm waters of this hedonistic corner of paradise and then move their exploration to the generously large *chaise longue* was…

'Well? Do you like it?' Cleo prompted, impatient at his silence.

'Good God, Cleo. *Like* is a very weak word to describe what I'm feeling at the moment. Full to bursting is closer.

Dangerously aroused is even more accurate.' He slipped his hands into Cleo's hair, threading through its warm silk. She often wore it down around the Hall, the chestnut waves covering her shoulders. Sometimes he missed her short hair, but playing with the warm tresses more than compensated for his occasional nostalgia. Like now, as he imagined it covering her bare breasts as she slipped into the water. 'Is the water warm yet? Actually, I don't care. Lock the door...'

'Bah!'

They drew apart and Rafe turned to face the wide grey eyes of his niece and the equally wide grey eyes of his sister-in-law and the very amused green-grey eyes of his brother.

'Bah!' little Charlotte announced again, waving a glistening fist towards the water. Edge shifted his daughter from one arm to the other, his other hand closing around Sam's as they entered the *hammam*.

'No, Charlie, I'm afraid you'll have to wait your turn going for a swim. Your uncle and aunt look as though they need a cooling dip first.'

Sam laughed, her eyes taking everything in.

'This is amazing, Cleo! Oh, Edge, look at the hieroglyphs!'

'I'll be damned,' Edge said, a new light entering his eyes as he strode over to the wall with his daughter.

Rafe sighed with resignation, shelving his fantasies, and followed his brother towards the far wall. As he inspected the carving on the wall the memory returned of an evening two years before in a half-fallen temple in Kharga. There were the Pharaoh and the Queen, arms extended, each standing on a royal cartouches, and surrounded with lotus flowers, palms, and a row of...jackals?

Rafe smiled and laced his fingers through Cleo's, drawing her against his side, his throat tight.

'I can't remember. Are those the symbols from the temple in Kharga?' he asked Cleo, pointing to the cartouches, but Edge shook his head as he inspected them.

'Not unless you believe in colossal coincidences. Have you been studying Champollion's *Precis*, Cleo?'

She laughed, brushing her cheek against Rafe's shoulder.

'Dash is in Paris and sends me all the latest news on the decipherment of the hieroglyphs. But I put this together myself. What do you think?'

'Do you mean these squiggles actually mean something?' Rafe demanded. 'All I can see is snakes, lions and falcons. It looks like a menagerie. Actually that looks more like a slug than a snail.'

'A slug for a great big lug,' Edge said. 'That's you, Rafe. The empty eye, the slug and the lion. R-F-L.'

'Huh. And this?' Rafe asked Cleo.

'The one with the lion and falcon is my name, Cleopatra. And this...' she murmured, pulling him to a row of the hieroglyphs between the cartouches showing a crouched figure and a long-tailed snake. 'This part reads *iu-meri-y-chu*. Together it says Rafael and Cleopatra love for ever. At least I hope it does. It would be very embarrassing to discover it says Rafael and Cleopatra like snakes.'

'Rafael and Cleopatra love for ever,' Rafe repeated, tracing the symbols. 'Carved in stone.'

'Greybourne stone. I had this quarried from the same stone they are using to build the new school in the village, which is a rather worthier project than the *hammam*,' she added guiltily.

Rafe turned and brushed his fingertips down her cheek, resting for a moment on her dimple.

'I find this project eminently worthy. At least I think I will if only I am allowed to assess it properly...without an audience.'

Sam laughed and slipped Charlotte from Edge's arms, pulling her husband away from his inspection of the carvings.

'Come along, Edge. Charlie is also in need of a bath, though I doubt she will enjoy it quite as much as her uncle.'

'Finally,' said Rafe as he locked the door behind them and turned to look at his wife. She wore a low-cut, loose-fitting morning dress gathered below her beautiful breasts, showing the growing bulge of their child. Her head was slightly to one side as she watched him, her smile warm and loving.

'Come here, Rafe.'

'You're looking rather dangerous at the moment, Cleo-Pat. What have you in store for me now?'

'Another great adventure, Mr Grey.'

* * * * *

A MATCH FOR THE
REBELLIOUS EARL

Chapter One

'Useless fops…' *thump* '…the lot of them!' *thump* 'What is the point…' *thump* '…of having a stable of stallions…' *thump* '…if not one of them has sired an heir?'

Thump, thump, whack!

Genny straightened the small table that had fallen victim to Lady Westford's enthusiastic cane-wielding. Her tantrums were always accompanied by a militant tattoo, but today she seemed intent on wearing a hole in the carpet. It didn't help that Carmine, Her Ladyship's off-key canary, accompanied the thumping with contrapuntal warbling and frenetic leaps about his large gilded cage.

Mary and Serena sat stiffly in their chairs, dark and light heads bowed, hands folded in their laps. With their lovely profiles aligned they looked like women posing for a tableau of penance.

Genny plucked a stalk of hay from her skirt and began stripping it into slivers, imagining it was Lady Westford's cane she was shredding.

Or, better yet, Lady Westford.

'And now the family is headed by a wastrel and a rogue who did not even see fit to attend his grandfather's funeral, and never cared one snap of his fingers for the Carringtons.'

'To be fair, Lady Westford, other than Emily and Mary, I haven't seen that the Carringtons have ever cared one snap of the fingers for him either. Quite the opposite, in fact,' Genny intervened—and immediately regretted her impulsive comment. Her object was to soothe the dragon, not throw oil on its fiery breath.

Lady Westford's cane slashed the air towards her. 'We gave that doxy's boy everything and he repaid us by shaming us even further! This is what we are brought to... Oh, go away, all of you!' she exploded, her voice cracking. 'You are no use to me. You've had your chance and failed. You two...' her cane slashed the air again, now towards Mary and Serena '...you were gifted the finest of the Carrington men and you brought them both to nothing. Now all you do is feed off the Carrington teat like the empty vessels you are. Soon I shall follow Alfred to the grave and leave the Carrington tree bare of fruit. I'm surrounded by nothing but fops and rogues and barren women and hangers-on and... Oh, go away!'

They did as they were told and Genny sighed as she closed the door behind her.

'Well, that will teach me that silence is golden,' she said far more lightly than she felt as she surveyed her sister.

Serena Carrington was ashen, her hand pressed tellingly to her abdomen, as if the pain of her third stillbirth was as sharp inside her as it had been two years ago.

'Come out to the garden, Serena,' Genny suggested, but her sister gave her a slight smile and shook her head.

'I think I shall rest a little, Genny.'

Mary and Genny stood in silence until the door to her room closed.

'Well, this cannot continue,' Genny said, taking Mary by the arm and guiding her downstairs to the library. 'Serena will never recover from losing Charlie and her babes if that harridan keeps flaying her every single day.'

'Lady Westford is suffering too, you know, Genny,' Mary reproached gently. 'Losing three sons, her favourite grandson and a husband is enough to turn anyone sour.'

'I know she is suffering, Mary, but that is no excuse to torment Serena. I know Lady Westford never thought my sister good enough for the heir to the title, but she has the biggest and truest heart in the world. When Grandfather died she fought for me to come live with her, despite their objections. I cannot stand by and watch her ground to dust by that Medusa. I *will* not. She deserves better.'

'Of course she does.' Mary clasped Genny's hand between hers and their comforting warmth sparked a long-gone memory of her mother, holding her hand as they walked down to the village.

'I'm tired, Mary.' The words burst out of her before she could stop them. 'I'm tired of watching the person I care for most in the world suffer. I'm tired of living on the fringes of Lady Westford's charity. Soon there will be nothing left of Serena and nothing left of me, and I want... I need to *breathe*...'

She choked the words to a stop. The urge to lean against the older woman and cry was so strong Genny pulled her hands away and went to look at the rainbow of spring colours out in the garden.

'I know we must do something—but what?' Mary asked. 'We cannot change Lady Westford.'

'I don't intend to change her. My grandfather always said that if you cannot choose your enemy, try and choose your battlefield. Lady Westford is most bearable when surrounded by her cronies and whist partners in London. We could convince her to hold a...a ball for Emily in Town, perhaps to celebrate her upcoming marriage.'

Genny watched the idea take root in Mary's mind, her handsome face softening. Envy flicked at Genny's heart— partly for herself, but mostly on Serena's behalf. She'd seen how her sister watched the bond of love between Mary and her daughter when she thought no one was looking.

Finally, Mary smiled. 'You're tired, I'm frightened, and Serena is…lost. What a trio we are, Genny. You are quite right: it is high time we return to the living. But how shall we convince Lady Westford? She might consider it a betrayal of Alfred's memory.'

'The way to convince Lady Westford is to offer her something she wants. Leave that to me.'

'The only thing she seems to want is for her grandsons to produce an heir. And that, unfortunately, is highly unlikely. They are all well past thirty, and none of them has shown the slightest inclination towards matrimony.'

'Yet,' said Genny, and headed towards the door.

'Where are you going?' Mary asked behind her.

'To make a deal with the she-devil. And then I shall have a word with one of her useless fops.'

'Useless, perhaps, but I take offence at being called a fop,' Julian said as he shifted some papers off the sofa.

Genny raised her veil and sat down in the cleared space, glancing around the room. She'd never been to Julian's rooms on Half Moon Street. They were not quite what she'd expected. The place looked as if a whirlwind had just passed through and left it littered with papers, books and instruments.

'I suppose there is some method to this madness?' she asked and Julian leaned against the table, a rueful smile on his handsome face.

'There is always method to my madness, Genny. I hope there is some to yours? It would be much safer to stick to our arrangement and summon me to Dorset.'

'Desperate times call for desperate measures.'

'I'm not going to like this, am I?'

'Probably not. I told your grandmother I might accept your proposal after all.'

Julian's abrupt movement almost knocked over a precariously placed miniature orrery. The planets set to dancing giddily and he steadied it, glaring at her.

'That was three years ago! And, as you may recall, you turned me down, Genny.'

'I never actually turned you down. I merely pointed out that marrying me to gain your aunt's legacy was a poor bargain for both of us. And since it turned out she meant to leave it to Marcus all along, it is lucky we didn't wed.'

'Well, you cannot just resurrect a proposal when it's convenient. Why don't you stop beating about the bush and tell me what it is you really want, Genny mine?'

She smiled. 'I need your help to appease your grandmother.'

'How?' he asked, still suspicious.

'She is lonely and bored and hasn't had a decent game of whist in months...'

'I am *not* playing whist with my grandmother, Genevieve Maitland. I would rather walk naked down Piccadilly.'

She wrinkled her nose. 'That's not a pleasing image, Julian.'

'I protest. Some would call it a very pleasing image indeed.'

'I'm sure they would,' she said placatingly. 'In any case, I don't expect you to play whist—you are a terrible player. What I mean is that I plan to bring her to London, where she can meet all her old cronies.'

'That sounds sensible. Where is the catch?'

'There is no catch.'

'Of course there is. There's always a catch with you, Genny.'

'Well, it is not precisely a catch... The Carrington

women have been in mourning and away from London and society for two years. They will need a supporting arm to ease them back into society. If you could convince Marcus to come to London for a show of familial solidarity...'

Julian grinned. 'And there it is. So this whole proposal nonsense was merely to make the alternative seem more palatable.'

'Julian Carrington, how ungallant of you!'

'Genevieve Maitland, how devious of you!' he replied, in a falsetto that had little in common with her husky voice.

She laughed. 'Well, will you help? You might even find someone new to finance your projects.'

'I doubt it, but I promise to attend a couple of entertainments of your choice.'

'Not a couple. Nine.'

'No, you madwoman. I said a couple.'

'A couple is hardly anything at all. Eight, however, is a nice round number.'

'Eight isn't round.'

'It is—it goes round and round like a snake.'

She traced a slow figure eight on the table, leaning forward to provide a nice display of her low bodice. Julian had always told her she'd been blessed with one of the loveliest bosoms of his acquaintance, and at the moment she was not above using any weapons at her disposal.

Predictably his gaze flickered between her suggestively sweeping finger and her bodice. 'For heaven's sake, Genny, you are shameless. Three, and not one more.'

'Seven.'

'Four.'

'Six.'

'Five.'

'Seven.'

'Six... Damnation. That's not fair—you reversed direction.'

'Oh, very well, only six,' she said demurely.

He planted his hands on the table. 'You are lucky I am fond of you, you cunning pixie.'

'I am not only lucky, but grateful. Will you try and convince Marcus to come as well?'

'I'll try. Why not command me to go down to the docks, prostrate myself before our new Lord and Master and beg him to attend as well, while you're at it?'

'Lord Westford is in London?' she asked in surprise. Mary had told her he planned to attend Emily's wedding in Hampshire, but she'd said nothing about him arriving in London.

'Docked only yesterday.'

'Oh, no—that isn't good.'

Julian's brows rose. 'I agree, but I didn't think you shared my distaste for my very inconvenient cousin and the new head of the misbegotten Carringtons. You and Charlie used to leap to his defence every time any of us dared speak ill of your precious Captain Christopher Carrington.'

She raised her chin, a little embarrassed. She had been very careful to patrol her true thoughts on the Carrington clan when she'd gone to live with Serena and Charlie, well aware of the tenuous nature of her position. But she'd been so shocked by the way they'd vilified Captain Carrington that she'd been goaded more than once into defending the man her grandfather had considered his most trusted officer during the year he'd served with him.

'I defended him because I thought it terribly unfair and disrespectful the way you and Marcus and your grandparents spoke of him, when in truth it appears you hardly knew him, since he'd spent so little time at the Hall.' She saw Julian gather himself to argue old grievances and hurried on. 'But, in the interests of fairness, I admit his behaviour since he sold his commission has hardly been exemplary—and as Lord Westford he is abysmal. Do you know that neither the lawyers nor the steward have heard from him since your grandfather died, apart from a perfunctory letter from some solicitor in London to direct all correspondence to him?'

'Ah. So you have discovered your idol has feet of clay?'

'I have never idolised anyone in my life—not even my grandfather, and I respected him more than anyone I know. I admit I did expect a modicum of accountability from Captain Carr—from Lord Westford, but since he seems to have shed his scruples along with his uniform, I must find other means to pursue my ends.'

'Meaning me?'

'Precisely. So concentrate your efforts on bringing Marcus. If you find it rough going I shall have a word with him.'

'The threat of that alone should be enough to convince him to come, darling.'

'Thank you, Julian.'

'Huh. Now, you'd better be off before I'm tempted to demand recompense for being so useful.'

She smiled and lowered her veil once more. 'Now, now, Julian. Think of how much worse it might be.'

'It might?'

'Yes, I might have agreed to marry you three years ago, and you would have been saddled with my devious ways for good.'

Chapter Two

'A month ago I was swimming stark naked in the Bay of Alexandria,' Kit said as he leaned against the bulwarks of the *Hesperus* and surveyed the fog. He could see no more than a few yards into the noxious soup, but occasionally the outline of the warehouses formed, like a hulking beast pacing the docks, waiting for the unwary to step ashore.

It might be April in the rest of the world, but it was darkest, dankest December in the London docks. Beneath him Kit could feel the sluggish pull of the Thames towards the sea. The temptation to weigh anchor and slide just as sluggishly out of the grip of his home town was powerful.

'This fog—it is a bad omen, *Capità*,' Benja said, and spat into the sluggish water of the Thames below.

'Why is it you always turn superstitious when we come to England, Benja?'

'Because it was on a day like this that your father brought his ship to England for the last time.'

Kit grinned. 'No, it wasn't. I may have been only eleven, but I remember well we docked in Portsmouth in full sunshine.'

'I remember fog. There is always fog in England…' Benja stopped as a voice called up from the dockside.

'You there, is this the *Hesperus*?'

An equally muffled voice answered from the deck. 'And what will you be wanting with the *Hesperus*, my fine cock?'

Kit smiled at the surly Kentish tones of his bosun, Brimble. He suspected people rarely, if ever, addressed Julian Carrington with that degree of disdain.

He nudged Benja. 'Do me a favour and fetch that fine cock and bring him to my quarters, Benja.'

Benja leaned over the bulwarks to get a better look and clucked his tongue. 'I don't like it. He looks like a Borgia. You know him?'

'I do. That, *amic*, is one of the two men at the top of the very long list of those who would like to see me feeding the fish at the bottom of the ocean.'

'You wish to invite your enemy on board the *Hesperus*?'

'He's worse than my enemy, Benja. He's my cousin.'

'Huh. Looks expensive. Are those rubies real?'

Kit watched as Julian held the filigreed music box to the lamp, turning it under the light. His cousin might be something of a wastrel, but he clearly had a good eye for value. Kit wondered if he'd have to do an inventory once his cousin left the ship.

'Of course they are real. I keep all my forgeries in the false hold, in case any excise officers decide to come calling.'

Julian replaced the box with the same swift, charming smile Kit remembered from his childhood. And had mistrusted just as long.

'Yes, I've heard you've turned respectable of late, Cuz.'

Kit sat down by the wide wooden table, fingering the edge of the map of the Mediterranean spread out on it.

'And I've heard the opposite of you, Julian. We neither of us should believe everything we hear.'

'Or read, apparently.'

Julian sat on the other side of the table and pulled out a folded sheet of a newspaper from his pocket and tossed it across the table.

There was nothing particularly informative written on it—merely broad hints that the new Lord Westford had not even been invited to his own half-sister's ball, so as to spare the family's blushes.

Kit didn't know whether to be annoyed or amused. There was something juvenile about the whole archly told tale—like children whispering behind a hedge.

'I knew you were a favoured target of the gossip columns, Julian, but I didn't know you read them.'

'I don't. This was brought to my attention by Marcus. He is part owner of the *Gazette* and he plans to have a sharp word with the author of this piffle. But that is hardly the point. The point is that they have a point.'

'Of course they do. I'm an uncouth, low-born pirate and our grandmother would as soon spit at me as be in the same room with the black sheep of the family. That is hardly a newsworthy revelation and I don't see why it should bother you. In fact, I would think you would be delighted to see me reviled. You've done it often enough yourself.'

'In private. However, family gossip is bad for business.'

'What business?'

'Our business,' Julian said flatly.

Kit went to fetch a bottle of wine, pouring out two glasses.

Julian sniffed at his, his dark brows rising. He drank and gave a surprisingly happy sigh. 'The rumours are not completely wrong, then. Your taste in wine is impeccable. Where is this from?'

'A day's ride from Rome.'

'What a happy life you lead, Lord Westford.' Julian's voice was light, but as acid as a third-rate vintage.

'Why have you come tonight, Julian? The last time we

saw each other you called me everything short of Beelze-bub himself. Now you're here, on enemy territory, compli-menting my wine and showing a completely disingenuous concern for my reputation. What is it you want? Money?'

Julian's hand tightened on the glass, his handsome mouth twisting. Strange, thought Kit, that his cousin looked far more like Kit's father than he himself did. If he hadn't had the Carrington eyes, Kit had little doubt his cousins would have thrown the slur of bastardy at him, as well as low birth.

'I'm no happier coming here than you are to see me, believe me,' Julian said at last. 'I admit our last encounter was unfortunate. It was very bad taste to air old grievances when your father had just been buried.'

'I appreciate the near apology. But, since I am certain you still haven't told me the reason for your presence here, I'll reserve judgement.'

'You always were a suspicious bastard, Kit.'

'And you always were a devious one, Julian.'

'You should be grateful I'm employing those skills in your favour at the moment.'

'Are you?'

'Yes. You asked why I'm here... I'm here to determine if you're presentable.'

'If I'm...what?'

'Presentable. To polite society. Our last encounter was inconclusive. None of us was at our best. Except poor Charlie—but then he was always the only ray of light among the heathens, as Grandmama would have said.'

'I wouldn't insult heathens by comparing them with the cursed Carringtons. And as for presentability—I don't see why it matters. The only society I plan to encounter is the family of Emily's betrothed in Hampshire, and they, unlike London society, apparently do deserve the epithet *polite*.'

'Damn, I'd forgotten you talk like a book when you're

angry. Just like your father. My point is that it won't do. You can't hide here in the fog while everyone knows you're in Town and practically on their doorstep. If you're so concerned for Emily and Mary, it would have been far better for them if you'd docked somewhere else entirely and sneaked up to the wedding and away again without anyone being the wiser. By the time the ball comes round they'll have you painted as a misshapen ogre holding pagan rites at the rise of the new moon—if you could ever see any moon through the sludge they call air down here.'

'Aunt Mary never said anything about gossip when I met her only yesterday.'

'That's because she's Mary. She's been putting a smile on things ever since her family sold her to our grandparents to take your father's mind off your mother's death. She wouldn't risk scaring you off, in any case, would she? You can always sail away, but she has to live with the old bat. Oh, and I doubt she appreciates you still calling her *Aunt Mary* as you did as a boy. It might have been a fine compromise when you refused to call her *Mama* back then, but she's only a few years older than you, and it's a tad aging to have your grown stepson calling you Auntie.'

Kit felt a sharp twinge in his jaw and realised he was grinding his teeth. Damn, he hated his cousins.

Julian's mouth quirked into a smile. 'I daresay your sweet stepmother didn't even meet you at Carrington House, did she?'

'That was at my suggestion,' Kit said, aware that he was sounding defensive. 'I don't wish to see my grandmother any more than she wishes to see me.'

'Well, once the festivities begin, either leave Town until she returns to Dorset, or do your bit for the family.'

Kit smiled, slowly. 'Are you ordering me to leave London?'

'That was my intention when I came aboard, but I've changed my mind. I think you should come to the ball.'

'Is this some new attempt to make my life hell?'

'At least in this instance, making you miserable isn't my primary objective. I've been asking around, and it seems you haven't been trading in contraband recently. Is that because you aren't, or because you've bribed the excise officers?'

'If you're asking whether my trade is above board, it is. Whatever sins I've committed, I've kept them far from England. In any case, I've become tediously respectable in the last few years.'

'Good—it would put a damper on the festivities if you were hauled out in the middle of the ball for smuggling, or worse.'

'I'm not coming to the damned ball. Putting me in the same room with Lady Westford is a recipe for disaster. Doing it in front of the whole of the London Ton, which is only waiting for the stain of my birth to out, is a recipe for the apocalypse. I don't want Emily's wedding tainted by scandal.'

'Well, it's a little late for that. As you can see, now the inhabitants of our little social swamp know you're in Town their cauldrons are bubbling with cackling conjecture. And a ball is the perfect place for the two of you to face each other across the green, since that's the one occasion she'll not risk showing her true face. You want the rare experience of Grandmama holding her tongue? That's practically the only time you'll find it, *Pretty Kitty*.'

Kit tightened his hand on his glass, breathing carefully.

'Oh, I forgot you didn't like your pet name,' Julian said with his most disingenuous smile. 'Marcus and I never meant for it to reach your school. Bad luck that. If you hadn't been such a pretty little thing it likely wouldn't have stuck. Still, I think it was rather extreme of you to force everyone to stop calling you Kit and call you Christopher instead.'

Kit was very tempted to show Julian precisely how he'd forced everyone to stop echoing his cousins' epithet. The only benefit of their mischief was that he'd learned to defend himself at a very young age, but for years he'd allowed no one to call him Kit other than Mary and Emily.

To everyone else he'd become Christopher Carrington.

And now, unfortunately, Lord Westford.

He sighed impatiently.

'If you're done drinking my wine and trying to goad me into losing my temper, Julian, you can take yourself off.'

Julian laughed. 'Foiled. You used to be so much more susceptible once. But don't let your dislike of me dissuade you from coming to the ball. I'm curious to see how you and Marcus rub along. At least I think Marcus will be there. He also has no intention of attending, but no doubt Genny will find a way of twisting his arm.'

'Genny?'

Julian stood and gave Kit a quizzical smile. 'Serena's sister—Genevieve Maitland. You've been away a while, but don't tell me you've forgotten Charlie's widow and her sister? The granddaughters of your old commanding officer General Maitland?'

'No, but what have they to do with any of this?'

'Since they live with Lady Westford, they will obviously be at the ball.'

'I didn't know they were living with our grandmother.'

'Where else would they be? Since Grandfather swore after the umpteenth time Charlie invested in some ill-fated agricultural venture that he'd not give him another chipped farthing, Serena has been left with all his debts, poor woman. And of course Genny wouldn't leave her to face Grandmother's bludgeoning alone.' He drained his wine and went to the door. 'Don't forget you promised me a case of that wine.'

Kit didn't bother to point out that he'd promised no such thing. Still, a case of wine was cheap compared to the funds Julian had received from the Carrington coffers over the years.

He was standing as the door closed and was still staring at it when Benja entered.

'Well, *Capità*?'

'Not well at all, Benja. In fact, I'm afraid I shall have to visit a tailor. My wardrobe does not stretch to acceptable evening wear.'

Benja clucked his tongue morosely.

'I knew it. The Borgia—they always bring bad news.'

Chapter Three

So far, so good.

Genny stood by the musicians' dais at the end of Carrington House's crowded ballroom and surveyed the product of her plotting. She didn't know what was more impressive: the fact that Emily's ball looked set to be one of the Season's successes, or that Lady Westford was actually smiling.

She was most pleased to see that Mary and Serena were occasionally leaving the matrons' corner to dance, and that even Marcus and Julian were behaving. Thus far. Well, Marcus was his usual reticent self, but Julian's easy charm was fast convincing many ambitious matrons that perhaps his lack of funds might be overlooked after all.

There was only one fly in the ointment, and she very much hoped it didn't transform itself into a whole hornets' nest.

One of the chief reasons the Ton had thronged to Carrington House tonight was not because of the Carringtons who were present, but because of the one who was absent.

For the past few weeks the gossip columns had continued to jab their poison pens into the enigmatic figure of Lord Westford as he'd lurked in the London docks. Genny had been particularly impressed with one of the engravings, depicting a cloaked and masked hunchback skulking along a darkened dock as brawny sailors scattered in fear before him. The text was hardly any better. An improbably salacious tale of his misdemeanours interlaced with what the Ton would probably consider even more scandalous facts about his origins and occupation.

They might smile at Lady Westford, but behind their fans they clucked their tongues because the once respectable Carrington name was now in the hands of a man whose maternal grandfather might well have been a bastard, whose mother had been not only a shopkeeper's daughter but an actress, and whose only protection from gaol and transportation might be the title he had never been meant to inherit in the first place.

It was all simply *too* delicious.

And Genny might curl her lip at the Ton's avid prurience, but she had to appreciate its effect—the ballroom was full to bursting. So long as the cause of that gossip kept himself to himself, Genny was content.

Still, she kept a close watch on the circling of the vultures, and was just beginning to relax her vigilance when the buzzing began—like a swarm of wasps shifting direction across the dance floor.

She knew that sound—it was the sound of gossip rippling across the fetid pond of London society, and it usually boded ill for someone. She had little doubt that this time it boded ill for the Carringtons.

It was at times like this that she wished she were taller.

She pasted a cool smile on her lips and worked her way towards the centre of this rising swarm. It was a bevy of eligible young women, many of whom were on her list of possible brides for Julian and Marcus. If either of them was fomenting trouble, this would be a good place to hear of it.

The girls had gathered in one of the alcoves that lined the ballroom wall, where weary dancers could rest be-

tween sets. Each alcove was flanked by tall Doric pillars
which provided ample cover for Genny's eavesdropping.

'I'm telling you, Papa recognised him,' said Lady Sarah
Ponsonby. 'Just as we stepped out of the carriage, we saw
him walking up the street.'

'Is he truly a hunchback?' This excited whisper sounded
like Lady Calista, the Duke of Burford's youngest granddaughter.

'Heavens, no. He looks nothing like the illustrations in
the newspaper. In fact, he is by far the handsomest man I
have ever seen. *Far* handsomer than Lord Byron.'

'No!'

'He is also far more scandalous...' whispered another
voice.

'They say he's a *pirate*!' Lady Calista contributed again.

'Not a pirate—a privateer,' clarified Calista's sister
Lady Sophronia, with a careful little cough. 'Though there
are tales that he has engaged in...smuggling.'

'Well, I heard the men on his boat are escaped prison-
ers, even *murderers*.'

A hiss of satisfied gasps rippled through the small
group.

'And *I* heard he has a harem on board.'

'What is a harem?' asked a timid voice. 'Is it some kind
of animal?'

'Animals. Plural,' answered Lady Sophronia. 'It means
women, Miss Caversham. *Not* respectable women.'

'He sounds dreadfully exciting. It is such a pity Grandpapa wouldn't approve of him,' said Lady Calista, and
sighed.

'Why not?' Lady Sarah demanded, a trifle defiantly.
'He might be all those things, but now he holds the title
and the estate he is bound to put all that behind him and
settle down.'

'There is, however, the issue of his...birth.' Lady Sophronia lowered her voice and there was a swishing of skirts as the group huddled closer. 'His maternal grandfather was not only a foundling and a shopkeeper, but he trod the boards. There is some talk his mother did the same.'

'She trod on what?' asked the timid Miss Caversham as the others gave a gratifying gasp.

'She was on the stage,' Lady Sarah Ponsonby said impatiently. 'An *actress*.'

'*And* she was five years older than his father. They say she bewitched him. Truly! They eloped and set out to sea, and the present Lord Westford was born on a *ship*. That is how he became a pirate—just like Captain Drake.'

'Ooh! How thrilling!'

'Thrilling' wasn't the word Genny would employ.

She left the safety of her pillar and headed towards the entrance to the ballroom. Halfway there she was intercepted by the head footman, Henry, his face carefully devoid of expression.

'Mr Howich wonders if you could be spared for a moment, Miss Maitland.'

Genny followed him into the hall and Henry closed the door behind them, muffling the rumbling rush of human noise.

'What is it, Henry?'

'His Lordship, Miss Maitland. He is *here*.'

This was said with such a portentous tone Genny couldn't help smiling. Henry would have made a fine chorus for a Greek tragedy.

'Here...where?'

'In the library, miss. He asked for Mrs Carrington, miss, but she's in the lady's retiring room with Miss Emily, who's gone and torn her flounce, so Mr Howich sent me to fetch you, miss.'

'Very good, Henry. You needn't wait.'

Henry nodded and hurried off, rather in the manner of

someone being released from a cage shared with a prowling lion.

Genny entered the library, thinking fast. She had not gone to all this trouble to bring Serena back into the land of the living only for Lord Westford to waltz in and scupper all her efforts. There was too much at stake.

She stopped just inside the door, her thoughts stuttering to a halt. The man by the library window had turned at her entrance, candlelight shifting over his face and distorting its sharp lines. For a moment she was certain that Howich had made a mistake and admitted the wrong man. Eight years had passed since she'd last seen Captain Carrington, but she must have been a child indeed to have forgotten how handsome he was.

Strange.

And—even more strange—she felt a stab of inexplicable disappointment.

She pushed it aside and focused on the man who held her sister's fate in his hands. And therefore hers as well.

Lady Sarah was right—even in the gloom there was no denying that he was an exquisite specimen of manhood. Julian and Marcus were unfairly attractive men, but Lord Westford was close to being an ideal of thoroughly male beauty.

Scandalous or not, Genny sincerely doubted the new Lord Westford was about to receive the cold shoulder—at least not from the female half of the Ton. And perhaps not from a good portion of the male half as well.

His dark brown hair caught the candlelight, shining with the faintest hint of auburn, and his sun-darkened skin made the famous Carrington blue eyes gleam like shadowed sapphires. He was dressed in the height of fashion, but without a glint of colour to break the chiaroscuro landscape. Even the pin in his cravat was made of something dark, obsidian, perhaps.

If those young ladies were expecting a pirate, they might be surprised by the reality of Lord Westford, but Genny doubted they would be disappointed.

He moved away from the window and his eyes narrowed as they inspected her, a little puzzled. He probably was having difficulty placing her—which didn't offend her in the least. She would rather not be instantly memorable as the scrawny, taciturn seventeen-year-old he'd known while serving under her grandfather in Spain.

Then a faint smile that would most certainly please the likes of Lady Sarah curved his mouth.

'Well, well… Genevieve Maitland.'

Ah. She remembered his voice. Her grandfather had always said he had a natural voice for command.

'Lord Westford,' she replied, moving into the room. 'You choose your moments.'

His mouth quirked and those dark blue Carrington eyes narrowed, flashing with either annoyance or humour. 'Shall I leave?'

'That might be a good idea…'

His eyes widened, surprise wiping away the smile, and Genny continued.

'However, I think it is a little late for that. You were seen entering the house and the ballroom is already buzzing in anticipation. It would only make matters worse.'

'Worse for whom? And worse than what?' His smile was back as he approached the table, where she saw Howich had cleverly set out a decanter of wine. 'Would you care for some wine? I have a feeling I shall be needing it.'

'Probably.'

'That bad?'

'That depends.'

'On what?'

'On you, Lord Westford. We did not know you were planning to attend.'

He poured her a glass and approached her. His smile was still there, but it had changed into something of a warning, and in a way she was grateful for that. He was an intelligent man—there was little point in playing games. There was also very little time to beat around the bush.

'This is my house, Miss Maitland,' he said with quiet emphasis as she took the glass from his long fingers. 'I am not required to announce my comings and goings.'

She smiled at the rebuke. Her memories were returning with each word he spoke. 'Certainly not, my lord. But unless it is your express purpose to put Lady Westford… and thus your family…at a disadvantage, I think it is best that we ease her into the knowledge of your arrival at her first big social appearance since coming out of mourning. Which, unless I am mistaken, is why you sent for Mary rather than going directly to the ballroom.'

He leaned back against the table, gently swirling the wine in his glass as he listened to her. 'I can almost hear your grandfather when you speak, Miss Maitland. Where *is* Mary, by the way?'

'I believe she is helping Emily with a torn flounce. Howich will fetch her the moment she is available. I think it best that she and Emily accompany you into the ballroom, and after I have a word with your grandmother I shall ensure Marcus and Julian are on hand for a show of family solidarity. This is best done during the pause in the dancing and before everyone goes in for supper. When the dancing recommences after supper you should dance with several of the young women, starting with the Duke of Burford's granddaughters as the Duke is a particular friend of your grandmother. Mary will make the introductions. Marcus and Julian have already done so, and it will be expected. Oh, and you should take Her Grace the Duchess of Firth in to supper. She has precedence.'

His brows rose and rose as she spoke. 'Anything else, Miss Maitland?'

'No. My grandfather always said that of all his officers you were the one with the greatest degree of common sense and self-discipline, and I trust his judgement implicitly. I also infer from what Mary has told me over the years that you care deeply for her and Emily and would do nothing to jeopardise their happiness.'

'Good God, you do nothing by half-measures, do you?'

'There isn't time. By now everyone in the ballroom will be waiting for your grand entrance. Some are expecting a hunchback. Others are hoping you have brought a few members of your harem with you.'

'Hell and damnation.'

'Yes. Now I must go and prepare your grandmother and your cousins…' She paused as the door opened and Mary hurried in, a smile lighting her face.

'Kit! I didn't think you would come!'

Lord Westford straightened away from the table, his smile changing again, softening.

'I wasn't going to—but then guilt overcame good sense. I should have warned you.'

'Nonsense! I'm delighted you decided to come after all, and Emily will be *aux anges*. Come…'

She took his arm. But Lord Westford merely threw Genny a slightly cynical look. 'In a moment. Miss Maitland has to smooth my path first, apparently.'

Mary, utterly guileless, smiled. 'Oh, that is probably best. When should we follow, Genny?'

'Ten minutes—no more.'

'Such faith in oneself is admirable,' he murmured. 'Go to it, Miss Maitland.'

Genny ignored the undercurrents in his voice. She didn't need Lord Westford to like her. He was intelligent enough to do what was right without being coaxed. Still, his tone pinched at her as she left the room, as if her laces had been tugged by an inexperienced maid.

She found Julian and sent him to prepare Marcus, then went in search of Lady Westford. That lady was still holding court in the dowagers' corner, a densely packed jungle of jewelled and feathered turbans, shawls and politics. Two patronesses of Almack's, one duchess, and three countesses flanked Lady Westford, and it was evident from their watchful smiles as Genny approached that they had heard the gossip. Genny, who had hoped to speak with Lady Westford in private, realised that would be a mistake.

She widened her smile. 'Wonderful news, Lady Westford, Kit has arrived!'

Her tone sounded a little over-bright to her own ears, and for a moment she wondered if Lady Westford would spoil her hand. Then the heavy lids lowered, and when they rose Genny knew that Lady Westford's self-interest had won over her antipathy.

For the moment.

'How marvellous, my dear Genevieve. I don't believe you have yet met my grandson, Lord Westford, have you, ladies? He has been much away these years.'

Genny happily fell into the background as the seasoned dames of society made polite enquiries while they awaited the grand moment. Again she tensed at the sound of society ruffling its feathers as Lord Westford finally entered, but to her relief he exhibited none of the antagonism she'd felt roll off him in the library. He looked completely at his ease, with Emily on his arm and Mary by his side.

Julian, bless him, approached them, and the two men spoke with every external sign of amiability. Marcus didn't follow suit, but came to stand beside Lady Westford as the cavalcade proceeded, a faint smile playing at his mouth as he watched. Genny was tempted to poke him in the back with her fan, but remained where she was. There was al-

ways a point at which any additional act was likely to do
more ill than good.

Talk rose and fell like gusts of wind about the room,
and the musicians, as instructed, played a subdued but
cheerful tune in the background. Lord Westford finally
reached Lady Westford and stopped, his gaze holding his
grandmother's.

'Good evening, Grandmama. You must tell me your secret. You haven't changed at all since last we met.'

There was the faintest grunt of amusement from Marcus, and Genny waited in mute agony for Lady Westford's
reaction. Finally, her gloved hand was extended, quivering a little before Lord Westford took it and bowed over it.
The silence felt a trifle too long, but then it was over, and
Lady Westford was introducing him to the ladies seated
beside her.

Howich, with impeccable timing, opened the doors to
the supper room and Lady Westford rose. The Duke of
Burford's corset creaked as he hurried towards her, while
Lord Westford extended his arm to the Duchess of Firth
and all the rest fell into their designated pairings with the
ease of long practice.

Genny watched the procession, her shoulders lowering
as it advanced. She realised she had a death grip on her
fan, and eased her hands before the poor thing cracked
under the pressure.

Chapter Four

Genny had always agreed with Wellington's words after Waterloo: *'Next to a battle lost, the greatest danger is a battle gained.'*

It was precisely what kept her from declaring the battle gained, despite supper passing without incident and nothing horrid happening as the new Lord Westford led damsel after damsel on to the dance floor for the next hour.

If he noticed her watching him like a hawk, he gave absolutely no sign. Like Julian, he possessed the skill of seeming to bestow his total attention upon his partners, and as she'd predicted, the Ton was at least temporarily bowled over by his external attributes, more than willing to be indulgent of this new and exotic toy dropped into its pen.

Finally, exhausted from her vigil, Genny relaxed enough to leave the ballroom in search of Howich. Barring any disaster yet to occur, the final verdict on the success of the Carringtons' return to society would not only be measured in the family's behaviour, but in the quality of the supper, the musicians, and the uninterrupted flow of spirits. There was no more she could do in the ballroom, but at least she could ensure the flow of wine to the card rooms.

She had just reached the hall leading to the servants' entrance behind the main staircase when a voice hailed her.

'A moment, please, Miss Maitland.'

Oh, dear, what now?

Genny didn't speak the words aloud as she turned to face Lord Westford, but her face must have expressed her thoughts quite faithfully.

His smile was mocking as he surveyed her, and there was no sign of the charm he'd recruited in the supper room and on the dance floor. The shadow cast by the rise of the stairs softened the hard-cut lines of his face. It should have dimmed the impact of his unfairly handsome visage and imposing size, but it merely added a predatory threat.

But if he meant to intimidate her by looming over her like that, he would be sorely disappointed. She'd never responded well to intimidation.

'Well, Miss Maitland?' he asked as she remained silent.

'*Well*, Lord Westford?' she echoed.

'*"Well"* as in did I pass muster?'

'Surely you don't need a subaltern's opinion on that, Captain Carrington?'

'Hardly a subaltern. Come.'

'Where?'

'Time to face the music, Genevieve Maitland.'

'What does that mean?' She frowned, her nerves tingling.

'It is a phrase I learned from an American friend after the wars. It means answering the call of the bugles into battle.'

'Oh, no, what has happened now?' She was too weary to keep the exasperation from her voice, and a strange look, almost of satisfaction, crossed his face.

'You shall see.'

She squared her shoulders and allowed him to lead her back into the ballroom. She scanned the landscape, but nothing horrible was apparent. There were fewer people than before supper, but that was to be expected as some of the older guests had left after supper, or gone to sit down and ease the effects of overeating in one of the dimly lit drawing rooms set up for that purpose.

She noted with resignation that Marcus was nowhere to be seen, but she wasn't overly surprised. At least Julian was still there. He was dancing with a rather dashing countess whose husband was always the first to populate the card tables. He caught her glance and his cheek twitched in something approaching a wink.

She sighed and frowned up at Lord Westford. 'I don't see anything…untoward. What is it?'

'Your penance. Come.'

He took her arm, directing her towards the dance floor and instinctively she resisted.

'No.'

His hold tightened. 'That frightening Mrs Drummond-Burrell is watching us. You wouldn't wish to blight Emily's chance of entering the hallowed halls of Almack's by leaving me standing on the dance floor, would you?'

Genny snapped her mouth shut and they moved forward again. To her further dismay, the musicians, who had finished a sedate country dance, were beginning the first strains of a waltz. Unlike the waltzes before supper, this was not at *trois temps* but at *deux*, its slower tempo more suited to the now pastry-and-champagne-heavy guests. Now she wished she'd not requested this modification from the musicians—the faster waltzes made talking rather difficult, and she was not feeling amiable enough to smile and converse with Lord Westford.

'It cannot be helped now, but in future you should ask a lady before presuming she wishes to dance,' she said under her breath.

'Just as you asked each and every one of us if we wished to be dandled from your puppet strings this evening?'

'I see. So this is by way of revenge?'

'For making Emily's first ball a success? I am not so petty. Besides, I don't think any of my partners these past couple of hours considered their dances with me punitive.'

'I am certain you can be charming when you wish, Lord Westford. But, although I am also certain you did not notice, I have chosen not to dance tonight. Dancing with you now, and in particular a waltz, will occasion precisely the kind of comment I was hoping to avoid during this already challenging evening.'

'You are wrong.'

'You may be an expert in many fields, Lord Westford, but this is not one of them.'

'I wasn't referring to my social skills, or lack thereof. Merely that I did notice you were not dancing. Mary has told me you prefer to focus your energies on ensuring that the grand return of the Carringtons to the bosom of the Ton goes smoothly.'

'Then why insist on dancing with me?'

'Because I wished to?'

She didn't reply to this blatant provocation, and fixed her gaze on the dark grey fabric of his waistcoat.

It was hard to remain aloof when one's hand was resting on one's partner's shoulder, and their differing heights were forcing one to lean one's forearm against the soft fabric of his sleeve.

He and his cousins were all tall men, and she'd danced with Julian often enough in the past, but the simmering tension and anger Lord Westford masked so well was beginning to slip its leash, and it intensified the impression that he was looming over her.

'Why *did* you come tonight?' she asked at last. 'It would have been far more sensible to conduct your first meeting with Lady Westford in private.'

'I don't wish to see her in private. I came for Emily and

Mary. My memory of my grandmother led me to believe she would not risk showing her distaste for me in public.'

'I see. So appearing in the middle of her ball was by way of forcing her civility?'

For the first time that evening he gave her a wholly genuine smile. The deep blue eyes caught glints of gold from the chandeliers, and the thin lines fanning out beside them added a human frailty to what in repose was a far too statuelike face. She'd watched him use this weapon to excellent effect that evening, in order to push back at society's deep suspicion of chimeric half-breeds like him.

She resisted the urge to smile back, though it was hard. When he finally spoke she realised that the smile might be genuine, but so was his dislike of her.

'You should appreciate my tactics, Generalissima, not condemn them,' he murmured, using the nickname that had sometimes been tossed at her in Spain by her grandfather's soldiers. 'In fact, I have been waiting all evening for some sign that you approve of my performance. If there is one thing I learned from your grandfather, it is that one should always show one's subordinates appreciation where it is due. Especially if you wish to encourage your men to fulfil your every need in future...'

His voice kept going lower, trickling like warm honey down her back. Her shoulders rose, as if to shake it off, and under cover of a turn in the dance she tried to put more distance between them.

He clearly noted her resistance, and his hand slipped a little lower, coaxing her into a twirl. She had no choice but to follow his lead or end up colliding with him. He returned her deftly to their original position, but now they were even closer than before. Worse, his hand kept shifting slightly against the small of her back, mirroring the rhythm of the music in a way that was probably not apparent to observers, but would have merited a sharp rebuke from any respectable partner.

She knew he was waiting for her to comment, which was precisely why she didn't. She also knew that there was nothing more to this mild seduction than a typical male show of power, like a peacock flashing its tail. She'd been through this with the other Carrington men at one point or another. It seemed second nature for them to make use of their considerable physical charms to get their way. To their credit, neither Julian nor Marcus had held a grudge when rebuffed.

She shouldn't be offended Lord Westford was like his cousins, but strangely she was. She had told Julian she had let go of her high opinion of Captain Carrington years ago, but it seemed some of her grandfather's high expectations lingered.

Not that she was surprised he was as smooth as his cousins at this game. Someone with his looks, innate charm, and intelligence was likely to have played it often enough. She just didn't like it that he was playing it with her. Still less did she like the fact that her body disagreed with her. In fact, it was now humming happily at the friction, and trying to make her breathe in the warm scent of sandalwood and musk that emanated from him.

Just a couple more minutes, she told herself, and then this little reminder of who was in control would be over. If she was wise, she would allow him this victory after an evening that must have been rubbing him the wrong way in a hundred different directions. Then he would be so much easier to manage.

So said her mind. Her tongue, however, had other ideas.

'I *am* appreciating your tactics, my lord. They are most…persuasive. Though at the moment they are sitting rather a shade too low on my back. I think if you shift your hand a tad higher, you will achieve the same effect without risking gossip.'

His smile turned inwards again, assessing. 'Like this?'

His words were as smooth as his hand as it eased the silk of her gown against her back, his fingers finding and tracing her spine until they reached the stiff barrier of her stays. His finger teased that line and the tingling continued, its path unimpeded, wrapping around her ribs, over her shoulders, creeping up her cheeks.

It was all done as he turned her from the very edge of the dance floor, and by the time they were back in the fray of the other dancers his hand was decorously settled precisely where the strictest of dancing masters would approve.

Genny's colouring did not lend itself to blushing, but she could feel an uncomfortable pinching sensation cresting her cheekbones. She refused to drop her gaze, locking it with the angry challenge in his dark blue Carrington eyes. She knew full well this was no attempt at seduction. He was paying her back.

Against all the advice she would have given herself, had she been in a more amiable frame of mind, she went to cut him off at the knees. 'I hope… I very much hope, Lord Westford…that you haven't been practising that particular sleight of hand with your other dance partners. It is shockingly bad Ton.'

His hand flinched against her back, dragging her momentarily too close and almost making them stumble. Then it relaxed again, and although there was a slight darkening of the tanned skin of his sharp-cut cheekbones, there was no other sign of discomfiture or anger when he spoke.

'I know it's been dogs' years since we met in Spain, but unless you have changed drastically it's not like you to antagonise people unnecessarily. Certainly not people who have a hold over you.'

She was about to deny that he had a hold over her, but since she lived in what was actually his home, and was currently wearing clothes that had been indirectly paid for by him, she kept her mouth shut. In fact, she was beginning to wonder why she was finding it so hard to play her own game with him.

No, she knew why. Julian had been right about her. She was angry with Captain Carrington. More than angry—she was *furious* with him.

She could not get over her almost childish expectations of the Captain Carrington her grandfather had so admired. When the old Lord Westford had died, so soon after Charlie, Genny had been convinced it was merely a matter of time before the new Earl arrived to untangle the mess left after his grandfather's death.

But, although she knew he had learned of it, arrive he hadn't. Instead, Mary and Emily continued to receive letters with tales of Askalon and Stamboul and Alexandria and Nafplio, and Genny had wondered at what point Mary and Emily might begin to doubt, as she did, his priorities.

But as months had passed and their little cage had shrunk, 'Darling Kit' had remained Darling Kit, unblemished by expectation and disappointment. Genny wouldn't have been surprised if his half-sister and stepmother had thought of some excuse for him, had he decided he was too busy to come to Emily's wedding.

She took a deep breath and forced a smile. 'You are quite right, Lord Westford. I apologise. It has been a long day. Thank you for the dance.'

His smile held, but now it was purely surface—under it she felt something flicker…perhaps an echo of the anger she hadn't even realised was boiling so hotly inside her.

'You're welcome, Miss Maitland. And thank *you*. This was by far the most…enlightening dance I have had this evening.'

The music slowed and faded. He still held her hand, and now tucked it over his arm as if to lead her back to Lady Westford, but for a moment they stood unmoving at the edge of the dance floor, like two wary dogs.

She meant to move away, back into the orderly motion of the evening, but for a moment she could not remember what it was she was supposed to do next. It was as if she had walked into a room and now stood there, wondering what on earth she had come for.

She knew hesitation was to society what a rustling in the bushes was for a hunting dog. Every alarm bell in her head was pealing, but she couldn't think of the right course of action.

Without turning her head, she could see Lady Sophronia and Lady Sarah Ponsonby watching her and Lord Westford with unmasked curiosity. Then she saw Julian approach and gave an audible sigh of relief. Lord Westford watched him as well, with that same half-smile on his face—not unpleasant, but certainly not pleasant.

He nodded to Julian, and Julian returned the nod but addressed Genny. 'My turn, Genny?' he asked, holding out his arm.

She placed her hand on it with relief, and was surprised to see Marcus back in the ballroom as well, watching them without a flicker of expression on his face. Clearly Julian had been orchestrating some action of his own since he'd seen Kit lead her onto the dance floor. No doubt he'd lined Marcus up to dance with her next, and perhaps some other cronies of his.

She felt like a fox that had tumbled into a wolves' den. Her newly discovered dislike of Lord Westford rose a notch.

'Thank you, Julian,' she said softly as they went down the dance.

'No need. I thought it would be best to spread us Carringtons about a little. I thought you weren't planning on dancing tonight, though?'

'I wasn't. He forced my hand.'

Julian glanced over his shoulder. 'Strange. Perhaps he doesn't enjoy being ordered about by you as much as I do. Never mind—he'll get used to it if he hangs about long enough.'

That stung as well, but she tried to smile. 'I was doing it for you lot, you ungrateful wretch.'

'Sheath your claws, love. I *am* grateful. Resistant, but grateful. Difficult combination to carry off well. Marcus is doing rather poorly with it, and I think my unwelcome cousin is at the end of his rope as well—which is understandable, given this evening's baptism of fire. You'd think people would refrain from gossiping about a man in his own home, but this vicious flock of carrion crows can't seem to help themselves, and I've no doubt he was meant to overhear quite a bit of it. It's like bear baiting for the Ton—prod the beast and see what he does. All told, I am impressed with his performance, since as far as I can tell he hasn't bitten off anyone's head…yet. But if you'd like me to thrash him for you I'll be happy to oblige,' he said hopefully.

Genny smiled at his light-hearted nonsense. She felt better already, and was wondering why on earth she'd allowed herself to become so unsettled.

It was merely the natural outcome of her concerns for Serena.

Nothing more.

Chapter Five

Kit resisted the urge to snatch his grandmother's cane and toss it out of the window. The constant tapping was almost as aggravating as her words.

'I would have preferred…' *thump* '…you give warning…' *thump* '…of your arrival…' *thump* '…last night…' *thump* '… Christopher.'

Thump, thump, thump.

She looked like a wizened dancing master, marking out the rhythm for a group of disappointing pupils. Or perhaps the steward at a medieval court. Kit did rather feel like an errant courtier, summoned to an audience before an aging queen. Instead of a court jester she had Carmine the canary cackling in a cage by her armchair. And on the other side she had her three ladies-in-waiting, seated in a neat row, watching him being dressed down.

Three heads—corn-yellow, honey-brown, and dark wood—were bent over three embroidery frames. Two of the ladies were even embroidering.

Serena's design was an abundance of flowers in sedate lavenders and blues. Mary was completing a shepherdess, surrounded by a rather overweight flock. Both were rich in detail, and would no doubt bloom into fine cushions or screens one day.

Genevieve Maitland, on the other hand…

Kit wasn't in the least surprised to see that she wasn't doing much more than prodding her stretch of fabric with her needle. The result was either a surly cat or a shifty-looking toad.

He turned away from the monstrosity and sighed. He'd been annoyed to find that his grandmother had assembled an audience for their first *tête-à-tête* in almost ten years. He didn't mind Mary's presence—she'd always been a calming influence on the stormy Carrington sea—but he wished the Maitland girls weren't there.

Thump, thump, thump.

'Having stayed away this long, Kit,' his grandmother continued after she had recalled his attention, 'it is rather unfortunate you could not have postponed your return until closer to Emily's nuptials. Still, now you are returned it is highly improper that you remain living in the docks like a common sailor. There is nothing for it but that you shall have to come and stay here with the family.'

He squeezed his hands more tightly behind his back. He'd been in plenty of skirmishes with hostile navies, and even more hostile pirates, but his preferred tactic had always been to elude, not engage. He resorted to brute force only when necessary, no matter how satisfying it could be. One always paid a price for violence.

He reminded himself of how well this had worked for him over the years even as he dreamed of turning a good three hundred guns on his grandmother. He couldn't resist a shot across her bows, though. Just a warning…

'Thank you for the invitation to stay in my own home, Grandmother.'

'Do not be flippant, Kit. It was always understood that I shall have use of the Carrington House for my lifetime.'

'It being *understood* is not a contract.' He knew before the words were out that they were a mistake.

She gave a slight superior smile. 'Not in *trade*, perhaps. But a gentleman's bond is above such vulgar considerations.'

Damn. Brute force was looking as seductive as Aphrodite rising from the waves right now.

He gave a slight bow. 'Thank you for the clarification, Grandmother. I shall consider your invitation.'

'I don't see that there is anything to consider, Kit. Surely we both want what is best for Emily? You are not *au courant* with society's ways, but I assure you that now you have stepped into its world, were you to immediately retreat to your...*boat*...and attend no more events, the brunt of society's thrust would be felt by your half-sister.'

He didn't answer. He couldn't think of anything he wanted to say that he wouldn't later regret.

'I am certain Emily would be delighted if you joined us here before she departs with Peter for his grandparents' house in Hampshire, Kit,' Mary said, searching in her sewing bag and extracting a pair of silver scissors. 'And she does worry that you must be dreadfully uncomfortable, sleeping in a ship's cabin.'

'My cabin is very comfortable, Mary, and the docks are not very far away. Carrington House is actually quite conveniently situated, so far east of the fashionable centre of town.'

'Berkeley Square is eminently fashionable,' Lady Westford protested, rising to the bait like the most succulent trout.

A slight dimple formed in Miss Maitland's cheek, but she kept her head bent over in her pretence of embroidering. He had no doubt the last thing she wanted was anyone interfering with her sway over this all-female household.

'I will consider your invitation, Grandmother,' he repeated, wandering over and picking up a Sevres figurine of a shepherdess with a sheepdog half hidden by her broad skirts. It was one he'd bought for Emily for a long-ago birthday. He turned to Mary. 'Where is Emily, by the way?'

'She has gone with Peter's mama and his younger sisters to visit the Menagerie,' Mary replied. 'The younger girls have never been to London, and are trying to see as much of Town before they depart. Tomorrow we are attending a lecture on Roman treasures at the museum. Do say you will come.'

He smiled at her enthusiasm, weighing the blushing shepherdess in his hand. 'Tomorrow, I am afraid I cannot, but I shall try to come here in the evening if you aren't engaged elsewhere.'

Mary hesitated, and Miss Maitland's head dipped a little further. This time it was Serena who spoke, her pale blue eyes lighting with sudden and surprising pleasure, like a child waking and remembering it was her birthday.

'Oh, but we are going to see Kean play Sir Giles Overreach at Drury Lane tomorrow. We have not been to a play in…in years, and only last night Miss Dalrymple was telling us how marvellous it is now they have rebuilt the theatre after the fire. She said it is as pretty as a music box—all white and gold, with tableaux from Shakespeare and the most opulent boxes. Oh, you *must* come…'

'I do not think Kit would care to attend a theatrical entertainment,' Lady Westford said with finality, her cane hitting the floor with a sharp snap.

It knocked Serena out of her reverie and sent a flush up her pale cheeks. It was such a sharp transformation that Kit stepped into another pit he would have never thought he would enter in a hundred years.

'On the contrary, Grandmother. I am curious to see how Drury Lane has changed since I was last there… How long ago was it? Twenty years? You might better remember. We were there together, weren't we?'

He saw the memory rise along with a faint flush on her papery cheeks.

'I do not recall.'

'Don't you? Perhaps once we are all there tomorrow evening it will spark your memory.'

He turned away from the flash of anger in his grandmother's eyes and caught sight of Serena's face. Her pale blue eyes were wide and a little red, as if she was about to cry. He noted too that Miss Genevieve Maitland's hands were tight on her tambour frame, her gaze on her sister's profile.

He pulled tight on his temper and smiled at Serena Carrington. 'Thank you for the suggestion, Mrs Carrington. It is not a play I am familiar with, but I am certain that anything with Mr Kean is well worth watching. I shall depend upon you to tell me what the play is about.'

The three women in a row smiled in unison. Serena with relief, Mary with pleasure…but most surprising of all was Miss Genevieve Maitland. Her smile was utterly different from any he had seen her wear the previous night. Gratitude lit her face, softening her carefully held mouth and bringing two dimples to full life in a way her society smiles hadn't.

So he had inadvertently discovered how to tame the little general—defend her pack.

But Lady Westford was not done with him yet. Having been foiled, she abandoned subtlety. 'Do you think that wise, boy? People are bound to comment on your choosing to appear at the theatre of all places. I think it best to confine your appearances to less contentious settings.'

There were limits.

He turned back to his grandmother, but Miss Maitland spoke first.

'Perhaps you are right and that is best, Lady Westford.

We shall already be quite crushed in the box, as Julian will be joining us, as well as Lord Ponsonby and Lady Sarah.'

'That is hardly reason for Kit not to be present in his own box, Genny,' Mary reproved a little sharply.

Lady Westford looked between the two of them with a rather malevolent smile that made Kit's jaw clench even harder.

Before he could comment, Genny Maitland rose, her eyes downcast as she folded her embroidery and laid it in the basket. 'I didn't mean... Of course you're quite right, Mary... Pray, excuse me. I must go. I must see Mrs Pritchard about the menus...'

When the door had closed behind her, Lady Westford turned to Mary. 'Well done, Mary Carrington. Do her good to have her wings clipped. Too used to having her own way by half.' Several decisive thumps of her cane sent Carmine trilling in a rare show of harmony.

'I didn't mean...' Mary looked contritely at the door.

'But Genny *agreed* with you, Lady Westford.' Serena said hesitantly, a thread of hurt in her voice.

'I don't need people agreeing with me, girl. If there's one thing I can't abide, it's toadies!'

Carmine broke into syncopated chatter and Lady Westford rapped his cage with the knob of her cane, silencing him.

'Help me upstairs, Serena. I am tired. And, Mary, you ring for Mathers and tell her to come up to me.'

The two women sprang into action with an alacrity that Kit would have commended in any of his men, but now made him wish more than ever that he could toss both his grandmother and her cane out of the window.

He waited for the door to close behind her before turning to Mary. 'How the devil can you stand it?'

Mary shushed him with her hands, her worried gaze on the door. 'Hush, she is not that bad. Losing your grandfather has been dreadfully hard on her. It is a good thing Genny convinced her somehow to end her mourning and come to London, for she looked likely to stay there sunk in a brown study indefinitely. She has not yet recovered her spirits.'

'She seems plenty recovered to me. I had forgotten what a poisonous snake she is. You *cannot* stay with her, Mary.'

'I cannot leave her. Where would I go? I do not wish to become a burden to Emily when she is about to begin her married life, and I cannot imagine setting up house alone. And, more to the point, I cannot leave poor Serena all alone with her. That would be quite unfair.'

There was a finality in her voice that checked Kit. His stepmother's soft-spoken kindness was often mistaken for weakness, but he knew better. When something mattered to her, she could be as stubborn as his grandmother. It was a pity she'd chosen this hill on which to make her stand.

Still, he made another attempt to dislodge her from it.

'She wouldn't be alone. Having seen Genevieve Maitland's *modus operandi* last night, and today, I would say she provides ample protection for her sister. I'd back her against the old crone any day.'

'Pray do not make fun of Genny.'

'I'd as soon make fun of Napoleon. But that is beside the point—which is that guilt is a poor reason to remain in purgatory.'

'It's not guilt, Kit. It is duty.'

His skin must have thinned considerably since his return to London, because her comment pierced it and prodded his temper back into life. 'Ah, here comes the reprimand.'

She flushed. 'I did not intend it as a reprimand. It is a fact. The one balm of my existence during these years, other than Emily, has been my friendship with Serena and

Genevieve. I will not leave them here at your grandmother's mercy.' She hesitated. 'Or her at Genny's.'

'Are those two constantly at war?'

'Oh, no. Nothing so obvious. Genny is…' She frowned, her eyes on the row of figurines, and pointed to the one he'd set down. 'She's like that sheepdog. She herds. And when there's a fox prowling she can…well, she can be protective in her own way.'

'So you and Serena are the sheep?'

'You are being harsh again. Oh, I do wish I had not chastised her as I did. You do not know how much she has done for us since she came to live with Serena. She is the only one who could manage your grandfather and grandmother.'

'All the more reason to leave her to it.'

'But that is wrong—can you not see? She isn't even a Carrington. Perhaps if she had married Julian when he offered…'

'*Julian* offered for her?'

'Oh, several years back. But it came to nothing and they remain good friends. My point is that, unlike Serena and myself, she has no duty to your grandmother.'

'Nor do you. That old bat treats you worse than she does her cacophonous canary.'

'That is only because she is unsettled. I think she feels guilty that she is enjoying coming out of mourning and seeing her old friends after so long. We must be patient.'

Kit realised that at least was true. As had been Mary's comment about her lack of choice. She had been living for other people since her marriage to his father, when she was seventeen, and the birth of her daughter the following year. He could see that, for her, the thought of setting up her own household must be almost unbearably daunting.

If he wished to remove Mary from his grandmother's influence he would have to provide a suitable alternative.

The only problem was that he had no idea what that alternative might be. The best thing for her would be to marry again, but playing matchmaker was well beyond the scope of his skills.

'Very well,' he conceded, rolling back his guns. 'I won't press.'

'Thank you, Kit. And you will come with us to the theatre?'

He looked down at her pretty, hopeful countenance and felt a wave of gratitude roll over him. She'd been younger even than Emily when she'd found herself in a marriage of convenience, and yet she'd tried so hard to be a good wife to a grief-stricken man and a caring stepmother to his equally grief-stricken son.

She was still trying. He ought to do the same.

'Of course I will come, Mary.'

Chapter Six

'He's drinking, Miss Genny,' said Mrs Pritchard as she gazed down at the basket resting on a bale of hay in the stables. 'And he had a little sliver of mutton just now.'

Genny smiled at the housekeeper and crouched down to inspect the tiny cat. The basket was a trifle large, for it had recently been populated by three ginger kittens a stable hand had found abandoned in the alley between Carrington House and the mews stables.

Likely their arrival at the house had scared the mother away, and only one of the litter had survived the week. Genny had learned not to name them until they could feed on their own. Even now she hesitated, waiting for some sign that it wouldn't suddenly weaken and fade as the other two had.

'Well, I'd best be about my duties, miss. I'll keep an eye on him.'

'Thank you, Mrs Pritchard.'

When she had left, Genny sat on the bale of hay and plucked the tiny cat from the basket. It circled itself into a ball on her lap, the agate eyes slitting and razor teeth flashing as it yawned.

'Did you like your mutton, you stubborn little ball of fluff? You did, didn't you, sweetheart?'

She purred encouragingly as she ran her finger from its little bony head down the curve of its soft back. She could feel its vertebrae shift like a bead necklace as she traced it again and again, murmuring foolish words to this sole survivor.

The kitten stiffened suddenly and Genny stopped, re-alising someone was standing in the alley. She turned, ex-pecting to see one of the servants.

'This is an unusual place to hide, Miss Maitland. I take it your need to see the housekeeper was an excuse for a strategic retreat?'

His voice was even deeper in the confines of the stables. Genny considered standing as he approached, but remained where she was. She was at distinct disadvantage, seated on her bale of hay, but standing in this confined space would be even worse. His tone clearly indicated that he was intent on attack, and if she must be loomed over she preferred to do it from her throne of hay with a kitten between them.

'If you wish to think so, my lord, then it was.'

'What I wish for and what I am likely to obtain around here are evidently two altogether different things.'

'Dear me—should I feel sorry for you? How quickly you have fallen from prodigal son to mere sacrificial lamb.'

He sank down on his haunches with a suddenness that made her lean back slightly.

'Don't mistake me for a lamb of any kind, Miss Mait-land. I'm not a good subject for whatever herding games you like to play in this household.'

His eyes, more silver than blue in the gloom, were fixed on hers, a hint of a smile softening his sharp-cut mouth.

'I don't play games, Lord Westford. What I do, I do for a reason.'

'Which is?'

She wanted to look away, but strangely she couldn't.

She also felt the urge to swallow, but knew he wouldn't miss that tell-tale sign of unease.

'To get through the day,' she replied, keeping her voice light.

'Yes, I remember that,' he said slowly, his gaze moving over her, his cheekbones catching the faint light from the doorway. 'You were always on your guard. Your grandfather said you could have made your mark in the army, had you been a boy.'

A stab of pain pierced her between abdomen and chest. It was cruel of him to use her grandfather's words and unfulfilled wishes against her. She didn't want him talking about her grandfather as if he owned part of him.

'I'm well aware of my failings, Lord Westford.'

'He meant it as a compliment,' he said, and his voice softened, as if in regret. 'He also said he was likely to go off tilting at windmills like Don Quixote, if not for his Sancho Panza.'

'That is certainly not a compliment to either of us. I may be short, and secondary, but no one could say of my grandfather that he was a deluded romantic.'

'Don't twist what I said, Genny. Your grandfather was a brilliant and generous man, but like everyone he had his blind spots, and he trusted your judgement, despite your youth. It might have upset some of the men under his command to have you hovering in the wings, but anyone with an ounce of sense knew better than to underestimate your impact on him.'

'I think I prefer the comparison to Don Quixote and Sancho Panza. Now I sound like a scheming harridan and he a malleable fool.'

'Now you are merely twisting my words in the other direction. You understand me very well.'

'You certainly appear to think *you* understand *me* very well, Lord Westford.'

'Let us say I am beginning to remember quite a bit from those days.'

'Surely you have better things to occupy you than my relationship with my grandfather?'

'I do, but since you appear to be impacting upon most of those "better things", in a rather surprising manner, I find I am curious about my old commanding officer's *eminence grise*.'

'So now I am not only short, and scheming, but also grey? And there I was, believing Mary when she said your reputation for deadly charm was well deserved.'

He smiled—his first real smile for her.

'You must have some French fencing blood to go with that name, Genevieve. You parry beautifully—though a little forcefully. If I were a gentleman, I would have been grovelling a dozen times by now.'

'Well, I'm glad you're not. I hate grovelling. I'm too tempted to kick snakes when they're down.'

'Ouch. I've never been likened to a snake before.'

'It's better than a peacock.'

His smile widened, causing the same softening about the eyes that had had such an unsettling effect on her on the dance floor.

'Nothing pea-sized about me, sweetheart. Certainly not my—'

'I don't need you to flash your feathers for me, Lord Westford,' she interrupted hastily, grateful for the gloom of the stables. 'There are plenty of young women in Town all too willing to oblige if you need your vanity fluffed.'

'It's not my vanity that needs fluffing, Generalissima.'

'No, that needs a good flattening.'

'You're doing a damn good job of that,' he said musingly. 'You're still winning this parrying game.'

'It's not a game, Lord Westford, and I'm not your enemy.'

He didn't answer, his gaze holding hers as if he would force some revelation out of her that she herself wasn't aware of. She tried very hard not to waver, but her breath began to fall out of rhythm, as if she was forgetting the most basic of physical actions.

Finally, he moved—but only to sit on a bale of hay next to her.

She wished he would leave. *She* should leave, but somehow she didn't want to. It was damnably confusing, and she didn't like feeling so stretched and pulled in opposite directions.

She especially didn't like feeling suddenly so young. As if somehow his vision of her as a taciturn, cautious, almost-eighteen-year-old was forcing her back to that strange time where she'd been clinging to her world by untried claws like the little ginger cat.

She stroked the ball of fur and the kitten, which had been happily asleep, gave a mewl, its tiny claws pressing into her skin.

He glanced down at it. 'I remember that too. Genevieve…patron saint of strays.'

His voice was low and soft, and the undercurrent of hostility was gone. She felt a strange flush spread out from the knot between her abdomen and lungs.

He leaned closer, stroking the arching back of the ginger cat with one finger. The kitten's eyes narrowed to blissful slits as he ministered to it, making long, gentle strokes from the crown of its scruffy head to the brash burst of its tail, stopping just short of her fingers. She held herself against the need to tighten her hands about the kitten as its purring went from silken to rough velvet against her palms.

'Where did this fellow come from?' he asked.

'He was found with two other kittens in the alley by the stables. The mother never returned and now he's the only one left,' she murmured, keeping quite still as the kitten wallowed in shivering bliss. She felt Lord Westford's gaze shift to her, but his stroking didn't lose rhythm.

'He's a good size already. He'll make it.' He spoke in a voice almost with the timbre of that purr. 'I'm sorry about the others.'

'There's no point in being sorry. They rarely survive. This one shall have more mice to choose from in the stables. And too many cats upset the dogs.'

He looked around. 'There are dogs here as well?'

'Not here. At the Hall in Dorset. Milly and Barka. Barka is too old to chase anything, and spends most days dozing in the stables, but Milly has enough energy for both of them. Hopefully by the time we return there Leo will be large enough to stand his ground.'

He stopped stroking, resting his elbows on his knees as he remained leaning towards her. 'Leo? He doesn't look like much of a lion.'

'Leo is short for Leonidas.'

'Good God, poor fellow—' He broke off with a soft laugh. 'Are Milly and Barka also named for long-dead warriors?'

'I'm afraid they are. Militiades and Hannibal Barka. I had to name them something...'

'What is wrong with dog names like Bouncer, or Dancer, or Rover?'

'I've used them all through the years. Also Juno, Thunder, Lovely, Lady, Lovely Lady, Hector... That one gave me the idea of going to the Greeks, so then there was Mars, who was a brute, and Zeus who was spoilt and ill-tempered, and Athena, who was quite the least intelligent dog I ever had.'

His laugh was every bit as beautiful as he—a warm rumble that reverberated through her far more deeply than Leo's purring.

'I remember you gave some odd name to that great scruffy brute who adopted you in Talavera. What was it?'

'Oh, Archidamus! Archie was a dear, but already quite old by the time he found me.'

Kit smiled, leaning back to look up at the wooden beams of the stables as if they were opening up and beyond them was a view of some long-ago memory.

'That's true. Strays of all forms did seem to find you. Your grandfather used to grumble that whenever we barracked for longer than a few days the place soon began to resemble a menagerie.'

'That wasn't my fault. Soldiers always attract foraging animals during a war. I didn't feed them any more than the others did.'

'Yet they always seemed to follow you about. Like that Archie fellow. I never did understand why he left the village with us; he must have lived there all his life.'

'The mayor's wife told me his family had been killed. Maybe he wanted to start anew, go on an adventure before…' Her words ended on a strange intake of breath. She let it out slowly, stroked the ginger kitten once more, and replaced him in the basket, where the little ball of fur curled up into soft sleep.

'Before he died,' he completed.

The shaft went home, surprising her with its sharpness. And with a strange hurt that *he* had driven it home.

His hand touched hers briefly and drew away just as abruptly, leaving a trail of sensitised fire and her nerves twanging like an angrily plucked harp.

She shrugged. She had no clear idea how he had gone from an inquisition to this strangely intrusive sympathy. She didn't *want* his sympathy. The inquisition had been less unsettling.

'They all do. It was a long time ago.'

'Two trite rationalisations that have little to do with the pain of losing someone you care for,' he said.

She bent to pluck straw from her skirt, pressing back the completely unexpected threat of tears.

She'd never succeeded in putting Captain Carrington in a safe box, so she'd done her best to keep her distance from him during that year in Spain. Now she could see her instincts had been completely justified. He did not play by any rules that she could see. He seemed to adapt himself to whatever situation he found himself in and yet remain aggravatingly, impenetrably, the same.

She had no idea why he seemed to think she'd succeeded in parrying his thrusts. She felt like an emotional pincushion. Perhaps he'd learned that annoying skill as the Captain of a less than respectable ship—adjusting to capricious oceans and whatever political games were being played out on the grand chessboard of the world's powers.

Whatever the case, she knew he wasn't…*safe*.

'I'd best go inside.' She stood and then hesitated. '*Are* you coming to the play tomorrow evening? I didn't mean to dissuade you.'

'I'm aware of that. Now. That little manoeuvre was aimed at cornering me into agreeing to attend, wasn't it?'

'Not cornering. Prodding. Society will make a deal of it whether you join your grandmother at the theatre or stay away. Sometimes bold is best.'

He remained seated on the bale of hay, looking up at her, his eyes catching the faint light from the stable entrance. Like the sea under a heavy cover of cloud. She felt absurdly nervous suddenly.

'Sometimes it is…' he replied at last, with surprising hesitation. 'I admit I allowed you and my grandmother to goad me into saying I would come, but I don't wish to do Emily any harm.'

'If there is one thing I have learned since I came to live

with the Carringtons, it is that you should never give society the upper hand. That means never revealing a weakness. Individually, people can be kind, but as a group they are vicious and unforgiving.'

'All the more reason not to tempt them to lash out. I don't care what they say of me, but I don't wish my contribution to Emily's nuptials to be an even heavier cloud of scandal.'

'You should come.' The words were out before she could think them through, and she scrambled to explain them to herself as much as to him. 'Last night was a success because you appeared to take it for granted that they would accept you.'

He gave a short laugh. 'I take nothing for granted.'

'I know—which is excellent and precisely why it worked. It might just as easily have been a complete disaster, but you have several serious advantages, Lord Westford. Your title, your inheritance, and your good looks. Not to mention the dash of romance your piracy brings to the table.'

He shifted on the bale of hay, his gaze falling from hers, and she wondered if she'd embarrassed him.

'I was never a pirate. And, believe me, that is not something one should consider romantic.'

'I don't. But then much of society—including our esteemed and rotund King—consider war to be the height of romance.'

'True… Idiots. I'm glad Emily found herself a nice country husband and not one of those dandies.'

'Peter is a darling, isn't he? But the point is, I think it best not to allow the one weakness in your flank to become your Achilles heel. If you try to hide it, that will only make the enemy all the more determined to pitch their arrows at it.'

'So you suggest I flaunt it?'

'No. Merely treat it—or rather their opinion of it—as a matter of no great import. You wish to go to the theatre, so you will go to the theatre.'

'I *don't* wish to go, but you are right.'

'Why don't you wish to go? Do you dislike plays?'

He seemed a little surprised by her question, and for a moment she thought he wouldn't answer.

'Did Mary tell you I was raised on a ship?' he asked.

'Yes. Until your mother died—' She broke off, wondering at her insensitivity.

'Yes. Well, the *Hesperus*…the original one…was a rather unusual ship. My father loved the theatre—which was where he met my mother. My maternal grandfather was, amongst other things, an actor, and she often went to help at the theatre. She was several years older than my father, to add to all her other sins, and if my father was Captain of the *Hesperus*, she was definitely captain of everything else on board. She regularly held plays on deck, and made all the sailors take part.'

Genny felt her jaw slacken at the image of a theatrical pirate ship and she shut her mouth, trying not to smile. 'How marvellous! What roles did you play?'

'None. I didn't inherit a smidgen of her or my grandfather's talent. Our star was Benja, who is my first mate now. The best I could do was fetch and carry, and then I would climb the mizzen mast and play audience.'

'I see…'

His mouth quirked. 'What *do* you see, Genevieve Maitland?'

'Drury Lane. All that pomp and grandeur and scent and noise compared to a wind-blown seaborne stage with sailors playing Hamlet and Ophelia. It won't be the same.'

In the silence she could hear the huffing of the horse in the adjacent stable, and Leo's rumbling purr.

'No, it won't be. But you are right. It is probably best to grab this bull by the horns. I hope the play is worth it.'

'Kean's playing of it is likely to be well worth it. But I must go now. Do tell Emily if you are coming—she will be delighted.'

'Yes, miss. Anything else I must do?' he asked with utterly unconvincing meekness as he leaned back further on the bale of hay.

'No, that will do for now,' she replied, unable to resist adding, 'But you really must learn to play by the rules. Such as not remaining seated when a woman stands.'

He grinned up at her. 'But I was being chivalrous, Miss Maitland. You should commend me.'

'For what?'

'I have noticed you dislike being loomed over.'

He rose from the bale of hay and she had to admit he had a point. His superior height seemed to shrink the already confined space.

'Besides,' he murmured, 'I rather liked looking up at you. You look good from all angles, Genevieve Maitland.'

'You aren't required to flirt with me, you know,' she said, hating the uncertainty in her voice.

'You should be happy. I'm honing my social skills. Drilling makes the soldier.'

'"Drilling" doesn't involve shooting at the side of a barn at five paces.'

'I had no idea you were that susceptible, Genny,' he said, with utterly unconvincing surprise, before adding, 'And I would never be so ungentlemanly as to think of you in terms of a barn—though you *are* rather liberally covered in hay at the moment. You might want to do something about that before you go inside, or the servants will get the wrong idea.'

Genny searched for something suitably cutting, and

then decided that ignoring pests was sometimes the best policy.

'Thank you for your concern, Lord Westford. Good day.'

Kit watched her brush the hay from her skirts as she left the stables. The material stretched against her hips and legs, and for a moment, as she swung open the gated door, sunlight permeated the summery fabric and outlined a figure that made it clear she'd changed a great deal since Spain...

The image was overlaid with another from years ago, of a much younger version of Genevieve Maitland, brushing dust from her skirts after helping clear one of the General's billets in a small hill town by the Pyrenees. She'd been only a girl then, but already seeming far older than most.

He couldn't remember Serena ever pitching in to help. But then it probably hadn't been her fault. The General had split his paternal and maternal instincts between his two granddaughters, and to be fair both had appeared quite content with the division, and had expected it to be replicated within the cadre of officers.

Serena, with her pure English beauty, pale blue eyes and corn-gold hair, had expected and received universal admiration. Genny had snapped impatiently at anyone who'd tried to flirt with her, but immediately fallen in with anyone who came to her with a problem to solve.

People new to the General's command had often been surprised to learn that Serena and Genevieve were sisters. Genny must have inherited some of her grandmother's Latin blood, and though her hair had been a broad palette of browns, from chestnut to pale honey in the light, her skin had used to take the sun like a Spaniard's, making her deep grey eyes look even larger in an almost gaunt face.

Well, she was gaunt no longer. In fact, she'd filled out

very nicely indeed. Serena had remained fashionably reed-thin, but Genny was a pure pocket Venus—small, but perfectly proportioned, and with a bosom worthy of a portrait of its own.

And yet she still possessed that strange quality that managed to keep curious males at bay. He'd seen them watching her the night of the ball, their eyes flickering over her lush curves, but amazingly not one of them had dared breach the invisible but very palpable battlements she carried about her.

No, that wasn't true—she'd let Julian in with a smile, which wasn't perhaps surprising if they'd nearly been betrothed. Marcus as well, though not quite as happily—there had been more resigned acceptance than affection between them. Still, it showed she had the capacity to let men in if she chose.

Strange…

She was strange. He could not understand what she was still doing here. She was not a beauty, like her sister, but she was far more interesting—and leagues more intelligent. Strange that someone with her skills at manoeuvring people had not yet married.

She must be…what? Twenty-five or six? Given the less than impressive scions of some of the nobility, he didn't doubt she could have found herself a husband to mould to her needs. Still, it appeared that for the moment all her skills were being used in aid of his family, for which he should be grateful.

For which he *was* grateful, he told himself. Reluctant, and uncomfortable, but grateful.

War made strange bedfellows, and it appeared he had just slipped into bed with Genevieve Maitland.

He waited for the rush of warmth that swept through him at the unfortunate analogy to fade.

Not a good idea.

Not that there was much to be read into his physical reaction to the pleasure of a battle well played and a very luscious figure and stormy eyes. Little Genny Maitland had been transformed into a very attractive woman and, more significantly, a puzzling one.

He had a weakness for puzzles. Especially those scented like orange blossoms.

Still, she'd been right to call him to attention—just as she had been right last night, when he'd stepped over the line into a literally heavy-handed attempt to test her defences.

Well, he'd best step back behind it. Uncharted waters might be enticing, but they were far more likely to hide treacherous reefs than treasures.

Chapter Seven

'As pretty as a music box' was an appropriate description for Drury Lane Theatre. Everything was designed to impress and awe—the grandiose foyer with its Doric columns, the brightly lit rotunda, crowded with the cream of the Ton, the boxes lit with rows of gaslight chandeliers, and finally the forty-foot-high stage.

Kit, who had entered the theatre with all the wariness of a man entering a scorpion-infested cave, wasn't certain whether he was relieved or disappointed that it looked nothing like his vivid memory of the place. But if it was relief, the feeling was very mild compared with the other emotions seething inside him.

Only a fortnight ago, if anyone had asked what it would take for him to accompany his grandmother to a play at the Drury Lane Theatre, under the viciously watchful eye of the Ton, he'd have said it would take an act of God to do the trick. He wondered if acts of God came in the guise of his sister's happiness coupled with a little devious manipulation by a general *manqué*.

Still, the happiness on his sister's face now, as she settled into her seat in the box between him and Peter, was a balm to his rumbling temper. She was practically bouncing, her gaze moving with patent awe over the theatre and her hand holding Peter's tightly.

'It is simply enormous! There must be *hundreds* of people here!' she whispered.

'Don't gawp, girl!' Lady Westford admonished, and Emily sat back, abashed.

Peter, his pale cheeks turning rather red, placed his hand on Emily's and leaned forward, clearly preparing to take up arms in his beloved's defence. But Kit's wish to see Emily's serious-minded betrothed tackle Lady Westford was dashed as Genevieve, seated on Peter's other side, touched his arm, drawing his attention.

'Do you know, Peter, I think Drury Lane was the first theatre in London to introduce gas chandeliers? It is rather amazing to think they are all connected to a warren of gas pipes. It seems quite impossible—and rather frightening.'

Peter, his clever, practical mind latching on to this engineering challenge, rushed into a reassuring speech about temperatures and pipes and counterweights. And Kit was rather amused to see Emily regard this serious monologue with far warmer admiration than she'd shown for the *Who's Who* of London society filling the theatre.

He was even more impressed when she interrupted with an objection about Archimedean points of leverage. The happy couple then descended into a heated but amicable discussion of how best to prevent all this piping from causing another catastrophic fire, and the rest of the world— the theatre included—was clearly forgotten.

His gaze briefly met Genny Maitland's. Her mouth was primly holding back a smile. It was let loose for a moment as he looked at her, and her eyes lit with shared laughter, a momentary flash like faraway lightning.

Then Julian walked in, paused for a moment to listen to the heated discussion, and then bent to whisper something in Genny's ear. The look she cast him over her shoulder would have felled a tree, but he merely raised his hands with a grin and settled deeply into his chair.

Lady Westford threw him an exasperated look. 'Sit up, do, Julian. What is it with you young men these days? You dress like footmen, lounge like hackney drivers, and behave in all manners as if you were the hoi polloi.'

'Hoi polloi, Grandmama,' Julian said with suspicious meekness.

'That is what I said.'

'No, you said *the* hoi polloi. *Hoi* is the plural for *the* in Greek, and *polloi* is *many*. Saying *the* hoi polloi is unnecessarily repetitive.'

The cane hovered ominously above the floor, but then a party including the Duke of Burford entered the box opposite them and the cane was lowered. When Lady Westford spoke again it was with a wholly unconvincing smile.

'I don't know why you bother to come at all if you mean to be unpleasant, Julian.'

'I don't *mean* to be, Grandmama. It just happens.'

She snorted and turned her back to him. Julian caught Genny's frown, winked at her, and raised an imaginary quizzing glass to ogle her bosom. Her frown dissolved into a rueful smile and she shook her head and turned her back on him too. Julian, balked of his view, sighed and settled into his slouch.

At least in this respect Kit could empathise with his cousin. Genny Maitland might not be a beauty, like her sister, but she had been endowed with a body that could launch quite a few ships.

She'd worn a relatively modest evening gown during the ball, and although her present gown was also far from elaborate, its simple square-cut bodice and silky material the colour of ripening Turkish apricots moulded over her curves and displayed her exquisite bosom like the work of art it was, promising that what lay beneath was a hundred times more appetising than that sweet fruit.

Kit was not in the least surprised that a connoisseur of feminine charms like Julian would appreciate the view. What surprised Kit was the degree of ease between Genny and Julian. Perhaps even intimacy?

Not that there was anything wrong with that. Genevieve Maitland was of an age to do as she willed, and she had a degree of maturity to her that outstripped her widowed sister, and in a way even Mary. As far as he was concerned, so long as it did not adversely impact upon Emily and Mary, she could—and probably would—do as she wished.

Kit forced his attention to the stage as a buzz of cheering signalled Edmund Kean's entrance. He hoped the performance of the actors on stage would compensate for the performances off it.

To his surprise, it was excellent. As Sir Giles Overreach, Edmund Kean was ambition and rancour personified. He reminded Kit a little of Lady Westford. And the crowd, from the boxes to the pit, was enthralled with Sir Giles's vicious destructiveness towards everyone around him. He had no redeeming qualities but the sheer force of his will to win.

Kean's portrayal was so convincing Kit found himself completely in accord with the muffled cries of 'Shame!' and 'Poor show!' that punctuated his increasingly convoluted attempts to destroy and discredit everyone about him.

'Why, he is the most contemptible worm that ever was! If I were his daughter I would set the dogs to him!' hissed Emily, practically writhing in her seat. She looked ready to descend onto the stage, fill his pockets with chops, and drag him out to the dogs herself.

Kit smiled at his half-sister's uncharacteristic bloodthirstiness and let his gaze slip past her to Genny. She appeared as engrossed by the play as Emily, her whole body canted forward in a manner that might have drawn his grandmother's condemnation if she hadn't already slipped into a fitful doze.

Like this, Genny looked years younger—as if surrendering to the passion of the drama had peeled years off her. One fisted hand was clenched to her sternum, pressing her bosom into an even more impressive display of perfect curves as she leaned forward. Kit realised his own hand had fisted too, and he released it. But it fisted again, involuntarily, as she raised her hand to her mouth as if to stifle a gasp at Kean's latest masterpiece of evil.

He turned back to the stage himself, a little annoyed at his green response to her surprisingly girlish show of enjoyment, coupled with her wholly female show of curves.

She'd had those rare moments in Spain as well, when she'd been caught up in the heated discussions that had often brewed around her grandfather's dinner table in the barracks. Her careful mantle of control would slip, and her excitement and determination would be bared in service of whatever cause she'd felt worth defending. Then some comment would check her, and she'd withdraw like a fern, furling back as night fell, her gaze glacial, as if challenging anyone to remind her she'd been on fire only a moment before.

The contrast with the soft and frothy Serena had been even more obvious during those vivid eruptions and retreats. From his lofty age of twenty-five he'd thought it merely a sign of a girl hovering on the tricky bridge between youth and womanhood, and he'd felt both sorry for her and strangely proud, as if he was as invested in her awkward intelligence as her grandfather had been.

But she had not appreciated his stilted attempts to smooth those moments over and, looking back, he couldn't blame her. Charlie had done it much more successfully by poking fun at her at the same time as making his awe of her unburnished intelligence clear.

She'd certainly managed to leash that awkwardness over the years, but right now she looked precisely as she had in the heat of passionate argument. Her eyes glistened a strange vulpine silver, like snow deep in the shadows, and her generous mouth was parted and moving faintly, the sheen of the chandelier dancing on the soft curve of her lower lip. She seemed to be echoing the soliloquy below, and in a strange twist of acoustics he seemed to hear the words emanate from her—a tortured, hopeless call to arms against everything and everyone.

As if aware of being watched, she turned, her face alight with surprising excitement, her light grey eyes catching the gold flickers of the chandeliers like sun flicking off an ice-bound sea. She seemed hardly to see him, caught wholly in the deep human drama on the stage.

He turned away, rubbing his tingling fingers surreptitiously on his trousers, a little ashamed to have distracted her with his schoolboy gawking. He was here to watch the play and make Emily happy—not to ogle the woman who had become his unexpected nemesis.

He managed to insert himself back into the play, but was relieved when the crowd rumbled in a mix of protests and cheers that marked the departure of Sir Giles Overreach from the stage.

Genny Maitland sat back with a faint exhalation and in the same moment turned. Their eyes met once more. Her smile, already soft and faraway, deepened, encompassing him, inviting him to appreciate something extraordinary.

It caught at him. The immensity of the theatre, the strange abandonment that came from being told a bedtime story on a grand scale. He could feel the beating heart of the audience, the wonder, the passion, the escape...

That sensation was strange enough, but then her smile

made the theatre shrink and fall away, and he saw only a young woman freed for a moment from everything that held her down. It stripped him raw, and he had the unsettling conviction that she was looking right inside him to something he hadn't even realised was there.

It was merely a short, sharp moment. Then Julian rose, blocking his sight of her.

By the time he passed towards the door of the box she had turned back to the stage, her head tilted as Serena spoke to her. Though she was still smiling, the wonder was gone from her face, replaced by the slight crease between her brows that she'd worn for most of the ball.

The managing Miss Maitland was back.

'Is it true that pirates bury their treasure?'

This question, blurted out by the youngest of the Duke of Burford's granddaughters, caused a sudden break in the buzzing voices that surrounded them in the foyer of Drury Lane Theatre. Several pairs of eyes, from the brown of the two Burford girls to the blue of Lady Sarah Ponsonby and the pale green of a young woman whose name he could not recollect, were all fixed on him, awaiting his clarification on this crucial issue.

Kit, having twice already in the conversation disclaimed being a pirate, stifled a sigh. 'Burying is a rather risky way to treat your valuable belongings, Lady Calista. I don't know what pirates do, but I prefer to place mine safely in a bank.'

'Oh,' she said, clearly disappointed.

Her sister and the green-eyed girl appeared only slightly less disaffected with this prosaic approach, but Lady Sarah Ponsonby smiled a trifle condescendingly.

'I told you burying treasures made no sense, Cally. It is shockingly risky. Anyone could be watching and might make off with it the moment you sail away.'

'But you don't *have* banks at sea, do you?' Lady Sophronia pointed out, hurrying to her sister's defence.

Lady Calista perked up. 'That is quite true, Ronny! Perhaps you could place a curse on your treasure to stop other pirates from making away with it?'

'My mother taught me that it is impolite to curse,' Kit replied, once again debating and abandoning the idea of arguing with the 'other pirates' categorisation. Denial only appeared to fuel conviction.

He cast his gaze over the perfectly coiffed heads surrounding him and searching the crowd in hope of salvation.

His grandmother, who'd positioned him in this crowd of debutantes and then wandered off with the Duke of Burford, would be no salvation, and despite his height he could not see the other members of their party.

'Was your mother a pirate as well?' asked Lady Calista, and was met with a hiss of warning from the other young women. The youngest Burford flushed and added hurriedly, 'Oh, I forgot…she was an actress.'

Dead silence.

Now all the young women were all red as lobsters—even Lady Sarah Ponsonby, usually as cool and biting as ice. He took pity on them even as he cursed Genny Maitland for manoeuvring him into coming tonight.

'No, my grandfather was the actor, as well as being a bookbinder. Though my mother did enjoy the theatre very much. I learned my appreciation of Shakespeare from her—as well as my manners,' he added a little pointedly. 'Now, if you will excuse me? It has been delightful conversing with you, but I must find my sister.'

He ran Mary to ground behind one of the Doric columns, watching over Emily and Peter who stood in a small group of younger people.

She smiled at his approach. 'I cannot believe this is Emily's first time in a proper theatre! I have been very remiss.'

'From what I know of Emily, she is more likely to enjoy a visit to a foundry than a theatre. Still, I am glad she is enjoying herself.'

'Oh, dear. I take it you aren't?'

'I am surviving. Though if one more doe-eyed young woman asks me about pirates and treasure I might do something drastic and tell them I keep mine under my bed, along with the skulls of my enemies.'

'Kit! Pray be patient. They mean well, you know.'

He turned away before he told her what he thought of her naiveté. He spotted Serena Carrington, in conversation with two women by the stairs leading up to the boxes, but there was no sight of Genny.

'Where is Miss Maitland? I haven't seen her in the foyer.'

Mary glanced around her.

'Oh. I daresay she has remained in the box with Grandmama.'

'No, Grandmother is over there, with His Aging Grace. It was she who threw me to the sharks among the debutantes. Genny wasn't with her.'

Mary frowned as she scanned the crowded rotunda 'Perhaps she prefers to remain in the box on her own. She is like that sometimes.'

Kit felt a twinge of offence on Genny's behalf at Mary's casual unconcern for her whereabouts. Then he remembered Genny sitting in the stable at the house, conferring with the kitten, and how lost in rapture she'd been during the play. Now he thought of it, she had played the social game with consummate skill at the ball, but at no time had she looked to be enjoying herself. Perhaps she truly did prefer her own company. He of all people should be able to respect that.

'Or perhaps she is with Julian,' Mary continued, with

the same blithe unconcern, even as she turned away to greet two women approaching her.

Kit left her before he was roped into more piratical queries. They still had the second performance to sit through and he was already itching to leave.

He moved towards the stairs, wondering where Julian had gone. The Green Room, where actors entertained guests, was unlikely to be open for the usual influx of admirers until after the second play or musical piece, but no doubt Julian would find a way to wheedle himself into whatever room her liked.

Or perhaps he was, as Mary had said, with Genevieve Maitland.

He noted that Lord Ponsonby and his daughter were now standing with Serena by the stairs. Passing by them without stopping would be clearly rude, so instead he slipped into one of the side corridors and took a set of stairs leading upwards, hoping they would eventually lead to the boxes.

There were few lights here, and the narrow corridors were hushed. He smiled as he climbed the narrow stairs. It was fitting that he had turned into what was probably the servants' passage, or perhaps one of the passages where actors like his grandfather had once navigated the warren-like structure.

He'd barely heaved a sigh of relief at the quiet when he stopped. Two shadowy figures stood at the end of the darkened corridor, outlined by the hazy light coming through a window darkened with grime. They were standing quite close, their voices hushed, and they had not yet seen him.

Kit knew it was poor form to eavesdrop, but he stood silently, watching the dark-on-dark outline of Genevieve Maitland's profile. His cousin Julian was lounging against the wall, his hands shoved deep in his coat pockets, his chin tucked into the folds of his cravat.

'You promised me, Julian! I won't allow you to back out now.'

'I'm not backing out, love. Merely renegotiating. I gave in far too easily.'

'There is nothing to renegotiate.'

'There is *always* something to renegotiate.'

The same ease of long familiarity that he'd seen at the ball was even more evident here. Genevieve Maitland might be radiating annoyance, her arms folded like a disapproving headmistress and plumping up her bosom, to Julian's evident appreciation, but her voice was more resigned than angry, and the affection beneath it was as clear as her enjoyment of the play.

'I think you are being difficult for difficulty's sake, Julian.'

'All I am saying is that I think I deserve some incentive for being so…biddable.'

'Really, Julian. You do choose your moments.' She sighed with resignation, but there was a peculiar relief in her voice, as if she'd been expecting something worse.

'Do you know how much I adore being scolded by you, Gen…?' Julian's voice dropped as he moved even closer.

Kit moved into the corridor.

Genny turned and Julian stepped back. For a moment no one spoke.

Then Julian gave a rueful laugh. 'Your timing leaves a lot to be desired, cousin.'

'I could say the same of you, Julian. Wouldn't it be wiser, or at least safer, to conduct your flirtation at Carrington House?'

'Wiser, perhaps. Not quite as enjoyable. Knowing Grandmama is in the house is bound to put a dampener on one's enthusiasm.' He turned to Genny. 'Though we could continue our discussion at my rooms? I'll even clear the sofa for you this time.'

'Julian!'

Genny's voice snapped down on his name but he merely laughed and sauntered off around the corner.

For a building humming with hundreds of people, this corridor was as quiet as the hold of a ship. The murmur of the crowd from somewhere inside was like the soothing sound of water against the hull.

The comparison did nothing to ease the strange burning of anger inside him. He knew full well he was being irrational, and that if anyone was accountable for the charade he'd been forced to play out in the foyer it was his grandmother, not Genevieve Maitland. But all his frustration, exasperation, impatience, and discomfort homed in on her like light through a piece of glass. Its concentrated heat was searing a hole in him as surely as it would burn through wood.

He struggled for composure, but the words came out anyway. 'Are you in the habit of meeting Julian in darkened corridors in very public locations?'

'That is none of your concern, Lord Westford.'

'No? Since you are living in my house, I rather think it is.'

His eyes were now accustomed to the gloom, and he watched colour rush up her cheeks. But her tone remained as calm as before.

'Julian was trying to get a rise out of you. Apparently he has succeeded.'

'I will take that as a yes. Does Mary know?'

'Does Mary know what?'

'That the two of you are having an affair.'

Her indrawn breath was long, and gave him another display of her bosom that would likely have delighted Julian.

'It is amazing to me that men rule the world and yet they can never seem to think past their libidos. Or perhaps that is *why* they rule the world. Life is so much simpler when you are stupid.'

He ignored this clear attempt to divert his fire. 'You do realise that if it had been anyone else who had come up those stairs you and Julian would be in the centre of a very unpleasant little scandal?'

'Then we are lucky it was you, aren't we?' Her words were light but her eyes were still watchful.

'I would rather not depend upon luck protecting my family's reputation.'

'Interesting... I was rather of the opinion that was precisely what you have been doing ever since you sold your commission and adopted your...itinerant lifestyle.'

Damnation. The brutality of that thrust was only matched by the fact that she was absolutely right.

Still, what surprised him was the realisation, as sharp as a knife piercing flesh, that she was furious. With him. And she had been from the moment she'd walked into the drawing room the night of the ball. No, before he'd even returned to London.

Just as he made that discovery, he realised why.

'You think I'm irresponsible.'

She had turned away, as if to follow Julian's exit, but now she gave a strange little huff and turned back to face him. 'Yes.'

'I daresay you think Julian the soul of accountability?'

She shrugged, and turned again in the direction Julian had disappeared in, but he strode after her, capturing her arm and stopping her on the bottom step of another staircase leading upwards.

'Damnation, you don't get to throw around accusations—'

'I didn't accuse you,' she interrupted. 'I answered your question. Then *you* replied with a completely irrelevant statement. Now it is time to return to the box. The sheep are returning to their pens, and in this particular case I'm not a shepherd but a nice fluffy little sheep—and so are you. If you wish to meet me at dawn with pistols or cutlasses, Captain Carrington, I will be only too happy to oblige, but not now.'

He was so damn tempted to use every inch of his superior height and strength, but that in itself shocked him. He couldn't remember ever being tempted to use his physical superiority against anyone other than his cousins since his schooldays—let alone a woman. Genny Maitland was bringing out the worst in him.

He moved away but didn't quite let go of her arm. 'Damnation—how do you win each and every round?'

'I've won nothing.'

Her voice wobbled and his temper fell right off its high horse.

His hand slipped down to capture hers. It was cold. He was keeping her in a draughty corridor in a dress that probably weighed less than his waistcoat, doing his damnedest to force something out of her he didn't even understand.

An admission that he wasn't as black as she thought him?

He didn't need absolution from her, but he was still here, holding her hand, while she wished him in Hades and while the rest of the world was probably taking their places in the boxes.

With that realisation came a sly, unsettling thought... What would happen if they walked in together after the second play had begun? All that eager buzzing that surrounded him like wasps around a jam tart would turn deafening. And vicious.

He stepped aside. 'You'd best return to the others.'

She glanced down at the hand he still held. It didn't feel cold now. He let it slip against his as he withdrew, sensation shooting up his arm. She curled it into a fist and for one long moment he tensed as if for a blow, his whole body thudding with anticipation.

Then she slipped into the darkness.

Chapter Eight

'I'm so glad you decided to attend the theatre last night, Kit. Though I must say the second piece was not at all of the same quality as Kean's performance. But Emily found it engaging—especially the spectacle with the waterfall and the dog jumping out of the water. I still cannot understand how they did that, even after Peter's explanation...'

Mary's gentle flow of words accompanied Kit as he prowled the morning room. He'd arrived early, knowing his grandmother rarely descended from her rooms before the afternoon, but now he felt somewhat disappointed. At the very least he'd hoped that Emily would be there. She never failed to lighten his mood. But Mary had come down alone.

'Where is Emily? Is she worn out after her late night or off with Peter's family, exploring London again?'

'Neither. She and Genny have gone to Hatchards. Emily has discovered that Peter's library is composed primarily of scientific tomes, and though she shares his interests, she loves novels as well, and so has set about rectifying that fault before the wedding. You both inherited your father's love of literature, though Emily hasn't inherited his interest in history.'

As always when she mentioned his father, there was an

edge of sadness to her voice. Kit took a sharp turn towards the window. Sometimes her tendency to melancholy aggravated him. Today, it grated against his nerves. He wasn't in a mood to soothe her.

'She will be married in under a month. I think it is time we discussed your plans, Mary.'

'We have discussed this already, Kit,' she reproved. 'I shall remain with your grandmama. I know you are concerned, but I must say she is much improved this past week. Perhaps now she has had a chance to accept your grandfather's death she is coming to appreciate our presence—'

'Ballocks,' he interrupted indelicately. 'Don't fool yourself. She doesn't respect sweetness, Mary; she respects strength. If you'd once told her to shut the hell up, you'd have a better chance to stop her constant needling.'

Mary's pale cheeks flushed with mortification. He felt a complete bastard, but he couldn't seem to stem this newfound anger at his stepmother. Her sweetness might bring her much in life, but rarely what she most needed. He'd watched her allow her needs to fall to the very bottom of the Carrington pile time and time again, and he couldn't seem to convince her that she had the power to alter that order.

'I appreciate your concern, Kit, no matter how you express it... But I assure you she is not always as free with her criticism as you have seen her be these past days. In fact, her mood was much improved yesterday. She hardly made any cutting remarks at all.'

'Because we all obeyed her edicts and behaved ourselves on the social stage. And because—' He stopped, warned by the clicking of the cane on the marble of the hall. 'Ah, hell...'

Mary sighed and folded her hands.

Howich opened the door and Lady Westford entered, surveying the room.

'Where is Genevieve?' she demanded of Mary, not even bothering to acknowledge Kit's presence.

'Gone with Emily to Hatchards, Mama.'

'Huh…' Her gaze weighed Mary like a wolf eyeing a doe. 'Wasting my money again, eh?'

'Mine, Grandmother,' Kit corrected, drawing her fire, but she merely shrugged.

'Should have gone yourself, Mary. I need a word with Genevieve.'

'Perhaps I could help?' Mary asked.

Lady Westford gave a snort. 'Not likely. None of you have an ounce of her sense. Charlie should have married her instead of that golden sheep with no hips, then everything would have been a sight better all around. It's not looks we need; it's brains.'

They both watched as she limped out, and then Kit went to close the door behind her, resisting the urge to slam it.

'It's amazing none of you has shoved her down the stairs yet. She's the three witches all rolled into one and dipped in vinegar. And don't offer more excuses for her, Mary, or I might lose my temper.'

Mary kept her eyes on her embroidery, but her fingers shook. He took a deep breath and went to sit beside her.

'I'm sorry, Mary… I don't know why I'm being such an ass. Coming back here always brings out the worst in me. It's like being shoved back into the skin of a twelve-year-old. But that's no reason to make you miserable.'

'You aren't,' she said, not very convincingly. 'And I do understand it is hard for you. They truly were always horribly beastly to you. But I wish you could make your peace with her…with us. Keeping away is no solution. You need to come home—now more than ever.'

'It isn't my home, Mary.'

'It *could* be if you wished it.'

'Therein lies your answer. I wonder what the devil she's up to.'

'Who? Your grandmama?'

'She and the little field marshal.'

'Field mar...? Oh, you mean Genny? She probably wants her for something to do with the housekeeping. She's very hard on housekeepers, and both she and Mrs Pritchard find it easier to use Genny as intermediary. Mr Fletcher, the steward at the Hall, does so as well. It is easier that way.'

'I have no doubt. Clever how Miss Maitland has made herself indispensable...' His temper was beginning to climb, so he changed tack. 'Why hasn't Serena married again? She is still a handsome woman; she must have admirers.'

Mary's mouth twisted a little. 'You forget—we had not yet come out of mourning for Charlie when Lord Westford died. Besides, admirers aren't suitors. A widow burdened with debt, who has shown she cannot carry a child to term, is not in high demand, no matter how pretty.'

Nor was a woman of thirty-seven who had had but one daughter in a dozen years of marriage.

Those words remained unsaid, but they sounded loud and clear.

'Well, it doesn't help that you have both been immured at the Hall for the past year and a half. Now you are in London for the next few weeks it might be different. Men are not all cut from the same cloth.'

Mary frowned. 'That was what Genny was hoping.'

'She was hoping to find a husband?'

'Not for her. For Serena. And for me. She doesn't wish for either of us to remain with your grandmother alone.'

'Why not for herself? Because of Julian?'

'Julian?'

'Is she holding a candle for him? There is definitely something between them.'

'It is true they have been good friends from the start, but I do not think it is any more than that. I certainly don't think Julian wishes to wed her—or anyone, for that matter. He only offered for her because he hoped his maternal aunt would grant him a legacy if he were betrothed, but in the end Marcus inherited it all. Poor Julian was quite put out. Your grandfather always said he was shockingly expensive, and I happen to know he has borrowed funds from Marcus. If he did marry it would most likely be for a dowry, but Genny hasn't a penny, you see...'

No, he didn't see. Since the moment he'd become entangled in the workings of this strange female-driven household he'd felt as if he was sailing through a fog and far too close to the reefs.

He hated that feeling.

Mary turned her head, listening, and he heard the murmur of voices in the hall.

'Speak of the devil...' he muttered.

Mary cast him an imploring look. 'Please don't cross swords with her again in front of Emily.'

'Again?'

'The two of you were so viciously polite to each other at the theatre after the intermission it was evident to all that you had had words. Emily spoke of it when she prepared for bed last night. She was very upset that two people she loves were at loggerheads.'

'We merely disagreed about the merits of the play.'

'Huh.' Mary gave an uncharacteristically indelicate snort.

He stood, moving restlessly towards the fireplace. 'You may enjoy being herded. I don't.'

'She isn't trying to herd *you*, Kit.'

'Well, I don't like her herding *you*, either.'

'I see. Only you are permitted to do that, then?'

'I don't... That is different,' he bit out, annoyed at the truth behind her words.

Before he could continue, the door opened and Emily hurried in, followed by Genny.

'Kit! We've had the most marvellous morning. I think we have cleared all the shelves at Hatchards and I have bought you the loveliest illustrated edition of Swift's *Travels*. Would you believe the clerk tried to dissuade me? He said it was not at all the thing for a young woman to read, but Genny soon routed him—didn't you, Genny? And in the sweetest possible way, so that the poor fellow was quite smitten and spent the next half-hour carrying around our purchases like a little lamb.'

Kit raised an eyebrow, throwing Mary a wry look over Emily's head. At least she had the grace to blush a little.

Unfortunately, Genny herself looked up from drawing off her gloves and intercepted their exchange.

He was damned if he would ascribe the same omniscience to her that Mary and Julian seemed to, but when those chasm-deep grey eyes were fixed on one, it was damned easy to believe in it oneself.

He took the book from Emily and opened it to the illustration of Gulliver tied down by the Lilliputians. Right now he felt a double dose of sympathy for the helpless fellow.

'It's beautiful, Emmy. Thank you.'

She touched the dark brown spine of the book. 'Some of my very first memories are of you reading to me whenever you came down from school. I would keep myself awake, watching for the light of your candle under the door as you came with one of your books. Mama would read to me too, but she couldn't do the voices like you.' She smiled at Mary. 'Sorry, Mama.'

Mary smiled back. 'Don't apologise, love. It is quite

true. I admit I would listen at the door when you read, Kit. George said you had Kathleen's gift.'

Had his father said that? It wasn't true, of course, but it felt like a rare gift. His memories of his father before and after his mother's death were of two different men: one strong and often laughing; the other silent and bowed.

Mary had received an ill bargain with only Emily as compensation. It was time to repay her. And that meant removing her from under his grandmother's dark cloud.

He looked past Emily and Mary to where Genny was sorting through a stack of correspondence by the desk. The sun filtered through her hair, creating a gold and amber halo. She seemed utterly absorbed in her task, and yet he could feel her awareness of everything that was happening in the room.

Now she gathered the correspondence and excused herself. Emily and Mary barely noticed—Emily was chatting to Mary about her new books, while Mary watched her daughter with a combination of love and wistfulness.

Kit excused himself as well, and went in pursuit of the Generalissima.

Chapter Nine

'Miss Maitland.'

'Yes, Lord Westford?'

Damn, he hated that tone. If there was anything less deferential than Genny in this mood, he had yet to encounter it.

He went to lean against the writing desk which dominated the study, watching as she sorted and stacked letters.

'How long have you been my grandmother's secretary?'

'I help when I can, Lord Westford. Serena and I are living on her charity, after all. Or rather, on yours. It soothes my conscience to make myself useful.'

'More straight dealing?'

'It is merely the truth.'

She laid out the correspondence in neat piles. Most, as far as he could see, was addressed to his grandmother. There were a couple of letters for Mary, and one Genny had placed face down. He reached for it but she placed her hand on it.

'That is mine.'

Her voice was without inflection, but a slight burn of colour feathered across her cheekbones. The temptation to slip it out from under her hand was sharp, but instead he focused on the others.

'I didn't know my grandmother was such an avid correspondent.'

'These are mostly invitations.'

'And these?' He tapped another stack.

'Responses from tradesmen regarding enquiries I have made about a Venetian breakfast.'

'Venetians don't eat breakfast. I've yet to meet a Venetian who wakes before noon.'

Her mouth quirked and a near-dimple hovered into being. 'A Venetian breakfast takes place in the afternoon and has nothing at all to do with Venice, unfortunately.'

'Have you been there?' he asked

She shook her head and the same wistful light sparked for a moment and was extinguished.

He picked up a bill, raising a brow. 'Three dozen lanterns?'

'Lady Westford wants to hold it in the garden. There are few houses in London with grounds like Carrington House.'

'But why lanterns? I thought you said it is held in the afternoon.'

'It might last well into the evening. One must be prepared.'

'You plan to entertain guests for a whole day in the garden? In April? In England? What if it rains? Or have you put in an order for sunshine as well?'

'It shan't rain.'

Her response was so bland he felt a momentary loss of balance. Not even a dimple quivered in her cheek now, but he knew, absolutely, that she was laughing at him. His resentment against her, which had been riding so high the past few days and had peaked sharply last night, faded like a fog lifting.

As if she sensed his lowering of some internal barrier she finally smiled. Not the vivid, almost blissful smile of last night, but a mix of relief and laughter still carefully held in.

'I would hate to play cards against you, Genevieve Maitland,' he admitted.

'I thought that was precisely what we were doing, Lord Westford. You did not follow me here to discuss your grandmother's social plans. You want something from me, correct?'

You want something from me.

It was the truth, but an unfortunate choice of words.

At the moment, with that playful challenging smile tilting up her eyes and softening her mouth so that is showed its full, lush promise, he could think of one thing in particular he wanted from her.

It was as disconcerting as hell that she could spark in him this mixture of confusion and attraction. In Spain he had thought of her only as his commanding officer's granddaughter. Yet his memory of her was quite a bit sharper than he would have thought reasonable. She'd had freckles then, coaxed to the surface by the Spanish sun that had lightened her wavy hair. She'd looked like a waif but acted like one of the Prussian mercenaries who served under Wellington—cool, focused, and as prickly as a hedgehog.

Except when she'd been with animals. With them she'd always been as soft and cooing as she'd been with the little kitten in the stables.

He had no idea which of those warring personas was at her core and he doubted she'd allow him to find out.

Not that it mattered.

She hadn't moved during his silence, but the light of laughter faded from her eyes and left them guarded. He had the strangest sensation of looking through the deep grey to something else entirely. But whatever it was, it was as elusive as ever.

On impulse, he touched her chin lightly. She didn't pull away but stood there, impassive and waiting.

'You used to have more freckles,' he said, simply for something to say.

His fingers were barely touching her skin but he felt it humming. Her throat worked, as if she was trying not to swallow, a sign of nervousness that gave him far too much satisfaction—he didn't want to be the only one unsettled.

He moved away to the other side of the desk. 'You are right, Miss Maitland. I followed you here for a purpose. First, I wish to apologise for my behaviour last night. I realise you think me the lowest of slackers...'

Her eyes widened and her hands flew up, stopping him. 'No, that is not... I had no right to say that.'

'As I recall, you didn't actually *say* anything aloud.'

'I made my sentiments clear, which is even worse than saying them aloud.'

'That is debatable,' he replied, a little mollified. 'But it brings me to the second reason I wish to speak with you. The truth is, I need your help.'

Once again the shield fell away. Her lips parted and he had the pleasure of watching Miss Genevieve Maitland surprised. Unsettled, even. Her eyes darkened as her pupils dilated, crowding the grey into a dusky violet at the rim. It reminded him of the deep waters of the ocean in the slow hours before dawn—when sailors felt most at the mercy of the endless emptiness.

'I don't understand.' She lowered her chin, her long lashes curling upwards in a wary question.

He glanced at the door. The last thing he wanted was either Mary or Emily bursting in on this conversation. After a quick glance into the empty corridor he locked the door. Her eyes had widened further during this manoeuvre and the faint flush that had warmed her skin had darkened.

Unsettling her hadn't been part of his agenda, but seeing her less than cool and collected was a pleasant change.

'I want Mary out of this house.'

Surprise was transformed into outrage. 'Kit Carrington! That is…beastly!'

'Hush! Damn—I keep forgetting this is my house. I mean I want her out of my grandmother's clutches. I want to find her a husband.'

Genny's flush turned livid and she pressed her hands to her cheeks. 'Oh, dear. I'm so sorry. I thought…'

'Yes, that I am a beast and an ogre and I toss widows out on the street in the cold dark hours of the night.'

She dropped her hands, her dimples flashing. 'No, that is not what I thought, but…'

She hesitated and he forged forward. 'I know you will say I am interfering, but she is still young, and now Emily is leaving she will be lonely. I don't want to return in five years and find her still crushed under my grandmother's thumb. She deserves better.'

'True, but…'

'And I know you wish to find someone for Serena as well.'

'How do you know that?'

'I saw you herding her towards Lord Ponsonby and Gresham—apparently two eligible widowers with independent means and a measure of charm. But though your methods are impressive, your information is flawed. Gresham is deeply in debt. I wouldn't encourage that connection.'

'I have heard no such talk.'

'Because you move in polite circles and Gresham is clever enough to secure his loans from sources that are anything but polite. It won't last, though. I would give him perhaps three months before he is forced to rusticate.'

'A pity. He is very knowledgeable about rhododendrons.'

'A man can like rhododendrons and yet be a villain,' Kit misquoted, and won a quick smile.

'So, Lord Westford, what do you want in exchange for saving my sister from an impecunious rhododendron-lover?'

'I told you—your assistance in finding Mary a husband. I am no hand at matchmaking. What do you say?'

'I don't know…' she replied a little helplessly.

'Don't know if you want the trade or don't know if you can use your considerable skills to find a match for Mary?'

He was beginning to enjoy the peculiar revelation of Genevieve Maitland utterly unmoored. Her colour was coming and going like a drunken sailor in a storm.

'That is not the point, Lord Westford.'

'Then what is? Is she beyond all hope? Too hideous? Old cattish?'

Her eyes flashed with silvered laughter. 'You know full well she is lovely and any sensible man should be delighted with someone like Mary. But men aren't sensible. They are too often either practical or romantic. Neither works in Mary's or Serena's favour. All men see when they look at them are two portionless widows of mature years. However…'

Her eyes turned murky and faraway again. Strange that he'd thought her cool and controlled—one had only to watch her eyes to see a whole panoply of tales being played out.

He watched her toil along some inward path for a while. Finally, she gave a sigh, not of despair but of resolution, and he allowed himself to prompt her. 'However…?'

Her gaze focused once more—determined, decided, and direct. His nerves, already clanging like fog bells, snapped to attention.

'I will do it.'

For a moment he felt a wave of relief, which was quickly followed by annoyance at himself. It was a bad sign if he was beginning to regard this pint-sized woman with the same blind faith as Mary did.

'What, precisely, will you do?'

She leaned against the desk and crossed her arms. 'I have some ideas, Lord Westford. But you may not care for them.'

'If it makes Mary happy, I'll bear the cost.'

'It wouldn't merely be monetary. You would have to do your part. And I cannot have you arguing with everything I do.'

What was he letting himself in for?

'Why don't you share your ideas and then I'll decide whether I want to come on board?'

'Very well. I am afraid the kind of entertainments I have been organising aren't enough for our purposes. You saw what happened at the ball, and again yesterday at the theatre. Mary lavishes most of her attention on Emily, and even when she doesn't she mostly relegates herself to the company of matrons and elderly men. She will never meet anyone eligible in that manner, let alone engage their interest.'

'So what do you suggest?'

'I suggest we concentrate on entertainments that attract the right kind of men and conduct them in settings where Mary and Serena have no choice but to interact with them.'

He almost felt sorry for these faceless fellows. 'I presume you have already have a list of likely candidates waiting to be summoned to their marital doom?'

'Of course—in the drawer right between my list of men guaranteed to bore you with their hunting exploits and my list of men who can dance a quadrille without breaking your toes.'

He crossed his arms, mirroring her stance, and smiled. 'Sarcasm is not an attractive quality, Genevieve Maitland.'

'You started it.'

'You sank to my level without a peep.'

'I thought it would be easier for you to converse down there. Being polite is evidently a strain on your faculties.'

'I will have you know that I have always been noted for my good manners.'

'Pointing out your own good manners is the very definition of ill manners. It implies I am either too vulgar to recognise civility or the cause of you losing yours.'

Her teasing cut uncomfortably close to the bone, but he couldn't help laughing. 'Then I shall try to recover my reputation by accepting full responsibility for any unpleasantness between us.'

'Excellent. Now you have put me in the wrong while redeeming yourself. A masterly move, Captain Carrington. Oh, dear, I apologise... I keep forgetting... I mean, Lord Westford.'

'I keep forgetting myself. I wish I could do so categorically.'

'Most men would give their eye teeth for a title and a fortune.'

'I'd take that trade if I could. It never should have been mine. If I'd known Charlie was in such straits...'

'I don't see what you could have done. If your grandfather had no luck dissuading him from investing in those ventures and travelling to Argentina, how could you?'

He was about to comment that he was surprised *she* had not managed to curb his worst tendencies, but thought better of it.

'In any case, we are straying from our task,' he said. 'Which is finding a husband for Mary. I'm afraid I don't know her taste in men, though.'

Her smile turned a little sad. 'Men like your father.'

He moved away from the desk and wandered over to the shelves. 'He was a fool.'

'I never met him, so I cannot attest to that, but from what I have heard he was hardly that. Just…lost. Perhaps he should have stayed at sea after your mother died. Giving up too much of the familiar when you are in pain can be hard to bear.'

He shrugged. He had opened the door to confidences. He could hardly object now to her delving into his father's psyche.

'In any case, I hope we can find someone more suitable for Mary. She hardly shared his naval interests. I remember she never even wished to come down to the bay.'

'No, but she certainly shared his interest in antiquities. I know you aren't acquainted with people in society, but surely your…dealings…have brought you in touch with men who share your interest in art and antiquities.'

'How do you know I share those interests?'

'Aside from the tales you told in the letters you sent Emily and Mary, there is the damning evidence at the Hall. One cannot enter a room without encountering one of your baubles.'

'Baubles?'

'Since Lord Westford passed, Emily has been placing the gifts you've sent her over the years throughout the Hall and it now resembles a museum…in the best possible way. I cannot believe anyone who trades in such artefacts doesn't know of men who share similar interests.'

The image of all those *baubles*, some of which were near priceless, being spread indiscriminately around Carrington Hall was a little unsettling. And before he could consider the wisdom of asking, the words were out of him.

'Did she place any of these "baubles" in your room at the Hall?'

She hesitated, lowering her eyes as she did when she

was uncomfortable. 'She let me choose. There are two jade dragons on my writing desk.'

'I remember those. I bought them in Macau. Qin Dynasty. They are almost two thousand years old, by all accounts.'

Her eyes widened. 'I should put them somewhere safe, then.'

'No, keep them there. They are meant to be appreciated, not tucked away.'

'I admit it seems sad to put them in a box. They glow so beautifully in the sun, and the way they are shaped, so that their bodies interlace…' She stopped, a wholly uncharacteristic flush rushing up her cheeks. 'In any case, once we produce a creditable list of eligible men we can arrange for them to attend our entertainments.'

'How precisely will we arrange that? You can hardly command their presence.'

'I never command. In this case I need not even manoeuvre. Not when I have the perfect bait for our trap.'

He smiled at the rather bloodthirsty relish in her voice. 'And what is that?'

Her gaze focused on him and she smiled. He added another facet to Genevieve Maitland—she could look as smug as a cat with a year's supply of mice.

'Why, you, of course, Lord Westford.'

Genny paused in the corridor outside Lady Westford's rooms. She needed a moment to gather her thoughts, which were still tumbling over themselves as she tried to make sense of her new pact with Captain Carr—with Lord Westford.

She'd made one clear discovery—he was just as unnerving when he was being playful and kind as when he was intent on attack.

She rubbed her hands against her skirts and breathed

in and out several times to push back at the tingling unease that had been chasing her since he'd appeared at Carrington House.

She was not at all certain she could trust him to see the campaign through. He might be charming and insightful, but he was also a drifter, and might at any moment change course and leave her stranded.

Which meant she must also pursue her own plans.

Now she only had to ensure Lady Westford was compliant.

She tapped on the door and entered. Carmine immediately set up a bouncing warble.

'Don't hover in the doorway, girl. Come in,' Lady Westford commanded from her bed, putting down the quizzing glass with which she had been perusing the newspaper.

Genny slipped a few seeds into Carmine's cage, buying a few moments of peace, and placed a chair by the bed. 'Is your hip paining you, Lady Westford?'

'Don't use that sweet tone on me, Genevieve Maitland. I'm not happy with you. I'll concede you made my grandsons show themselves, which is more than I expected. But a ball and a jaunt to the theatre isn't enough for those hungry young misses to tie them down. Those boys are too canny for that—blast them. Marcus has already hared off back to whatever he is concocting up north, Kit refuses to leave the docks, and Julian... I'm not blind, girl. He may flirt with you, but if he hasn't popped the question yet he ain't likely to do so now. The moment Emily weds they'll scatter, and it will all amount to naught.'

'I agree—which is why we must adjust our approach.'

Lady Westford's hand groped for her cane, but it was leaning by the bed, so she gave the covers a thump instead. 'Out with it.'

Carmine chimed in with a warning warble, poking his

beak through the bars. Genny scattered a few more seeds at his feet.

'I have convinced Lord Westford that it will be in Emily's and Mary's interests if we hold a series of select entertainments here at Carrington House, but that for them to succeed he must be in attendance. And in residence.'

'What do you mean, you have "convinced" him? How?'

'It hardly matters. The point is that both he and Julian have agreed to attend.'

'Marcus won't.'

'Probably not. But two out of three is fair odds.'

Lady Westford's pouchy eyes narrowed to slits. 'We shall invite the Burfords. Good blood, large dowries.'

'Yes. And I think Lady Sarah Ponsonby and Miss Caversham as well. Although we'll need some men to balance out the list. We cannot be *too* obvious.'

'Quite. But no dashing young bloods that might appeal to the Burford girls.'

Genny thought it would be hard to find *any* young men who could compete with the Carringtons, but since Lady Westford's concern paved the way for her plan, she nodded.

'Of course not. I think older men…solid but unexciting. The contrast, you see…'

'Yes, yes. But…' Lady Westford tapped her newspaper. Cleared her throat. 'Are you certain Kit is in agreement? He might pull a runner. He was a devil of a boy—always disappearing. George ran him down in Southampton once. He'd gone to look for that ship.'

Over the years Genny had occasionally come face to face with something elusive behind Lady Westford's crusted exterior. She had never been quite able to tell if it was love or pain or merely discomfort.

Genny's attempts to approach were usually firmly rejected, but she stepped tentatively onto the plank. 'How old was he?'

'How should I know? It was years ago. Eleven? Been at the Hall less than a year.'

'Before Mr Carrington married Mary?'

'Yes. One reason George remarried. Thought the boy needed a mother. Told us to choose someone nice. Well, Alfred found someone "nice" for him, didn't he? Pity she couldn't produce more than the one girl. But at least she was good to the boy.'

Poor Mary.

Poor George.

Poor Kit.

'Was it better for Kit after they wed?'

'I don't know. He was away at school, mostly.'

Genny steeled herself to ask the question she'd always wondered. 'Why did he not attend the same school as Charlie and Marcus and Julian?'

The pale blue eyes flashed to hers and away. 'Alfred thought it best. Didn't want the boys dealing with gossip.'

'I see.'

Lady Westford must have heard enough in Genny's tone to pull back behind her ramparts. 'Nothing wrong with Westminster. His best friend was a duke's heir.'

'But Kit must have known why you separated him from the others. He is no fool.'

'What else were we to do? If it wasn't bad enough for that dreadful grandfather of his to be a shopkeeper *and* an actor, he was also a foundling. For all we know he was born on the wrong side of the blanket—could be a Hotten-tot for all we know. When George eloped with that woman all of London was laughing behind their hands at us. At *us*! I'm the granddaughter of the Duke of Malby and the Carringtons can be traced back to the crusades! Now the Seventh Earl might well be of base blood, not to mention that he carries on like a veritable scoundrel.'

Genny rolled her shoulders, trying to remind herself

why she was here. Letting loose the fury pressing against her control would not further anyone's cause. Still, she could not resist a thrust.

'From what I have seen of the world, birth has very little to do with worth, Lady Westford. A man should be judged by his actions, not by his ancestors, and in that respect the Carringtons have every reason to be proud of Lord Westford. He was by far one of the best officers who served under my grandfather during the war, and that is saying quite a bit. My grandfather was an excellent judge of men.'

'You weren't born into this world, Genevieve Maitland, and you and I have different notions of pride. Why do you think my Alfred fell ill when poor Charles died? He knew what was likely to happen. That when his moment came the future of his family name would be in the hands of that…that vulgar hussy's son. You didn't know her. She hadn't an ounce of proper respect. Looked us straight in the eye and said she and George didn't need us and would make their own path in the world. Snapped her fingers at us as if she was a queen, no less. At *us*!'

Good for her, thought Genny, keeping her jaw tightly locked.

Lady Westford subsided with something between a sigh and moan. 'It killed my Alfred. Killed him!'

There was such confused pain in those words that, despite her antipathy and disgust, Genny almost reached out to touch her gnarled fists. Instead she sat in silence and waited.

Finally, Lady Westford unknotted her hands. 'Do what you need to do, girl. But I think you're wasting your time on Kit.'

'What?' Genny asked, startled.

'Trying to find a match for him. I'd like to see one of the Burford girls take my place as Lady Westford, but likely Kit won't be interested in either of them. I daresay if he ever marries he'll bring back someone wholly unsuitable, like a Saracen or one of those harem girls of his. If he lives that long. Still, you'd best invite Lord Ponsonby's daughter. Handsome thing—and clever. She might wheedle her way past his defences. But make your big push with Julian. He's a rake, but he needs funds for his hobbies so he's most likely to fall into the trap. The Ponsonby heiress might do even better for him. She's no one's fool and she'll keep his head above water. *And* she might not take offence at his flirting with anything in a skirt.'

'He is a touch more discriminating than that, Lady Westford.' She didn't mention that Lady Sarah, definitely no one's fool, had shown at the ball and at the theatre that her sights were set firmly on Kit.

'Hmm… Now, go away. I'm tired. And I don't appreciate you giving Carmine treats. He's getting fat.'

Genny left the room, accompanied by Carmine's shrill objections.

When the door had closed behind her she allowed herself a smile. There was nothing quite like recruiting one's enemies to fight one's battles.

Chapter Ten

Hell on earth.

Kit had been to many places that might have deserved that epithet. The top of his list was still the hold of a Barbary Coast pirate ship, where he'd spent three hellish weeks. But dinners at Carrington House were climbing to the top of that list faster than a monkey up a coconut tree.

And the night was still young.

The worst of it was that he had walked into this particular hell with his eyes, and his bank coffers, open. He had no one to blame but himself...

Actually, there was someone else with whom he could at least share the blame. He cast a reflexive glance halfway down the ludicrously long dinner table to where Genevieve Maitland was seated, between two of his grandmother's portly whist partners.

Since their discussion in the library, the pocket-sized Generalissima had taken the helm at Carrington House with a determination that had left the other members of the household, even his grandmother, breathless in her wake.

In the past week the threatened Venetian breakfast had not only taken place—in full sunshine—but had lasted well into the night as the famous songbird Madame Vestris had given a brilliant recital of Italian arias by the light of several dozen lanterns floating up into the evening breeze. Not a single cloud had dared make an appearance.

The following day Genevieve had transformed the ball-room into a lecture room, and half the directors of the British Museum had joined prominent members of the Antiquarian Society for a lecture on the latest developments in the deciphering of Egyptian hieroglyphs.

He'd actually enjoyed that—and not merely because Mary had been in seventh heaven. And, to be fair, not all the entertainments had been horrible.

It was mostly the dinners. They seemed to involve interminable hours spent discussing tedious topics and parrying even more tiresome questions.

Still, there were elements of interest even in the dullest of evenings. One was watching the inexorable tightening of Genny Maitland's net about a supremely unaware group of eligible men. The list of guests was being constantly modified as she reviewed, discarded and revised her objectives.

He didn't bother trying to keep track of the list—merely watched the dance with appreciation, trying to follow her moves as she slowly amassed an impressive group of eligible, intelligent and mature men. She was strict with her pawns too. When the hands of a brilliant and wealthy antiquarian had happened to rove casually to Serena's derriere, he had been promptly struck from the list.

There were other selections she had made that were more obscure to Kit. For example, he understood the imperative of inviting the Duke of Burford and his granddaughters, as the Duke was a close friend of his grandmother. But Kit could not see her reason to invite someone like Lord Ponsonby. He was relatively eligible, but he'd already gone through two wives and many more mistresses.

Not someone Kit would care to see choose Mary as his third wife.

There were also a few others who were regular invitees—possibly for reasons of familial connection that eluded him. Unfortunately, they too were possessed of an annoying number of daughters.

He would not have minded if only he did not have to sit next to them. But when he'd made that point to Genny after the first few days she'd brushed his objection away without a smidgen of sympathy.

'You are head of the family, so you don't have the luxury of choosing your dinner companions. And do remember you promised you wouldn't make a fuss.'

She'd wandered off with Mrs Pritchard before he'd been able to object, and so tonight once again he was flanked by Lady Sarah and Lady Sophronia. He had nothing against pretty girls—quite the opposite—and he appreciated beauty. But he was not in the mood for flirtation and that was pretty much all they wanted from him. That and tales of grand adventure he had no wish to indulge them with.

At least Julian was similarly besieged. The bubbly Burford chit—Lady Calista, or Calamata, or something—was doing her best to monopolise his cousin's interest, while on his other side was a pretty brunette someone had mentioned stood to inherit ten thousand pounds, who was casting him occasional birdlike glances of mixed interest and fear.

Kit watched in appreciation for a moment as Julian skilfully navigated both those very different flirtations. But then, in the moment of shifting his attention between the two women, he saw Julian fix his gaze upon Genny, who was seated opposite him.

It was the matter of a second—like a bird tipping its wing mid-flight before correcting course. Julian's smile changed from charming and attentive to rueful and real, and then went right back to one of flirtatious enjoyment as he engaged Lady Calista once more.

Kit's gaze went to Genny. She was entertaining the

elderly whist lovers while she kept an eye on the rest of the players at the table and remained in constant silent communication with the servants in the background. But, like Julian, for that moment she'd let her guard slip and smiled a real smile—also rueful, and a little weary. And in another moment, as Julian's attention was engaged elsewhere, her gaze fell to the table, her smile faded, and she looked...lost.

The clinking and buzzing and rumbling and chattering seemed muted, as if they'd all sunk below the water. Even the colours, bright and brassy in the light of dozens of candles, became hazy.

She didn't look like Genevieve Maitland at that moment, but the Genny she had been in Spain—slight, watchful, quiet, and much more that he hadn't seen then but realised now. She was full of fierce determination and carefully sheathed pain.

The officers had laughingly tolerated her hold over her grandfather, but Kit realised now that General Maitland had seen everything that his granddaughter was and everything life would never allow her to become and tried his best to give her...*something*.

It was not enough. All that force, and passion, and *need*—wasted on organising dinner parties, curbing his grandmother's temper, and now finding husbands for the Carrington women.

Then she straightened her shoulders, raised her chin, and turned and met his gaze. It felt like a slap. His whole body took the brunt of the blow, short and sharp and followed by a surge of molten heat, and he pressed back against his chair.

She held his gaze, held *him*, her cool grey eyes carefully blank. But her shields weren't doing their job. If she'd stood and upended the table—china, silver, crystal and all—it would have felt more natural than her sitting there in her pretty pale blue gown, with her rebellious hair tamed into Grecian braids.

He let the image come—her standing like Dido among the ruins of Carthage, her honey-and-fire hair set loose to brush over her skin, her cool eyes in full storm. She would come towards him and—

'Don't you agree, Lord Westford?'

Lady Sarah's question dragged Kit's attention back to reality as abruptly as the erotic image had dragged him out of it, and far less pleasantly. In the haze of confusion, he considered agreeing blindly to whatever politeness she'd offered, but something in her eyes stopped him.

He managed a smile. 'I apologise, Lady Sarah. What must I agree to?'

'I asked whether you preferred flower arrangements or epergnes as a centrepiece,' she replied with mock demureness.

He glanced down the dinner table to where a lovely arrangement of peonies did nothing to impede his vision of his grandmother. Thankfully his view of Genny was now blocked by one of the rotund whist partners. He turned to the fine view of his grandmother down the miles of linen. She glared at him.

'Whichever is taller,' he said, in reply to Lady Sarah's enquiry.

She cast a quick glance down the table and hid a giggle in her napkin. 'I quite see your point. I had never thought of an epergne as an aid to digestion, but one learns something new every day.'

'That is a positive outlook on life. What else have you learned today, Lady Sarah?'

'The same thing I learned yesterday, unfortunately. That my host would far rather be elsewhere.'

He raised a brow in surprise. This was a very direct approach.

He decided to meet candour with candour. 'I'm sadly deficient in that role, aren't I?'

'Not at all. You are usually engaged in discussions of greater interest than epergnes, or the weather, or the latest *on dits*. It is merely unfortunate that so many men with similar interests are assembled here. It makes it hard for those of us not up to snuff in matters of antiquity to compete for attention. I must endeavour to improve myself.'

He could almost hear his mother, chiding him for his ill manners. 'You do not need improving, Lady Sarah. You might equally claim that us old bores must improve *ourselves*, by broadening our horizons to matters other than musty antiquities.'

'But they aren't in the least musty. You have such beautiful treasures here.'

He smiled, waiting with resignation for some mention of pirates, but she surprised him again.

'For example,' she continued, 'that wonderful little vase in the drawing room that looks as if it has caught the sunlight, so you can see the little drawing as if the people are dancing.'

He frowned, trying to place it. 'Ah, yes. The alabaster vase. It is Egyptian, and probably some two thousand years old.'

'Oh! Was that when Queen Cleopatra was alive?'

'Close enough.'

'Goodness. It might have been a gift to her from Julius Caesar.'

He smiled at the awe in her voice.

'I don't think he would have been allowed past the first portal with such a modest gift. She was probably accustomed to her admirers presenting her with far more substantial offerings.'

'Size isn't all that matters,' she replied with suspicious

demureness, before adding, 'Though it is, of course, important.'

Kit was saved from replying to this suggestive comment by his grandmother, signalling that it was time for the women to withdraw. Lady Sarah impressed him further by showing no sign of regretting the interruption, but he had little doubt this had only been her first sally.

As the men stood he met Julian's gaze and his cousin raised his glass slightly.

Kit wasn't certain if his lopsided smile was mocking or commiserating.

'Damn the boy. He's disappeared again.'

Genny didn't even have to guess who Lady Westford was referring to. She'd noticed Kit absconding not ten minutes into the game of charades that was currently holding the guests rapt in laughing attention as Lady Calista and Serena tried to depict Hannibal's crossing of the Alps, elephants and all.

'He shall probably return soon,' she replied lightly, not in the least convinced that he would.

This wasn't the first time he'd slipped away from the after-dinner entertainments these past few days. He'd behaved admirably during the first week, but this second week she'd often had to run him to ground, either in the library or in the garden.

The first two times she'd been sympathetic. The coy picking over of his bones that society engaged in behind his back and sometimes not very far away was enough to put a strain on anyone's composure. But *she* was just as exhausted, and *she* did not allow herself to go and put her feet up in the library and read a book while the house was full to bursting with *his* guests.

'*"Probably"* won't cut it. The dancing will begin in half

an hour and he'd better be here,' Lady Westford replied. 'Tell Julian to fetch him.'

Tell him yourself, Genny thought mulishly, but kept silent. Just as she'd kept silent throughout most of this hellishly long fortnight.

'I don't wish to interrupt his flirtation with Lady Sarah. I'll go,' she replied.

Lady Westford gave a short snorting laugh. 'That little minx is making headway with both of them, eh? Good for her. You go, then. And have a word with my grandson. He listens to you. Society might have taken him to its bosom for the moment, but it's fickle and they're watching him. One misstep and they'll roast him over an open fire.'

Genny raised her brows at this image. 'I think we have a little more leeway than that. Lord Westford's entertainments have become the talk of the season.'

'For the moment. Title and wealth and a damned pretty face are excellent shields, but they aren't impenetrable, Genevieve Maitland, and his flaws run deep. Now, go and fetch the rogue.'

Genny did as she was told, happy to get away. But she knew Lady Westford spoke the truth.

It was true that *everyone* wanted to be invited to Lord Westford's entertainments.

Everyone spoke of how tasteful they were…how they married the right touch of intellectual interest with excellent food, wine, and music.

Everyone was now enamoured of this new jewel in society's crown.

Everyone wanted to see Lord Westford.

Lady Westford's now all too frequent 'At Home' hours had become a parade of ambitious matrons angling for invitations. Genny sat through them with a smile pasted to her face as she listened to the fruit of her labours being extolled by those hopeful mamas.

'*What a fascinating man Lord Westford is.*'

'*So cultured.*'

'*Such good taste.*'

'*Such surprisingly fine manners.*'

'*And so, so much more handsome than Lord Byron.*'

And on and on and on—until Genny felt queasy and found some excuse to leave the room before she let slip that, far from being as enchanted with them as they were with him, the handsome and charming Lord Westford was counting the days until he could escape.

All too often—like now—he had a tendency to disappear from his own festivities and had to be coaxed back like a skittish filly. And then, damn him, he had the audacity to look at her as if she was forcing him to do Latin declensions, when all he had to do was charm a bevy of beautiful women—an action which evidently came as naturally to him as breathing.

No wonder Julian envied and resented him. She envied and resented him herself.

The transition from light and laughter to dark silence as she stepped out through the library door into the garden was a blessing. For a moment she just stood there, soaking in the night. The quiet. The pleasure of being utterly alone. She walked to the end of the patio, where darkness hid the gardens, and leant her palms on the stone balustrade, breathing in the cool night air overlaid with the city smells of smoke and refuse, coming through the green scents of the garden.

Carrington House was set at the edge of town, its face to ever more tightly packed buildings, while its back still clung to the illusion of country, with a lush garden and trees beyond. From upstairs she could see the lights of houses in a very different part of London, to the south of them, but from here she could for a moment imagine she was back at the Hall in Dorset, with its far more impressive garden leading to open cliff faces and the bay.

Just the thought of walking down to the bay and sinking her feet into the cool damp sand where the waves kissed the shore calmed her jangling nerves.

She stood listening to the music from the house for a moment. Mozart sounded softer here, slipping beneath the gurgle of the fountain. Suddenly all the noise she'd left inside seemed brassy and discordant.

She gave a sigh of relief—and then almost fell off the patio as a dark form appeared beside her out of nowhere.

'Kit! You walk like a cat,' she admonished, her heart in full gallop.

'You scratch like one, so we're even. Have you come to herd me back inside?'

Even his smile looked feline in the dark, and his eyes caught the faint glimmer from the windows farther away in the house.

'Lady Westford wanted to send Julian, but I didn't want to interrupt his flirtation with Lady Sarah.'

She tried to gauge his response to that, but he merely leaned against the balustrade, his back to the darkness.

'They were making too much noise. I couldn't hear the music. Listen.'

The quartet of players were keeping to their instructions to be unobtrusive until called upon to play dance music, and so had chosen a slow, soothing tempo. But Mozart's genius defeated their aim—the violin sang in such sweet sorrow it was impossible not to be drawn in.

They stood side by side, listening, and when the tune slipped into another, warmer piece, she gave a little sigh, reluctant to let the pleasure of that moment go.

He shifted a little beside her, his voice a low murmur. 'Remember Los Dos?'

Genny gave a gasp of surprised memory. They'd been

two Spanish liaison officers who had served with her grandfather for several months and travelled with beautifully crafted guitars. They would play in the evenings as they sat in courtyards or on boxes beside tents. She could almost see the flicker of campfire and smell the dust, wood fire, and jasmine.

'Ramirez *y* Ramirez,' she murmured, smiling. The two men had been unrelated but had borne the same name, and had soon come to be called Los Dos. 'I missed their music when they left. I missed those evenings.'

'I miss music all the time—especially when we're sailing. I have some music boxes and my bosun plays the guitar, but not as well. I shall have to find some musically talented sailors before my next voyage.'

'Will you be leaving directly after the wedding?' she asked, keeping her voice light.

'Yes. I have to sail the *Hesperus* to Portsmouth for some repairs, but she should be ready by then. My grandmother will be relieved to see the back of me. Julian too.'

She didn't bother denying this. 'The Ton will be disappointed.'

He gave a low laugh. 'I daresay they will. Toddlers never like to have their toys snatched from them. But I prefer not to linger until they become bored and decide to toss me out of their perambulators.'

'I didn't realise you saw yourself as a baby's rattle.'

'I thought that was *your* opinion of me, Miss Maitland,' he said, and smiled, turning to look at her. 'All flash, no substance.'

'Now you are fishing for compliments. You know that is not in the least my opinion of you.'

'I admit I am not at all certain *what* your opinion of me is.'

'Does it matter?'

'Indulge me.'

'It strikes me that you have been indulged enough. I prefer not to fall in line with the rest of the female species.'

'It isn't like you to evade giving an honest opinion. It must be bad, then.'

'It isn't—and you know it. I have, for the most part, recovered my grandfather's opinion of you. However, he might have had a few words to say about your tendency to wander off in the heat of battle and leave your subordinates to hold the line.'

He laughed again, folding his arms. 'You have it topsy-turvy, Genny. You're the General here. I'm merely the battalion to be brought in with drums and flutes to make a great show at one end of the battlefield while you are engaged in flanking action on the other. It's all bells and whistles here.'

'That is arrant nonsense. If you are trying to make me feel sorry for you, you are failing miserably. You are luckier than you deserve, Kit Carrington. You have a life to go to. A life you love.'

'And you don't.'

It wasn't a question.

She turned away but he touched her arm, stopping her. 'I shouldn't have been so blunt. Forgive me.'

'What for? It is the truth. I don't love it, but I am content. I am luckier than most.'

'Resigned isn't content. Why don't you find a way to leave? You are intelligent enough to do so.'

A slash of fear struck through her and she almost asked him—where to? But she pushed it aside and clung to the one important thing. 'I won't leave Serena. Not when she needs me.'

He sighed. 'It is a waste for someone like you to set her life aside for another. And have you considered that Serena might not want this particular form of salvation? You cannot save people against their will, love.'

She squirmed at the casual endearment. It wasn't in the least complimentary. More pitying.

'I can do my damnedest,' she snapped.

He held up his hands. 'It wasn't my intention to upset you. Certainly not when I owe you so much.'

'No, you don't. What I do, I do for myself.'

Guilt joined the bubbling cauldron inside her. He wouldn't be quite so grateful if he knew of her pact with Lady Westford.

Suddenly it felt horribly wrong.

What would he do if she told him…everything?

She opened her mouth and raised her eyes to his. He was looking at her with that intent look she sometimes saw on his face when she caught him watching her—as if he was trying to decipher some runic inscription.

It felt invasive…dangerous.

'We should rejoin the others,' she said, her words rushed. 'The dancing will begin soon.'

'In a moment, little shepherdess. From the sound of those squeals they are still in the middle of one of those awful games. I have a few more moments of reprieve, and so do you. Your brief is to ensure I perform, so help me practise my quadrille.'

He took her hand and bowed over it, and as if on cue the musicians slipped away from Mozart and into a tune she did not recognise.

'What a talented quartet to anticipate my needs,' he murmured. 'This has the distinct flavour of a waltz to it. Come, let us see if we can't do better than our last attempt.'

Before she realised what he was doing, he slipped an arm about her waist.

'We can't dance here,' she whispered, even as her feet slipped into the rhythm.

'Shh…' he replied, and he guided her down the stairs onto the grass without losing the rhythm of the music.

The warmth of his body was a sharp contrast with the night air and the cool, springy grass beneath her soft shoes. All her objections gathered for a grand resistance and then fizzled as he guided her deeper and deeper into the darkness.

She had the strange sensation of dancing off the edge of the earth into an inky stillness populated only by them and the music. The scents of the night were joined by his—a deep, warm musk and a hint of something cool and distant.

'Damn, you dance like a dream, Genny. It's like dancing with a summer breeze scented with orange blossoms.'

It was such a lovely, whimsical thing to say that her panic faded and she smiled up at him. For the first time his steps faltered. Then slowed and stopped.

'No, don't stop smiling,' he murmured, and there was a strange urgency in his voice. 'You have no idea how dangerous that smile is, do you?'

She shook her head. His face was a pale chiaroscuro composition above her, the darkness both muting and highlighting his beauty.

'You smiled just like that in the theatre, when you were lost to the world,' he said, his fingers brushing the corner of her mouth, setting it tingling, as if the stars had sprinkled down on her. 'All those layers, Genny... No matter how many I peel away, there seem to be more. What would it take to lay you bare, I wonder?'

This is as bare as I've ever been.

His fingers moved over her face in a soft, feathery exploration that was lighting fire after fire. They skimmed down her cheek to trace the swell of her lower lip, and without thought she licked the tingle left behind by his thumb. He made a sound, muted but harsh, and it jarred through her body, bringing to life an answering urgency.

He breathed out slowly, shifting away from her. 'We should return.'

She didn't want to. It might be wise, but it felt unfair—ungentlemanly, even—for him to set a fire alight and then slither away. But it was precisely what he did, she realised. He'd charm some pretty young woman or other, or engage a guest in conversation, and then be off, leaving them tantalised but with no foundation to build on. It was as if he was playing out his life's pattern—sailing from port to port and settling in none. Always ready to leave.

She moved away from him, striding into the darkness. He caught her arm, slipping his hand down to capture hers and stopping her.

'It's the other way,' he murmured, his breath warm against her ear.

She turned, and somehow in the darkness found herself pressed full-length against him, her hand on his chest. He made the same sound, deeper this time, and his arm moved around her. But not like in the waltz.

She didn't wait to see what he would do; she leaned in, rising on tiptoe to find his mouth with hers.

She stayed like that, her mouth fitted against his, his breath filling her with a midnight promise that had nothing to do with the reality of day. It was like being filled with life, slowly, with the darkness melting into her, melting her against him.

She'd never felt anything so…right.

Then his mouth moved, his hand sank into her hair, and his lips brushed over hers in soft coaxing sweeps that forced her to follow, like a teasing breeze on an unbearably hot day. She heard herself exhale a soft moan as her lips parted and his body shivered against hers, his tongue tracing that parting.

That simple touch shattered the dreamy beauty with a surge of heat. It swept through her, expanding her, making her hands wrap around his back and tighten on the warm fabric of his waistcoat as they pressed into the rigid muscles of his back.

'Yes…' he whispered against her mouth. 'Take what you want…'

She kissed him, not thinking, just opening, her tongue tasting the firm line of his lower lip, retreating when his tongue came to meet hers, and then giving in to the need to explore, feel. He let her lead the kiss, encouraging her with warm, rumbling sounds of pleasure that were as addictive as his hands shaping her body. They swept down her back, curving over her backside as he raised her against him, their bodies swaying to the half-heard strains of the music.

But when one large hand brushed the side of her breast there was a strange burst of pain, almost as if she'd touched a voltaic cell.

It angled through her like an arrow, striking hard at her core, and she felt a welling of heat between her legs. It wasn't the tentative excitement that came from reading illicit books—this was molten, almost vicious.

Frightening.

She stiffened, suddenly afraid to move, and he stopped as well, his mouth still against hers but not moving. His hand was cradling her breast but nothing else.

Then he breathed in deeply and pulled away. She felt the draw of air cooling her burning lips.

'That went further than I planned,' he said lightly, but his voice was hoarse. 'I'm sorry.'

'Don't apologise.'

Was that her voice? In the darkness she sounded prim, like a governess reprimanding a child.

She cleared her throat. 'We should return.' She echoed his previous words, but this time she managed to head in the right direction.

He followed, but at the patio steps he stopped. 'You go first. I will follow in a moment.'

She didn't argue. If he disappeared again Lady Westford would have her head, but at the moment she didn't care. She couldn't feel much of anything through the chaos of sensations and the jumble of conflicting thoughts and the sheer burning haze of embarrassment.

'Where have you been?'

Genny jumped in alarm, pressing a hand to her chest. 'Julian! Must you sneak up on one?'

'I must if that "one" doesn't want anyone noticing that she looks like she's been dragged backwards through a hedge. You can't go in there looking like that—your hair is coming undone at the back.'

She flushed and reached up.

Julian all but shoved her into the library. 'Not here, where everyone can see you. They'll likely blame it on me and then we'd be in a fine fix, love. Here, let me do it. Turn around.'

She stood still and let Julian pull a couple of pins from her hair, too shaken to object. There was something comforting about his competent motions, and it struck her as both strange and rather depressing that Julian's touch felt as impersonal as her maid's. Her nerves weren't dancing or singing or doing anything they ought not to be doing.

She sighed. 'I think you're a lovely man, but I'm glad we never married,' she said abruptly, and winced a little as his fingers slipped and he poked her with a pin.

He said nothing until he'd secured the last pin and stood back. 'There, sweetheart. You look half presentable. And thank you for the compliment... I think. Now, will you tell me what happened?'

'No.'

'Did any of those bores try to take liberties? If they did...'

'No, Julian, really—they didn't. I doubt they even see me.'

He opened his mouth, closed it, and opened it again. 'Genny Maitland, for an intelligent woman you are shockingly stupid. If you gave the slightest sign of interest you'd have them lined up and down the hall, vying for your favours.'

She smiled at that nonsense and went to the mirror to inspect her hair. It did look presentable, but she didn't feel ready to return to the guests.

She sank onto a sofa and Julian joined her.

'You don't believe me, do you?'

'I believe you are kind as well as charming, Julian. I think I will sit here for a moment. You needn't stay with me.'

He took her hand. 'Listen to me, Genny—' He broke off as the door opened and a tall figure cast a long shadow into the room.

'What is going on here?'

With the light behind him Genny could not make out Kit's expression, but his tones were a mix between ice and acid.

'Close the door before someone sees you, man,' Julian remonstrated, waving his hand at Kit.

Kit shut it with a distinct snap. His gaze flicked over her and past her, settling on Julian, but she felt it like the snap of a whip.

'I know I suggested you conduct your flirtation at Carrington House, but I didn't mean while it was full of guests.'

The irony of his words after their interlude in the garden made Genny's jaw drop, and chased away both embarrassment and confusion. She sprang to her feet, but Julian spoke first.

'Then you should have been more explicit, Pretty Kitty. We'll know better next time.'

Genny had never seen Kit so furious before. He hadn't

moved, but something in his face had been transformed utterly.

Without thinking, she held out her hands, as if to put herself between the two men. Kit's eyes snapped to her, glittering like obsidian in the dark and she swallowed.

'I think you'd best return to the guests, Miss Maitland. Julian and I will continue this conversation alone.'

That woke her further.

'Don't be ridiculous. You two can't indulge in fisticuffs in the library while we are entertaining. If you must act like troglodytes, I suggest you prove your manhood at a boxing salon, or something with at least a pretension to respectability. And you, Julian, don't stand there grinning. I take back everything nice I said about you. You are not helping in the least.'

'Sorry, Gen,' Julian said. 'You're quite right. And you're way off the mark, Kit. I didn't do a thing to Genny but try to help her. Someone roughed her up and I was offering cousinly comfort.'

'Someone roughed—' Kit repeated, shock erasing the anger from his face.

'No one roughed me up,' Genny interjected hurriedly. 'Really, Julian, where do you learn these vulgar phrases? Julian was merely offering to help with my hair.'

Oh, God, she was making it worse. She had best leave before she began bawling and even more thoroughly disgraced herself.

She cast one last harassed glance at herself in the mirror and hurried out, back into the anonymous safety of the crowd.

Chapter Eleven

Kit stopped on the threshold of the library. Genny was half expecting him to excuse himself and leave, but he entered and shut the door. She remained seated on the sofa, her hands tight on the book she had been trying to read, unsure what she should do next.

'You are up early, Miss Maitland.'

'So are you, Lord Westford.'

'I don't sleep well here,' he said, moving restlessly towards the shelves.

Neither do I. Not since you arrived, she almost replied, but kept silent.

The library faced east, to the gardens, and light was streaming in, casting a golden light over him. Sometimes it struck her all over again how handsome he was. It was like coming across a painting and being caught by the skill of its creator.

'I am glad for the opportunity to speak to you before the others wake,' he continued. 'I wish to apologise. For last night. I know I should never have asked you to dance, let alone... You didn't object... But was what Julian said true? Did you feel I had...roughed you up?'

She could feel her cheeks become viciously hot. 'No! Of course not. That was Julian's supposition, because he noticed my hair and presumed one of the guests had... I told him it wasn't so, but naturally I couldn't tell him the truth...'

'I see... In any case, I must still apologise. I should not have taken such liberties.'

He looked and sounded as uncomfortable as she felt.

'You have nothing to apologise for, Lord Westford. Or rather we both do, for acting in a manner that might have caused concern had we been observed.'

'I think I bear a rather larger share of responsibility, Miss Maitland.'

'Nonsense.'

'I accosted you.'

'Clearly your memory is at fault. I kissed you first.'

'I...' He seemed to run aground, his cheeks darkening with either anger or embarrassment. 'That isn't how it works, Miss Maitland. Weren't you the one instructing me to act the gentleman? A gentleman assumes responsibility for such matters.'

'I don't think it very gentlemanly to paint me as a sad little flower with no power to reject unwanted advances or make advances of my own. I think it would be more honest merely to say you would prefer I didn't try to kiss you again.'

'Being honest and being a gentleman are evidently two vastly different things,' he snapped. 'And if we are being honest, I certainly wouldn't say that. However, I will say that I will be certain not do so again if I'm going to have my knuckles rapped like this while I'm trying to do what is right.'

She felt absurdly close to tears and she rubbed her forehead, pressing hard.

'The only thing I object to is the presumption that men can do as they will, but the moment a woman follows an... an impulse, something must be wrong—something must be rectified. Believe me, Lord Westford, had I objected you would have been well aware of the fact. You told me to take what I wanted, and I did. What is more, I did so on the presumption that you were mature enough to follow through on that offer without making precisely the kind of scene you are indulging in now.'

She was shaking a little at the end of her tirade and he seemed rather stricken himself. Then, to her further consternation, he gave a short, rueful laugh and shook his head.

'You are quite right, of course. My only excuse is that trying to play by the rules of this foreign world has skewed my sense of right and wrong. I meant no disrespect— either last night or now.'

She gave a huff of a breath. 'Good. We shall forget about it, then.'

'Must we?'

Her mind stuttered. 'I beg your pardon?'

'Since that kiss is one of my only pleasant memories since walking into Carrington House, I would rather *not* forget it. If you do not mind.'

'I… No… What I meant was… You *know* what I meant.'

'Yes, you meant that with good, *mature* Tonnish hypocrisy, having attained what you wanted, we are now to act as if it never happened.'

'That is not what I meant,' she said, aghast, a little shocked at finding herself in a corner.

'What *did* you mean, then?' he asked politely. 'Not being versed in these rules, I am not certain how to interpret your demand.'

'I am not *demanding* anything. I only meant to allay your fears that I…that you…'

Oh, God, this was going in an entirely wrong direction.

'That you might once again make demands upon me?' he suggested.

'No! That is…if you felt the need to…to make amends… drastic amends…that is…'

He settled on the sofa opposite her and crossed his arms, for all the world as if he was watching a rather choppy attempt at charades but was too polite to hurry her along. His expression was utterly bland, but she knew—she *knew*— he was laughing at her.

Well, she was grateful for it, because her temper finally rushed to her defence. 'Are you enjoying yourself, Lord Westford?'

'I am certainly feeling better than when I walked in here this morning,' he replied. 'I know I am once again betraying my ungentlemanly roots, but watching you flounder is rather…appealing.'

'I am so glad. Now, if you are finished watching me flounder, you may leave.'

He didn't move, and his voice had lost its smile when he spoke. 'Don't expect me to dance to your tune like the others, Genny. I won't do it.'

'I don't expect you, or anyone, to dance to my tune. I don't *have* a tune.'

'You certainly do. You've been playing it for the past two weeks, and all those fine gentlemen and ladies are capering along to it like a group of monkeys because it suits their purpose to do so.'

'That is not very respectful.'

'You have no more respect for the parasitical wastrels than I do. Possibly less, since I possess a far less excitable disposition than you.'

'Excitable!' she exclaimed.

Of all his facial expressions, she most disliked his ability to raise one dark brow without looking ridiculous. It was merely one more thing to list under *Unfair Advantages Possessed by Kit Carrington*.

'I am *not* excitable,' she said with deathly calm. 'Anyone will tell you I am dismally dull and devoid of all the normal female—' She'd been about to say *passions*, but that word felt far too close to the bone at the moment. 'Attributes.' That too had its pitfalls, but it would have to do.

'I find *"anyone"* to be an unreliable source of information,' he replied. 'I'm a Baconian at heart—I prefer to draw my own conclusions, from the evidence before me.'

'Well, so do I. And, putting today aside, I would say that you have proved far more temperamental than I!'

'Today and yesterday.'

'What?'

'If you wish to skew the evidence, you might as well do so thoroughly. Put aside today and yesterday evening from your observations.'

He was doing it again. Just when she'd managed to climb back on deck, he shoved her into the water once more. She *hated* floundering.

'I am not skewing the evidence,' she insisted, amending her approach. '*Even* taking into account today, *and* yesterday evening, you are more temperamental.'

'I wasn't measuring temperamentality…is that the noun? Never mind… I was discussing excitability. I may be more temperamental—though I would strongly debate that, especially given the new evidence before me—but I deny I am more excitable. You didn't see yourself all but swooning over Kean's performance.'

'I was *not*…'

'If you'd leaned forward any farther, you would have toppled into the pit.'

'That wasn't excitability.'

'What was it, then?'

What *was* it, then?

She hadn't even realised she'd been so obvious. The thought that he had watched her while she'd been unaware that she was showing her pleasure was not only embarrassing, but unsettling.

'It isn't kind of you to make fun at my expense, Lord Westford.' She'd meant to sound authoritative, but her voice wobbled.

He frowned and stood abruptly. 'I was not making fun at your expense. Enjoying something fully and honestly is nothing to be ashamed of.'

'It is embarrassing.'

'Only if you are embarrassed. You shouldn't be. Damn, it wasn't my intention to make you check yourself...you do that far too often already.'

As if on impulse, he came to sit beside her on the sofa.

'If you must know, watching you take pleasure in the play was another of the few times I have enjoyed myself since I stepped off the *Hesperus* in London. You made me forget how much I'd been dreading that evening, and you reminded me why my mother and my grandfather loved the theatre as much as they did.'

She was blushing again, in a completely foreign tug of war between pleasure and mortification. This whole conversation was utterly out of her control, and yet she did not want it to end.

Her curiosity rushed into the breach. 'Why *were* you dreading it? I remember you saying something to your grandmother about an incident that had occurred there...'

He smiled, but it was that careful, shielding smile. She wished she hadn't called it up again.

'What a memory you have. I don't know if it merits the name of "incident"...'

'It must, to have left such bitterness.'

He gave an impatient sigh. 'We went to see a play.'

'Which one?' she prompted.

'The Lives of Henry the Fifth.'

'Oh. That was one of our favourite plays as children.'

'It was one our favourites on the ship as well. My mother would play young King Henry, and Patton, our bosun at the time, made an excellent Falstaff.' He leaned forward, his gaze on the carpet. 'I saw the notice when we were in London, my second or third summer in England. I told Mary I wished to see it. She suggested it to my father, and it led to one of the rare battles between them. Certainly the first that she won.'

'What happened?'

'Nothing much. We all went—my grandparents as well. Perhaps they thought a show of familial solidarity at the theatre would put paid to the tattle about my father's first marriage. I remember entering the foyer... I was impatient because my grandmother had stopped to speak to a woman with a monstrous wig...and then I saw my grandfather. Not Lord Westford. My mother's father. Whom I had been told had died soon after my mother's death.'

Genny's breath caught. She'd had no idea about that lie. She could almost see the scene. A boy standing in the foreign but wondrous world of the theatre, that linked him to his mother and her family, feeling their loss. And then...

'Oh, God...' she whispered.

'That was close to my thoughts at the time. I believed I was seeing a ghost. He must have felt me staring, because he turned and froze...'

Genny watched in shock as hot colour spread over Kit's face, and without a thought she took his hand in hers. He looked down, but barely seemed to notice her transgression. He was present, yet miles and years away.

'I can still see his clothes...down to the embroidery on his waistcoat—intertwined grey and black and white lilies. My mother's favourite flower. He just stood there, staring at me. He looked...stricken. Miserable. It can't have been more than a few short moments, but I remember realising the magnitude of the lie. I knew it wasn't he who had perpetrated the deception, but them. I knew that he had wanted no part in it but had given in because they'd convinced him it would be best for me.'

'The poor man… I had no idea. What did you do?'

'I went to him. My father tried to stop me.' Kit rolled his shoulder, as if feeling the weight of a hand settling on it. 'They all did. My grandmother caught my arm and hissed something in my ear, Lord Westford had my other arm, and my father went and spoke to Nathan…my maternal grandfather. Nathan looked at me and said, *"I'm so sorry, Kit."* And left.'

The silence stretched again. While he'd talked she had unconsciously intertwined her fingers with his. His hand was much darker than hers and worn rough at the knuckles. Not a gentleman's hands.

'I ran away. Again. I had grand ideas of disappearing completely, but after spending a freezing night sleeping under a bridge I found my way back here. I was sent down to Dorset and then to school.'

'I'm so sorry, Kit,' she said. His hand tightened on hers and she realised she'd unconsciously mirrored his grandfather's words.

'Don't be. It was merely an interlude. I feel sorrier for Nathan. He lost his daughter and his grandson in one fell swoop.'

'I had no idea they severed your ties with him. That is unforgivable. I'm so glad you found him again, despite their efforts…'

He looked up with a frown. 'How did you know I found him again?'

She faltered. 'I… Mary must have mentioned something.'

'Did she? I daresay she is the only one who has ever mentioned his name.'

'How *did* you find him?' she asked hurriedly.

'I had a book he once gave me, and the publisher's name was written inside. He'd told me he often bound books for them, so I went there and some kind soul took me to his shop.'

He smiled, and Genny could see the echo of relief and happiness.

'He tried to convince me to return to the Hall, but not very hard. We compromised by sending a letter saying that a school friend had invited me to his home for the summer. He was a duke's heir, so they didn't object. My friend Rafe told his mother the same, and we both stayed at Nathan's house. The following winter Rafe ran away to the army, so I hadn't that excuse, but I went to Nathan's anyway.'

'Didn't your father mind?'

'If he did, he never said anything, and I think my grandparents were relieved to be rid of me. I was the one blot on the Carrington landscape at the time. This was before Charlie's parents and sisters died in India, when it was still expected that there would be more sons, so I was definitely expendable. Until I joined the army myself I spent a good part of my time away from school with Nathan. He was a good man. Everything he had he'd earned himself, and he was never bothered by his lack of roots. He encouraged me to explore the world and not to let others decide what I was worth. It was the best possible advice.'

'He sounds a little like my grandfather.'

He smiled, turning her hand absently in his, his thumb brushing rhythmically over the heart of her palm.

'I thought the same when I met General Maitland. My grandfather had all the flamboyance of a man of the stage and letters, but his roots were practical and kind. Your grandfather was the same under his martial façade.'

The pain of memory and loss, of sitting by her grandfather and holding his hand as he faded away, was suddenly so vivid she untangled her hand and went to the window, fighting long-forgotten tears.

'I miss him,' she said to the clouds skimming by. 'Every day.'

She heard Kit rise from the sofa and move towards her. But she knew she was in no state for any more excitability.

She turned, planting her hands on her hips. 'This isn't working.'

He stopped. 'What isn't working?'

'My plan. It has been well over a fortnight and neither Mary nor Serena is showing signs of any interest, let alone attachment. Other than when she is forcibly seated next to someone at dinner, Mary finds every excuse to sit with Emily and Peter or his parents, and as for Serena... Well, no one would believe she was once one of the foremost flirts of the Peninsular Army. I might not be very well versed in such matters,' she said, thinking of Julian's comment, 'but it strikes me that the men will need a little more encouragement than they are being given if we are to make any headway.'

'Quite true. But, to use an inelegant phrase, we may have transformed Carrington House into a trough, but we cannot force your sister or my stepmother to drink.'

The lump in her throat thickened and she swallowed. 'So there is no point, is there? We should stop.'

Stop and put an end to this. You will go back to your ship and I will go back to my comfortable uncomfortable life and Mary and Serena will have to find their own paths in life.

It would be safer.

She didn't like excitability. She didn't *want* it.

Liar, said another voice. *You like it far too much. And therein lies the rub.*

'We should stop.'

Genny was right. He'd seen it as well. When not forced

into proximity with one of the men on their list during dinner, Mary invariably chose to sit with Emily. He might have hoped that at least one of the male guests would see her reticence as a challenge, but, as Genny had said, men needed *some* encouragement.

The sensible course of action would be to admit defeat and return to the *Hesperus* until the wedding. It would put an end to his grandmother's cutting remarks and Julian's snide asides. Not to mention put some much-needed distance between him and the source of his increasingly unsettled nights.

All excellent reasons to do precisely as Genny was suggesting. To say, *You are right; let's put an end to this.*

Genny was waiting. She looked as she had that day she'd walked into the library and issued her first set of commands: resolute and resigned. And cold. As if she hadn't moments ago been almost in tears over her grandfather and his.

She would return to her life acting as buffer in his grandmother's household. Julian might toy with her, might even care for her, but it was unlikely he would extract her from that life. They would all exit this interlude precisely as they had entered it.

It should have been a relief, but it felt horribly wrong.

'Perhaps you are being hasty,' he said.

'Hasty?' she asked.

'Your grandfather wouldn't approve of abandoning a blockade without reviewing what went wrong, would he?'

'What I did wrong was try to impose my own wishes upon two women who are their own mistresses,' she replied tartly. 'You said yourself that I cannot save them from bondage if they do not wish to be saved. It is hubris.'

'It may be hubris, but it is well-intentioned, and I think it is too soon to admit failure. What *we* did wrong was provide our prey with too many degrees of freedom. It isn't a siege if your adversary is allowed to wander about between assaults, sampling pies in neighbouring markets and wandering back when he pleases.'

Laughter chased some of the coldness from her eyes. 'It is very ungallant to liken your stepmother to a pie.'

'Don't split hairs. Still, if you wish to concede defeat...'

'Of course I don't, but...' She sank onto the sofa with a thump, her shoulders sagging. 'I don't know what to do. I keep hoping I shall see that spark of...of true happiness on Serena's face. You must remember it from Spain. She was always so...alight. And I know everyone thought Charlie was rather staid for her, but she *loved* him. And I wish... I wish I could help her find even a little of that again... But I don't know what else to do.'

Kit had never reckoned that confusion and pain could act as a sensual stimulant, but Genny confused and did odd things to his libido. His pulse was quickening again, and his body was remembering precisely how she'd felt in the garden—warm, soft, with all those luscious curves her very proper gown had failed to hide pressed against him, her inner warmth bursting its barriers, sweeping him along.

'I still think we should make one final push,' he said, ignoring his mind's suggestive take on the phrase. 'With modifications.'

'Modifications?'

'Yes. We remove the degrees of freedom. We need to tighten our blockade.'

Her mouth curved in and out of a smile. 'I think we are carrying this martial analogy too far.'

'You started it. And blockades are naval territory—my speciality.'

She straightened. 'Very well—how would we tighten our blockade? Are you suggesting we kidnap those poor men and put them on your ship with Mary and Serena?'

'I wouldn't do that my precious *Hesperus*. I have my limits. I was thinking of the Hall. In Dorset.'

'The Hall... A house party!' she said, her gaze growing intent.

The Generalissima was back in command, he noted, almost with regret.

'Once Emily and Peter remove to his grandparents' house in Hampshire we can invite a select group to the Hall,' he said. 'Away from the distractions of London. You offered me as bait before...'

'I didn't mean—'

'Yes, you did,' he interrupted. 'You laid me out like a leg of mutton for the foxes. Well, on board the *Hesperus* I have a few other legs of mutton for our antiquity lovers, and I could arrange to bring them to the Hall as lures for a select group of gentlemen. I have to sail the *Hesperus* to Portsmouth in any case, so we shan't be too far from the Hall. And, since Mary and I must be in Hampshire in less than a fortnight for Emily's wedding, we have the perfect excuse not to extend our invitation for more than a week. Any more and I will likely lock them in a cellar. Or myself.'

'You wouldn't need to bring anything from your ship,' she replied with enthusiasm, her eyes growing hazy with plotting again. 'I have told you the Hall is already crowded to bursting with your treasures.'

He tried not to smile at the sight of Genny, back at the helm. Perhaps it was the lack of sleep, but he wasn't as resistant as before to the thought of returning to the Hall for the first time since his father's death. In fact, he could kill two birds with one stone. As Genny had pointed out, the cursed Carringtons were his responsibility now. It was time he went to the family seat.

'My grandmother might not agree to be uprooted from

London so soon after coming here,' he said. 'She appears to be thriving.'

Genny waved a dismissive hand, her eyes intent on some inner calculation. 'Leave that to me.'

He pressed his mouth firmly down on a smile. 'Don't mind if I do.'

'Good. Do I have your permission to send out invitations?'

For a moment he considered the wisdom of spending a week in a house he hated with his witch of a grandmother, a group of men who, though worthy, were hardly scintillating company, and the woman he was aching to bed.

In fact, there was nothing to consider. It was clearly, categorically, unwise. If any of his friends heard of this, he would lose for ever his reputation for calculated caution.

'Faint heart ne'er won decent husband for fair stepmother,' he said resolutely.

'"Once more unto the breach", then, Lord Westford?'

'Once more.'

He held out his hand and she smiled and placed hers in it. It took every ounce of his will not to pull her towards him and kiss that smile into something entirely different.

Chapter Twelve

'And this is the Capità's cabin,' the first mate announced in a heavy Catalan accent, motioning the visitors inside with a flourish that would have been comical if the room had not completely justified it.

Emily gave a gasp of appreciation which Genny echoed silently. It was the loveliest room she'd ever seen on board a ship. Kit certainly knew how to surround himself with the good things in life.

It was larger even than her room at Carrington House, with a wooden table at its centre covered in maps and books, and many more books filling the shelves along one wall. The floors were covered with carpets in deep, earthy colours that contrasted with a trio of watercolours of birds and mist-shrouded mountains.

There was also a bunk.

She'd thought that the bunks in the cabins assigned to them on the *Hesperus* for the short voyage from London to Portsmouth were quite generous compared with other ships she'd sailed on with her grandfather, but this…

This bunk should not in all fairness be called a bunk at all. It was far longer and larger than most beds at the Hall, and made even more imposing by a deep wine-coloured silk covering and tasselled brocade cushions the colours of a sunset. The light from the windows made the fabric shimmer, as if at any moment they might dissolve into warm liquid and spill towards them.

It was a bed made for pleasure.

And it had probably served that purpose well and often.

She turned to look at the paintings instead. If Kit lay against those cushions these were what he would see—the slight, light, almost wistful lines of birds and mountains. The sybaritic setting should have overwhelmed their fragility, but they were powerful counterpoints to the sensuality of the bed and the earthy tones of the carpets and the heavy furniture.

It was a disorientating room in more ways than one.

Just like its owner.

'Well!' Emily announced. 'That is the last time I shall feel sorry for Kit when he is on a long voyage. I would love a room like this—wouldn't you, Peter?'

Peter looked rather less enthusiastic than Emily, but perhaps that was due to the rising motion of the ship as it slipped out of the Estuary and into the Channel.

Mary sat down heavily in a chair, her hands tight on the armrests.

'Mary…?' Genny asked and Mary gave a wan smile.

'Perhaps I should have travelled by carriage with Serena and Lady Westford, after all.'

'Oh, no, Mama,' Emily protested. 'You know we have been wanting to see Kit's ship for ever and ever. It is not a long voyage to Portsmouth. We shall be there tomorrow.'

Mary's smile wobbled and Genny glanced at the first mate.

'Perhaps some fresh air would be a good idea, Mr Fábregas?'

Mary smiled with relief and Emily hurried to take her mother's arm. Peter followed, a little unsteady himself, and Genny and the first mate brought up the rear.

'You are feeling well, Mees Maitland?' he asked solicitously, and she nodded.

'I was used to sailing often with my grandfather between England and the Continent. It seems I have not quite lost my sea legs, Senyor Fábregas.'

'You must call me Benja, please, miss. Many men on this ship have no family and no past, so it is agreed we use only our Christian names. Even the Captain.'

'Captain Kit?'

'Ah… When he was a boy, on his father's ship, he was Kit. But when he bought this ship, after the wars, he did not wish to speak of old times. He is not Kit the boy, not Captain Christopher Carrington of the army. To us, he is only Captain Chris—or Capità Krees in my terrible English.'

Genny laughed at the first mate's obvious self-deprecation, a little surprised that he was being so open with her, and wishing he would be a great deal more so. Kit had introduced him as one of the sailors who had served under his father on the original *Hesperus* and there was evident affection between them—the same quiet but solid respect that seemed the order of the day among the other sailors. Another sign that this ship was more than a mere trading vessel.

It was like being back in Spain—she knew these men were used to risking their lives for each other. She'd missed this. Even if she'd always been outside that inner circle of male camaraderie, she'd lived with it so long that it felt like coming home.

Once they were on deck, Kit came to guide Mary towards the bulwarks, moving between the sailors and ropes with fluid grace.

'You'll be better on deck,' he said comfortingly. 'Keep your eyes on the horizon if you can. Meanwhile, Benja will prepare his magical mint tea.'

'But there are *waves*!' Mary objected, her hands as tight on the bulwarks as they'd been on the chair.

'But isn't the view marvellous?' Emily replied, though her hands also clung rather tightly to the railing. 'We are moving so fast...' she added wonderingly.

Genny had noticed the same; once in the Channel, the ship had seemed to jump forward, all but leaping over the choppy waves.

'Perhaps it is merely that I have not sailed for many years, but this seems much faster than the ships I remember ferrying us between England and Spain with Grandfather.'

Kit smiled at her, his face alight with pleasure. He looked younger—another side of him still. He was in his element, and his pleasure was infectious, but Genny also felt a strange pinching in her chest...perhaps envy.

'It is definitely faster,' he replied. 'The *Hesperus* has the same hull design as the dreaded *USS Constitution*— American live oak between layers of white oak. Though it is heavy, it sits very lightly on the water and is almost impenetrable to cannon fire. You will be happy to hear that, aside from being very fast, she is very hard to sink.'

'I'm glad to hear that,' Emily said. 'It is a little wet, though.'

A gust of wind confirmed this assessment by gathering an armful of spray and tossing it up at them. Mary retreated, spluttering, and Emily turned into Peter's shoulder.

'Perhaps we ought to go inside after all, until the storm calms?' Peter asked, looking rather worriedly across the choppy sea.

Genny caught the rueful amusement in Kit's eyes as he nodded and took Mary's arm, guiding her back inside.

Genny remained, watching the waves slip by faster and faster. Another burst of spray engulfed her and she laughed in sheer pleasure. It had been years since she'd felt so... so free.

She looked around the damp deck at the sailors going about their work. For a group of men with dubious pasts they looked surprisingly civilised and amiable, and not in the least put out at having women on board.

Just then Benja appeared from the hold, carrying a tray with impressive balance. He motioned her towards a strange construct which stood in the centre of the deck. She walked around a wooden partition and stopped in delighted surprise. Three wooden walls created a protected gazebo, and inside there were two armchairs and a table nailed to the deck.

She had never seen anything like it. It reminded her of a royal barge she'd seen in an illustrated book. The thought of sitting there as the world slipped by, under the shade of the stretched sails, perhaps with a book...

'Mint tea, Miss Maitland. It keeps your heart warm and your stomach cool. The Captain will join you soon.'

'Thank you, Benja. You are very kind.'

'It is a pleasure, Miss Maitland.'

Emboldened, she reached for her memory of Catalan. *'El plaer és meu,* Benja.*'*

His dark eyes lit with pleasure. 'You speak Catalan!'

'Not much, I am afraid. I have forgotten most of the little I knew.'

'Miss Maitland was in Spain during the war,' Kit said, appearing in the entrance to the gazebo. 'I served under her grandfather for a year—General Maitland.'

'Ah, yes. I remember you spoke of him, *Capità.* A wise man, and good to his men.'

Pain prickled at the back of her eyes and a surge of yearning for that good, wise man washed over her. She needed him now more than ever.

'He was,' she said, her voice hoarse.

Benja smiled and melted away, but Kit remained standing in the opening.

She felt absurdly embarrassed and rose to her feet. 'How are they?'

'They will be fine…just finding their sea legs.'

'Perhaps I should sit with Mary…?'

'No. Stay.'

She hesitated. 'You think I shouldn't intrude on them?'

'I think you should do as you wish. Do you wish to go inside or stay here?'

Again there was that strange shift in energy, like a moment in a play that presaged some portentous action. She looked past him out to the choppy grey surface of the sea, stretching into a sky of scudding clouds, and then to the scrubbed wood of the deck and the whimsical little study at its heart.

'I wish to stay.'

'Then stay.'

The ship tipped and a cloud of spray ballooned over the side like a cool kiss, commending her for her audacity. She laughed, and he took her arm and guided her towards the armchair.

'But this is *your* seat,' she objected.

'Not today. This seat belongs to the one who needs it most. Today that is you, Genny.'

She sat, her behind sinking into the generously upholstered cushions. It was a little stiff with dried salt water, but she could easily doze in such a chair, lulled by the waves, a book on her lap… She sighed.

'I feel I ought to issue a command,' she said.

'Try me.' He poured out a cup of tea for her and then leaned back in the other chair, stretching out his long legs.

The ship kept shifting, sometimes a little jerkily, like a rug being tugged and shifted beneath her feet, though Kit didn't seem to notice at all. The wooden partitions protected them from the worst of the wind and spray, and gave a strange sense of the two of them sailing alone, with only the masts and a strip of the sea in sight.

'I can't think of anything I'd care to command at the moment. I'm too content. I shouldn't be, I know—not when they are unwell—but…this is so much more pleasant than travelling in a carriage. I wish…'

He waited, and somehow she spoke the words.

'I wish we could keep sailing.'

He looked away, out to sea. She felt the flush of embarrassment spread over her cheeks. After their rocky beginning she'd become far too comfortable sharing her thoughts with Kit Carrington. Somehow, after every time they clashed, they seemed to reach a greater degree of understanding. She kept telling him things without thinking them through. She supposed he was becoming a…a friend. Like Julian.

No, not like Julian.

She was comfortable with Julian; what she felt when she was with Kit was not *comfortable*. And Julian, in his own way, would always be there for her. As soon as Kit was finished with Emily's wedding he would be on his way again. For a brief moment he'd entered her cage, just as she now sat at the centre of his. But nothing had truly changed except inside her.

It was not his fault, but he had done her a disservice worse than any enemy—he'd made her want more from life…from herself.

She leaned her head back and closed her eyes, raising her face to the sun dancing in and out of the clouds.

His touch on her cheek was so light she might almost have mistaken it for the caress of the breeze, or the sweep of her escaping hair across her cheek.

She opened her eyes, wondering if she'd imagined it. He was leaning forward now, his face intent and hard. Not with anger, but something that sent her nerves into alert far more readily.

He touched her again...just skimmed the back of his fingers down her cheek. 'You're crying.'

She touched her own cheek, a little shocked to discover he was right. 'It's the wind,' she said, her voice hoarse.

He shook his head and shifted, raising her off the chair only to slip under her and place her on his lap. She sat there, utterly shocked at this strange manoeuvre, and even more so at the feel of his body under hers.

'What are you doing? I cannot sit on you!'

'I certainly can't sit on *you*. I'd crush you.'

His voice was warm against her temple, and he compounded it by putting his arm around her and settling her more comfortably against his chest.

'There. Now I can offer you a shoulder to cry on in earnest. No, don't hold yourself stiffly like that. You'll get a crick in your neck. Relax.'

She tried not to, still clinging to her outrage—more at herself for not getting up immediately than at him.

'Is this common practice in your gazebo?' she demanded.

'This is the first time—to my knowledge, at least—that this seat has been occupied by two individuals at once. I wonder it has never occurred to me before. It is quite comfortable. Or at least it would be if you unbent.'

'I don't think it is wise.'

He sighed. 'It is certainly not wise, Vivi,' he said. 'But we are now outside the boundaries of society and will all too soon be back inside them. If you wish me to return to the other chair I will. Your choice.'

Her choice.

Perhaps it was the way he called her Vivi. No one had ever called her that. It made her feel...daring. *Vivi* would undoubtedly choose to follow her heart—or at least her body.

She relaxed against him, tucking her head into the curve of his shoulder. He'd dispensed with his waistcoat and wore only a linen shirt under his jacket, and he was warm…more than warm. She could feel his chest against her arm, the hard pressure of his muscles.

She closed her eyes and breathed in his scent. Beneath the wood and salt air there was an indefinable, magical spice that was beginning to haunt her. Now she could breathe deeply of it.

She canted her head so that her forehead rested against the warm skin of his throat. She could feel his pulse against her temple—swift and clear.

'This is shockingly improper,' she said, but in a different way from before, and he laughed.

'Let us imagine we have for the moment sailed off the edge of the earth and into another sea entirely. Where neither the Ton nor my grandmother reign supreme.'

'Where neither the Ton nor *men* reign supreme,' Genny amended.

'Where men *and* women are measured on their merit. We are becoming very revolutionary.'

'Why is it that revolutions so often begin with such fine ideas and invariably disappoint?'

'Because ideas are ideas and people are people.'

She sighed. 'Nasty, brutish things, people.'

'You aren't,' he replied gently, brushing aside a lock of hair from her face and gently twining it about his finger.

She smiled and let her eyes drift shut as he ran his fingers through the unravelled hair. So this was what Milly and Barka felt when she stroked them. Except that it wasn't truly soothing. His pulse seemed to grow around her, echoing inside her, carrying through her blood as if it was bringing her to life.

'This *is* comfortable,' she murmured, settling more

deeply against him, resting her hand against his chest. 'Though you are not as soft as the chair.'

His arm tightened around her, his other hand abandoning her hair and capturing her hand, threading their fingers together in an abrupt motion.

'No. I'm definitely not soft,' he muttered, his voice no longer playful.

He slid her a little down his legs.

'Am I too heavy? Should I move?' She forgot she was Vivi and began to shift, but his arm tightened further.

'God, definitely don't move, Vivi. Oh, the hell with it!'

He shifted her back again, so that she was once again pressed against his chest, her behind settled against his slightly splayed thighs. Her slow mind finally registered the hardening pressure of his erection against her thigh. It would have been obvious to any woman with a smidgen of experience. Even *she* realised its import.

He desired her. At least right here, right now, he desired her.

Her body went up in flames.

It had been simmering for the past weeks, flaring at the worst possible moments, reaching boiling when she'd kissed him, but this conflagration went far beyond that. It *ached*, with a hard, burning ache right at her core, tightening her breasts, making her skin tingle from her head to her toes.

The urge to touch his skin made her hands twitch. She might not know much about sensuality, but she knew what she wanted right then as clearly as she knew anything— she wanted to raise her skirts and straddle him so that she could feel him, hot and hard against that ache. She wanted to taste his skin. She wanted him to kiss her back into oblivion.

It didn't matter that they were on the deck of his ship,

exposed to anyone who walked by. It didn't even matter at the moment that there was no future to this.

He had said that this chair belonged to the one who needed it most.

This moment it belonged to *her*.

She touched her lips to the pulse at the side of his throat, brushing it in time with the shortening rhythm of his breathing. Then she drew her tongue along that beating artery, gathering his unique addictive flavour. He breathed in and out, deeply. Other than that, and a strange muted sound deep in his chest, he didn't react. But she could feel his body straining against his control like the sails above them, taut in the wind of the elements.

She was the wind—far more powerful than a mere man-made construct. Perhaps she could even tear through his defences if she wished.

She brushed her lips against the softness of the lobe of his ear and a shudder coursed through him, ending in another of those muted groans. She rather liked that sound. It rang something deep inside her, dragging an answering echo. So she ran her tongue along that soft curve again, and then, on impulse, caught it lightly between her teeth.

She hadn't expected the sails to tear quite that easily.

'Genny...'

His fingers splayed over her nape into her hair, canting her back to capture her mouth with his. It wasn't like the soft, teasing kiss in the garden. This was possession. It was begging and demanding and bringing this new Vivi to life like a wizard's spell. His tongue tangled with hers, caressing it as his hands moved over her body, then drew back to taste her unbearably sensitised lips.

It wasn't only the kiss that was conjuring her into existence, releasing wave after wave of need. His hands were doing as much damage—even more so. He was still holding hers and he ran their joined hands up her waist, brushing the curve of her breast, and a harsh groan was wrung out of her, as if the ship itself was being torn open.

It felt doubly wanton to feel the heel of his palm shaping it, his thumb skimming the bared skin above her bodice and her own hand moving with his, skimming the smooth fabric and the weight of her breast beneath it. Her skin tightened, her breasts turning heavy and needy, and when he shifted their hands to brush them over the taut, tingling peak she moaned against his mouth, her teeth catching at his lip, her legs pressing tensely against him as she tried to turn into the sensation.

She should have held still, because his body bucked under hers and with a strangled groan he pulled back from the kiss. For a moment he didn't move, breathing deeply, and she waited for him to stand up. But then he wrapped his arms around her again. He was caging her, but she didn't feel caged. She could feel the tension of his inner sails being drawn taut again, the quivering of muscle and nerve as he pressed down on the heat that was trapped between them. It was viciously frustrating to feel it, and viciously satisfying to know he felt it too.

'Hell, this is madness, Vivi,' he said at last, his voice hoarse and raw. 'If I had the power, I'd banish every last person off this ship right now.'

'That sounds dangerous. Who would sail it?'

'I don't give a damn.'

He touched his lips to her hair briefly, as if by compulsion. His voice was light, but hoarse, and there was still that rigid tension singing through every inch of his body she could feel.

The temptation to test his control was so strong she was just gathering her resolve to throw caution to the winds when she found herself suddenly seated alone while he was on the other chair. She hadn't heard a thing, but then with a clearing of his throat Benja appeared.

He cast an apologetic smile at Genny and broke into a spate of Catalan. Genny's Portuguese and Spanish had always been excellent, but Catalan was beyond her.

Kit cursed and scrubbed his hands through his disordered hair. 'Mary is asking for you. I'll go…'

'No.' Genny stood and brushed down her skirts. 'If she is feeling ill, I think she might prefer a woman to hold the basin for her. And you have a ship to sail, Captain Chris.'

Chapter Thirteen

'I prepare a feast and no one is here to enjoy,' Benja said morosely.

Kit smiled distractedly at the display of roast fowl, pies, and an impressive pot of Benja's speciality, *paella*.

The choppy weather had held, preventing Mary, Emily and Peter from finding their sea legs. And, since his step-mother drew the line at having either him or his sailors hold a basin for her, poor Genny had been recruited to tend to the sick. Luckily Emily and Peter had not passed from queasiness to outright illness, but they remained in their cabin despite his attempts to convince them they'd do better on deck.

'Well, at least that is the last time Emily will beg me for a pleasure cruise,' he said, heaping some food on a plate. 'Take this to Miss Maitland's cabin and remind her to eat while she can. Mary is likely to throw something at me if I show my face. I'll take a plate to my cabin and the men can come in here and do justice to this bounty.'

Benja sighed as Kit took his plate and glass. He could have stayed and eaten with his men, as he usually did. He *ought* to stay with them and take the distraction they of-fered. A lonely dinner and a bottle of wine while his cock was aching for satisfaction was not a good prescription for a sound night's sleep.

He even tried to insert himself mentally into Mary's sickroom, in the hope that envisaging the familiar sight of the contents of upheaved stomachs would douse the pulsing need he'd foolishly unleashed on deck.

Instead he saw in his mind Genny leaning over a bed, her rounded backside shaping what looked more like a nightdress than the proper gown and pelisse that had separated them on deck. He turned her around. But now she was wearing that unfairly low-cut peach-toned gown she'd worn to the theatre. He stood there in his mind, as hard as a mast, and reached out to set loose her hair, watching the thick honey-brown waves unfurl over her shoulders, covering her beautiful breasts...

No, not covering her breasts—he wanted those bared to his imagination. He reached out and gently brushed her hair aside. God, he could almost feel it between his fingers. He'd only touched that heavy, warm silk twice, but it was imprinted on him more deeply than an inked tattoo on a sailor's skin.

Her hair was now cascading over her shoulders, and he was free to take her hand, as he had on deck. But this time she guided his to her breasts, their fingers linked as they cupped the heavy warmth that rested in his palms— heavy, soft... But he could feel the skin tightening against his hand, just as it was tightening over his erection...

He opened his eyes and pressed his palms together. This was *not* a good idea.

Once they were safely at the Hall it would be easier to stick to the rules. There would be lots of guests, lots of servants...

Lots of rooms.

All those corners where he could...

No.

He kept forgetting that even though Genny might be unconventional, their worlds were utterly different. He might have begun by thoroughly disliking Genny Maitland, but somehow he'd come not only to desire her but to...to care for her...as a friend. He would not wish to see her harmed simply because he couldn't keep his hands to himself. It was not worth it. A flirtation, even a kiss, was all well and good, but everything else would come at a high price for both of them.

Still, he wished too that they could keep on sailing. A little longer. And while he had her in his world, he'd make damn good use of the armchair...

His mind grabbed hold of that pleasant thought: his ground, his armchair...his woman.

No—he amended—not his woman.

Genny Maitland was her own territory. He was merely toying at her edges. He didn't *want* to conquer her; all he wanted was to bed her.

But, *hell*, he did want to bed her.

The knock on his door was hesitant. He was about to send whoever it was to the devil when the certainty struck him that it was Genny. He was at the door and opening it before he realised he was dressed only in his trousers.

She stared at his chest, opened her mouth, turned away, turned back, and frowned at the floor. Luckily, her eyes skimmed past the evidence of his lack of self-control.

She planted her legs a little wider, rushing into speech. 'I'm terribly sorry to intrude. I did ask Benja, and he assured me I would not be disturbing you.'

He would have to have a word with Benja about his sense of humour. To Genny he said, 'Has anything happened? Mary?'

'No, no. She is finally asleep. But I'm afraid she will wake again and I thought it best to have a book with me when she does, to take her mind off her stomach. Mr Fábregas told me the books are in your cabin. I did ask if he could…but he said he had to hurry on deck…something about sandbars? I didn't know there were any so far out.'

Neither did Kit. Nor were there. And Benja knew full well there was a shelf of perfectly suitable books in the map room.

Damn him.

Or bless him, depending on the state of Kit's fast-fraying morals.

He opened the door. 'Come in and choose.'

'I… Perhaps you should?'

'I wouldn't presume. I'll even put my shirt back on.'

'I… Don't on my account. Though…aren't you cold?'

She stepped into the room and he shut the door before she could reconsider.

'No. No, I'm not cold.'

He went to pick up his shirt and she moved cautiously towards the shelf of books, her brows rising as she moved along the shelf.

'You have a great many books.'

'There is a great deal of time to read on a ship.'

'True. Are you ever bored?'

'Sometimes. I don't mind, though. Boredom is a privilege. Some of my best ideas come to me when I'm bored.'

She gave a slight laugh and ran her finger down the spine of one of the books. It seemed to shiver down his spine as well, and his erection rose against the confines of his trousers.

'I remember often being bored when we were billeted in one place for a long time,' she said to the books. 'I wanted to be *doing* something. Not sitting with Serena and the other women and gossiping.'

He could well imagine that. Genny had never belonged in such a setting any more than he had. He felt a twinge of heat a couple of dozen inches north of his erection and rubbed at it. Empathy was not what he wanted to feel right now. He wanted her to ask him to fetch a book for her from the top shelf, while she stood very, very close.

'Take a book or two,' he suggested. 'It might be a long night.'

Damnably long.

'I don't think I shall have time…' She took a book and clutched it to her like a Quaker with her bible, her hair a tangle of waves over her shoulder, glinting gold and dark wine in the flickering of the lantern.

He reached past her to pull out a volume. *'As You like It.'*

'As I like…?' she echoed, her voice hollowing.

'It,' he completed. 'Shakespeare. Rosalind is my favourite of his heroines. *"I shall devise something."'*

'Oh.' She took the book and added it to her shield.

He reached to her right, nudging her aside very gently. 'No, not *A Midsummer Night's Dream*, I think. That will likely give you nightmares. *Measure for Measure*? A little dark, and there's a beheaded pirate there, so we shall pass on that. What of…?'

'These two shall do, thank you,' she said hurriedly.

They both fell silent.

'I didn't tell you before, but this is a lovely room,' she added.

'Thank you. I bought the *Hesperus* from an American privateer. He liked his comforts.'

'Like you. It is impressively neat too. Everything in its place.' Her eyes flickered up to his with a hint of laughter.

'I was born and raised on a ship. When you live at the mercy of the elements and with hardly any room of your own you come to appreciate the benefits of order and comfort.'

'I wasn't making fun of you, Kit.' She looked absurdly contrite.

'No?'

'No. It is merely nice to see your human side… Oh, Lord, that didn't sound right…'

'My human side? You find me cold, Genny?'

'That isn't what I meant and you know it. Shouldn't you don your shirt?'

'Should I? One of the benefits of being on *my* ship, in *my* cabin, is wearing what *I* want. Or, in this case, not wearing it. If my state of undress offends you so, you can, of course, choose to leave. Yet here you are.'

'The books…'

'You are holding two perfectly serviceable books—masterpieces, even. Yet you are still here. Could it be you are contemplating another…impulse?'

'Right now I'm contemplating your chest,' she blurted out.

He planted his hands flat on the shelves on either side of her. 'I would love to do the same. Must you cover the most spectacular masterpiece in this room with all those layers?'

A laugh bubbled out of her. 'Kit. This is *very* improper.'

'If you were *very* proper, you wouldn't have sat on my lap and kissed me on an open deck just a few short hours ago.'

'I didn't…'

'You most certainly did. I was there.'

'I *meant* I didn't mean to be so brazen.'

'You weren't brazen; you were honest. You asked for what you wanted; I asked for what I wanted. So if you wish to play on equal ground, this is how it is done. At any time, no matter what, you can walk out through this door. I would never stop you.'

She swallowed. 'That almost sounds like a threat.'

'Freedom is threatening. We're beasts that like boundaries. We feel safe inside them.'

'*You* don't.'

'I mistrust them because they are too often used against

me. I'd rather risk my fate outside them so long as I don't hurt people I care for. But that's my choice; you make yours.'

She took a couple of deep breaths, her eyes fixed somewhere in the area of his right shoulder. 'So…if I would like another kiss, I could ask you?'

His elbows threatened to give way and close the distance between them. He almost said, *You could ask me anything.*

He pulled his sagging mental faculties back into some semblance of intelligence and nodded. 'You could. That isn't to say I would agree. The same applies to you.'

'Of course.'

She shifted her eyes up to his. They were a deep, metallic grey now, the pupils dilated. He very much hoped that meant she was strongly considering being impulsive.

'I really should return to Mary,' she said, hefting her books higher against her bosom.

Ah, damn.

'But first…fair is fair. Hold these, please.'

She gave him the books and then untied her cape, draping it over his braced arm as if he was part of the furniture. Beneath she wore a demure cotton nightgown, secured with blue ribbons at the neck. The simple cream-coloured fabric clung to her curves as lovingly as he would happily have done. She wore a chemise beneath, but no stays, and even through the double layer he could see the tight pressure of her nipples beneath.

Then she drove home the knife with a slow tug at the laces and the fabric fell open, revealing the plump curves all the way to the dark hollow between them.

'What is it with men and bosoms?' she asked as she watched him, her voice caught between laughter and embarrassment and a tamped heat that echoed his.

'I don't know, Vivi, but it's deep. Especially when faced with such perfection.'

'They're hardly perfect.'

'Exquisite.'

He allowed his eyes to sweep over her, gathering images—the outline of her thigh under the cotton, the rise of her hip, the faint echoes of freckles across the bridge of her nose, the warm, generous curve of her mouth. And her eyes… Perhaps they were the most damaging to his sanity. They glistened like liquid mercury…mystical and dangerous.

'And not just them, Vivi. Every inch of you. Utterly exquisite.'

'Now you are being foolish. Mary and Serena are exquisite. I'm short and passable, with a bosom that seems to distract men and make them say silly things. It is nothing to be proud of.'

'Mary and Serena are pretty like a hundred other women are pretty. Like that vase on the table is pretty. I have absolutely no urge to populate my wicked waking dreams with *pretty*. They are thoroughly occupied with absolutely…utterly…exquisite.'

He allowed himself to gently brush his fingers over her shoulders and the soft skin at the side of her neck before he regretfully tied the ribbons again and draped her cloak about her shoulders.

'Once we're at the Hall we won't be able to…to flirt like this,' she said, her eyes skimming past him to the rumpled bed.

A spear of fire cleaved through him—fierce and demanding—but instead of pushing him over the edge, it held him back.

The thought of exploring Genny's excitability might be threatening his sanity, but it wasn't the hypocritical Carrington morals that stood in the way of taking what she was contemplating offering.

Genny deserved far, far better—and that was precisely what he couldn't give her.

No, to be fair, it was not that he couldn't—he wouldn't.

If there was one thing his father's two marriages had taught him, it was that marriage should either be entered into with all one's heart and soul and conscience, or not at all.

'No, we won't be able to,' he finally agreed.

Fantasy would have to remain fantasy.

She nodded and took the books, pressing them to her chest again. Then she rose on tiptoe and brushed her mouth over his, lingering for a moment. His arms were already rising when she sank back down and slipped past him and out through the door.

He stood there for a while longer, staring at the books on the shelf. The gilt lettering of *Love's Labour's Lost* twinkled in the candlelight, mocking him and the long night ahead.

He put on his shirt and boots and went up on deck. With any luck it would rain.

Chapter Fourteen

How strange.

He'd forgotten how lovely Carrington Hall was.

In his boyish memories the house had been dark, brooding, oppressive. Since their arrival yesterday he'd only seen part of it, but he'd yet to find a dark corner.

The house was a large grey stone affair in the classical style with two wings, set in a slight valley that protected it and the lush spring gardens from the worst of the sea winds.

It was a resolutely English sight, cheerful and even comforting, but the jewel in the crown was the horseshoe-shaped bay which nestled below rocky cliffs and was accessible by a narrow and seldom used cliff path.

Tomorrow he would indulge in the only happy memory he had of the Hall—swimming. The cold water would be useful.

He felt strangely cheated. He'd been nursing a boy's resentment for well over a dozen years and now it had fizzled like a wet candle wick.

He walked through the gardens, wondering if he could identify the place where he'd constructed the fort Julian had invaded when they were boys.

'Good morning, Lord Westford.'

He turned at Serena's voice. She was coming out of the rose garden, carrying a basket filled with fully blown roses and peonies.

'We've missed the best of the peonies already while in London,' she said with evident regret. 'They were Charlie's pride and joy.'

'They are still beautiful,' he said, and she smiled happily at the flowers. It was the first time he'd seen a true smile on her face since his return to England, and he realised with surprise that Genny's sister was still deeply in love with Charlie.

In Spain he'd thought her rather shallow, both in intelligence and emotion. He still had no idea about her intelligence, but he rather thought her emotions ran deep—and they ran in the river bed she'd forged with sweet, straightforward, and ultimately gullible Charlie.

He encouraged her to talk about his cousin, watching the joy pour out of her just as the peonies were threatening to tip out of her basket, and he wished once again that Charlie had survived and was here, where he ought to be, as husband to this grieving woman and as rightful head of the Carringtons.

'He liked you, you know,' Serena said after falling silent for a moment. 'Very much. He always felt he'd been caught between you and the others and never quite knew how to be. That was why he was so happy when you both found yourselves in the same regiment in Spain. He even thought of asking your advice when he realised how bad matters had become.'

'Why didn't he?'

'He didn't know where you were at the time. Mary said the last letter she'd had was from somewhere in the East Indies. In any case he felt…he felt he had to fix it himself. To prove to everyone that he was not…weak.'

'Goodness isn't a weakness, though it is sometimes preyed upon.'

'Yes,' she said earnestly. 'That is what I told him. But he wished he were like you or Marcus. Men who insisted on what they wanted. But he was a *good* man—the kindest I knew. That is why I love him...but he never valued himself as I did.'

'Then he was a very lucky man.'

'I was the lucky one. I only wish...' Her smile wavered and she stopped by the kitchen path.

'Would you like to go live in the Dower House again?' he asked impulsively, and her face lit.

'Do you mean with Genny?'

'If she wishes.'

'I... No, we could hardly leave Mary with Lady Westford, and I don't know if we could convince her to leave her on her own. Oh, it would never work.'

'It strikes me that my grandmother would be far happier in London in any case. Racketing around there seems to suit her far more than it does you and Mary.'

'Oh, it does. But then *we* would have to stay with her there...'

'Why? I'm sure we could unearth some worthy but impoverished Carrington cousin who could organise her whist parties. Charlie wouldn't have wanted you fetching and carrying for that old witch for the rest of her life.'

'No... Charlie wanted us to have a large family and to live on one of the smaller estates where he could grow—' Her voice cracked and she shrugged and smiled. 'I must go and place these in water before they fade. Thank you, Lord Westford.'

Kit watched as she hurried inside and then continued towards the library. He'd ask Mary about Carrington cousins, and the steward about the Dower House, and Genny about—

'Hello, cousin!'

Kit stopped abruptly in the library doorway at Julian's salutation. His cousin was lounging in an armchair, looking through some papers, and the look he directed at Kit was half-smug, half-wary.

'What the devil are you doing here?' Kit demanded.

'I thought the past two weeks had rubbed off some of your rough edges, but apparently I was mistaken. Is this how you plan to greet all your guests, Kitty?'

'Guests are invited. You aren't.'

'I beg to differ. I most assuredly am. Well, if you wish to split hairs, it wasn't strictly an invitation. More of a command.'

'Whose?' Kit's voice snapped like a whip, though he already knew the answer.

'Who issues commands in this household? Or rather, who issues commands I'm likely to obey? Darling Genny, of course.'

Kit went to the sideboard, where Howich had cleverly placed a decanter at the ready for the new master. It was early yet, but he felt the need for a glass. 'Wine?'

'One of your purchases? Or the vinegar Grandfather indulged in?'

'Mine.'

'Then I will, thank you. It's been a long two weeks so far, and likely to be a longer week still. I need all the support I can garner, Kitty.'

Kit considered taking offence at Julian's needling him with the hated nickname, but decided that would only encourage the bastard. He took his glass and paced along the shelves, as he had last night when he'd reacquainted himself with the one room in the house he remembered fondly.

It was a graveyard by means of books, with each Carrington ancestor possessed of their own plot of land. His grandfather's collection of medieval Books of Hours was shut safely into glass-fronted shelves, his father's antiquarian tomes and plates covered part of the north wall, and then came Charlie's shelf, dedicated to agricultural tomes...

He moved away from Charlie's dreams and stopped. A book was leaning tipsily into a gap in the middle shelf. He set the book straight, momentarily distracted from his vexation.

'Did you take some books from here, Julian?'

'I haven't touched a book in this house for years. Why? Are they valuable?' Julian asked.

'Not in the least.'

'Oh.' The disappointment was evident. 'Pity. I could have used the hunt for a book thief to enliven the next few days. What books?'

'Three books. One on the battle of Thermopylae, Herodotus's *Historias*, and Chamber's *Life of Thucydides*.'

Julian's mouth quirked, as if at some secret thought, but then he shrugged. 'They will probably turn up on a table somewhere.'

Kit surveyed the rest of the shelves but there were no other gaps. 'Not that it matters. It is merely...curious.'

'I'm taking some more of this excellent tonic,' Julian said, wandering over to the decanter. 'Would you care for some more, or are you determined to keep your wits about you to meet the onslaught?'

Kit held out his glass to be filled. 'I'd rather have them dulled. I never would have guessed I'd prefer a forced march across the Pyrenees to another week entertaining the Ton.'

'God, yes. They're insatiable. If we have to play charades one more time... Other than the excellent food and wine, I'm regretting the moment I convinced you to show your face in society. I never realised how boring people obsessed with antiquities can be. Why the devil couldn't you

invite some guests with an interest in something useful?
Even an interest in pork jelly would be a relief at this point.
The way they went all spongey at the sight of the vase you
brought out that last night in Town made me queasy.'

'You're a damned waste of a good education, Julian.
That vase is over a thousand years old and probably worth
more than your horse.'

'Since I don't own a horse, you're undoubtedly right.
You'd best watch how you flaunt those baubles. I over-
head Lord Ponsonby telling his daughter how much it was
worth, and the lovely Lady Sarah's sapphire eyes lit like
bonfires.'

'Thank you for your concern, but I don't think someone like Lady Sarah would enjoy giving up her Tonnish
pursuits to become the wife of a scandalous merchant—
even one with a title.'

'Who says she'd have to give up her pursuits? Her type
would lord it in London while you were out on the high
seas providing the dibs.'

'You don't like her, do you?'

'I'm not particularly fond of schemers. Remind me of
my mother. Always scheming and never stopping to see
who they've stepped on along the way.'

'You say you don't like schemers but you seem very
fond of Genny, and she casts Lady Sarah's machinations
into a deep shade.'

'You have a point. Genny's ambitions may not be mercenary, but she's happy to sacrifice the two of us to keep
the old witch happy and off Mary's and Serena's backs,'
Julian continued.

The uncharacteristic shade of bitterness in his voice
caught Kit's attention as much as the words. 'What do you
mean, sacrifice the two of us?'

Julian leaned his head back in the chair, his smile mocking. 'I would have thought it was obvious. In between her

efforts to snatch one of those prosy gentlemen for Mary and Serena, she and dear Grandmama have us surrounded by a constant buzz of lovely ladies like bees around a honeypot. You didn't think that was chance, did you?'

'Neither Genny nor Grandmama had anything to do with my decision to come to the ball in the first place. *You* were the one who convinced me,' he said warily.

'*Mea culpa.* Genny forced my hand. I knew Marcus would prove damn elusive, and I didn't see why I had to suffer alone. I honestly never expected the chase to last so long—and certainly not to see it transposed from London to Dorset with your full approval. Which of the pretty and pedigreed parcels arriving today are you leaning towards?'

'Arriving today?' Kit echoed, still hoping he had misunderstood.

Julian raised a brow. 'Were you hoping for another day's reprieve? I saw the Cavershams stopping at the Green Giant in Guildford on my way here. The Ponsonbys were with them. I daresay the Ducal pack is not far behind. Your few days' rest is up, Cuz. The old witch would obviously prefer you pick one of the Burford girls, to please the old Duke, but I put my money on Lady Sarah. She's almost as cunning as Genny, and she and her ambitious papa have clearly decided you will do very well indeed for their purposes. If I were you I'd choose that sweet little Caversham lamb—pretty, quiet and outrageously wealthy, with an irreproachable name that goes all the way back to the dawn of time. She'll brighten your tarnished coat of arms and wait patiently at home while you do as you please. What more could a man want?'

Kit hardly even registered the slipping of Julian's urbane charm, revealing the angry bitterness he usually kept veiled. He was too occupied with realising what a complete blind fool he'd been. Why hadn't he asked who Genny was inviting? He'd left it to her and assumed...

He'd assumed a great deal about Genevieve Maitland. And in his lustful haze he'd forgotten precisely what she was.

Yet it still felt…wrong.

He made one last bid to redeem her. 'Why assume Genny orchestrated this and not Grandmother? You would think marrying us off would go against Genny's interests. She and Serena would be forced to leave the Hall and Carrington House.' He didn't mention his surmise that Genny had long been holding a candle for Julian himself.

'Well, that is what she wants, isn't it? Independence. Grandmama has her own funds, you know. And that is what she promised Genny in return for one of us walking up the aisle and signing the register. She'll pay Serena's debts and settle a generous sum on her. A very comfortable arrangement.'

'Who told you this?'

Julian's shrugged. 'What difference does it make?'

Kit wished he could dismiss this as a sign of Julian's malice, but it rang true. Such a pact would provide Genny with everything she wanted.

He should have told her that very first week that he had settled Charlie's debts and arranged annuities for Serena and Mary. He'd been tempted to tell her but he'd held back, afraid she'd think he was doing it as much to please her as out of duty.

Which was true as well.

Idiot.

But he shouldn't be angry with her. Genny Maitland was simply doing what she did best—surviving.

He wasn't angry.

He was *furious*.

At her, at his grandmother, and at Mary and Serena for allowing those two Machiavellian women to control their lives… No, for practically forcing them to do so by the sheer force of their passivity.

He was furious at Julian as well. Not for his part in the subterfuge, but for seeing more clearly what he himself should have seen from the moment he'd walked into Carrington House. He *had* seen it. He'd just allowed his suspicions to be lulled, allowed himself to believe that in joining forces with him Genny had somehow set her other alliances aside—his grandmother, Julian…

Unbelievably gullible.

'Kit? Where are you going?'

Kit didn't answer as he strode out of the library.

First he would set his grandmother straight. And then…

Chapter Fifteen

'Lady Westford has sent for you, miss,' Susan announced.

Genny looked up from her writing and sighed.

Susan's mouth hovered near a smile. 'Yes, miss.'

'Very well, Susan. Are my sister and Mrs Mary still resting?'

'Mrs Mary is, but your sister is out in the garden with His Lordship.'

'With Lord Westford?' Genny tried to mask her surprise.

'Yes, miss. Bess said as she just saw her and Lord Westford there, miss.'

'Thank you, Susan.'

Genny closed her books and went to the window. She had a clear view of the gardens and the path leading back to the house. As Bess had reported, two figures stood by the entrance to the rose garden. Kit was smiling down at her sister and Serena was laughing, her face bright with pleasure, her hands moving animatedly.

She looked years younger, like she had in Spain, full of joy and flirtatious light. Genny hadn't seen that expression on her face in a long, long time. They looked perfect together, both tall and beautiful, dark and light. Genny's heart gave a painful squeeze compounded of pleasure at

seeing her sister as she had once been, and sharp, undeniable jealousy.

She had resolved to accept whatever fate dictated, but
if fate dictated that something should evolve between Kit
and Serena…

*Nonsense. They don't suit at all. Serena needs someone
sedate and stable and cheerful, like Charlie. There is no
reason to worry simply because Kit is making her laugh…
and look happier than she has since…*

She turned away from the sight and left her study, her
hand pressed hard to her stomach as she made her way to
Lady Westford's room, where she took a few moments to
compose herself before knocking on the door.

She had barely crossed the threshold when Lady Westford's voice snapped out at her.

'I'm not happy with you, Genevieve Maitland.'

Genny took a deep breath and went to sit by the bed,
where Lady Westford lay still in her dressing gown and
lace cap. Carmine's cage was partly covered by an embroidered cloth, and his beady eyes glimmered accusingly
from the shadows. She'd forgotten to bring seeds, and most
likely Carmine was about to make her pay for her lapse.

'It's been over a fortnight and we've nothing to show for
it,' Lady Westford continued, reaching for her cane where
it lay on the coverlet beside her.

'A fortnight is not a very long period,' Genny replied,
feeling the lie. This fortnight had felt very, very long indeed.

'It's enough to see that he spreads himself about but
won't encourage any of them. I don't see what difference
this week will make.'

'He has spent a great deal of time with Lady Sarah,
during the past week in particular.'

'Aye, she sees to that! But sinking her claws into him
is a sure way of making him bolt. At our last dinner in

London he flirted with Burford's youngest instead—the one who wants him to carry her off on his ship like Scheherazade, or some other foolish female.'

Genny didn't bother correcting Lady Westford's literary allusions. She'd noticed the same, and so had Lady Sarah, who had very wisely stepped back and spent the evening flirting with Julian.

She wondered what Lady Westford would say had she seen Kit and Serena just now. Serena had barely been considered good enough for Charlie when they'd thought her able to provide an heir. Lord Westford marrying his cousin's barren widow would likely give Lady Westford an apoplexy.

'Yet you must admit he has behaved exceptionally well—'

Genny cut herself off, realising she was following Lady Westford's lead in speaking of Kit as if of a child invited to join the adults at the dinner table. If she didn't need Lady Westford's co-operation and goodwill, she would be tempted to tell her precisely what she thought of her treatment of her grandson.

She gathered her scattering resolve and continued. 'Playing hot and cold at this juncture is probably his way of reminding Lady Sarah who is in command, Lady Westford. He knows quite a bit more about seduction than you...' She trailed off that sentence and took a deep breath. 'I, for one, think we are doing quite well. You shall have to be patient. The more you press, the more resistance you arouse.'

'In you as well, eh?' Lady Westford cackled and Carmine followed suit, hopping about excitedly.

'Yes,' Genny snapped. 'In me as well.'

Lady Westford's eyes widened in surprise and she looked far more human. 'What's eating you, child? Worried about Serena? You'd think the gel would be sensible enough to cast out some lures to Caversham. He might be tempted into the parson's mousetrap by a pretty face and soft ways if she but exerts herself. Can't have her mooning about Charles for ever or she'll lose her bloom. Best have a word with her.'

'I will *not* have a word with her. She is old enough to make her own decisions and mistakes.'

Genny felt an absurd need to cry and hurried to the door. She'd had her fair measure of being tested for the moment. For the year.

As she opened it Lady Westford's cane rapped against the chair, but lightly.

'Wishing me at Hades, aren't you, Genny?'

'There is a great deal to prepare and I'm tired, Lady Westford,' Genny replied.

Her answer seemed to upset Lady Westford, as if she'd somehow been snubbed.

'I can see that. Go and do what you need to do. But make sure you keep your eye on the *rouleaux*, Genevieve Maitland. We have a deal, you and I. Don't think I won't hold you to your part of it. Remember what's in it for you.'

'I remember, Lady Westford.'

'Yes, I daresay you do. Don't forget—it was your scheme to begin with, but it's my money you won't see a penny of if you don't deliver results.'

Genny didn't bother responding, just stepped out into the corridor.

And straight into Lord Westford.

Her heart gave an almost audible squeak as his hands closed on her arms, steadying her. She was about to apologise when she caught the expression in his sea-blue eyes. His gaze held hers for a moment, then shifted past her to the still-open door.

He reached past her and slowly closed it. The faint *thunk* of wood on wood sounded very loud.

She waited for him to say something. Anything. She knew without a doubt that he had heard her last exchange with Lady Westford. She was not quite certain how it had sounded to him, but by the absolutely blank look on his face it was bad. He just stood there, saying nothing, his face so leeched of expression she might as well have been boxed in by a statue.

'Excuse me, Lord Westford,' she said, her voice a shade too high.

'For what, Miss Maitland?'

Good point. She was tempted to point out that people who eavesdropped rarely heard anything to their advantage, but thought better of it.

'Mrs Pritchard is waiting for me. To discuss tomorrow's menus.'

'Mrs Pritchard is proving endlessly useful to you, Genny Maitland, isn't she? By all means, run along. I shall find you after I have a word with my grandmother.'

With that ominous promise he set her aside and entered Lady Westford's room.

Genny did not wish to admit even to herself that she had found every excuse to remain in Mrs Pritchard's neat little parlour far longer than their business merited. They'd reviewed the linen inventory, the references of a new housemaid, and everything else that had been piling up in the busyness of opening the Hall to guests after almost two years of mourning.

By the time she returned to her rooms she hoped Lord Westford had calmed sufficiently and would leave her be.

That hope died abruptly when she saw him on the sill of her parlour.

The menu lists she'd taken to review for the rest of the week slipped from her hand and fluttered to the carpet.

Lord Westford turned at the sound of the door opening

and leaned down to pick up one of the sheets of paper that had settled by his boot.

Her surprise was transformed into alarm and she calmed only slightly as she realised she'd put her private notes in the drawer out of force of habit before leaving the room.

'This parlour has been set aside for my use and Serena's, my lord.'

'I'm aware of that—which is precisely why I am here. You took your time hiding in Mrs Pritchard's lair.'

Her stomach tightened at his clipped tones. He looked much as he had during those first days in London, before they'd forged their tentative truce and tested the boundaries of propriety with their flirtation.

He certainly looked nothing like he had on board the *Hesperus*.

She waited for the attack, but to her surprise he placed one hand on the stack of books on her table.

'I was wondering where these had gone.'

A shiver of alarm ran through her, but her voice was steady when she answered.

'I apologise. I did not know anyone was looking for them. I shall return them.'

'No need. Now I know where they are...'

He raised the book he had been holding. A different kind of tension caught her.

'I didn't know your grandfather had written a book,' he continued.

'It is a volume of essays first published in the *London Magazine*.' She swallowed and tried to smile, adding a little impulsively, 'I have several copies if you wish to take one.'

He considered her, but there was no lightening of his expression. She'd begun to forget how unfairly handsome he was. When he was aloof like this it was hard to ignore the sheer beauty of his face and physique. Every time she was reminded, the differences between them slammed down like a drawbridge clanging into place.

'Thank you.' His words were cold and something turned inside her—a flicker of welcome anger to press back at the confused heat.

'You are welcome. Now, if you do not mind, I must review the week's menus.' She waved the handwritten sheets she'd collected from the floor and scooted around him to sit at the writing table, pulling the inkwell towards her.

'An excuse, Genny?'

Far from leaving, he came to stand by the desk, picking up one of the entwined jade dragons and weighing it in his palm. She felt a tremor shimmer down her spine. It wasn't fear—it was that damnable awareness, made all the worse now it was backed by experience.

'It is no excuse, my lord, merely a care for details. It might have escaped your notice, but a house party is a nightmare of logistics,' she said with dignity, keeping her eyes on the menus but seeing very little.

'Not at all. I'm impressed by your skills, Madam Quartermaster. Even more so having seen you in mid-campaign. What were you and my grandmother discussing just now?'

That answered her question about whether he'd overheard. Her stomach sank to somewhere below her ankles. Which was suitable—she truly felt a heel.

'Lady Westford is naturally unsettled by the house being invaded. I merely reassured her I shall do my best to keep everything in order.'

He planted his hand on the menu she was trying to read. It was a very large hand, splayed wide on the white paper. She swallowed again as another potent memory arose— that same hand, entwined with hers, his calluses rough against her palm. She felt the warmth of his body as he leaned over the desk but she didn't look up. Not that staring at his hand was any better.

'Someone who lies as often as you should do a better job of it, sweetheart.'

His voice was as soft as silk and as menacing as a coiled snake.

'I'm not—'

'I am serious,' he interrupted. 'Whatever you and the old witch are concocting, I hope… I very much hope…it has nothing to do with me.'

She tried to tug the paper from under his hand, but achieved nothing more than a ripped corner.

'I told you I do not care to be loomed over, Lord Westford. If you are in a foul mood, please exorcise it elsewhere.'

'I'm in "a foul mood", Genny, because I don't like being manipulated. If you put so many pokers in the fire, don't be surprised when one burns you.'

A flush of sheer, brutal heat swept over her. She bent further over her lists, but he caught her chin, angling up her face.

'What are you two plotting?'

His voice had dropped into a hoarse, coaxing rumble. He wasn't exerting any pressure on her skin, but she felt his touch deep inside her, as if it was setting roots and spreading.

'I'm not *plotting* anything,' she said, a little desperately.

His fingers traced the line of her jaw, feathering the hollow below her ear. 'So what do you call it, then? Merely doing what needs to be done to *"get through the day"*?'

She realised he was using her own words from that day in the stables. They sounded all wrong like that. She shook her head, but that only made his fingers graze the lobe of her ear and she couldn't stop the answering shudder that swept through her. He felt it, closing his hand on her nape. A deep sound, almost of pain, caught in his throat.

For a second she couldn't breathe. Her lungs just

stopped, waiting out the wave of scalding heat that swept through her, setting fire after fire—in her cheeks, her chest, and again at that unfamiliar core inside her.

He spoke first, his voice a sensual drag across her nerves.

'You don't like being out of control, do you? You're like a cat, clinging to the ceiling, afraid to sheathe your claws for fear of the fall.'

'Cats land on their feet. I don't.'

'But you do. Or rather you somehow arrange for one of us mortals to lay a mattress precisely where you need it.'

The mention of mattresses was not fortuitous. She thought of his wide rumpled bed on board the *Hesperus*, and of her own bed behind the door not two yards from him.

She couldn't think of anything intelligent to say so she kept silent, waiting for him to stop the assault and leave her be.

'What were you and my grandmother discussing?'

This question was a whisper of coaxing warmth, spilling like silk down her spine. She knew what he was doing, but it made no difference to her body.

It was *aching* to be seduced.

'I will find out, Genny.'

This time she heard frustration, determination—and, she thought, hurt. That surprised her, and she looked up. His eyes were in full storm, dilated. She didn't see any hurt in them, only concentrated fire. Goosebumps rose on her arms.

'It's dangerous, not giving quarter, Generalissima. You should know that,' he continued.

I do.

She almost spoke the words, but nothing came.

He smiled. 'Defiance by silence, darling? You're not the only one who can be stubborn.'

His thumb brushed the cleft of her chin, and then the soft pillow of her lip. His eyes followed, his lashes lowering to shield the deep blue eyes. She let her eyes drift to his mouth; she could feel it on her still, in the gentle, sensuous kiss in the garden, the wild, drugging kiss on the *Hesperus*, even the kiss that had been promised but never came in his cabin. Each was a different aspect of this man.

This time he was using his skill on her consciously. He might not use his weapons as lightly as Julian, but when he chose to do so he could clearly play a beautiful seduction scene. It might have been a little more believable if he hadn't been radiating anger.

There was none of the teasing warmth she'd begun to expect when they crossed swords, when the battles were almost a pleasure as they skirted around the heat they sparked off one another.

'Tell me.' His eyes were icy, his voice raw.

She shook her head, the friction of his fingers dancing deliciously over her mouth and adding fuel to the fire. 'You should know I don't respond well to threats, Kit.'

'I'm not threatening. I'm asking,' he murmured, his hand slipping into her hair, cupping her head, his fingers moving gently against her scalp.

She laid a hand against his chest to push him away but stayed there, feeling his heartbeat fast and hard against her palm.

'Why don't you trust me?' he asked.

'Why should I?'

He gave a small laugh. 'Damn you. No reason.'

'I'm not the only one who doesn't like being out of control, am I, Kit?' she asked impulsively.

He shook his head, lowering it inexorably. 'No. No, you're not...'

The last word was a whisper against her mouth. But he didn't kiss her. Not like before. This soft brushing of his lips over hers, sweeping like a willow branch on water, wasn't quite a kiss. It felt more like a dance…like that waltz on the patio as the music had wound about them and carried them deeper and deeper into darkness, swaying only for the sake of the lightest of frictions.

'Such sharp claws and such soft lips,' he murmured. 'What a chimera you are, Genevieve. I never know if you'll command, condemn or tantalise.'

'I never tantalise,' she protested in a whisper.

Shaking her head only increased the friction.

'Yes, you do.' He kissed her gently, mouth closed, just nudging her lips with his before whispering against her mouth, 'You use whatever tools you have at your disposal.'

'Not this.'

'You did in the garden. On the ship.'

'*You* did that,' she protested, drawing back a little.

He shook head again, his eyes narrowed and slumberous. '*We* did that. You know you could have told me to stop and I would have. You can tell me to stop now and I will. Admit it, Genny. You enjoy this. Another field to test your powers.'

A shiver ran through her. Damn him for being right. Perhaps it was best to think of it precisely like that?

'So what if I do? Me and the rest of humanity. It is nothing extraordinary.'

A flash of challenge turned his eyes near black. 'Isn't it?'

He leaned forward again, his mouth hovering below her ear, his breath slipping down the side of her neck and setting it alight. Slowly, slowly his lips approached the lobe of her ear. She could feel the ebb and surge of warmth as his breath came closer.

'Can't you feel it, Vivi? I'm on damn fire here and it feels wonderfully out of the ordinary. This is what people live for. Not society, not propriety…this. *This* is beautiful.'

His lips came to rest on the peach-soft flesh of her lobe and she couldn't hold back the moan that rose from the deepest part of her. It *was* beautiful.

But it doesn't mean anything, her mind insisted. *He probably uses the same tactics with whichever female sparks his interest. Or whenever he needs to prise secrets from credulous women.*

I don't give a damn, replied her body. *Right now, I am the one sparking it.*

She turned her head, making his lips skim her cheek, stopping when they reached the corner of her mouth. His breath stuttered against her skin before he withdrew, sending the tiny hairs on her cheeks shivering.

'Show me,' she goaded. 'Show me something extraordinary.'

There was a thundery echo of anger in his eyes in the moment before his head descended to hers once more. She waited for that anger to be reflected in his actions, but his mouth settled on hers as gently as a dandelion seed on a pond.

'*Vivi...*'

The word was a slow exhalation of smoke against her lips and they opened of their own accord, letting him brush the parting with his lower lip.

'I want to do this…everywhere. Every inch of you. I can close my eyes and see you on my bed, your hair tangled, your thighs bare, the silk sheet slipping between them, begging me to follow. I should have thrown scruples to the wind and accepted your invitation on the *Hesperus*. Have you any idea how much I wanted you at that moment?'

She shook her head, a little shocked by the urgency in his voice, and more than a little mistrustful.

Kit would tell her what she wanted to hear, what any woman wanted to hear—that she was desired, that her powers in some way overcame his. He'd warned her that he meant to make her tell him the truth. This was nothing more than another negotiation—wasn't it?

She didn't know what to do. This was not a game she knew how to play. This was not a *game*. Not to her. All she knew was that she wanted him.

He still held her hand pressed to his chest and his heart beat against her palm, against her own hurried, tumbling pulse. She wanted that beat against her bared body, not a stitch of fabric between them and only the cool slide of the silk sheet beneath.

'I didn't know. I *don't* know. Show me...'

'If I do I'll go up in flames, Vivi. Just your scent... You smell like the orange blossoms that bloom on Capri—the scent of paradise. And the taste... I've never tasted anything so exquisite, Vivi.'

His fingers slipped down, tracing the outline of her breast, tightening the muslin over her skin until it dragged against the tightened peak, the friction sending a shower of tingling need right down to her toes.

She wanted him to bare it, to touch her properly, and while he was at it to do something about the insistent discomfort that kept surging and ebbing between her legs. She'd thought she understood a great deal about the interplay between men and women—what she hadn't gleaned from Serena and Mary she'd learned from books or by asking an amused but co-operative Julian. But she realised now that in this domain reality was very, *very* different from theory. She was still as green as the greenest of virgins and she was tired of her ignorance; she wanted to *know* in the most biblical sense.

His lips explored hers in a series of light, almost playful kisses, like a butterfly flickering on and off a flower, except each contact was like a strike of flint on flint, teasing, making everything tighten unbearably. Then he raised her from the chair and onto the desk in one motion, drawing her towards him so that he could stand between her thighs.

She'd felt his erection before, on the ship, but now it was a thudding presence against the flame-hot pulse between her legs. Her moan was lost in his own low, guttural groan as he held her there, his mouth against hers, his skin warm on hers, the rasp of his stubble making her skin tingle, a tantalising contrast with the velvet of his lips, making her wonder what that contrast would feel like…elsewhere.

The sensations, so foreign and so right, and the vivid images conjuring themselves in her mind, were both frightening and wonderful. She wanted so much more. She wanted to press deeper, impossibly deeper against him. Until there was nothing at all that stood between them… until she was nothing but these unnameable sensations… until they went up in flames.

Then he spoke, his words a whisper against her temple. 'Why won't you tell me what you and my grandmother were discussing, Vivi?'

Sometimes Genny woke from a dream with a harsh thud, quite as if she'd rolled off the bed. His words struck her exactly like that. They cut through the haze of lust and finally set bells pealing.

She gathered every shred of her control, put her hands on his chest, and pushed. His hands tightened on her behind, then released her. He moved away, towards the window, tucking his shirt back into his buckskins. She hadn't even realised she'd pulled it out.

She truly must have lost her mind.

She slipped off the desk but remained leaning against it. 'If I tell you…'

He gave a short, bitter laugh.

'Ah, here it comes. Tit for tat.'

'*You* began this negotiation.'

'It isn't a negotiation, damn it.'

'An interrogation, then.'

He didn't answer, but nor did he deny it.

Then, 'So, what price *are* you demanding for your confession, then, *darling*?'

The word was a slap but she ignored it. 'Serena.'

He frowned. 'Serena?'

'Yes.' She took a deep breath and forced the words out. 'I don't want you making her fall in love with you.'

His eyes narrowed. 'Are we talking about *Serena*?'

'Yes. I saw the two of you coming up from the gardens. You were laughing together and she looked…alive again. Like she did before everything went wrong.'

Her voice faltered and she could feel the unfamiliar burn of tears in her throat, in her eyes; even her cheeks ached.

'And you thought…? Do you want to know what we were talking of, Miss Maitland?'

His sudden formality stung, but she shook her head.

'My brilliant strategy of seduction was to inveigle your sister into telling me of the time Charlie tried to win the prize for the largest turnip in the village fête. How he finally grew one larger than Squire Felston but the night before the fête his favourite sow… I think her name was Annie…found her way into the garden and ate it.'

He gave a harsh laugh at her expression.

'You are right about one thing, though, Miss Maitland. It was the first time I had seen her come to life since I returned to England. Whether you wish to face the truth or not, Serena is still in love with Charlie, and I think the last thing she wants to do is find herself another husband. All she wants from me is someone who will talk to her of Charlie and not pity her. She is not interested in me and I am not interested in her. And if this…' he swept the room with his hand, encompassing everything that had transpired there '…was an attempt to keep me away from your sister, you have truly outdone yourself, sweetheart. You are so bent on winning this game you're playing against life, I think you forget what you are playing for.'

He went to the door and stopped, his hand on the knob.

'Intelligence isn't maturity, Genny. You're long on one and sometimes frighteningly short on the other. That's a dangerous combination and one day it will burn you badly.'

Kit closed the door as quietly as the explosive mix of fury, lust, and hurt allowed him. It was the dignified thing to do, but he was almost tempted to open it again and slam it shut so hard it shook the whole of Carrington Hall. Shook it right into rubble.

He strode down the corridor, but stopped at the sound of voices in the hall below. The deep voice of the Duke of Burford and the higher chatter of his granddaughters intermingled with Lady Sarah's laughing tones. Beyond them he could hear the rumble of carriages on the drive.

Now he could remember why he hated this house. He could feel it shutting the cage door, pressing him deep into a corner. Except this time, he'd walked voluntarily into this cage. Invited it, even.

He wished he could leave. Ride back to Portsmouth and raise anchor on the *Hesperus* and leave.

He'd known this visit to England would be difficult. He hadn't realised it would be purgatorial.

Chapter Sixteen

'And what ring of hell are we entering today?' Kit asked Mary, and she glanced around swiftly to see if anyone had heard. But only the two Burford girls had yet come down to breakfast, and they were surveying the dishes set out on the sideboard.

'Hush, Kit. We have a quite unexceptionable activity arranged for today.'

'You said that the day before yesterday, when we spent the whole day traipsing around the house as if it was a damn—dashed museum, and then you said it again yesterday when we spent the day in Weymouth, following in old King George's footsteps along the promenade.'

'The Duke and your grandmama have many fond memories of the town and you must admit it is a rather lovely place. I only wish it had been warm enough to try the bathing machines.'

'I don't. I much prefer swimming on my own in the bay.'

'Hush. If only you would at least *try* and enjoy yourself.'

'I am on my absolute best behaviour, Mary. I have never in my life made such an effort to be pleasant so far against my will.'

'I know it, and I appreciate it, but I wish you would try and *enjoy* yourself.'

Kit refilled his coffee. He should be on the *Hesperus*'s deck now. This was his hour, after seeing to the morning rote, to go to his deck study with a book and a cup of Benja's strong, bitter coffee. Everyone knew he was not to be interrupted unless they had run aground or were about to be boarded.

God, he missed his freedom.

To think that people actually wanted this life.

He wanted none of it. So far it had brought him nothing but headaches. And cock aches.

At least he'd held firm to his determination to steer clear of the little Field Marshal these past two days. They'd hardly talked, and when they had it had been either with the most punctilious politeness or with the sharp biting jabs he had promised himself he would not succumb to and kept succumbing to nonetheless.

At least until yesterday morning, when by a stroke of bad luck they'd found themselves alone together in the breakfast room. It had been absurdly awkward. They'd sat there like two painfully shy greenhorns, trying to think of something unexceptionable to say. Since then, they'd stopped sniping and moved to ignoring. Genny clearly shared his wish to get through this week as swiftly and painlessly as possible and forget that anything at all had happened between them.

Eventually that was what would happen: the same fate that overtook everything—it faded.

His heart hitched, stumbled down a hill, and then slowed again. He was becoming accustomed to these anatomical anomalies, but he hated it. It was like a gammy leg—it served well, nine parts out of ten, but the tenth...

He dragged his mind back to the matter at hand. 'You still have not told me what is planned for today.'

'Why don't we let it be a surprise?'

'Good God, no. Out with it. What horror have you planned?'

'It is no horror. It should be quite enjoyable.'

'This is sounding more and more ominous.'

'Nonsense. It is merely a treasure hunt.'

'A *treasure* hunt! You are jesting!'

'Shh! It was Lady Calista's idea.'

'Of course it was. Why don't I just bury a chest full of jewels for her to find and be done with it?'

'Now, now… It shall be great fun. What a pity Emily isn't here. She would have enjoyed it mightily.'

Kit decided it was politic not to answer and concentrated on his coffee. He should have asked for it to be sent up to his rooms—but, besides it being impolite not to share breakfast with his guests, he was too restless. And he needed the distraction.

Just not a damned treasure hunt.

'What does this damn—dashing idea entail?' he asked in calmer tones. Forewarned was forearmed.

Mary greeted Lady Sarah and Lord Ponsonby, as they too entered the breakfast room and went over to the sideboard.

'It entails,' Mary answered, keeping her tones low, 'the guests being divided into two groups. Each must search for a hidden object by following a series of clues. We knew you would be difficult, so Genny did not include you. Unless you wish to be included. We shall say you have hidden the clues and so cannot in fairness take part. You need do nothing more than follow along.'

'Does that mean they shall be crawling all over the house again?'

'They shall be exploring and enjoying themselves. And you shall be polite.'

'Yes, Aunt Mary,' he replied obediently.

The door opened and he prepared his polite face again,

but it was only Genny and Serena. Genny's eyes met his for a moment and fell away, a faint flush touching her pale cheeks. Serena went to join the others at the sideboard, but Genny sat next to Mary and pulled the teapot to her.

'Is everything in place?' Mary asked cheerfully.

'Yes. You needn't worry.' Genny's tones were as flat as the sea in the doldrums.

Serena sat opposite, casting a peculiar glance at her sister. 'Are you feeling quite the thing, Genny?'

'Of course.'

'Oh, I'm so excited!' Lady Calista exclaimed as she bounced into the chair next to Serena, the abundant contents of her plate very nearly finding their way onto the pristine linen. 'I am quite certain our group shall be the first to solve all the clues.'

'I would not wager on that, Calista. I saw the lists in the hall. I am in the competing group,' Lady Sarah said as she sat beside her with rather more decorum.

Lady Calista's eyes sparkled. 'Perhaps we ought to lay a wager.'

'You shall do no such thing, young woman,' the Duke said as he entered the room, but he patted her affectionately on the shoulder as he passed.

'Oh, Grandpapa!'

'I said no. You shall have enough excitement, hunting for that treasure. Learn to be content with what you have, child.'

Lady Calista's pout lasted only for a moment. 'Never mind. It will be enough to know we've beaten you to flinders, Lady Sarah. We have Julian… Mr Carrington… on our side.'

Lady Sarah's mouth pinched but Julian, who had settled on Genny's other side, raised his cup in salute to his bubbly teammate.

'You may console yourself with that dream until it is

rudely shattered,' Lady Sarah retorted and smiled across at Mary. 'We have Lady Westford and Mrs Mary Carrington on our side, and when you are a little older you shall realise that women are far better at clues than men.'

Mary laughed, and despite his sour mood Kit couldn't help smiling.

'I didn't see everyone's names on the lists,' Lady Sophronia intervened, her eyes flickering in Kit's direction and then dancing away. 'Which side are you on, Miss Maitland?'

Genny set down her still-full cup and folded her hands in her lap. 'Neither, Lady Sophronia. Since I hid the clues, my role is merely to grant each group a hint if they are truly stymied.'

'I thought Lord Westford hid the clues?' Lady Calista said, throwing him a disappointed look.

'I'm afraid I am as much in the dark as you are, Lady Calista. Miss Maitland is the true mastermind here.'

Genny's chin rose, her mouth flattening, but she was clearly the only one who had heard anything questionable in his tone. Lady Calista laughed and clapped her hands.

'Why, that is marvellous. Then you *can* play. You must be on our team.'

'I think it wouldn't be fair play to have both Carrington cousins on one team. Since they grew up here, they have an advantage, don't they?' said Mr Caversham as he sat beside his daughter.

Since Miss Caversham was in Lady Sarah's group, his suggestion was a trifle transparent and his poor daughter turned an unfortunate beet-red. Kit, who'd had no intention of voluntarily joining the game, found himself smiling across at the young woman.

'You're quite right, Caversham. I value fair play above all else—it is so hard to come by. I shall add my name to the list. Unless you would rather do that, Miss Maitland?'

'No.'

Genny's answer was bald enough to breach even Lady Calista's bubbliness. She threw Genny a rather puzzled look, and Serena hurried to explain the rules of the game, drawing everyone's attention.

Kit missed most of it. He was too busy kicking himself for succumbing once again to pointless, petty sniping. Whatever Machiavellian schemes Genny engaged in, and however much he resented them—and her—he should not allow it to affect his own conduct. What he should do was play the game and count the hours until he left all this behind.

'*"Enlightened One by any other name."* What can it mean?' Lady Sarah smoothed out the strip of paper they'd discovered in the music chest, where their previous clue had led them.

Kit was about to speak when Miss Caversham cleared her throat nervously.

'Roses?'

The team turned to her and she shrank back a little.

He smiled encouragingly. 'What made you think of roses, Miss Caversham?'

'The quote. *"A rose by any other name would smell as sweet"*?'

She seemed to finish most of her sentences with a question.

'I think you are right. Shall we go to the rose garden?' He held out his arm and Mr Caversham beamed with pride, which only made his daughter's blush deepen.

'But what does *"Enlightened One"* mean?' asked Lady Sarah as she fell into step on his other side as they entered the garden. 'Is that the name of a rose?'

'Sounds like what you'd name a saint, or something,' Lord Lansdowne replied as he helped Mary down the steps. 'Maybe one of the roses is called Bishop or Cardinal or something. They have Mrs Serena Carrington on their team for all the horticultural questions, so we'd best ask Lady Westford.'

'It's not a rose,' Kit answered.

He had no wish to draw this out any longer than necessary. Lady Westford and the Duke had very early on abandoned their respective teams to offer their support from the comfort of the card room, where Genny sat in readiness to supply the teams with their one hint.

'Oh, you know what it is!' Lady Sarah exclaimed, with an enthusiasm that would have done Lady Calista proud. 'Why did you not say?'

'Fair play. I thought you ought at least to work for it. And Miss Caversham has proved I was right to trust your abilities.'

They entered the garden and he led them to its centre, where a small pedestal that had once housed a sundial now supported a stone statue of the Buddha he had sent Emily years ago. The roses were in full bloom and the garden bathed in an intoxicating rainbow of scents. Once again he was struck by the almost reluctant realisation that Carrington House was a place where someone could, and should, be very happy.

The Buddha certainly looked content with his setting.

The group fanned around it.

'He doesn't look very enlightened,' said Lord Ponsonby. 'Saints usually look rather more serious. This fellow looks like he's contemplating a good joke. Either that or picking a thorn out of his finger.'

'This *fellow* is called Buddha. He lived well over two thousand years ago and was the founder of the religion of Buddhism. He is often called the Enlightened One or the Awakened One.'

'Well, I don't see how we were to know that. And he certainly looks more asleep than awake.'

'Papa!' Miss Caversham reproved as he and Lord Ponsonby laughed at the jest.

Lady Sarah went over to inspect the statue. 'Whatever the case, here is our last clue.'

The group clustered round her and Kit gave a silent sigh of relief.

'Almost over,' Mary whispered to him—just as there was a distinctive cry from the direction of the house.

They all turned as Lady Calista's high tones carried joyfully through the air. 'We won! We won! Oh, I do wish you had let me place a wager, Grandpapa.'

'Oh, dear,' said Lady Sarah with an uncharacteristic slipping of her mask as she balled up the strip of paper with the clue and tossed it back onto the pedestal. 'She is going to be more insufferable than ever now.'

'Julian was marvellous,' Lady Calista said as they all gathered in the conservatory, having completely discarded formalities in the excitement of the chase. 'We had already used our hint, and were convinced we were all done for, when suddenly he practically rode to the rescue on a great white steed when he remembered that marvellous portrait of the Fifth Earl in the hallway. Why, I must have seen it a dozen times since we arrived, but I never noticed there was the dog at his feet. And I certainly had never looked at the name on its collar.'

She cast Julian an adoring look as she took another grape from the fruit bowl.

'What can I say?' Julian smiled as he sat on the sofa next to Genny. 'I love animals. Of all kinds.'

Lady Sophronia actually tittered, but Lady Sarah's fine lips curled a little in distaste.

'I don't think "love" is quite the correct verb to employ in your case, Mr Carrington.'

Surprised silence followed this uncharacteristically blunt blow from Lady Sarah, and then her father rushed into speech.

'Hard to believe the week is almost over. You shall be leaving soon for your sister's wedding, won't you, Lord Westford?'

'Yes. In three days.'

'And then? Back here or to London?'

'To Portsmouth,' Kit replied. 'My ship is there.'

Again conversation floundered, and then Miss Caversham's sweet and seldom heard voice piped up.

'You are leaving England again?'

Kit knew the answer to that, but for a moment he couldn't seem to find it. He latched on to the one certainty—the *Hesperus* was waiting for him. The life he knew and trusted.

'Yes. Of course. We are sailing for France and then Italy.'

'I hope you will bring back some more of that marvellous Montepulciano,' Julian said with a mocking smile as he surveyed the guests' responses to this news.

They were varied, and swiftly hidden behind polite masks. But Kit could see disappointment, annoyance, distaste, and—touchingly—on Miss Caversham's face, regret.

Genny's face showed no expression at all. She was still looking as stiff as she had at breakfast.

Julian leaned towards her to ask her something, but she shook her head without answering. Her hands, Kit noted, were still folded in her lap, but they didn't look in the least restful. They were held tightly, her knuckles slightly pale. It struck him that she too was pale and had been since breakfast.

Not that it was any of his concern. His concern was to reach the quiet of his rooms and refresh his store of patience and good manners so he could survive three more days of this…

Howich entered, his gaze seeking Genny, and she stood stiffly and after a moment's hesitation went towards the butler.

With a word of excuse Kit rose to join them.

'Is something wrong?' he asked, and Howich gave a slight bow.

He seemed to expect Genny to answer, but when she remained silent he shook his head. 'No, my lord. I was merely enquiring whether we should set back dinner half an hour to give the guests time to rest, seeing as the treasure hunt took longer than expected. If so we had best decide now, so that Cook may adjust her timetable.'

Still Genny said nothing so Kit spoke.

'If Cook can manage it, then I think that is wise, Howich.'

Howich bowed and left, and as Genny turned back towards the others Kit touched her arm, stopping her, lowering his voice.

'If this silence is some form of punishment for what you imagine to be a slight against you, I should tell you I'm damned if I'm apologising, Genny. You were utterly at fault and you know it.'

'I have the headache,' she said, and he laughed, all the resentment he'd managed to tuck away during the day's activities filling his vessel to the brim.

'Surely you can do better than that threadbare excuse, sweetheart?'

'Don't call me that!' Her voice sounded as raw as his nerves.

'No, you're not very sweet, are you? You might smell like orange blossom but you have the bite and sting of a lemon. Are you certain it is a headache, or are you merely finding it hard to stomach Lady Calista winding her ivy around Julian?'

She finally looked at him. Her face was pale, but there were harsh spots of colour on her cheeks and the fury and loathing in her eyes were utterly unveiled.

'You say one more word to me today, Lord Westford, and I will…' She stopped, shoving a hand hard against her temple. 'Stay *away* from me.'

'With the utmost pleasure, Generalissima.'

Chapter Seventeen

'Genny? It's time to dress for dinner...'

Serena's voice, though low, shoved the hot steel nail in Genny's temple an inch deeper. She gave a faint protesting moan, but even that made it worse.

A soft hand rested for a moment on hers where it was fisted on the blanket, and then an even softer voice spoke somewhere above her.

'Rest.'

The curtains were blessedly pulled shut and the door closed. Genny gave a little mewl of relief and let go of consciousness.

'Is Miss Maitland not joining us this evening?' Lady Sarah enquired as she inspected the piano, running her fingers along the ivory keys.

'My sister has the headache,' Serena replied, not looking up from the music sheets she was inspecting with Miss Caversham. 'I cannot seem to find the Northern Garlands ballads you asked for, Grandmama.'

'What's that? A headache? Genevieve? Nonsense,' declared Lady Westford, putting down her cards and waving her cane in Howich's direction. 'Howich, go and see what is keeping the girl.'

'Let the poor gel rest, Amelia,' the Duke of Burford said soothingly, over his cards. 'It's no wonder she's feeling out of sorts; she's been run ragged these past weeks. Dashed competent girl.'

'Genevieve hasn't had a headache in her life,' protested Lady Westford. 'And she will know where the ballads are. Why can no one remember where everything is? Send one of the maids for her, Howich.'

'There will be no need for that, Howich,' Kit intervened. 'I am certain whatever music Serena has for the pianoforte will do.'

'I think perhaps the ballad sheets are in the cupboard in the blue drawing room. I shall go and see,' Serena said swiftly, and both she and Howich beat a hasty retreat.

Lady Westford's cheekbones were mottled with colour as she faced her grandson. He smiled slightly, wondering if she would manage to rein in her temper. Her cane hovered ominously a few inches off the floor. The conversations around them dipped in tone. Everyone was waiting.

He was spoiling for a fight after his clash with Genny, and it was high time his grandmother had her wings clipped. He was damned if he would have her ordering everyone about as if they were her serfs.

'If you wish, Lady Westford, I know several of the ballads by heart,' Lady Sarah interjected, her voice a soothing breeze in the heated atmosphere. 'I could play them while we wait for Mrs Carrington to find the music. There is no need to bother Miss Maitland.'

For a second longer Lady Westford's temper teetered. Then the Duke of Burford gave a slight, almost imperceptible *tsk*, and she lowered her cane, turning to Lady Sarah and Lord Ponsonby with a smile.

'What a dear, accomplished girl you are. You are to be commended in your daughter, Lord Ponsonby. Yes, do come and play something for me, my child. And perhaps dear Calista and Sophronia could sing for us. Such lovely clear voices.'

The Duke beamed at her and Kit leaned back, half-amused, half-wishing she'd picked up the gauntlet.

He watched Lady Sarah take a seat at the pianoforte. She and the vivacious Lady Calista and Lady Sophronia presented a lovely tableau: three English beauties polished to a high sheen of perfection.

All he had to do for Society to bestow upon him its seal of approval was choose one of them and lay her pedigree like a silken cloak over his tainted roots. *Unite with us and all will be, if not forgotten, then at least only whispered behind fans when we are bored or feeling more spiteful than usual.*

Lady Sarah laid her hands on the keys and glanced up, meeting his gaze, her lips softening in the slightest of smiles. If he'd been at all impressionable he'd have melted into a puddle by now.

He switched his gaze to Lady Sophronia as she began singing, her clear high voice bringing the ballad about a shepherdess and her lost flock to life. She too met his gaze but, not possessing Lady Sarah's poise, faltered for a moment, her cheeks warming.

He sank his chin into his cravat and turned his gaze to the second singer. Lady Calista twinkled with all the bravado of an eighteen-year-old accomplished flirt. He rather thought that by twenty she would either be ruined or, more likely, married to a pleasant, tame man who would let her run rings round him. She would probably live a long and happy life.

The thought cheered him a little, but then he caught sight of his grandmother's complacent smile, her hands rocking her cane.

'Three on a silver tray...take your pick,' Julian whispered as he settled on a chair beside him. 'At least they're musical. That's an advantage.'

Kit shifted in his seat, leaning his heel heavily on Julian's toes. His cousin grunted, but sank into silence.

At the end of the ballad Serena entered with a stack of music sheets and Julian went forward to help her. He was promptly dragooned by Lady Calista into turning the pages for them.

The three pretty blonde heads followed Julian like sunflowers turning to the sun. Kit watched his cousin smile and charm them, and might himself have been convinced that Julian was truly taken with their charms—except that he'd seen his cousin smile very differently at a far less beautiful woman. There was charm aplenty in his current smile, but not even a hint of the affection evident in his eyes when he spoke with or about Genny.

Affection, ease…intimacy. So much so that Julian was even willing to forgive her for trying to marry him off to another woman. Perhaps that was even what he wanted? A wealthy bride would give Julian a degree of freedom…

Kit shifted in his seat. It was damned uncomfortable. Why did they have to produce seats that made sitting for more than half an hour a penance? He missed his armchair on the *Hesperus*.

He missed the *Hesperus*.

No, he missed his uncomplicated life before he'd ventured onto the Carrington web.

He damned his cousin again for drawing him into this world. It was as brutal and competitive as navigating the Barbary Coast, and it had brought him nothing but headaches.

Not only him, apparently.

Did Genny truly have a headache? Or was she tired of facing him, knowing she'd been caught? She hated being in the wrong—he was certain of that. It didn't suit her vision of herself. She was probably up there, reassessing her campaign. Perhaps even planning how to turn this defeat to her advantage.

Probably.

The girl was relentless. If she'd been one of his men he'd probably be commending her determination and enterprise, not hating her for it. And she owed him no allegiance, so it wasn't even worthy of being called a betrayal.

But it felt like it.

It felt…vicious.

Chapter Eighteen

When Genny woke again she had no idea whether she'd been asleep for a day or a week. She shoved aside the blanket, but someone pulled it back up. Serena.

Her sister was dressed in her travelling pelisse, and Genny remembered the excursion planned to the Osmington White Horse. The thought of tramping through the countryside with the gaggle of young ladies while they made eyes at Kit made Genny groan, but she tried to put back the cover once more—only to have Serena stop her.

'You are not rising from this bed until you are well, Genny.'

'But the guests…'

'Will do perfectly well without you. Mary and I shall see to them. You have just come through a megrim, love. You are in no state to do anything but rest today.'

Genny slowly shifted onto her back and tested her forehead, then placed a hand over her right eye where the pain had been unbearable yesterday. A dull, faraway thud answered her with a Parthian shot—*I might be leaving but I'll be back when you need me least.*

She sighed. 'I thought I'd left these behind with childhood.'

'So did I,' Serena answered, sitting carefully on the bedside. 'Why did you not say anything? I wondered what was wrong yesterday, but a megrim didn't occur to me, not after so many years. What happened?'

I made a dreadful mistake and I'm tired. And scared. And hurting dreadfully.

She turned onto her side, her back to Serena. 'A megrim happened.'

'Well, you should have gone to rest the moment you felt the first sign, love. You have been doing far too much recently.' Serena sighed. 'I am glad to be back in Dorset, but I wish you hadn't begun this.'

Genny squeezed her eyes shut. *I am doing this for you.*

'I know you are doing this for me, and for Mary, but it has to stop, Genny,' Serena said softly.

Genny turned over cautiously. She hadn't spoken aloud, had she?

Serena smiled at her. 'You are so like Grandfather sometimes, but you don't always know best. I would rather live under Lady Westford's thumb than marry again. Thankfully, there is another option. Lord Westford has offered to let us return to the Dower House and I think it best we accept. I will ask Mary if she wishes to join us.'

Genny pressed her hands to her eyes—not because her head hurt but because this weakness was making her weepy. 'Is that enough, Reena?'

'It is for me, Genny. I still have hopes that you at least shall marry one day and provide me with nieces and nephews to spoil. If you would only lower your guard long enough to allow a man over it.'

Genny shook her head. The burning in her eyes was worse and her head was thumping again.

The bed creaked as Serena stood. 'Stay in bed today, love. We'll speak later.'

* * *

Lady Westford looked up from the card table with a smile. It disappeared promptly when she saw Kit standing in the doorway.

'I thought everyone had gone to Osmington,' she said a trifle sullenly.

'Almost everyone has,' he replied, closing the door behind him. 'The steward called me back just as we were leaving, with the excuse of urgent estate matters.'

Across the room the garden door was open, and he could see the absurdly named Milly—Militiades—spread like a furry rug on the lawn, no doubt missing his morning walk with Genny.

He'd been more than a little surprised when Genny had missed breakfast as well. It wasn't like her to hide. Still, she could not be very ill if both Mary and Serena had departed on the excursion to the Osmington White Horse and the Roman wells. It was probably merely that Genny wished to avoid him as much as possible. Had she known he planned to remain at the Hall, no doubt she would have gone with the others.

'You really must have a mind to your manners, Kit,' his grandmother said behind him. 'One would think you could manage a week without shirking your duties.'

He wrapped his hands around the back of one of the spindly gilded chairs she favoured. It wasn't much of an anchor, but it was better than nothing.

'You should be grateful, Grandmother. The reason I am shirking my duties is so that we can hold this discussion while everyone is out. I would prefer we are not overheard.'

Her back straightened. 'I don't see what we have to discuss. You made your disapproval clear when you stormed into my rooms the other day.'

'So I did. But today I would like us to establish some rules, Grandmother.'

The cane wobbled a little. Carmine peeped, but with a wave of Lady Westford's hand he fell silent.

'Rules, Christopher?'

'Rules. If you wish to remain at Carrington House in London, you are free to do so—on the understanding that you never again interfere in my private life.'

'Interfere!'

'Do you have another word for conspiring to manoeuvre me into marriage with one of your carefully chosen titbits?'

'I do indeed. *Duty.* My duty to the Carrington name. It should be yours too but as you are too lax in your morals to see that as clearly as I, I decided to act.'

'Putting my morals aside for the moment, I understood it was Miss Maitland's suggestion to auction us off.'

'Her suggestion was sparked by my concerns, and quite frankly I didn't put much stock in it. But if there was even but the smallest chance of success, I thought it worth pursuing. In any case it has kept her occupied and hopeful that she might yet secure Mary's and Serena's futures. Her efforts have been commendable—her results less so.'

Several epithets were burning on the tip of Kit's tongue, but he held them back. 'You don't appear very bothered by her failure,' he said.

'I did not say that, but since I hold the trump card I am resigned to playing it.'

'What trump card?' he asked with deep foreboding.

'My pact with Genny is that should she find a bride for one of you, I will secure Serena's and Mary's financial freedom. If she fails, she has offered to marry Julian herself.'

'She has *offered.*' He couldn't manage more than that.

His grandmother smiled. 'She did. In fact, after watching your rather dismal performance yesterday I spoke with Julian, and since he seems no more inclined than you to progress from his empty flirtations with the young women here to a more settled state, I told him I would settle a lump sum of ten thousand pounds on him if he weds Genny.'

She paused, searching Kit's face, but when he said nothing she continued.

'Since her lineage is not up to Carrington standards I opposed the idea when there was talk of them marrying some years ago, but I've come to believe someone like her is precisely what Julian needs. They certainly spend enough time in each other's pockets. They think no one notices them scurrying off together whenever he comes to the Hall, and that I don't know she went up to see him in London when she said she went to visit an old friend of the General last month. Well, I have noticed, and I don't like it. There will be a scandal and then where will we be? So, if all that comes from this rigmarole is that those two finally cease shilly-shallying and wed, then at least I shall know one of my grandsons has married a woman capable of securing the Carrington legacy.'

The chair creaked ominously beneath his hands. He'd never felt such an urge to throttle someone...not even a Carrington.

'You manipulative, conniving bi—'

'May I join you?'

The deep voice cut through Kit's and he turned. The Duke of Burford stood in the doorway, an uncharacteristic frown on his florid face.

Kit took a deep breath, dragging his temper down. 'If you don't mind, Your Grace, this is a private matter between Lady Westford and myself.'

'I gather as much, young man. And I shall not apologise for eavesdropping as I think it is best I join this discussion.'

'There is no need, Robert,' Lady Westford intervened, her voice softer than it had been up to that point. 'I do not need your protection. We can have our hand of whist later.'

'I think there *is* a need, Amelia. And I am not here to protect you; I happen to agree with Lord Westford.'

'Robert!'

'If what I have heard is true, you are sorely at fault, Amelia. I was under the impression we had been invited here in good faith—not as the result of some convoluted plot. A plot which would never have been necessary had Alfred made fair provision for the members of this family. I told him often enough that when you hold the reins too tight, the weak might buckle but the strong will bolt.'

He turned to Kit.

'If I have one complaint to place at your door, young man, it is that it was your duty to return and set matters right directly when you inherited the title and estate. You may not wish to shoulder the burden. You may—and rightly—resent your family's treatment of your mother and yourself. But to indulge in pique by continuing on your merry way as the others struggle to find their way out of the swamp left by your grandfather's mismanagement of his family's affairs should be beneath the man I have come to know these past weeks.'

Kit raised a brow at this softly spoken but sharply delivered reprimand. He waited, half-annoyed, half-amused, for his grandmother to let slip her dogs—or canaries—of war, but she merely sat there, twin spots of colour on her cheeks.

He gave a slight bow to the Duke. 'You are quite right, Your Grace. I have been remiss in my duties. However, since my return I have tried to make some amends. I have already settled Charlie's debts and arranged annuities for Serena and Mary. I will do the same for Julian…with no strings attached so he shall have no need to succumb to extortion. As for you, Grandmother, you may have the London house for your lifetime. I don't want it. I'm sure there is some Carrington relation who will be more than happy to stay with you if Mary…understandably…chooses not to.'

The Duke cleared his throat. 'As to that, I think Amelia will be better off with me and the grandchildren at Burford Manor rather than racketing about in that big house with no one but some poor relation to order about. Don't you think so, Amelia?'

It took Kit a moment to register the meaning of the blandly spoken words.

It took his grandmother even longer.

Then her eyes went wide as saucers, her cheeks pale, only a sharp streak of colour standing out across each cheekbone. 'Burford Manor?' she whispered.

'Indeed. I would not wish to show you or Alfred any disrespect, but he has been gone for over a year and I think it is high time I spoke. You and I have not many more years on this earth, Amelia. I think you enjoy my company as much as I enjoy yours—foul temper and managing ways notwithstanding,' he added with a smile. 'It would make me very happy if you would accept my hand in marriage. That would remove at least one of your concerns, wouldn't it, Westford?'

'It certainly would…if Lady Westford is agreeable.'

'Yes, that is the crux of the matter. And *are* you agreeable, Amelia?'

Kit didn't wait to hear the outcome of the Duke's proposal, not even for the pleasure of watching his grandmother rendered speechless. He shut the door and stood for a moment in the hall, until Julian's voice dragged him out of his stupor.

'You look as if you have just witnessed a murder, cousin.'

'No—a proposal.'

Julian's face was suddenly wiped clean of expression. 'Congratulations. Who is the unlucky lady?'

'Our grandmother, you idiot. We cannot speak here.

Come into the library. I need a brandy. This family is driving me to drink.'

'What do you mean, our grandmother?' Julian demanded as he closed the door behind them.

'Burford has proposed to her.'

'Good God! Bless the fellow. Please tell me she accepted.'

'I rather think she will. What are you doing back so early?' Kit asked suspiciously.

'It doesn't feel early. They stopped for refreshments at Falworth and I realised that I preferred not to spend another two hours evading that little minx Calista. So I got on my horse...sorry, *your* horse...and rode across the fields back to Carrington. I haven't had such a good ride in years. Do try and flirt with her a little so she returns her allegiance to you, Cuz.'

'No, thank you. I'm quite happy having her enthusiasm directed elsewhere.'

'Yes, you have your own fish to fry, don't you?'

'What does that mean?' Kit paused in the act of pouring two glasses of brandy.

But Julian shrugged, looking a little sullen. 'Nothing.' He took one of the glasses and raised it. 'Here's to gullible dukes. Cheers.'

'I don't think he is in the least bit gullible. Amazingly, he appears to know precisely what deal he is brokering. To each their own.'

'Well, well... I wonder if Genny planned this too. It does solve quite a few of her problems in one fell swoop.'

'You seem to credit her with omnipotence,' Kit snapped.

'No, merely superior tactical skills.'

'Yes. That deal is off the table, by the way.'

'What deal?'

'Ten thousand pounds if you marry her.'

'It...it is?'

'It is. I'm making you another offer. If you accept it, when you leave Carrington Hall with the rest of the guests you don't come back.'

Julian set down his glass. There was danger on his face, but Kit didn't care. He was beyond caring about much at the moment. If they wanted him to play head of the household and set them all to rights, he damn well would.

'Twenty thousand pounds and you will never receive another penny from the estate. Unless, of course, fate favours you and Marcus and someone does away with me. Then you can touch up Marcus for more. You will also stop whatever game it is you are playing with Miss Maitland. While she lives under my roof she is under my protection. No more furtive meetings in town, in theatres—anywhere.'

Julian shoved his fisted hands deep in his pockets.

Kit wished, ardently, that his cousin would take a swing at him. Playing by the rules meant he could hardly attack the man while in his home, but he was so tempted to he could practically taste blood.

'So…' Julian drawled. 'Grandmother offered me ten thousand to wed Genny and you are offering me twenty thousand not to?'

'I am offering you twenty thousand to go away and stop moaning about being treated unfairly. Burford said Grandfather enjoyed keeping everyone on short strings and he was right. It cost my father his happiness, it drove Charlie into debt and an early grave, and it has turned you into a resentful malcontent. Take the damned Carrington money and do something with it.'

'So… I can have the money and Genny too?'

Kit's blow took both of them by surprise.

Julian stumbled back against the door and they stood for a moment, glaring at each other.

Then Julian wiped his mouth, smearing blood on his chin. '*Damn*, I've been spoiling for this, Pretty Kitty.'

'So have I, you petulant brat. Let's see if you're more than talk.'

Julian snarled and launched himself at Kit. He had clearly spent a good many hours at Jackson's boxing salon. He had good science and was quick, blocking the worst of Kit's blows—at least in the beginning.

But Kit was stronger, all those years of sailing and swimming giving him an advantage, and it wasn't long before he got a blow over Julian's guard, sending Julian crashing into a delicate table that held a figurine of a mother and baby elephant connected trunk to tail.

The figurine flew up and Kit made a grab for it, but missed. It hit the floor, splitting in two, with the babe's grey trunk still wrapped about its mother's tail.

'Was that expensive?' Julian asked, his hands on his knees as he drew panting breaths.

'No, but it was one of the first gifts I ever sent Emily, damn you.'

'Sorry,' Julian said, abashed.

'What the devil do you care?' Kit snarled, wiping away a trickle of blood from his temple. 'Do you want the money or don't you?'

'Yes, damn you!' Julian snarled back, all contrition gone. 'And, for your information, I don't know what that old witch told you, but she doesn't know everything.'

'She said Genny has been to see you in your rooms in London. Do you truly wish to see her ruined?'

'Blast you—of course not. I told Genny that was a mistake. We usually… Look, this isn't what you think, but it's not my place to tell. Why don't you ask her? You seem to have everyone telling you their business anyway.'

They glared at each other until finally Julian shrugged and glanced down at his bruised knuckles.

'This wasn't as satisfying as I'd hoped.'

'No,' Kit agreed, the fight going out of him as well.

Everything seemed to have gone out of him. Like an empty ship's hold—dark, dank, empty.

'We're too old for this.'

'Speak for yourself, old man.' Julian's mouth quirked, then flattened again. 'It feels wrong, taking money from you.'

'Well, too bad. It should have been Charlie's in any case. If it makes you feel any better, I'll offer the same to Marcus. I don't need it.'

Julian grinned and winced, gingerly touching his split lip. 'I'd pay to see Marcus's face when you make that offer. In fact, I could probably raise a crowd to watch the fight. You have a mean left hook, man. The benefits of life on board a ship, I daresay. I ought to try it.'

'I would be only too happy to put you on a vessel to the Antipodes, cousin.'

'No, thank you. I'll make good use of the funds right here.' He hesitated. 'Genny told me years ago that Marcus and I were fools to blame you for Grandfather packing our parents off to India. I have to concede she was probably right. My mother made her own choice when she took advantage of your father's melancholy, and we shouldn't have blamed you for crying bloody murder when she slipped into his bedroom that night. But it was easier than admitting one's mother was an arrant flirt who enjoyed taunting my father with her conquests.'

Kit took a deep breath. 'Grandfather blamed me as well, so I don't see why you should have been any different. He told me outright that a true Carrington would have known better than to air family mistakes in public. Another lesson on how you Carringtons were superior to dregs such as my mother and myself.'

Julian winced. 'Charming fellow. Almost as bad as dear Grandmama. I pity poor Burford. Well, I'd better be off, before I start liking you. I'm definitely not ready to do that.' He paused by the door. 'And do remember that although the old she-devil sees much, she understands little. Try not to emulate her, old man.'

He gave a slight salute and left before Kit could give in to temptation and demand an explanation his cousin was highly unlikely to provide.

Chapter Nineteen

Kit could do with a less honest mirror in his dressing room. His hair was damp and spiky with perspiration, reddish rivulets from the cut on his temple streaked his cheek, and his poor cravat looked as if he'd tied it underwater.

He wondered what his men would have thought, had they witnessed his behaviour these past few weeks. He wished Benja or Rafe were here. Anyone who knew him as a sensible individual. Reliable, detached, unflappable…

He pulled off his shirt and sluiced his face and neck with water from the basin. He had just put on a new shirt when he heard a tapping coming from his study. He debated ignoring it, but then it came again, a little louder, and he strode through to open the door.

'What—?' His teeth snapped shut on the word. For a moment his mind went blank as he stared at Genny.

'Lord Westford? Howich said you might be in your study and I thought… I thought it would be best for us to speak…in private…before everyone returns.'

Her voice was hardly above a whisper and her warm-toned skin was sallow and leeched of colour, as if she'd been cupped by an over-enthusiastic surgeon. She looked nothing like Managing Miss Maitland.

An unfamiliar shiver of fear was followed swiftly by

remorse. He'd truly thought she was shamming, but she looked fragile, almost waxen. 'You *are* ill.'

She shook her head and a thick tress of hair slipped from the ribbon that held it back and fell over her cheek. She tucked it behind her ear and winced. His fingers twitched. Surely anyone with a headache would be more comfortable with their hair released from its bondage, spread out…

He quashed that thought. Whether she had a headache or not should make absolutely no difference to the magnitude of her betrayal.

As the silence stretched, her cheeks began to suffuse with colour, but it merely made her look wearier…and more miserable.

He stood in the doorway, damning both of them. If this was another ploy, it was working. The anger he'd been nursing skulked away in shame, ignoring his attempt to grab it by the scruff of the neck and shove it back to the front line.

'You don't look recovered yet, Miss Maitland. You should be resting. In your room,' he added pointedly.

'It was only a megrim. I am better now.'

'Well, I'm glad you are better, but I'm in no mood for any more…games.'

She raised her hands, rushing into speech. 'I won't stay. I thought you had gone with the others to the wells, but then Susan mentioned you were here and I thought… I thought it best not to wait…to make my apology. I should have done so right away, but… You were right. It was foolish…ch-childish.'

She stumbled over the word, and when she shoved the thick tress of hair behind her ear again he noted her hand was trembling.

He struggled for a moment with common sense and then, with a quick glance up the corridor, he stepped back. The worst that could happen was that he would solve most of Genny's problems in one fell swoop. And cause quite a few others.

'We cannot talk like this. Come inside.'

'I don't… I think…'

'Don't think. Or, if you must, don't do it in the corridor. That is inviting trouble.'

Her flush deepened but she stepped inside, flattening herself against the wall as he closed the door. He moved away to the other side of the room, leaning back against the writing desk and crossing his arms. She took a deep breath and plunged into speech, her eyes on the carpet as if her tale were woven into the blue and brown geometric design.

'You are right. About me. I struck a bargain with your grandmother before you even came to Carrington House. It wasn't… I am not making excuses… Well, yes, I am, but…'

She floundered and glanced at him, but when he kept silent she continued.

'Since your grandfather died Lady Westford has become obsessed with an heir for the Carrington line. But instead of taking you men to task she has been flaying my sister and Mary, making them feel like…like failures as women, with no regard to their own pain—especially Serena's.'

She stopped for a moment, rubbing her cheeks as if she'd only just come in from the cold, but she did not look up.

'My sister lost three children to stillbirth. It shattered her and it shattered Charlie and I think it drove him even more deeply into those foolish ventures. Your grandmother never says so outright, but it is clear she holds Serena accountable for Charlie's debts and his death. The worst is that poor Serena has come to believe it herself, and it is…it is destroying her. I couldn't bear it any longer, so I promised Lady Westford I would do everything I could to ensure one of her grandsons married in exchange for Serena's and Mary's freedom. If either of you became betrothed, she would pay Charlie's debts and settle funds on Mary and Serena.'

There was nothing he did not know here. It should not make any difference. But the impotent, wounded anger he'd felt was melting faster than ice in an Egyptian summer. He wanted to keep hold of it, but it was useless in the face of the raw pain in her husky voice. The best he could do was remain silent.

Her eyes flickered up to his and fell again. There was no guile there, no calculation, only a brief, rather desperate appeal for clemency. She looked far younger than her years now—far more like the little Genny Maitland of Spain, held together by nine measures of determination and one measure of cunning.

'I also told her that if I failed I would marry Julian,' she burst out, as if determined to make a clean breast of all her sins.

His anger fired again, in a visceral resistance as old as childhood. He managed to ride that out in silence too—which was just as well, for she continued.

'I didn't mean it, of course.'

'Why suggest it if you didn't mean it?'

'I wanted her to feel there was always something to fall back on.'

'Would he have agreed?'

'Not unless there was some serious monetary—' She broke off at his expression. 'It isn't that he is mercenary… merely…' She stalled again.

'Merely that he needs the funds,' he completed dryly.

She sighed. 'He has his reasons. And I had mine. Which brings me to my other admission.'

God, he didn't know if he could take any more admissions.

'This.' She held out a copy of her grandfather's book. 'It isn't truly my grandfather's, though he had a hand in it. I had trouble sleeping for years after my parents died, so every night, after Serena fell asleep, my grandfather would tell me about battles.'

'Battles as bedtime stories?'

'He didn't know any other tales. We would read from his books together and wonder what went through the mind of a Trojan soldier who woke from his sleep to shouts that the Greeks had penetrated the impenetrable city. How he must have felt when only the evening before he'd celebrated victory after years and years of suffering under siege.'

She paused, her eyes searching his.

'When Grandfather died, and I came to live with Serena, I began writing the stories down. One day Julian found one and read it. After I had torn strips off him for reading other people's private writing, he convinced me to send it to an acquaintance of his at the *London Magazine*. They asked for more. So Julian oversaw the correspondence and we split the proceeds. At some point Julian suggested compiling them into a book, and this is the first of them. There are two others, and I am working on a fourth at the moment—which is why I took those books from the library. No one else knows of it—not even Serena and Mary—so I would appreciate you not...'

She shrugged and held out the book. He had to force himself to move and take it. Strange that this revelation affected him more than her deal with the devil.

The book felt heavier than when he'd taken it from her table yesterday. He brushed his hand over the cover. The binding was marbled, the words *A Soldier's Tales* and *Maitland* engraved on the spine. He opened it and looked again at the frontispiece.

A Soldier's Tales or
A Collection of Tales of Historic Battles
as Told by a Common Soldier
By Gen. Maitland

He'd naturally presumed it was *General* Maitland. Here too Genevieve Maitland had hidden herself in plain sight.

Then his eyes caught the publisher's name at the bottom of the page—and the year. As far as coincidences went, this was…strange.

Genny noted the placing of his finger and took it as a question.

'Julian and I didn't know any publishers, but Mary had once mentioned your grandfather's name, and that he had a bookbinding shop in Cheapside. So when I was in London I asked a hackney driver to take me there. He was a lovely man, your grandfather. He arranged matters with a printer and oversaw those bindings personally. This is the very first copy he printed for me. I would like you to have it.'

Her voice was becoming choppy again.

His own insides were far choppier.

'Did he know you were connected to the Carringtons?' His voice was harsher than he'd meant, and her now empty hands were clasped together so tightly her knuckles gleamed a pale yellow.

'I didn't tell him. I didn't want him to feel obligated in any way. But, you see, he recognised my name, or rather Grandpapa's name, from your letters. When he asked me if I was any relation I realised there was little point in subterfuge. He was so proud of you… I enjoyed my visits with him—he was like a version of my own grandfather, only with a sense of humour and…and easier in his skin.'

She smiled, her gaze now inward, and it took him a great effort not to move towards her. Then she focused, and the hesitation returned, and her hands resumed twisting into each other.

'I had hoped to earn enough to settle Charlie's debts and set up house for Serena and Mary. But I'm afraid I shall likely never earn enough merely with my books, and every year Serena remains... I am not making excuses... Well, I am. In any case, I owe you an apology. You were right about me. Sometimes I think I'm older than anyone here, and sometimes I feel like I'm still the same as when Grandfather came to fetch us when our parents died. I cannot seem to find the in between.'

Her voice hitched and caught and he set aside the book and took her tense hands in his. They were shockingly cold.

'You're frozen.'

'No, my hands are always cold after a megrim, and when I'm nervous.'

Her voice was as rough as gravel, but she didn't pull her hands away. He took her towards an armchair and went to find a blanket.

He'd never credited confessions could be seductive... One learned something new every day.

But she was unwell and vulnerable... Hell, *he* was vulnerable. He would not take advantage of either of them at the moment. All he would do was warm her, calm her, and send her on her way.

He repeated this to himself, just to be absolutely clear. *Warm, calm, send away...*

He brought the blanket and crossed the line a little by smoothing it over her primly pressed together knees, then he stepped back behind the line and went to sit in the armchair opposite.

'If you wish to make amends, you can sign the book you gifted me. Not Gen. Maitland. Your full name.'

She opened her mouth, did some more damage to his

resolve by licking her plump lower lip, and then gave a nervous smile.

'My full name? Genevieve Elisabeth Calpurnia Maitland?'

'Calpurnia? Good Lord. Genevieve Maitland will do. You shouldn't hide behind your grandfather's name.'

'I cannot write under my own.'

'Why not?'

'Why *not*? That should be obvious.'

'Not to me. These are your books, not his. You can dedicate them to him, but they are yours.'

'No one would read a book about battles written by a female.'

'It might be a trifle difficult at first, but you might actually gain some readers due to the novelty—in particular female readers. I read the first two essays while I was waiting for you to exhaust your Mrs Pritchard excuse. They are far more than dry accounts of battles; they are deeply wrought human tales.'

'I don't *want* anyone knowing I write books. Other than your grandfather, and Julian who sees to all the interactions with the publishers, no one knows.'

Her mouth had flattened completely. Stubborn Genny was back. Genny the General might pen part of these stories, but the rest was by the young girl who'd sat up into the night spinning tales with her only anchor of safety.

He set aside the issue for the moment. It did not matter now. The only problem was he wasn't quite certain what did. Not any more.

Two weeks ago he'd known full well what mattered. His list of responsibilities had been quite clear—his sister and her mother, his friends, his men, his ship. The Carrington title and responsibilities had been nothing but irksome duties, imposed upon him by a family he despised and which despised him, to be evaded for as long as possible. Perhaps he had even believed what his so-called family had always seemed to convey—that in time either he or they would conveniently fade away.

Nothing had truly changed since his return. He might play at being Lord Westford, but he wasn't. A proper Lord Westford would wed Lady Sarah Ponsonby and do his best to obliterate the tarnished stain of his birth and occupation.

His guests might enjoy his wine and admire his art collection, but they couldn't completely hide their distaste. He was a novelty, and he was tolerated, but not accepted. Nor did he wish to be. He would never sit comfortably in Lord Westford's life. This…this performance was a temporary illusion—a what-might-have-been-but-will-not-be. Because at heart he didn't wish it to be. Soon he and Mary would attend Emily's wedding and then he would join the *Hesperus* and be on his way again.

That plan had not changed simply because he'd found himself temporarily entangled in Genny Maitland's web. Neither her plots nor this confusing, unfamiliar, sometimes painfully aggravating pull she exercised on him should make any permanent change to the trajectory of his life. It would not be wise for either of them.

Genny gave a sigh, her knees sinking a little from their rigidity. But her hands were still tangled in the blanket.

'Are your hands warmer?' he asked, resisting the urge to test for himself.

She touched them to her cheeks and his own tingled.

'Yes. Thank you. I was so nervous.'

'I'm not an ogre.'

'You were furious. Rightly so.'

'Upset,' he corrected. He didn't add hurt.

'Upset and furious,' she corrected.

'Do you wish for me to apologise?'

'No, of *course* not. I was merely explaining why I was… why I *am* nervous.'

'Still?'

'Are you still…upset?'

'I'm absorbing everything you have told me. I'm not angry.'

Bruised, battered, confused…but not angry. Not with her, anyway.

She smiled. 'I promise no more plotting. It isn't working, anyway. What you said earlier, about Serena… You are right. She isn't ready. I think… I think I've known all along that she is still in love with Charlie, but I hoped perhaps… And Mary… I don't think there is anyone here she fancies, either. Perhaps she too is still…' She stopped and sighed again.

'Still in love with my father?' he continued. 'I hope not. I think Serena's affection for Charlie was far truer and more grounded than what Mary thinks she felt for my father. Unlike Serena she was very young and untried when she married him—and unlike Serena she never had the experience of being loved. I'm hoping that when she finds someone who feels love for her she will see the difference and be drawn to it. This house party might yet do her some good. With Emily away she cannot cluck about her like a mother hen, so she is being forced to enjoy herself all on her own. If that is all that comes of this week, then it is well worth it.'

Her smile grew. 'Thank you for rescuing that ember from the ashes of my ambitions.'

'You're welcome, Genevieve Maitland. Thank *you* for fighting for her. As for the rest… Well, I should perhaps have taken everyone into my confidence earlier about my actions, but quite frankly I planned to leave it until after I departed, so there would not be unnecessary discussion around it. I've already settled Charlie's debts, as well as set up funds for Serena and Mary. If you three decide to continue to live together at the Dower House, that will be your choice—*your* choice.'

Her smile fell away, her hands twisting back into the fabric of the blanket. 'I didn't tell you this to force you... This isn't...'

He pulled his chair closer and closed his hand over hers. Her hands were warmer, but only just.

'This has nothing to do with you, Genny. I realise it will take you a while to cut yourself loose from the moorings of responsibility, but you didn't create my duties and you are certainly not forcing me to honour them. The only thing you did was draw my attention to them. If in a rather convoluted and uncomfortable manner.'

She was still looking a little stunned. 'What of your grandmother?'

'Are you guilty at how happy you feel to be shot of her?'

'A little.'

'Well, don't be. She is about to become a duchess. Burford proposed.'

Her mouth spread slowly into her lovely smile. 'Oh! I am so *happy*. He is so very right for her.'

'You don't seem very surprised.'

'I am not surprised that he cares for her. I wasn't certain she cared for him—though I was hopeful, since he is the only person she seems to wish to please.'

'I saw as much today. I feel a blind fool not to have realised that before.'

'You have been...distracted.'

'True...' He took a deep breath and placed his last card on the table. 'I am giving a substantial amount to Julian as well. Grandfather ought to have done that long ago.'

Her smile faded and her hands dug deeper into the blanket. 'I hope he took it. I'm afraid it will make him resent you even more, though.'

'He took it. As for resentment—that is his problem, not mine.'

He only hoped Julian didn't tell her either of their grandmother's offer or his own stipulations.

She nodded, her teeth sinking into her lower lip. It set his own lips tingling and he wished he had something to sink his fingers into as well...preferably warm and soft.

Without the defensive barrier of anger, lust was seeping through the cracks. Not that she would notice. She was still looking dazed, and there was certainly nothing on her face to indicate that his proximity was affecting her as hers was affecting him.

Perhaps, as he'd suspected, whatever impulses he sparked in her were more the product of circumstance and curiosity than anything deep and lasting. It was probably eminently better that way. In a couple days he would leave for Hampshire and then join the *Hesperus* and be on his way to France within a week. All this would be behind him.

'That's the lot of them, isn't it?' he prodded, trying for lightness. 'Unless there are some bequests for the servants you wish me to make? No? The dogs, perhaps? Carmine the canary?'

She smiled and shook her head, her eyes warming from pale grey to liquid mercury, driving up his temperature with it. He gave in to temptation and took her hands in his, untangling them from the blanket and rubbing them in a pretence of warming them as he spoke.

'So now you'll have to find some other strays to succour—or, better yet, don't. Think of all the energy you could expend on your writing if you had nothing to think about but Thermopylae. Which side are you writing, by the way? Persians or Spartans?'

'Both...' she said dreamily.

She looked as if the concept of being unmoored from

the anchors which had held her in his family's port for so long was both tantalising and terrifying. His heart gave another of the annoying squeezes it had become prone to recently.

He kept his mind firmly on other battles. 'I have never read any records from Xerxes' side of the battle. Are there any?'

'I only know of Herodotus's account.' Her gaze focused back and she was Genny the General, surveying her troops with a critical eye. 'It may be the fashion to revile the veracity of his reports, and compare him unfavourably with Thucydides, but I think he is sorely maligned. He may be more colourful than Thucydides, and less objective, but he is no less valuable as a recorder of history.'

'I never said he wasn't,' Kit said meekly, still gently rubbing her hands between his, despite her increasing agitation as she spoke. 'I happen to enjoy reading them both. Two of the books you purloined from the library are mine, you know. I'd only just put them there the day we arrived, which was why I was surprised to see them gone. The Greek copy of Herodotus was given to me by a woman named Laskarina Bouboulina—one of the leaders of the Greek war of independence. Now, there's a tale for you to write about—although most people would find it too fantastic to be true. She's an Albanian widow with seven grandchildren and eight ships to her name.'

Genny's eyes lit like a kitten with a stretch of yarn dangled above it. 'You were there?'

'I didn't take part in it, if that is what you are asking. Unlike Laskarina, many of the *klefth*—the warlords—are little more than pirates themselves, and I don't deal with their kind, however much Lady Calista might be disappointed to hear that. Not that they wanted me there. They were afraid I might be part of the English Navy's attempt to replace the Turks. But I did bring arms and provisions to her on Spetses, and I was also there when she took Monemvasia.'

'Oh, how I wish I could speak with someone like her myself.'

Her hands had warmed and softened in his as he spoke, her eyes turning dreamy again. If he could have produced Laskarina at that very moment, he would have. But it was a very bad sign if he was contemplating outrageously unrealistic chivalric gestures…

'I could write her story,' she murmured, the dreaminess gathering into purpose. 'What it must be like for a woman to take those risks—her family, her possessions, everything at stake. It would be different than for a man. There is no distance…'

He didn't answer, merely watched the thoughts and ideas chase across her face. Was this how she wrote her tales? Boarded her mind's ship and sailed into those other worlds?

There had been that same intimacy and presence in the essays he'd read. She might as well have been standing by Tiberius Longus's side as he watched Hannibal's monstrous-seeming elephants charge the plain along the Trebbia River and destroy three-quarters of the Roman army. It was a sign of his addled mind that he was beginning to believe that Genevieve Maitland would have found some clever way of routing Hannibal's enormous army without harming a single elephant in the process.

She smiled at him, her eyes focusing. That now familiar, near-unbearable surge of energy gripped him, demanding action, outlet—something.

He sat this out as well.

He was glad to have cleared the air between them, but it had not resolved the real problem—Genny Maitland was disastrous for his equilibrium.

This was new territory for him. It wasn't the first time

he'd been attracted to the wrong woman, but he'd always been able to solve those situations quite readily, merely either by distance or by finding more convivial company to soothe his libido and his pride.

Those reliable solutions no longer felt practicable.

There was one potentially practicable solution, of course—he could offer marriage.

His hands tightened on hers, his hunger threatening to spill over.

'Never go to the market hungry,' his mother had used to tell him when they'd dock at a new port and he'd want to run ahead and see what treasures awaited them. *'Shopping with your stomach is the best path to indigestion.'*

A breeze twitched the curtains and with it entered the distinct sound of carriages coming up the drive. Genny glanced down at her hands in his and with a slight shiver withdrew them, lighting each nerve-end in him.

'They have returned,' she said, her voice muted. 'Mrs Pritchard has arranged for an early dinner as they will be tired. I'd best go.'

'Of course.' He rose and went to the window. 'You needn't come down to dinner if you are still unwell, Genny.'

'I'm not...' She stood hurriedly, the armchair grunting a little as it was shoved back. 'Of course. Goodbye. Thank you.'

'I didn't mean you *shouldn't* come down...'

But she was already out through the door.

Blast the girl—he couldn't do a damn thing right around her.

Chapter Twenty

Genny woke in the dark, but immediately knew that it was almost dawn. The birdsong had a clear, faraway sound, carving the air into crystal notes. She lay on her side, listening to their avian conversation for a long while, postponing the moment when she must think.

At least her head was clear of the last remnants of pain. She hoped another dozen years passed before another such assault.

A dozen years...

She lay on her back, staring at the blank ceiling. She'd always been careful not to think of the future. She had her writing, her sister, her friends, a home...of sorts. It had always felt enough.

Now it felt like a chasm. No...a desert. A great, empty, parched expanse. Nowhere to stop, no one to talk with, no one to hold her hand or kiss.

She covered her burning eyes with both hands.

She'd never felt this before, and she rather feared that it was a sign of something very bad. If this...all of this...was love, then it was horrid. And stupid. It made one maudlin and weak and unable to think clearly except of deserts and loneliness and other foolishness. No wonder some poets wrote such pap.

Yes, but most of those foolish poets weren't really writing about love, but about lust. They made a great show of feeling desperation and loneliness, but they hardly seemed to know the objects of their desires beyond having seen them in the village square or across a dance floor. One could probably exchange their particular maiden with another and they would hardly know the difference.

Perhaps that was all this was—her first encounter with lust. After all, he was so damnably beautiful, and he kept walking around in nothing but a shirt, and on the ship not even a shirt, and...

She turned over and shoved her face into her pillow.

It was definitely, unequivocally lust.

But what frightened her most was that it was more. Far too much more.

He mattered.

She shoved her face deeper into her pillow but it was no good. The list kept growing.

His opinion mattered, his wellbeing mattered, his presence calmed something deep inside her even as it sent other parts into chaotic confusion. He'd brought her to life when she hadn't even realised she'd been hibernating.

She fisted the soft linen of the pillowcase against her burning eyes. Her head didn't hurt but she felt exhausted and battered. She wished her grandfather was alive. She needed him to tell her that all would be well. That she was strong, that she needed no one but herself, that life would still be good and full when he left.

He's only passing through, Genny. You've never been a dreamer...don't start now.

She sat up abruptly and tossed away the blanket. She needed to clear her head, and there was one place on the Carrington estate that always did that for her.

Outside, Milly came dancing along the path at her whistle, delighted that his mistress had finally come to her senses and resumed her early morning walks.

The breeze was blowing in from the sea, bringing salt-water promises, the sun still too low to soothe away the chill of dawn. The ground too was wet with dew, weighing down her hems, but they would likely soon be even wetter with sea water so it hardly mattered.

She passed through the gate in the garden wall and the wind welcomed her with a burst of tangy exuberance. She loved the extreme transition between the lush abundance of the garden and the bare clifftops, kissed with hardy clumps of sea pink and nothing beyond but endless shades of blue and cloud.

At the bottom of the cliff path she removed her shoes while Milly sniffed at a clump of seaweed before prancing off in search of something more rewarding.

Genny sighed with pleasure as her bare feet settled on the cool, gritty sand. She hitched up her skirts, securing them into a knot about her waist with her hair ribbon, and set out across the sand.

The first contact with the lapping waves made her whole body curl in shocked resistance, but within moments she was striding happily along that magic line between water and land. By the time she reached the edge of the bay her internal cloud had lifted a little, and she gave a happy sigh and ran her hands through her hair. Whatever pain yet awaited her, it could not take away all pleasure. Even if all else in the world was ill, *this* was good.

She gazed out over the gentle waves and gave a slight gasp as she saw an arm rise from the water... Her heart slammed to a halt and then stuttered on.

Someone was swimming.

Someone was swimming very well.

He was far out, but his strokes were long and he was heading directly for the bay. She looked along the horizon for a boat but there was none. She could make out a head now—dark hair—and arms glistening in the rising sun.

Muscled arms, brown from the sun.

Kit.

She realised far too late that at any moment now he would reach the shallows. She'd already seen him shirtless, but he might be rather more than shirtless...

The thought of Lord Westford rising from the water as naked as Adam...

She had enough of a challenge with memories of him in a state of partial undress. She did not think surveying him naked was a prescription for battling lust.

There was no time to reach the cliff path, so she whistled to Milly and climbed over the boulders to where a natural ledge was shaded by the overhanging cliffs. Milly leapt from boulder to boulder, very pleased with this new game, and settled beside her, panting happily as he surveyed the shore below.

Genny did the same, realising that the shadowed ledge might protect her from being seen, but it did nothing to block her view of the man rising from the water like a god being formed from the foam of the sea.

Though a divine being would not be wearing breeches.

Well, she was surely a hypocrite. All this effort not to view him naked and all she could feel was disappointment that he wasn't. Not that the short, light-coloured breeches hid much. His skin had the warm, honeyed tone of a man accustomed to sun and sky. It was glistening with the water that ran down over his shoulders and chest. He shoved his dark hair back and began drying himself with a length of towelling he'd picked up from a boulder. He stretched, his arms high, his abdomen hollowing and the muscles of his chest gathering.

The urge to walk over and lean against him, capture

the cool dampness of his skin, the hard length of his body against hers...

Goosebumps spread over her skin as she watched, knowing it was a sore mistake to knowingly add fuel to this fire. She shifted deeper into the shadow and waited for what seemed like an eternity. Finally, she risked a peep, and the stab of disappointment at the sight of the now empty shoreline damned her for a besotted fool.

She began her descent, wondering why climbing down was always so much more treacherous than climbing up. It certainly required more concentration—which was probably why she had no forewarning.

'Genevieve Maitland. I should have known you'd come to plague me here as well.'

The shock hit her with the force of a gale.

She might have regained her balance if Milly hadn't chosen that moment to leap onto Genny's boulder and shove past her in his attempt to reach the new master, who always scratched precisely the right spot behind his ears. Genny felt her sandy feet slip, and with a cry of warning she went over.

If Kit meant to catch her, he failed. If he meant to break her fall, then it might be considered a success—though a rather more painful one for him than for her.

She lay winded for a moment, staring at the sky. She was half on him, half on the sand, his arm tight around her waist. Then the sky was blocked by Milly's panting grin and waving tail. Kit nudged him aside and raised himself onto his elbow with something between a croak and a grunt, his eyes the shade of deep, unsettled water.

'Are you hurt?'

She shook her head, taking stock of her almost-saviour. To her disappointment he was now wearing a plain linen shirt and buckskins, instead of the wet breeches. His hand was still on her waist, but he didn't seem to notice.

'I am sorry I fell on you,' she whispered. Her lungs felt as if they dropped from the cliff and bounced on every boulder along the way.

'I'm sorry I didn't do a more elegant job of catching you,' he replied, brushing sand from his hair. 'But you know my chivalric skills leave much to be desired.'

'Perhaps you should practise.'

'You would like to attempt that again?'

'I don't think so. You could practise on Milly. I'll watch.'

Milly, hearing his name, shook himself vigorously, spraying them with wet sand.

Kit cursed. 'Go away, you canine catapult. You've done enough damage.'

'He is usually better behaved,' Genny said.

'That's because he spends more than half the day snoring in the sun. I'm also very well behaved when I'm asleep.'

Genny's mind went inexorably to the silk-covered, cushion-festooned bed on the *Hesperus*. She would dearly love to check that assertion for herself. What would Kit look like asleep?

'No retort, Genny?'

His hand softened on her waist. His gaze moved down the length of her and then, more slowly, back up.

He smiled. 'I seem to find you in a some very... interesting circumstances, Genevieve Maitland. I wonder why that is.'

'I don't know,' she answered foolishly.

'Hmmm... You're covered in sand,' he said, and brushed at the fabric of her dress. She could feel the grains of sand shiver off...thought she could even hear the scrape of tiny crystals against cotton. She felt a slight pinch at her waist as he raised a piece of dark green seaweed and flicked it onto the sand.

'I think that it is best these skirts earn their keep now,'

he continued, his voice pitched somewhere below the waves.

There was another, more definite tug. The knotted ribbon slithered free with a hiss of friction as he pulled it away. Then he slowly lowered the ribbon so that it spooled into a damp coil on her abdomen. She watched as if it was a venomous snake rather than a strip of cloth. It felt far heavier than it ought, and suddenly it was hard to breathe again.

His hand slipped over the warm curve of her hip, raising her a little to release her bunched skirts. For a moment his fingers sank into the warm fullness of her flesh as he gathered the hem of her gown. Then he drew it down her legs with excruciating slowness.

She could feel everything: the weight of the fabric shifting against her, the way it sent sand cascading off her bare skin… And then his fingers slipped under the softness of her inner knee and stopped.

Her whole body clenched. Her toes pressed into the sand. It was the same thing all over again—her body taking control, shunting her to the baggage train and riding into battle, drums beating.

A sound between a moan and a mewl formed deep inside her. She tried to stifle it, but he heard, tightening his fingers, his own breath hitching. Then his hand skimmed upwards, his palm riding up her thigh, tightening on the damp fabric even as he bent over her.

His mouth settled on hers and she sighed, half in relief that it was finally happening, and half in anticipation. His lips were cool, as she'd known they would be, and she couldn't resist the urge to test her other hypothesis by gently tasting the curve of his lower lip.

Yes, sea salt and the ineffable, addictive flavour of Kit Carrington.

She pulled his lower lip between hers, tasting it, laving

it with her tongue and slipping past it. The tip of her tongue encountered his and a jolt of lightning coursed through her. Without thinking she wove her fingers through his hair, pulling him towards her. She wanted that dance again; she wanted him to make good on his wish to taste every inch of her. She wanted to do the same.

A raw, feral growl swept through him and his body covered her, pressing her into the sand, his chest heavy against her breasts, his leg sliding up between hers to press against that agonising heat. She abandoned all control of the embrace, meeting the demand of his kiss with more of her own. She wanted *more*.

So, apparently, did he. His mouth became almost savage in its intensity as it plundered hers. This wasn't careful, civilised Kit. His raw exploration of her mouth and body was nothing like his previous kisses. He dragged up her skirts with no finesse this time, his hand curving around her thigh and raising it to cradle the hard pressure of his hip. Without thinking she hooked her leg about his, her hips rising against the pressure of his erection.

God, she loved that groan, coming from that same deep well as all this heat inside her. She rose again, reaching for it.

His teeth nipped and licked her lower lip, sparking fire wheels of pleasure as his hand eased the bodice from her breast, his palm, rough with sand, brushing against the sensitised peak. The combination was more of a shock than her tumble off the boulder. Her whole body arched towards him with a cry of need, her nails pressing into his back…

She had no idea what might have happened if Milly hadn't returned and tried to join this new game. With a happy bark he sank down on his front paws and stuck his muzzle into the fray, panting in pleasure and expectation.

They pulled apart and Kit let loose a curse she hadn't heard since Spain as he rolled off her and into a sitting position, hooking his arms about his knees. She rose rather more slowly, brushing sand from her hands and wondering how she kept making the same mistakes over and over.

'I keep forgetting how dangerous you are, Genny,' he said to the cliffs, and she almost laughed at the absurdity of that.

'I'm not dangerous.'

If anyone is dangerous it is you, Kit Carrington. Not merely dangerous—utterly, catastrophically, calamitous.

'I'm not dangerous.'

The fates were clearly toying with him. Dropping the half-dressed object of his erotic dreams on top of him was an act of Greek retribution. Having her then proclaim herself 'not dangerous' was a double affront.

God, help him, he was in trouble.

'That wasn't wise,' he said, trying for cool common sense. 'Anyone on the cliff might have seen us. I know I said you could indulge your impulses, but doing so on an open beach is…risky.'

'You kissed me first this time,' she replied primly as she rose and headed towards the cliff path.

He shoved himself to his feet and followed, feeling like a reprimanded schoolboy. 'I might have kissed you first, but you kissed me into oblivion.'

'I did no such thing. I wouldn't know how.'

'Coyness doesn't suit you, Genny. I don't know where or from whom you learnt to kiss like that, but I take my hat off to them.'

It was a petty thing to say, but it was out of him before he could stop it.

'You may do so next time you look in the mirror, then,' she said tartly as she extracted her shoes from behind a stone.

He stared down at her in shock. 'What does that mean?'

'You are an intelligent man. Sometimes. I am certain you can decipher the puzzle.'

'You expect me to believe you have never kissed anyone before…before me?'

She shrugged and began pulling on her stockings but he was too shocked to appreciate the show.

'You had *never* kissed anyone before that night in the garden?'

'No,' she replied baldly, cheeks flaming.

He stood silent for a moment, too stunned to move. Somehow he'd assumed…

He had no idea why. Genny's age…her competence and cool responses both to his and Julian's flirtations… and then that utterly, inexplicably explosive conflagration just now…

He'd expected… He didn't know what he'd expected.

'You're looking at me as if I've grown two spare heads at least,' she snapped as she straightened and headed up the path.

'I was only… You were…' He cleared his throat and followed, searching for solid ground in this sudden marsh and finding not an inch of it.

He couldn't possibly have misread her enthusiasm after that hesitant beginning in the garden. Unfortunately, he remembered every second of it. And now in the bay… She'd opened to him, her body arching against his with that deep, almost lost moan he could still feel singing through him, twisting him into knots of frustrated lust.

He'd presumed…

Taking that presumption out of the equation, his behaviour had not merely been ungentlemanly, it had been wrong.

The realisation doused the remaining embers of the firestorm. He'd never, *ever* taken something from a woman— not even a kiss—without the rules being absolutely clear.

'I never should have—' he began, but she cut him off impatiently.

'Please. We have already held this conversation, if I recall correctly. Let us not make a drama of it. I daresay it was high time I finally kissed someone.'

It was a welcome splash of cold water and he tried to feel grateful for it—but mostly he was still trying to assimilate the revelation.

'All those years surrounded by soldiers…how did you manage to avoid being kissed…?'

God, he should keep his mouth shut before she pushed him off the cliff path. But she smiled over her shoulder, surprising him.

'I never said I hadn't been kissed. Only that I had never kissed anyone back. There is a difference.'

He definitely should not have this conversation while his cock was still cocked. A mix of physical jealousy and protective instincts rose like a snarl through him, and he had to stop himself from demanding name, rank and regiment. A choking suspicion reared its head, and though he knew he should keep quiet the words kept coming.

'They didn't…harm you?'

'Goodness, no, of course not. I think they were mostly curious. Except for the last one. He was drunk and mistook me for Serena, because I'd borrowed her cloak. I mostly found it annoying and rather unpleasant, and couldn't in the least understand why Serena made such a great deal of it. No doubt I was too young to appreciate it—or perhaps they just weren't very skilled. Perhaps both. And since I've come to the Hall there hasn't been anyone even to be curious about.'

They passed through the gate to the gardens, where the wind dropped and the air was full of the scent of roses. He knew he should not keep prodding this open wound, but he touched her arm, stopping her.

'But…what of Julian? I thought you two had almost been betrothed?'

'Yes, but that does not mean I wished him to kiss me.'

'That does not make any sense. Why would you consider marrying him if you didn't wish for any…intimacy?'

'I didn't think it was important. Many women marry without wishing for intimacy. And still many more do wish for it, but don't receive it. It strikes me that it is a seriously problematic area in relations between men and women.'

Kit was saved from stepping into the quagmire attendant on that philosophical observation by a burst of frenetic barking from Milly, who had stopped by the fountain, his front paws braced on the rim as he addressed the lily pads with full-throated woofs.

'What do you see, Milly?' Genny asked, scanning the water. 'Oh, no!'

'What is it?' Kit fully expected to see a kitten flailing in the pond, at the very least, but there seemed to be nothing there but sedate lilies.

'He's fallen into the water.'

'He…?'

'If I could only reach…' She tugged a branch from a shrub beside the fountain and sank to her knees on the rim, bending over the water.

He caught her waist as she teetered, pulling her back. 'Careful! What the devil is in there?'

She settled back with a frustrated cry. 'A bee. My arm is too short. Here—you try.'

'A bee?'

'A bee. He is drowning.'

Now he could see it. Floating in an indentation on the calm surface, wings outspread, was a bee. Kit's nerves, strained to snapping, gave way to amusement, but one look at Genny convinced him that laughter was not politic at the moment.

'It's probably already drowned, love.'

'No, he hasn't. He was moving, and he tried to climb onto that lily before he floated farther away.'

She began unlacing her sand-speckled shoes.

'You cannot mean to go in after it?'

'If you cannot reach him, then of course. Bees are important.'

He sighed and took the branch, leaning out over the water. His size was a distinct advantage for bee-rescuing, and he soon managed to scoop a leaf under the prone bee and draw it towards the shore.

'Put him amongst those flowers by the wall. He can dry himself there in safety.'

'Yes, ma'am.' Kit did as he was told. 'When I suggested you find other strays to tend to, I didn't think you would start with Apidae. I wouldn't be doing this for a wasp, you know.' He laid the branch between the flowers, with the bee clinging to the side of the leaf, its rump and wings glistening. 'There. Let's hope he dries before the birds find him.'

'*He* might be a *she*,' she said, kneeling on the grass to arrange some flowers to provide cover for her near-drowned victim.

'Even better if it is. I feel very gallant now. I probably saved you from a dunking too. I think I have earned my breakfast. Shall we…?'

He held out his hand to help her up, but she looked about the trees around them with a slight frown at the chattering birds.

'Perhaps I should wait until he…she…is dry.'

He conceded defeat and joined her on the grass. The bee hadn't moved. If he…she…hadn't been clinging so decisively to the leaf Kit might have suspected their rescue had come too late. He wondered how long they would have to wait to discover if the insect was alive or dead. He had no intention of testing the fates by prodding it.

'How long does a bee usually live?' he asked.

'Oh, two months or so.'

He wrapped his arms around his knees. 'We might be here awhile, then.'

She threw him a grin that did more to dispel his embarrassment at his behaviour than her assurances.

'You needn't stay, Kit. You must be hungry after your swim.'

'You saw me swimming?'

She nodded, her eyes back on the bee. He watched her profile, the strong line of her chin and nose and that lush pout of her lower lip. His mouth watered.

He wasn't hungry; he was *ravenous*. He'd come down to swim precisely to counter this plaguing hunger, only to have the fates drop its cause on top of him. And now he was engaged in a bee-watching vigil with his tormentor while imagining her beside him in the water, their bodies hot against each other in the cold bite of the sea. He would stretch her out on top of him, the cool sand at his back, her warm, firm thighs encasing his, her breasts glistening from the sea…

'Do you know how to swim?' he asked, trying to prise his mind from that image.

'Yes. Grandfather's batman taught us when we were in Portugal. I am quite good. Not as good as you, of course.'

She gave him another quick, sidelong smile. Half-shy, half-teasing. He tightened his hold around his knees.

Milly, realising his masters were going nowhere for a while, plumped down between them. He stretched to the full extent of his wolfish frame, then gave a contented sigh and panted into canine abandon.

This was how he could be, Kit thought. If they were married. Keeping vigil over near-drowned bees with a woman who could write as if she'd walked through history and manage people as if she'd taken lessons from Napoleon. A woman who was fiercely loyal, who cared for people far more than she wished to, and whose body was a source of agony for him in a way he had never experienced.

And who had chosen him for her first kiss.

That shouldn't matter in the grand scheme of things, but it did. It was like a hand reaching through fog. The urge to clasp it and let it guide him was almost overpowering.

He'd been from one end of the known world to the other and he'd never felt...*this*. He was more content to sit with her in silence, watching over a bee, than going to explore the world in search of his next treasure.

He had no idea if this was what his parents had shared or what poets went on about. It felt outside the bounds of the known. A mix of dark and light and deep, deep water.

He was afraid it was here to stay and that scared the hell out of him.

It scared him even more that he had no idea what she felt.

For all he'd come to know her, she still kept rooms and rooms of her fortress carefully under lock and key. She'd explained her tie with Julian, but that was only on the surface. Underneath she was passionate, excitable, and she was fighting every one of those tendencies—had probably been doing so for years.

It would be something of a miracle if Julian—who cared for her, no matter what he might say—hadn't sparked some answering emotion. For all he knew, the two of them, equally defensive and defiant, frightened of the future and themselves, were a hair's breadth away from that tipping point that might bring them together.

And he had just given Julian the means to explore that possibility.

He shouldn't have.

He tried to focus on the rhythm of Milly's puffing breath, on the chatter of the birds that was becoming less energetic as the sun rose in the sky. On anything but the chaos the silent woman next to him kept unleashing.

It would be madness to allow this strange sinking to continue. Seductive and dangerous. It was time to kick his way back to the surface, fill his lungs with fresh air, and assess the situation in a rational light.

He couldn't do that around her. Whatever this was—rampant lust, love, a reaction to finding himself wallowing in the cursed Carrington swamp—he needed distance.

'Oh, look!' she exclaimed, pointing to the bee.

The furry, tubby little thing was flicking its wings.

'There,' she said, her voice rich with contentment, her lips parted in a smile. 'I told you she was alive. She merely needed to recover her strength.' Milly buffed her hand and she smiled down at the dog. 'Yes, you're a good dog. You have more than atoned for knocking me onto your master, haven't you, love?' she cooed, her voice pouring warm honey over both of them.

Kit gave a silent groan and sank his head onto his knees.

Genny watched Kit bowing his head and thought of the last time he'd caught her cooing, over little Leo back in London. It felt so strange that they were the same people. If someone had told her that love could transform her, she would have scoffed.

But she felt different.

Happy.

She knew it was about to end...that tomorrow the guests would leave and so would Mary and Kit and that the clock was ticking down to heartbreak. But right here, right now—she was happy.

Her throat tightened. The sun was burning her eyes.

She gave Milly one last pat and stood up. 'I'll have

Cook give you a fine bone, Milly. And you've earned your breakfast too, Lord Westford.'

He stood as well, stretching, his eyes glinting in the sun. 'Thank you, Generalissima.'

That stung a little—she hadn't meant to sound high-handed.

'I wish you would stop calling me that.'

'I meant it purely as a compliment this time, Genny. It is a tribute.'

'It doesn't feel like that.'

He shook his head. 'I don't understand why you are ashamed of being brilliant. You won't tell anyone you've written some of the most wonderful tales I've read in a long while. You roll into a ball like a hedgehog the minute I pay tribute to your considerable skills...'

'Scheming skills are hardly something to be commended for.'

'Of course they are. Politicians and generals are commended for them all the time. If you were a man you wouldn't be hiding your light under a bushel. The only reason you couldn't give Napoleon a run for his money is because you're too compassionate. Believe me, he wouldn't have stopped to pull a bee from a pond.'

Embarrassment and curiosity warred with a strange sense of hurt. She didn't want him to admire her. She wanted him to love her.

Quite desperately.

He should have known praising her intelligence would send her running. She was beet-red now, and looked ready to kick something in embarrassment. She was already shrugging off all the pleasure of the moments they'd shared, tucking herself away.

Except he wasn't ready to let this moment slide. He wasn't ready to let *them* slide. Because there was a *them*.

Where they were heading he didn't know, but there was, for the first time in his life a *them...us*.

He should let her go, but instead he crowded her against the garden wall and cupped her cheek, angling her face so that she had to look at him. Her eyes were shadowed, wary, but there it was—that wistful need that was always there. Carefully hidden, but there. That was the bridge that would either let him in or keep him out.

'Genny Maitland is smart,' he half sang, his eyes holding hers. They were defiant, but he could see the hurt beyond the defiance and didn't stand down. *'"What is it to be wise? 'tis but to know how little can be known, To see all others' faults, and feel our own."'*

She blinked, and he saw curiosity warring with hurt. 'Who wrote that?'

'Pope, sweetheart.'

'Well, it is not accurate at all.'

'Of course not. You are a model of arrogance and selfishness, employing all your considerable powers for evil ends. I daresay you only rescued that poor bee so he could help you infiltrate the hive and secure all the honey for your nefarious purposes.'

'Oh, the bee...' she said worriedly, trying to move past him, but he caught her waist, stopping her.

'She flew off while you were busy claiming how evil you are. Another plot foiled.'

Her mouth flickered into a smile. 'You must be dreadfully bored if you are resorting to flirting with me again, Lord Westford.'

He knew very well what flirting felt like—and seduction, and lust. This felt like all and none of those. He wished it did. He didn't want to accept the implications of it being something else entirely.

'I'm not bored in the least, Genny,' he said in all honesty.

Terrified, but not bored.

He bent his head, just grazing her cheek with his mouth.

Not smart, not smart, sang the voice of caution—and was tossed into the pond.

She shivered against him, and her voice was breathy when she spoke, but her words were pure Miss Genevieve Maitland.

'I don't think this is wise, Lord Westford. If any of your guests were to wake and glance out of the window you might provide them with rather more entertainment than you wish.'

He glanced over his shoulder at the row of windows twinkling in the sun. He was tempted to throw caution to the winds. More than that, he wanted *her* to want to throw caution to the winds and surrender to impulse. He wanted some sign that she was as confused, overwhelmed, and entangled as he.

But Genny, with her cautious eyes on the windows and her cautious mind on consequences, was not that.

He sighed and stood back. Sailing into the wind required a great deal of tacking. And patience.

'Come. Breakfast. I feel I've earned it twice.'

Chapter Twenty-One

'That morning walk certainly did you good, miss,' Susan said as she secured another pin in Genny's thick hair. 'You're looking much more the thing, if you don't mind my saying so. Now, hold still while I fasten your gown.'

Genny sat obediently, staring at the tell-tale colour in her cheeks. It had been flowing and ebbing all morning. As had her mood.

The morning had turned out to be quite, quite different from her expectation. She wasn't quite certain what to make of Kit Carrington's attitude to her, but she knew, as clearly as she could feel her heart thumping away, that she was in love with him.

He'd saved a bee for her.

She ought to be more affected by his actions on Serena's and Mary's behalf. Well, she *was*. By freeing them, he'd freed her. But he'd saved a bee for her and sat with her while it dried. And in that calm, companionable silence her heart had ceded its last plate of armour.

She loved Kit Carrington. It was no longer avoidable, negotiable, deniable. It just was.

He'd been good to Julian, though she was quite certain Julian had done his usual best to be annoying.

He thought she was smart, and not merely in a devious way.

He'd even found some merit in her devious ways.

He was, quite simply, marvellous.

And she was a fool.

She wished she were far more devious. Then she wouldn't have drawn his attention to the perilousness of their position in the garden. She would have kissed him in full view of whoever cared to glance out of their window on a beautiful sunny morning.

It would have been quite a scandal, and Kit, being Kit, would have offered to marry her. Poor Lady Sarah would have had to roll up her tents and cannon and depart the field.

Society would have been sorely disappointed, of course. Probably even vindictive. Charlie's impeccable birth had balanced out Serena's indifferent Maitland lineage, but that lineage would do nothing to help Kit's standing in society. He might believe he did not care, but he might yet change his mind. Especially if there were…if there were children.

She'd never indulged in the thought of children. But now the idea caught her by the throat with yearning and terror. She didn't want *any* children—she wanted children with *him*.

He would be a good father. She'd never been on any other ship where the men didn't merely respect their captain, but love him. Kit would know what to do when she was weakest. He would love their children when she was afraid to. He would check her when she tried to rule them for their own good.

But they very well might look like her, not him, and they too would have to negotiate the shoals of society. While his and Lady Sarah's children would sail through the eye of a needle with their perfect looks, and their wealth, and their much-mended pedigree. Lady Sarah would be another perfect piece for his collection. The jewel in the Carrington crown.

'There you are, miss. As pretty as a picture.' Susan stood back, pleased.

Genny eyed herself, thinking that there were all kinds of pictures, not all of them pretty. But she thanked Susan and hurried downstairs towards the breakfast room.

She wanted and did not want to see him again so soon. She…

'Good morning, Miss Maitland.'

Genny closed her eyes briefly before turning, donning a smile as she did so. Lady Sarah even descended the stairs like a work of art.

'Good morning, Lady Sarah. Did you enjoy the excursion yesterday?'

'We did indeed. Though you were missed. As was Lord Westford. I trust nothing serious occurred to keep him here?'

'I don't know, Lady Sarah. I spent the day in my rooms,' she lied.

'Ah, of course. I do hope you are recovered?'

'It was merely a megrim. Nothing serious.'

'But not pleasant.'

'No.'

Lady Sarah paused two steps from the bottom and did not seem inclined to proceed. 'I was wondering if I might ask your advice, Miss Maitland.'

No.

The word jumped into Genny's mind and she very much hoped it did not show on her face.

'I was about to go in to breakfast.'

'It will only take a moment.'

'Very well. This way.'

Inside the library, she stood by the door while Lady Sarah wandered along the shelves.

'Papa said you were raised in Spain. With all the soldiers.'

'My sister and I lived with my grandfather when we were young, that is true.'

'It doesn't show in the least on your sister.'

Genny didn't know whether to smile or spit. She opted for the smile. 'Thank you.'

Lady Sarah turned and smiled back—a surprisingly warm smile. 'I like you better.'

Genny blinked.

'I like it when I don't know what people think. It's boring otherwise. You're only a few years older than I, but you are...different. You do not seem to need anyone. I wish I was like that. Maybe if I'd grown up like you I would be.'

Well, this was a turn-up for the books.

'I don't think you would have enjoyed that, Lady Sarah.'

'You have no idea what I would enjoy.'

'At the moment, I think you would enjoy becoming Lady Westford.'

The words were out of her before she could check them.

Lady Sarah's eyes widened. 'You *are* direct. Yes, you're quite right. I don't think life with Lord Westford would be boring.'

'It might be when he returns to sea and leaves you here.'

'Not at all. I rather fancy having such a lovely house to myself, to rule as I see fit. Papa has very definite ideas about his household, and one reason I am still unwed is because I do too. I won't exchange my father's house for another cage. When I leave it, I want to go somewhere I can breathe. You can understand that, can't you?'

God, yes, she could.

'Wouldn't you worry about what he was doing while he was away?' she asked.

'You mean other women?'

Genny prayed the thump of heat she felt in her chest

wouldn't bloom into a blush. She had actually been referring to the danger of Kit's enterprises but, as Lady Sarah
had supposed, it was probably the women that would occupy her mind.

Lady Sarah frowned at the tip of her pink silk shoe. 'I
think I might—a little. But men always have mistresses,
don't they? Papa does. His current one is quite nice…
certainly nicer than Mama ever was. I feel sorry for her,
though. She isn't his first and she won't be his last. That
is the wife's advantage.'

'True.'

'Are you Lord Westford's mistress?'

'I beg your pardon?' Genny said, her voice a little
hoarse.

'I saw the two of you this morning. In the garden.'

Oh.

'Have…have you told anyone?'

'It is hardly in my interest to do so, is it? He would have
to marry you—which isn't in his interest either. If it were
he would have done so already. I noticed it from the start.
We were in the garden, and you were carrying a basket
of flowers, and he took it from you and…smiled. He has
a different smile for you. So does Julian Carrington. I
learned to watch for those signs from Mama. She was good
at spotting those things. I daresay it came from watching
Papa all those years.'

A confused mix of anger, guilt and the sharp piercing
pain of hope shoved through Genny's heart.

'Why are you telling me all this?' Genny managed.

'I don't even know…' There was a strange cadence to
the younger woman's voice. 'Papa says Lord Westford
wishes to contract a marriage of convenience or he would
not have invited all these families with their daughters.
When I told him what I thought about you he said that
your birth, though respectable, won't balance out Lord

Westford's own parentage. That he needs someone from a family of the first order of respectability. Like one of the Burford girls. Or myself. I think I suit him better than Sophronia, and certainly better than that minx Calista. Don't you agree?'

The best Genny could do was nod. The girl's gaze was relentless.

'Papa said the best outcome is that Lord Westford marries me and takes you as his mistress until he tires of you. Papa says one must always be looking ahead and not be trapped by details. By "looking ahead" he means thinking of title and wealth, and by "details" he means loyalty and morality. They are for the vulgar, apparently.'

Genny held herself still through this barrage. She felt like a mouse trapped under the floorboards while a cat's paw groped through the cracks, swiping closer and closer. She no longer liked Lady Sarah. What she felt was very close to revulsion.

No—it was pain. The truth hurt.

'If you believe this…if you really believe this about Lord Westford…that he would do what you so despise in your father…you should not marry him,' Genny said.

'Why not, if every other man in our class would do the same?'

'Because even if that were true—and I don't believe it to be true—there are some men…worthy men…who wouldn't. Don't you wish for a man who would not dream of doing that? Not even because he respected you, but because he did not wish to hurt you.'

Lady Sarah's usually cool complexion mottled with sudden harsh colour. Unlike Genny, with her Mediterranean skin, blushing was not Lady Sarah's friend. Her eyes too had reddened, and Genny's sympathy sparked again. Lady Sarah and she were not that different. Both were a little lost in their search for safety.

'You ought not to marry Lord Westford, Lady Sarah,' she said.

'I'd be a fool not to. If he offered.'

'You wouldn't be happy.'

'I would be happier than remaining in Papa's home for ever and ever.'

'I don't know… There is something that happens to a person when hope and choice are removed from the table. Even if Lord Westford is not like your father, I'm afraid you would become more like your mother than you would wish if you married him without love. I hope that doesn't happen to you.'

'You're saying this because you want him for yourself.'

'That is not why I am saying this. But it is true that I don't wish to see him hurt, and I'm afraid you would both suffer if you married him for the wrong reasons.'

'You aren't denying that you want him.'

'I think we've gone beyond that with all this honesty. But I don't think he will marry anyone—not yet. I think he will return to his ship and his old life the moment his sister weds. He is comfortable there.'

'Lucky him.'

'Yes. Now, we should go in to breakfast. I do wish you well, Lady Sarah.'

Lady Sarah gave a slight, unhappy laugh, but did not follow Genny.

At the entrance to the breakfast room the sound of Kit's low, warm laugh reached her from inside and Genny stopped short.

'Miss?' Howich said from behind her in surprise, a large teapot in his hand.

Genny moved out of his way. 'I have forgotten some… letters I must write, Howich.'

She didn't wait for him to comment. She needed to escape before anyone saw her looking as shattered as Lady

Sarah. She needed to think—alone. Today the guests departed, and tomorrow Kit would leave for Hampshire. After the wedding he would leave altogether, and it might be years and years before she saw him again.

Pain lurched through her like a poorly thrust spear, and she pressed a hand to her sternum. The pain would probably fade. It must—like all pain. And she should be grateful to him for giving her so many memories to hoard. She *was* grateful.

She just wanted more.

Chapter Twenty-Two

Kit watched until the ducal carriage was swallowed by the shadow of the beeches and then let the curtain fall back into place with a sigh of relief.

It was finally over.

Except that now the real challenge awaited him.

He was halfway across the library when the door opened and Genny slipped inside, closing it behind her.

'The Duke and your grandmother have departed for London.'

'About time. I was afraid he might toss her out of the carriage at the last minute. Please tell me they took Carmine with them?'

She nodded, her dimples appearing and disappearing just as quickly. She was staring at the floor, the crease between her brows warning him that all was not well.

'What is it, Genny? I don't think I can bear any surprises at the moment.'

Her chin went up and she shook her head. 'It is nothing. Merely… Never mind.'

He reached her before she slipped out, easing her back into the room and closing the door again. 'I didn't mean to be abrupt. Tell me what it is.'

She was as tense as a topsail in a gale and his heart, already rocky, picked up speed. It was something serious.

'Is it Julian?'

The words were out of him without thought and she frowned, finally looking up at him.

'Julian?'

'Has he…? He's left, hasn't he?'

'Yes, he left this morning.' She gave a slight, distracted smile. 'With your letter to the Carrington solicitors in his breast pocket. I don't know if he thanked you properly, and he probably never will, but he is grateful.'

He didn't give a damn about Julian's gratitude or lack thereof, but her tone reassured him. Whatever this was, it wasn't either a proposal from Julian or her concern about him.

'Then what? Your sister?'

'No, no… She is already happily planning our removal to the Dower House.' She looked around the library, her frown returning. 'May I still come to the library for books sometimes?'

His much-maligned heart dropped with a wet splat onto the wooden floor. 'Of course. Whenever you wish. Is that what is bothering you?'

She shook her head, her gaze sliding to the floor again. 'No. It isn't bothering me precisely… That is to say, it is… But not… The thing is…' She took a deep breath. 'The thing is, I have a request to make.'

'What request?' he asked, without much enthusiasm.

'After Hampshire will you join the *Hesperus*?'

It was close enough to the truth, so he nodded.

She nodded as well, just once.

'Where are you sailing?'

'France and then Italy. Why?' he ventured.

She raised her chin. 'I would like to request something of you, Lord Westford.'

'I'll make a pact with you, Genny. I shall stop calling you Generalissima if you cease with all this Lord Westford nonsense.'

Her mouth curved and she looked up. 'Captain Carrington?'

'Kit. Say it. It rhymes with kiss, in case you were wondering how to pronounce it,' he said, a trifle testily.

'It does not rhyme,' she replied with that swift smile he loved, making his insides clench in confused yearning.

'If the first word is cut off by the second it does. Shall I demonstrate?'

She swallowed and leaned back against the door, as if the hordes of hell were beating down the other side. As far as he was concerned the hordes were right inside the room, engaged in pitched battle inside him.

'Pray stop distracting me, Kit. This is important.'

He didn't like the sound of that, but he shrugged and motioned for her to continue.

She gave a sharp huff of resolution and fixed her gaze on the floor once more. 'Before you sail, I would like to... to spend the night on the *Hesperus*, Kit. If it is possible. I could make my way to Portsmouth and after the wedding... before you sail...if it is agreeable with you, of course...' She stopped and then added a little explosively as he remained silent, 'You said it was honest to ask.'

'Honest...?' He woke from his stupor. 'Yes, it is very honest to ask. But just so I understand... You wish to spend the night on the *Hesperus* before I sail?'

'Yes. In your bed.'

'In my bed? With me?'

'Yes.'

'Not sleeping, I presume?'

'Precisely.' She was now a hot, dusky red, but her expression was as stern as ever.

'This is rather more than an impulse, Genny.'

'I am aware of that. But I trust you, and this is something I wish to do. I think… I think you are attracted to me…'

'You *know* I am attracted to you.'

She shook her head, as if that was one of life's mysteries. 'Then it wouldn't be distasteful to you.'

He rubbed his hand over his mouth. He'd wanted Genny to throw caution to the winds and this, in inimitable Genny fashion, was as caution-throwing as it came. It just wasn't enough. Genny discovering her considerable sexuality with him was an intoxicating fantasy on its own. But he wanted…he *needed*…to know she cared. He wanted her need to be as overpowering as the need he could no longer deny he felt for her.

He wanted her to love him.

That was a rather more serious request than hers, and one neither had any control over in the end. But he could do his damnedest to try and ensure she did.

Genny hurried to fill the silence. 'I… I didn't say this for you to feel obliged.'

'This is not something I would ever do out of obligation, Genny.'

'Oh, devil take it—I never should have said anything.'

She groped for the doorknob but he flattened his hand against the door. She wasn't going anywhere yet.

They both started at the jerk of the knob on the other side.

'Kit?'

Genny was halfway across the room by the time Mary opened the door.

'*There* you are, Kit. Where is your jacket? The carriage is waiting. We must leave now if we are to reach them in time for dinner. Oh, Genny—you are here.' She came forward and enveloped Genny in a hug. 'I do wish you and Serena could come. It is a sad pity that Peter's grandparents' house is so small and his family so big. We should have—'

'It is quite all right, Mary,' Genny reassured her.

Mary gave her another hug and picked up Kit's jacket from where it was slung over the back of a chair.

'Come along, Kit.'

Kit took the jacket and ushered Mary towards the door. 'I shall be out directly. Wait for me in the carriage.'

'But—'

He shut the door on his stepmother. Now it was his turn to lean back against the door, his hand on the knob. Genny stood with her hands clasped before her like a prisoner in the dock.

'That wasn't very chivalrous,' she said, her voice wobbling a little.

'No. You do choose your moments, Genny Maitland. Unfortunately, we shall have to wait until I return to discuss your request in more detail.'

'Return…? I thought you were going directly to the *Hesperus*?'

He didn't tell her that that plan had flown away with her rescued bee.

'And leave Mary to travel home on her own after seeing her only child wed and dragged off to the wilds of Leicestershire? That would be even more unchivalrous than shutting the door in her face.'

She finally smiled. There was definitely relief there.

'So, will you consider my proposal while you are away?'

Every waking moment, most likely, he thought. *And probably quite a few unconscious moments as well.*

Aloud he said, 'I will. Will you?'

Her dimples flickered. 'I already have. Hence my request.'

'Come here.'

She stepped forward. Stopped. 'Does that mean you are interested?'

'That means the carriage is waiting and I require some more material for consideration.'

It was lucky he had the door behind him as support. Genny wrapped her arm about his nape without hesitation, went up on tiptoe and kissed him until they were both breathless. He held her against him, wishing against fate that he could consign Hampshire to hell. Words were burning inside him, but even more than that was the need to hear something from her.

'Now this is not only going to be a hellishly long drive, but a damned uncomfortable one,' he muttered against her hair, breathing in orange blossoms.

'I'm sorry,' she murmured against his chest, but her hands caressing his back were utterly unrepentant.

'Liar.'

'Kit!'

Mary's peremptory cry penetrated the door and Genny moved towards the window, straightening her dress.

'Godspeed, Kit. Give my love to Emily.'

I'd rather keep it for myself, he thought, but nodded, opening the door.

'Do try not to fall onto anyone or rescue a wounded tiger while I am gone, Genevieve Elisabeth Calpurnia Maitland.'

Chapter Twenty-Three

Surely she was seeing things?

No. It was *definitely* a longboat coming around the edge of the bay.

Genny stood and shaded her eyes to watch the apparition as it turned into the bay.

Her heart set off at a run. She knew that dark head, that broad back. She had no idea where Kit was coming from, but at the moment that didn't matter. He was coming.

The boat finally rode up onto the shallow sand and Kit jumped out and strode towards her.

'Well, this is convenient. You've saved me a climb.'

'I was walking,' she said foolishly. And then, equally foolishly, 'You and Mary weren't expected back until tonight. Where did you come from?'

He pointed towards the eastern cliff. 'The *Hesperus* is anchored in the deep waters around the head. I'm surprised you didn't see it from the cliff.'

'I've been down here awhile,' she said. She didn't add that she'd been so caught in a brown study she'd likely have missed a hot air balloon landing on Carrington Hall.

'Hmmm... Brimble?' Kit turned to one of the sailors who'd stepped out onto the shore with him and handed him the thick sheaf of folded papers he'd pulled from his pocket. 'Take this up to the house and present it to Howich. When he takes you to Mrs Serena Carrington, inform her that her sister is quite safe with me.'

He held out his hand to Genny.

'Come.'

She stared at it. At him. At the longboat. 'Now?'

'Now. It won't take long.'

Oh. That didn't bode well. Well, they would see about that.

He took her arm. 'I'd best carry you over the surf. Not that I object to seeing what happens to that pretty dress in water, but I'd rather not return you all salt-encrusted when we're done.' He picked her up with a cheerful grunt. 'You are more of a handful than you look, Genny Maitland.'

'That isn't a very nice thing to say,' she objected, and his arms tightened as he walked into the surf.

'It's a very nice thing. I happen to enjoy handfuls. In you go.' He settled her on the bench and hauled himself in, taking her hand as he sat beside her.

The grinning men in the longboat began their rhythmic rowing and she watched the bay recede, the waves hurrying away from them as they rose and fell, the water turning darker. She was out of her depth in so many more ways than one.

The *Hesperus* came into view, its sails vivid against the cerulean sky. Perhaps one of her daydreams had become rather too vivid. Perhaps it was the sun…

The longboat pulled up alongside the Jacob's ladder and Kit helped her to her feet.

'There is yet time to turn back,' he murmured. 'Once aboard you are in my domain once more and must accept the consequences.'

His tone was playful, but she felt the tension beneath it.

'*Would* you take me back?'

He paused, her hands in his. 'Of course. I told you—it is always your choice.'

She nodded and took hold of the Jacob's ladder. 'A gentleman would look away while I climb.'

There was relief in his smile. 'What if you need help?'

'Then I shall ask for it.'

She did not look back to see if her wishes were being obeyed. Some things were best assumed.

When Kit joined her on deck he looked suspiciously angelic. 'Come,' he said again.

This time she didn't object, but placed her hand in his and followed.

His cabin looked different. Or perhaps *she* had changed.

A tray with wine and fruit sat on the table. There was also a small wooden box she had not seen before, with painted panels of flowering gardens and a cover inlaid with mother of pearl.

'Oh, how beautiful!' she exclaimed, reaching out to touch it.

But he placed a hand on it. 'Sit down.'

She sat, feeling all at sea. His lightness had flown and he looked distant and rather stern. This definitely did not bode well. But if all he wanted to do was reject her advances, he could have done that on the shore.

'Did you consider?' she asked, annoyed at how feeble her voice sounded.

She picked up her glass and set it down again. He did the same.

'I did.'

'And what is your answer?'

'That depends.'

'On what?

'I am considering two courses of action at the moment,' he began, swirling his wine. 'I could accept your proposal and then leave with the *Hesperus* for France tomorrow...'

She clutched her hands together. Her heart was thudding so hard her ribs ached. 'And the second possibility?'

'I could go home.'

'Home?'

'Carrington Hall. It is not quite home. But it could be. I am considering staying. For a month. Maybe longer. It depends.' He took a deep breath, turning the wooden box round and round in a parade of luscious gardens: butterflies and roses, palms and honeysuckle, peonies and willows, orange blossoms and a single red-breasted robin, wings spread.

'For a month?' Her voice was calm, which was a miracle, because she was shaking like blancmange inside.

Oh, please. Please, please, please.

'It depends,' he said once more.

'What...what does it depend upon?'

There was a faint knock at the door and Benja's apologetic voice. 'Sorry, Captain. We need you for a moment.'

Kit's jaw tightened. 'Blast. Wait here, Genny... No, best come with me.'

Genny followed him, still feeling completely at sea. Which proved to be far more than a figure of speech—because the moment she stepped onto the deck, she realised the truth.

'We're sailing!'

'Took you long enough to realise that, Gen.' He looked up at the sails. 'Pretty strong against the current, Benja. We'll need to come around.'

'Yes. But it will take longer, *Capità*.'

Kit finally smiled. 'We have time. Do it.'

For a moment Genny felt a strange welling inside her, almost like grief, but then she realised what it was—joy. It made no more sense than what was happening, but still... The thought that he was taking her away, just the two of them...

But Managing Genny Maitland knew better. 'Why?'

'Maybe I'm kidnapping you,' he said, watching as Benja issued orders to the men.

'Depositing me on a desert island so I will cease my pernicious meddling with your family?' she asked.

'Hmmm…' he murmured, his eyes on the sails as they wavered and pulled.

Her voice also wavered when she spoke. 'I don't understand.'

He glanced across at her, his face turning serious again. 'Come, we'll leave the men to it,' he said abruptly. 'It's hard work, sailing into this kind of wind.'

He took her hand again, and this time she felt he hardly noticed he was doing it. She thought of that strange conversation with Lady Sarah. Of her sharp, bitter eyes, catching the tell-tale signs of intimacy.

'Where are we sailing?' she asked, her voice hurried.

He stopped and let go her hand. 'A little south…a little west. Why? In a hurry to return?'

She shook her head. 'No. I was thinking.'

'What were you thinking about?' he asked.

And she shut her eyes and threw herself overboard. 'I was thinking of that beautiful bed.'

Silence.

Waves splashed, gulls cried, sails flapped and wood creaked—but what she heard was that silence.

She kept her eyes shut.

His hand, warm and rough, took hers.

'Come. I want to talk with you.'

Talk.

She didn't want to talk. Talk was sensible. And sensible was what she'd been for so, so long. She wanted to *live*.

Inside the cabin he pressed her back into a chair and refilled her glass. She drank, grateful for the billow of warmth that filled her icy insides.

'If amethyst and gold had a flavour, this would be it,' she murmured. 'With blackberries too.'

He smiled and touched his glass to hers before he drank. Then he sat and pulled the wooden box towards him, turning it idly in his hands once more as he watched her.

'This is harder than I thought, Genevieve Maitland. You are a difficult woman to read. Here you are on my ship, and we are sailing, and other than your interest in my bed I am not certain what you feel. That places me in a quandary.'

'What…what kind of quandary?'

'My options. If the sum of your interest is in my bed, in theory we could resolve that during this voyage and then you can send me off to France.'

'But… I… You said you might yet remain at Carrington Hall a month.'

'Yes. I did. I was thinking… These last weeks have been eventful, to say the least. Quite a great deal has happened… God, this is hard.' He sank his head into his hands, shoving his fingers into his hair.

She clasped her hands together to stop herself from following suit. Her leg was bouncing from nerves.

He dropped his hands and said, almost explosively, 'Would you like me to stay at the Hall?'

Like?

Her wide-eyed silence seemed to exasperate him.

'Do you even like me, beyond your interest in my damn bed?'

'Of course…of *course* I do. You *must* know I like you. I would never have mentioned your bed if I didn't.'

'Forget the damned bed.'

'*You* mentioned it just now.'

'Very well—as of this moment, and for the next quarter-hour on the clock, there will be no mention of beds.' He shoved himself to his feet. 'What I am trying to say—extremely poorly—is that if you are agreeable I would like to spend the next month at Carrington Hall so that we may become better acquainted. Without my grandmother making mischief and without half the Ton in attendance, trying to suck my Carrington blood. At the end of that month, if you agree, I would like to make you an offer of marriage.'

Genny's thoughts tumbled in their chase of this speech, trying to make sense of what he was saying.

Better acquainted?

Marriage?

'If, on the other hand, this prospect does not appeal to you,' he continued, still pacing, his voice still stilted, 'I shall see you safely back to the Hall and be on my way. I think we are both mature enough to...'

He faltered and stopped in front of a painting of a long-tailed bird sitting on a branch heavy with cherry blossom. She could hear her heart thumping. Great big thuds echoing in her ears.

Marriage.

It wasn't wrong to want that, was it? They were friends, could be lovers... And if he wasn't in love with her, as she was with him, it could still be good...for both of them. She could give him something he lacked—something she felt he needed. She knew he was not asking lightly, or out of consideration for honour, and yet...

She wanted so, *so* much more.

'I would like you to stay,' she blurted out.

He turned and she hurried on, stumbling over her thoughts and her words.

'I would like you to stay and for us to be able to explore our...our friendship. But I think it is wrong to establish in advance that it must lead to a...a marriage of convenience. The truth is...the truth is I don't want to marry you for propriety's sake, Kit. *You* shouldn't want a marriage on those terms.'

'I don't.' He turned back to address the painting and for a long while neither spoke.

Finally, she couldn't bear the silence. 'Where does that leave us?'

He shook his head without turning. 'I don't know.'

She swallowed. Any minute now he would put her back in that longboat and…

'This isn't something we can resolve right here, right now,' she said.

'No. Probably not,' he replied, still in the same empty voice.

'Will you stay at the Hall a little while longer, then? Or will you sail?'

She saw his jaw tense but still he didn't turn.

'Stay. I don't seem to have much choice in the matter.'

She didn't quite understand what was happening here, whether to be happy or scared, and so she settled on both.

She had been prepared for the worst, but now Kit was to stay a little longer, and she was precisely where she wanted to be—alone with him in his cabin. She would concentrate on that and on her objective.

If she'd known she was to be kidnapped she would have worn something far more appealing, but at least her morning gown was easy to remove. It took less than a minute to slip off her dress and her stays. Her chemise was sheer muslin, with two thin straps, and ended about her knees. She debated making away with that as well, but lost her nerve. She went to the bed and sat down. The silk was warm and viscous, almost liquid. She rested her hands on it.

'Now that we have settled that, do you wish to join me? Or shall I put my dress back on? Your choice.'

He finally turned, his blank gaze coming into startled focus. 'Genny, what are you doing?'

She spread her arms, a little confused by his confusion. 'You *agreed*.'

He stood dumbly for a moment, his gaze moving over her, but already she could see the heat entering his gaze as it lingered over her form, moving down to her feet and then back, slowing as it went.

He took a step closer and stopped. 'Definitely better than my imagination,' he murmured.

A hitched sigh of relief escaped her and his eyes rose to hers, intent now. He took her hand and turned it over to touch a light kiss to her palm.

'Your hand is cold,' he murmured against her, his tongue testing the ultrasensitive skin of her palm and sending silvered shocks down her arm and sparking over her breasts. 'Are you nervous?'

'Terrified.'

'Don't be. I won't hurt you.'

You will.

'I need you to warm me,' she moaned, and the words were smothered as he bent to fuse his mouth with hers, pressing her back against the cushions as he lay beside her.

'I've been on fire ever since you ordered me into the ballroom,' he said urgently, and that strange distance that had so confused her was completely gone now. 'I've dreamed of stripping you bare, spreading you out on my bed, tasting every inch of you...'

She shuddered at the image. The contrast between his words and the languorous progress of his fingers as they moved over her, tracing the sweep of her hips and thighs and rising to stop just short of her aching breasts, had her stretched tauter than piano wire, vibrating as she waited for another chord to be struck.

'I didn't think you would agree...to this...' she said.

'I can't seem to help myself...' His laugh was shaky and it spread heat over the swell of her breast as he slid down the strap of her chemise, very gently exposing her breast, like an archaeologist extracting a precious find. 'I *need* to touch you…'

Cupping it in his large warm hand, he bent to brush the swell with his lips in hot, feathery kisses, never settling. Then his teeth scraped very gently over the sensitised peak and a wave of heat surged through her. Even in the haze of desire the intensity of her need scared her. But not enough to stop. And not enough to keep her words safe inside her.

'Kit… I want you. I *need* you.'

He groaned, his erection surging against her thigh. He caught her hip, holding her against him so she could feel the full pulsing heat of him against her. His mouth hovered above her nipple, his breath teasing it, taunting her.

'Say that again.'

She drew breath, her chest rising to scrape her erect nipple against his lower lip, but he didn't move.

'I want you…' she repeated obediently, and his indrawn breath dragged cold air over her nipple, adding pain to pleasure.

'I *need* you…' he prompted, pulling down the second strap and raising her so that the chemise slipped to her waist. He leaned back a little, his hand gathering her breast and brushing the tense peak with a feathering caress.

'Oh, God… *I need you*…' she breathed.

'I need you, *Kit*…' he coaxed, but his voice was hoarse.

He pulled away, abruptly discarding his own clothes and then slipping back onto the bed, pulling the wine-coloured silk over them as he gathered her full length against his body with a broken groan.

His body was fire against hers, and his hands and mouth were doing wonderful and dreadful things. She clung to him, surrendering utterly to the storm he whipped up about her, inside her. The whole universe was only this—nothing else mattered.

'Tell me.'

His words were harsh, but even through the fog of pleasure she knew them for the plea they were.

'I need you, *Kit*.'

I love you.

She managed to keep those words to herself, but she thought them again and again as he continued his voyage over her body. Her hands tangled in his hair as he moved with infuriating slowness over her body. The air was cool against her heated flesh, and everywhere his mouth touched her skin leapt as if branded.

She floated in a haze of confused pleasure until his hand slipped between her thighs, easing them apart. Then her hands tightened in his hair, trying to pull him away.

He raised himself onto his elbow, his eyes warm and slumberous as he smiled at her. 'Freckles.'

'What?' she whispered hoarsely.

He trailed his fingers along her thigh. 'You have freckles here. I knew I'd find some.'

She laughed, embarrassed and strangely pleased. 'Were you looking for them?'

He shook his head, his fingers tracing up and down, just teasing the soft inner flesh and stopping short of the pulsing need between them.

'I'm not *looking* for anything. I'm exploring this wondrous new land where everything is beautiful, and lush and...' His fingers grazed the soft curls at the apex of her thighs and another flare of almost unbearable new sensation made her body clench and her knees press together. 'And very, very responsive,' he continued, his voice hoarse.

'I can't seem to stop it,' she said apologetically. 'It's like those frogs.'

'Frogs?'

'Emily took us to an exhibition about electricity once.

The man was making frogs' legs dance with a voltaic cell and… And I should be quiet now, shouldn't I?'

'No, don't stop.' He grinned down at her before sliding lower on the bed again. 'Do tell me all about electricity and frogs' legs while I continue counting freckles. Here is one,' he murmured, his mouth brushing the skin just above where he held her knee. 'And two more here…and another here…'

He worked his way up, slowly smoothing aside her legs with teasing licks and kisses. His hand was on her breast too, his thumb teasing the sensitive peak and adding to her agony.

She didn't continue her discourse on Galvanic impulses. She couldn't. She couldn't seem to do much of anything other than lie there, one hand anchored in the silk cover and the other biting into his shoulder as he drove her higher and higher on a wave of agony.

'You can touch me…you can touch yourself,' he murmured against her thigh. 'You can do anything you want, Vivi.'

Without thinking she released the silk sheet and tentatively touched his hand where it stroked her breast.

'Yes…' He breathed warmth against her. 'Show me what you like.'

'This. I like all this. Only more.'

He laughed, and his breath finally feathered over the centre of her heat. She pressed her head back against the cushions, trying to twist her hips away—or into the sensations he was unleashing. She'd never, ever imagined anything like this.

Her whole body rose in the shock of pleasure. It crashed through her body, connecting all his assaults like veined bolts of lightning. Suddenly it was unbearable, impossible, beautiful. She gave a long, tense cry and he rose to catch it against his mouth as she shattered inside.

* * *

Genny woke to the sensation of his fingers trailing slow circular patterns over her abdomen and she smiled without opening her eyes. She stretched, testing the strange new awareness of her body. He'd rearranged her…no, *they'd* rearranged her. It felt so much better…*truer.*

She finally opened her eyes to his smile.

She could become addicted to that smile…no, she already was.

'That was amazing, Kit.'

'It was.'

She frowned as her scattered senses gathered. 'But I don't think you… Did you?'

'Did I what?'

He was teasing her, but she didn't mind. Not when he looked at her like that.

'You know perfectly well what I mean. You didn't… have pleasure.' She cringed at how stilted she sounded, but he didn't seem to mind.

'You have no idea how much pleasure it gave me to see you like that, Genny. If I had to trade my pleasure for the privilege of watching yours I would do it without regret.'

She shook her head, embarrassed and pleased. 'That is a very gallant thing to say, Kit.'

He kissed the corner of her mouth and drew back, inspecting her. 'I knew you would look beautiful in my bed,' he murmured. 'These are the colours you should wear… all the shades of wine and warmth.' He drew the edge of the silk cover over her midriff, moulding it to her. 'Yes, we could make do with you wearing nothing more than this for a month at the very least.'

She smiled, brushing her fingertips over his exploring hand. 'I didn't realise mistresses were required to go about in nothing but sheets.'

'You aren't my mistress; you are my lover. That is a whole different matter.'

She warmed from head to toe. 'Is this what it is like? Having an affair?'

An affair.

The words caught Kit like the swipe of a cat's claws—sharp and stinging, scattering the slumberous satisfaction of bringing her to orgasm. She had such a casual ability to cause pain, and the worst thing was he never knew when it would strike, or how.

She looked so beautiful—her cheeks flushed from lovemaking and sleep, her hair a tangle of honey and wood. She looked beautiful. Vivid and utterly unique.

His Vivi.

It was time to make it perfectly clear what this was and what this wasn't.

'You said you aren't interested in a marriage of convenience, Vivi. Well, I am not interested in an affair.'

Her eyes widened, shot through with pain and dismay. 'I didn't mean to imply that you wished to do this again…'

He caught her, pinning her down with his arms and his body. He was done with having her slip away the moment she felt the ground pulled from under her.

'I wish to do this many, many times, in many, many places—but not like this. Not an affair. Not with you. Did you honestly believe I could contemplate that? Or a cold-blooded marriage of convenience?'

'But…'

'You are happy at the Hall, aren't you?'

'Yes, but…'

'And you enjoy…this…?'

His hand trailed up from her thigh, over the dip by her hipbone and across the warm softness of her abdomen to her beautiful, luscious breasts, lingering there. His erection hardened against her thigh. He couldn't resist leaning down and pressing a light kiss just above the dark areola. It gathered to a hard peak, and goosebumps rose along the arm that was trying to stop him.

He loved how responsive her body was, shifting towards him almost against her will as she tried to remain impassive. He wanted to reach the point with her where she would finally trust him enough to let slip that control. It would take work, and trust, and many, many days and nights, but it would be well worth it. If it took a lifetime it would be well worth it.

'You enjoy *this*,' he repeated with emphasis, holding her gaze. Her eyes were misty now, the hurt ceding to desire.

'Yes, you know I do,' she murmured, her leg rising against his. 'But you cannot…'

He trailed his hand down again, resting it on her hip, his thumb brushing the soft valley between her hip and navel,

'What can I not?'

'Marry me.'

'Not good enough for you?'

'Don't be ridiculous. You ought to marry someone like…like Lady Sarah. She wants to marry you, you know.'

'Huh… She told you, I suppose?'

'She did, actually.'

He pushed away a little, a slight smile on his mouth. 'People tell you everything, don't they? Why would she do that?'

'She wanted advice. And to determine if I was your mistress.'

The smile faded. 'Those two subjects strike me as contradictory. And why would she think you were my mistress?'

'She saw you take a basket of roses from me in the garden.'

'In the…?' He frowned, his eyes narrowing. 'I would have done the same for anyone.'

'She said you have a different smile for me. She learned to look for it from her mother. The woman apparently had an eye for philanderers.'

He shifted over her, nudging aside her legs to slide one of his much larger legs between them.

'Is that what I'm doing? Philandering? You do know the word means being fond of men?'

'I don't require a lesson in Greek right now. Lady Sarah—'

'Devil take Lady Sarah! Do you really believe I would be happy with someone like her?'

'I… You might. She's beautiful, and intelligent, and not unkind—and she would be the right kind of Lady Westford.'

'I don't like her. I like you. I don't stay awake at night hoping she will be on the shore when I come in from my swim. I don't wake up as hard as a damn mainmast and realise I have to make do with my own company because of her. I don't go searching that monstrosity of a house when I'm in a foul mood, hoping to run her to earth so I can be dragged out of whatever pit I've cornered myself in. I've never felt anything even close to this.'

He watched the expressions chase themselves across her expressive face—worry, want, and that awkward helplessness that was still little Genny Maitland.

He stroked her cheek gently. 'She doesn't truly wish to marry me. And I certainly don't wish to marry her. I have other plans. And if you don't wish to study Greek right now, we could try Italian. Do you speak Italian?'

'No, but…'

'Pity… But your Spanish is a good base. It won't take you long to learn if you set your agile mind to it.'

'Why…why would I learn Italian?'

'So you will know how to order everyone about when we sail there for our honeymoon. And quite a few of my men are Venetians. A good general knows how to communicate with his...sorry, *her* troops.'

'They aren't—'

'Yes, yes,' he interrupted. 'Say after me: *Mi chiamo* Genny. My name is Genny. Go ahead, say it.'

She sighed. *'Mi chiamo* Genny.'

'Beautiful. Your accent is a little on the Iberian side, but we'll soon change that. Now say, *Mi chiamo Genny e ti amo.'*

'Mi chiamo Genny e ti...'

Her breath left her, falling as dead as the wind on a hot day.

Genny fixed her eyes on his, sinking into that deep dark blue.

'It's j-just like Sp-Spanish,' she stuttered.

He nodded. 'Say it.'

His voice was a purr, almost menacing, but she heard something else in it and it made the world shrink to the space of their two bodies.

She swallowed and wet her lips. *'Mi chiamo* Genny and I love you.'

His lashes fluttered down to cover his eyes, his head lowered, and his forehead came to rest on hers very lightly. But there was tension in every inch of his body. It was endless, the wait—either for the trap to close or the world to open.

'Genny... God, Genny. You had better mean it.' He turned his head, his lips just touching her temple, his words low and raw. 'I need you to *mean* it.'

'I couldn't say it if I didn't mean it,' she whispered, laying her palms against his cheeks. She slid one hand down to press against the beat of his heart and touched her lips to his, felt them shiver. 'Kit. I *love* you.'

'Ah, sweetheart, don't cry,' he said, his voice hoarse and she realised she was. She brushed at her eyes but the tears kept slipping out, slow and inexorable.

'I'm sorry. I've been trying not to for weeks. I'm so sorry.'

'God, don't be sorry, love. Come here.'

'I'm already here. If I come any closer, I'll be inside you.'

'I'd rather be inside you. And now you have finally admitted you love me I will be inside you soon enough. You *can* come closer…here, like this.'

He sat, pulling her onto his lap and tucking her head under his chin. Then he tucked the silk blanket about them like a cocoon, one arm warm about her waist, one hand curling around her feet as he held her against him.

'It's very useful, you being this small.' He brushed a kiss over her hair, rubbing his mouth against it.

'I hate it. I always wanted to be tall and beautiful, like Serena.'

'You are far more beautiful than Serena.'

She rubbed her wet cheek against his chest. 'Your eyesight is fading; that cannot be good for the Captain of a ship.'

'My eyesight is excellent. I've told you before: your sister is the very definition of pretty, and I wish her well with it, but she isn't beautiful. Beauty is another thing entirely. Those paintings you like on the wall here—I bought them because I kept going back to look at them…they kept playing on my mind. I've never once looked at them and thought, *How nice*, or *How pretty*. Beautiful is what is vivid, alive, demanding. Everything *you* are, Genevieve Maitland—soon to be Genevieve Carrington and, God help you, Lady Westford.'

She shook her head. Her throat was too tight for her to answer and the tears kept leaking out of her.

'I think, love,' he continued, threading his fingers through hers, 'you should just let go and wail. It's long overdue. I'll survive.'

'I don't know if *I* will,' she croaked.

'Oh, you will. Trust me.' His arms tightened around her, his voice dropping. 'You *do* trust me, don't you?'

'With my life.'

'Good. Maybe one day you'll trust me with your heart too.'

Sometimes things could break in the strangest way. You could drop a glass a dozen times and it would just roll across the floor. Then one day you'd set it down on the table, just as you had a hundred times before, and it would shatter.

And just like that she shattered into a thousand sobbing pieces.

He murmured all kinds of wondrous things at her, just as she did to Leo and Milly and all the other strays she'd gathered. But mostly he held her, rocking her like a boat on a gentle swell...

'It is my birthday today,' Genny said, much later.

She'd wept her heart out and he'd put it back together with slow, gentle lovemaking that had almost driven her to tears all over again.

She'd expected pain, but there had been none, just a strange stretching as he filled her, a sense of finally growing to encompass her own body. The pleasure had been different too. She'd been carried higher and higher on a rising swell that had refused to let her loose, and pleasure had flowed through her like a wave within a wave, depositing her like a shaking mass of jelly on the other side.

He raised himself now, leaning over her, with the smile

she loved so much curving his lips. Then he stood, walking across to the table, his body caressed by lamplight.

'I know,' he said. 'Mary told me. I have something for you. Here.'

He brought the wooden box from the table and set it on the bed, before slipping back under the cover with her.

'It is beautiful,' she whispered, caressing the box.

'Open it.'

She opened the lid. On a bed of milky silk lay a delicate filigree gold ring with a deep, almost red amethyst surrounded by seed pearls.

'I bought this long ago in Naples. They said it had belonged to a princess, but I don't know if that's true. I just saw it and had to buy it. I had no idea that I would keep it, let alone one day make use of it myself. I probably should have found you a great big Carrington heirloom, or something, but—'

'No,' she interrupted, touching the cool stone. 'No...'

'"No" as in no good? Or "no" as in you like it?'

'No, as in I am about to cry again.'

He smiled and took the ring. 'And you said you weren't excitable, my love...'

'I was wrong.'

He paused with the ring halfway on her finger, his eyes rising to hers, the deep dark sapphire sparking with heat. Then he slipped it on the rest of the way, his thumb brushing over it like a seal.

'We were both wrong about quite a few things. But not about this.' He kissed her finger just above the ring and then, very gently, her mouth. 'Make a birthday wish, Genny mine.'

'You have just fulfilled it, Kit.'

'Make another, then.'

'I wish to go swimming with you every day.'

'In winter too?'

'Don't ruin my wish with practicalities!'

He laughed. 'Every day. You can warm me afterwards. What else do you want?'

'You.'

His chest rose and fell. 'You ask for so little, Genny.'

'You aren't little at all, Lord Peacock.'

'Ah. You remember…?'

'Of course I remember. You thoroughly disliked me that first week, didn't you?'

'*Dislike* isn't the right word. You…rubbed me the wrong way. It merely took me a while to find out why. And what to do about it.'

'Seduce me?'

'May I remind you that you seduced me? Several times. And, no, when a spitting kitten is rubbing you the wrong way, all you have to do is turn around and then you discover that the rubbing is just right…'

His hand brushed down the length of her spine and she couldn't stop the reflexive arching of her back into the caress.

'Yes, just like that,' he murmured, pressing the words against the sensitive skin below her ear as his hand curved round her waist, turning her over. 'Just. Like. That.'

Epilogue

'Well, this is a sad disappointment,' Genny said.

Kit took off his other boot and watched as his wife stepped further into Julius Caesar's fabled Rubicon River. She stood, hands on hips, frowning at the grassy incline and the woods beyond.

'Not what you expected, love?'

'Not at all. I had this image of a great river, like the Thames or the Tiber, and Caesar glaring across it at the wealth and power of Rome that were denied him. I knew it could not be anywhere near Rome itself, yet somehow… Fantasy can be so much more satisfying than reality.'

Kit stepped into the stream, sighing with pleasure as the cool water engulfed his feet.

'I beg to differ. I far prefer reality to the fantasies I had to indulge in until I came to my senses and kidnapped you.'

'Is it kidnapping if I came willingly?'

'Kidnapping or not, I've not regretted a moment since,' he said, planting his feet and sweeping her into his arms. She gave a yelp of surprise. '*Alea jacta est,* Genevieve Maitland. The die is truly cast, and this is the fate you've drawn—two perfect children and one imperfect husband. Resign yourself to it.'

She laughed. 'Kit! We'll fall in.'

'If Caesar had had so little faith in the Thirteenth Legion as you have in me, my little field marshal, history would have played out quite differently.'

She wrapped her arms around his nape and settled more securely against him, her lips brushing against his neck, just where she knew how to do the most damage. 'That's not true, Kit. I trust you wholly, without boundaries, with my life and my heart *and* our two horrid children.'

'I happen to be quite fond of the little devils—especially when they are far away in Venice with their aunts. Your daughter, Genevieve Maitland, looks likely to rival you in tyranny.'

'Why is it that when she is being brilliantly managing she becomes *my* daughter, yet when everyone says how sweet and beautiful she is, she is your daughter?'

'It is one of life's mysteries. Stop that, or we shall both end up in the water.'

She gave his ear a playful nip and blew gently on it. He groaned and let her slip down his body, holding her tight against him before leading her to the other bank.

'I told you my skirts would get wet.'

He eased her back onto the grassy incline and stretched out beside her, running his hand down her thigh and then slowly gathering the damp fabric so that it slid up to reveal her legs.

'You should have tied them up as you did that day in the bay. Then I could have the same pleasure untying them... smoothing them down...or up...definitely up.'

She sighed and stretched happily as his hand followed word with deed.

'I'm so glad we decided it was better that I accompany you on your voyages again now that Tom is old enough.'

'It wasn't a decision; it was a necessity, Vivi. You have no idea how much I missed you on my last voyage.'

'I beg your pardon; I have a very good idea. You had

your voyage to distract you. I had to spend every night in our bed alone.'

'I should hope so. And I had to spend every night in our other bed, alone, freezing my backside off in the Baltic Sea, with a ship full of snoring and shivering men. After a week I was ready to turn back. After a month I promised myself that next time you were coming with me—even if we had to let the children fend for themselves. After two months I was convinced you were quite happy not to be constantly disturbed by my carnal lust. After four months I was crying into my wine…a pitiable sight.'

She smiled, her fingers trailing patterns on his back and sending shivers of anticipatory pleasure to all the right places.

'That is very poetic—though a trifle dramatic and not quite accurate. After three months you were safely back in your bed with me, being mightily disturbed by a three-month accumulation of *my* carnal lust. In fact, I am feeling mightily disturbed right now.'

'You don't mind the ghost of Caesar watching on, then?' he asked.

'Not in the least. He might learn something from the best lover on earth, ever…'

He laughed and slipped his hand higher up her thigh, curving it over her warmth. Somehow her skin felt different from anyone else's. It made no sense, but there it was.

'Perhaps this was why he crossed the Rubicon—the poor fellow was looking for this.'

'This?' she sighed, her eyes closing again as he trailed kisses down her throat.

'This…' He eased her bodice down, punctuating each word with a kiss as he revealed inch after inch of warm skin. 'Happiness. Contentment. Challenge. Joy. Pain. Pleasure…'

He slipped the last inch from her tightly beaded nipple and bent to lavish a slow kiss over the sensitive peak that made her twist towards him with a moan, her fingers threading through his hair. But then he drew back, blowing a gentle soothing breath against the damp skin and looking up at her, holding her gaze as he spoke.

'…and love.'

She rested her palms against his cheeks. Her grey eyes were magnified by the welling of tears and her voice was hoarse when she finally spoke.

'I would cross any Rubicon for this, Kit. Fight any battle for you. You know that, don't you?'

Kit waited out the tightening of his throat. He hadn't completely lied. Perhaps he hadn't quite cried into his wine, but the depth of pain and fear that had caught at him all those miles from her had been as much a shock as falling so desperately in love in the first place. He had *needed* to return.

'I know that, Vivi. That is why I need you with me. I need you to remind me that you care for me almost as much as I care for you.'

She smiled his favourite smile—full of joy and promise and trust. 'Dear me, Kit. Are we competing again? I'll win, you know.'

'I'm afraid I outshine you there, sweetheart.'

She nudged him onto his back, tucking her bare leg between his, slipping her hand over his abdomen and under his waistband.

'We shall see. I *do* so love a challenge… Especially a hard one.'

* * * * *